Lee and Miller's *Tomorrow Log!*
The #1 Science Fiction Trade Paperback in America
March 2003!—*Locus Magazine*

"Finished reading it in the small hours...and, to pun ungracefully, it's a Gem."

"All the lovely language they seem to specialise in as well as marvelous characters and a good plot (with obviously more installments to follow to wind this up.) Such a nice surprise."

"It goes on my comfort shelf."

"Imagine! Landing a Garden with that many acres from outer space. I chuckled so over the Combine ship not believing their eyes when a forest went by them!"**—Anne McCaffrey**

The Tomorrow Log: No, it's not Liaden. Yes, it's got all the wonderful elements that Liadan readers have come to expect. Beginning with the first line, "His name was Gem and he was a thief," we know we're on a roller-coaster of fast action, interesting futuristic societies, high tension, ricochet plot twists, humor, horror, weird science, space ships...and romantic tension, with a strong heroine in Corbinye, and some villains we really, really love to hate. More, more!"
—Sherwood Smith, author of the *Crown* and *Court Duet*

"Readers familiar with the Liaiden novels will not be disappointed.
Lee and Miller are consistently deft and smooth. The tale has momentum from the first page (or screen) and never lets it lag."—***Analog***

"No, *The Tomorrow Log* does not take place in that familiar universe, but in an entirely different setting, which befits an entirely new series."

"Panic not though (if you were about to) all of the duo's

magic is here in *The Tomorrow Log*. Just get ready to see a whole new world of adventure."

"Lee and Miller are masters at raising danger, action, passion, and loss to an irresistible pitch, keeping the plot moving ahead at a breathless pace. No one in the genre handles the romantic aspect of science fiction with such a deft and subtle touch, never letting it overpower the storyline or appear tacked on."

"Is it better than the Liaden® books? Worse? Would anyone listen if I told you that it is quite simply completely distinct? The comparisons are inevitable, but the wise readers are going to be the ones who simply revel in yet another layer in the richly textured writing career of Sharon Lee and Steve Miller."—**SFSite, MEviews**

"Fans of Liad will find a setting that is similar enough to easily settle into, with familiar emphasis on the responsibility of belonging to a clan/family/lover/crime syndicate/ ship's crew. Yet unlike the Liaden books, which feature a system that for the most part works for mutual support and advancement, *The Tomorrow Log* describes a system in decay, allowed to feed upon itself until it merely codifies social structures that enforce the ability of the strong to prey upon the weak. This is no gentle comedy of manners but a hard-hitting look at a single man's ability to alter destiny by remaining independent and not succumbing to mob mentality, as well as how true love requires individuality. Well worth reading."—**Science Fiction Romance**

THE
TOMORROW
LOG

SHARON LEE & STEVE MILLER

The Tomorrow Log Copyright © 2002 by Sharon Lee & Steve Miller

THE TOMORROW LOG

Published by Meisha Merlin Publishing, Inc.
PO Box 7
Decatur, GA 30031

Editing by Stephen Pagel
Copyediting & proofreading by Teddi Stransky
Interior layout by Lynn Hatcher
Cover art by Christian McGrath
Cover design by Kevin Murphy

ISBN:	Hard Cover	1-892065-86-X
	Soft Cover	1-892065-87-8
	Mass Market	978-1-59222-127-1

www.MeishaMerlin.com

First MM Publishing trade edition: February 2003

PRINTED IN CANADA

10 9 8 7 6 5 4 3 2 1

Dedication

For Archie, who loved adventures

THE TOMORROW LOG

SHARON LEE & STEVE MILLER

CHAPTER ONE

HIS NAME WAS Gem and he was a thief.

With stealth and in utter silence, he slipped down the darkened hallway to the door he sought. Gently, he brought the specially etched glove from his shirt and laid it, palm-flat, against the lockplate.

The door sighed gustily as it opened, and Gem crouched, ears straining to catch the slightest hint of unrest from the household slumbering about him.

Silence in all parts of the house. The telltale on his wrist showed no surge of energy, as from the triggering of a remote alarm. The room itself was dark, slightly cool and smelling of must. Gem slid the infraglasses down over his eyes and stepped inside.

His information from here forward was nerve-wrackingly vague, so he went slowly, alert to the possibility of pressure-sensitive tiles, sending the tiny electronic spiders ahead of him, step by cautious step, until he was at the case itself, and never an alarm had been raised.

A less wary man, or a thief yet short of mastering the craft, might have grinned his triumph here, and laid his hands upon the case. Gem hunkered down before it, adjusted the lenses to maximize detail and began a painstaking study of the frame and the shatterproof crystal, while the little spiders perched on his shoulders and clung to his hair.

Close scrutiny revealed no trip-wires or alarm-grids; readout from his wrist was uncompromisingly flat. Gem frowned and sat back on his heels, mindful of the passing of time; mindful, too, of the value of the object within the case, which none but a moonling would allow to sit, all unguarded, except for the laughable outside intruder-net.

Mordra El Theman was no moonling, despite that Gem was even now well within her house, with neither her invitation nor her permission. He stared at the case and that which was within the case, felt the skittering of spider claws at his nape and frustration in his heart.

The case was not booby-trapped, unless the trap was so sophisticated that the very advanced equipment he carried on his person detected no hint.

Gem stood up and lifted the lid, carefully locked it in the raised position and was still, barely breathing, ears strained to the ultimate, eyes on the telltale.

All was quiet in the house; the readout showed not even the tiniest spike of energy that might be a cry of warning to the police.

He bent his attention to the object of his desire, minutely, and found no webs of light or wire indicating that it was itself a trap. He sent a spider to perch on the rosette rim. It glided down the gilded, arching side to the floor of the case and discovered no pressure-plate there.

The same spider clambered back up to the lip of the urn and slipped down inside, suspended by a line of synthetic silk. Its tiny half-chip brain sent impressions to the telltale, which refined them for the man's understanding.

There was something within the urn, but not yet the alarm he had begun to hope for. Instead, his instruments showed something organic; unalive; uncontagious. Gem called the spider home, barely noticing as it climbed across his hand and took a firm grip on his sleeve.

No alarms. None. Unbelievable.

Unbelieving, Gem extended a plas-gloved hand and curled his fingers around the urn's neck.

Revulsion erupted within him; revulsion and a fear so consummate that his heartbeat spiked, sweat beading his face, sheathing his body; his bladder threatened to fail and he shook so hard that three of the spiders fell from their perches to the floor and scrambled to ascend his trousers.

Terror built, firing his imagination so that he heard the whole household roar awake and come running toward this room; and heard sirens in the front court; felt the irons already on his wrist—

"Ah!"

Barely a sound at all, loud in his fevered ears, he bit his lip to keep another from escaping, jerked his hand away from the urn, brought the lid clumsily down and went across the room in a stumbling shamble. Instinct alone closed the door; sheer animal wiliness got him silently down the long, darkened hall and to the window he had breached; the stern discipline that made him a master craftsman closed that window and erased all signs of his entry.

He reached the street, heart still stuttering, shivering as the sweat dried and the dawn breezes found him; and he walked for a long time, rubbing the hand that had touched the thing down his thigh, over and over, as if the palm were burned.

CHAPTER TWO

TWO DAYS LATER, he was at Iliam's, admiring the view and a certain aquamarine necklace, when a man stepped to his side and lightly touched his sleeve.

"Gem ser Edreth?"

He turned slowly, for the voice was not familiar, nor, once faced, was the man: Tallish, stocky, middleaged and genteel; exactly the sort of person one expected to find at Iliam's Curiosity Shop of an afternoon.

"You have the advantage of me, sir," he murmured, smiling courteously and slipping his sleeve away from the other's fingers.

The man bowed slightly. "I have come from Saxony Belaconto," he said softly. "She greatly desires a favor from your honor."

"I am, of course, overwhelmed by the lady's condescension, but I am not in the habit of doing favors."

"Ms. Belaconto," said the genteel individual smoothly, "repays her favors—generously."

"I would not have thought otherwise," Gem answered; "and I am desolate to disappoint her. If it were anything but a life-rule, sir, laid down to me by Edreth himself…Convey my very heartfelt regret to your lady, and my certainty that she will easily find another able to oblige her."

The man's face showed that which might not be considered quite genteel; then he was bowing, as others came to admire the aquamarine necklace.

"Good-day, sir," he said tightly.

"Good-day," said Gem, and moved off to look at the other displays.

He did steal the aquamarine set. Later, he wondered if it had been an omen.

The second contact was less auspicious: two burly individuals, conspicuously armed, waiting in the dimness of Third Noon, blocking the narrow courtway to his house.

"Gem ser Edreth," snapped the burlier of the two. He bowed, trying not to measure his slightness against their bulk; or to weigh his skill with the sorl-knife against their probable accuracy with the jutting rapid-fires.

"Gentles."

"Ms. Belaconto sent us. You know why." The slimmer of the pair held a truncheon, which she slapped rhythmically against her palm. Gem stared at her with what coldness he could muster and the bully hesitated; glared.

"I was told," he said to the spokesman, "that Ms. Belaconto desired a favor. I have already explained that I could not oblige her. Henron houses several members of my profession—and Zelta is not that far to send, if no one on-world meets the lady's requirements."

"Ms. Belaconto wants you," the one with the truncheon said, and grinned. "She said to hurt you, if you weren't—obliging."

"Oh, nonsense," he snapped. "What possible good would it do to beat me? If I agreed to accommodate your mistress at the end of it, I'd hardly be in shape to fulfill my guarantee. And if I still refused—even if you killed me!—she would be faced with the same problem. I cannot believe the Vornet is as inefficient as that!"

The truncheon-holder blinked and turned to her partner, who sighed. "That's right. But we could hurt you without *hurting* you, if you take my meaning."

Gem shook his head, mentally working the moves; measuring how far they stood from the door to his house; measuring how far he might be able to run.

"If you're going to beat me," he said irritably, "then get on with it; but I assure you my answer will be no different at the end than it is now: My sincere apologies to your mistress, but I simply cannot oblige her."

She was very fast: he sensed, rather than saw the truncheon snapping toward his head and spun in the move Edreth had drilled him in until he danced it in his sleep.

The stick whizzed by and the sorl-blade was out in the same instant, slicing back along the line of attack; drawing blood on his assailant's upper arm—the merest pinprick, but she grunted surprise.

The stick sang again and he twisted, danced under it and sideways, his arm snaking up and over her shoulder, until the blade rested, gently, against her throat.

"Drop it!"

She did, noisily; and her partner raised empty hands. Gem considered his position, blade absolutely steady, just nicking the skin.

It did not do to wantonly kill the servants of the Vornet; and this pair were doing nothing more than their duty to their leader. He looked at the man; saw the rapid-fire still in its holster; saw the empty hands and nonthreatening stance.

"You'll carry my word to Ms. Belaconto?"

The other nodded. "The message is that Gem ser Edreth declines to perform a service for Saxony Belaconto. Forcefully."

"That is," Gem agreed, "the message." He stepped back and slid the sorl-knife away. The man turned to go; the woman bent to retrieve her truncheon.

"Leave it!" he snapped; and she looked at him in surprise before glancing at her mate.

"Leave it," the man said and she did, the two of them fading down the narrow courtway and out into the main street.

When he was sure they were gone, Gem picked the truncheon up and hurled it with all his strength to the roof across the court.

CHAPTER THREE

EVENTS QUIETED. GEM went about his several businesses, though he kept a wary eye out, and on the evening of the third day he allowed himself to believe that the Vornet had relinquished its interest in him. Nor, indeed, did the next disturbance in his life come from that quarter.

He was at Kayje's Concourse, having a light nuncheon and watching the play, when Phred approached and bowed.

"Master Gem, there is one here who asks to share your table."

He frowned, because here, of course, was the Vornet again, when he had dared to think them safely settled.

"The young person in scarlet, sir;" Phred murmured, under the guise of refreshing Gem's wine.

He turned his head slightly to look and found his glance captured across the room by a pair of enormous black eyes, sparkling bright in the dimness of the club; he broke the contact and picked up his glass.

"Send her away."

"Yes, sir. Your pardon, sir."

Gem returned his attention to the action at the Spyro, sipping now and then, but abruptly without taste for his nuncheon. Out of the corner of an eye, he saw Phred speak to the young person in scarlet, saw her begin to protest; saw the discreet intercession of the bouncer. Confronted with both headman and bully, she hesitated and finally left, shoulders defiantly straight in the bright cloth.

Gem joined the crowd in the center of the Concourse; wagered a bit on the Wheel; had another glass of wine and bought a deck at the Knave's table. In due time he collected his winnings and turned his steps toward home.

He had barely stepped away from the brightly lit pedstrip and onto the DownRamp when he felt her fall in beside him; heard a young, firm voice:

"Anjemalti Kristefyon."

He neither quickened his pace nor slowed it; nor did he glance aside or give any sign that he had heard.

"I am Corbinye Faztherot," she continued, hurriedly, matching him, stride for stride. "I know that this is not done seemly, but the need is great, and I ask that you forgive the informality forced upon me. My rooms are nearby, if you would but step aside…"

Still, he did not alter his pace; her voice might have been the whisper of river wind against his ears for all the heed he gave it.

"We are kin!" she cried, shockingly loud in the stillness of the 'Ramp. "Of the same Ship and Captain! You *must* hear me—the courtesy, at least, of a reply—" Her hand was on his arm and at last he did stop and spun to face her in the dimness; saw with noontime clarity the space-tanned face; the huge light-sensitive eyes; the short pale hair and the long, lithe grace of her; felt the strength in her fingers and ripped his arm away.

"I do not know you," he said coldly, "and I do not know your kinsman. I am Gem ser Edreth and I have no kin, and none to order me, now that my master is dead. *You* should mind your manners and not be snatching the arms of strangers in the dark, young miss, or you'll find yourself hurt—or wronged and in the Blue House."

"You are Anjemalti Kristefyon," her voice was low; exultant in its surety; "child of Captain Marjella Kristefyon of the Ship *Gardenspot*. You carry the genes of the Crew; you are the Captain-to-Be, who is now the Captain-in-Truth. The Ship is in danger and you are foretold in the Tomorrow Log—"

"And you," he snarled, "are mad! Good-night, moonling, and may the gods conspire to allow you live through the night!"

He spun away then, and ran to the base of the 'Ramp; going from there through all the back ways home, trying with all his skill to lose her. When he finally did reach Jilvon Court, he hovered long at the entrance-way, straining ears and dark-seeing eyes.

At last, convinced that she was no longer with him, he entered his house, went straight to the bar, and poured himself a brandy.

CHAPTER FOUR

HIS NAME WAS Anjemalti Kristefyon; he was nine years old, his mother was dead, and his Uncle Indemion hated him.

There were blows, and hard words about faulty genes, for his mother had mated with no man of the Crew, but with a Grounder, and had exulted in the spindly, half-blind boy that union produced, to her brother's cold disgust.

The blows were hard to take, but the words were harder, especially when they dealt with his mother, so that he cried aloud and felt acid in his own heart. And the acid grew until the day he drew his boy's blade and launched himself at the man, surprising both by drawing blood, by the strength and determination of the attack.

The beating that time was very bad.

Not long after, his uncle took him to Prongdil. They walked a dismal port-fair to a stinking tavern, his uncle's hand brutal about his arm. The place grew quiet as they entered, then erupted noisily as they marched toward the back of the room.

"Hey, Olbi, look at this! A father and son act!"

"A half-wheel for the little one, don't he look fresh!"

"Fresh! Unplucked, I'll warrant—a *whole* wheel for the virgin!"

"As if you'd know what to do with him! Beautiful mouth, eh?"

This last drew a bit of laughter and he felt his face heat, though he barely knew why. His uncle pulled on him roughly then, and he stopped.

The person behind the table stared at him, then shifted her gaze upward, eyebrows lifting.

"He's a bit undergrown, for twelve."

"His father was thus, mistress; and the child favors him."

"I see." She raised her glass and drank, placed it carefully aside, and beckoned with a broad-fingered hand. "Come here, boy."

His uncle pushed him and let go. Anjemalti hesitated, reluctant to go to the woman, willing almost to run through that noisy mob....

"Ah-ha!" The woman laughed, extended a long arm and drew him close. "He thinks he may not like me—and he knows he doesn't like you." The hand on his arm was neither cruel nor kind; the fingers that tipped his face toward the meager light and stroked his cheeks and hair flesh— warm and efficient.

"What's your name, boy?"

"His name is Anjemalti," his uncle said hurriedly, and the woman glared at him.

"Can he speak for himself, or are you peddling damaged goods, as well as underaged?"

"He can speak, mistress." His uncle's voice was almost subdued.

"Good." She brought her gaze back to him, ran judgmental fingers down his throat, casually unsealed the first several fastenings of his shirt. "What's your name?"

"Anjemalti Kristefyon," he said, and jerked his head irritably. "Stop that."

"A touch of spirit, is it? Now, Anjemalti, who is the man who brought you here?" She continued to unseal his shirt, slipped her hand against his flesh and probed, laughing when he flinched away.

"My Uncle Indemion."

"Is he?" She touched a bruise and frowned slightly; began to close his shirt. "Do you know that your uncle has brought you here to sell, Anjemalti? He beats you, I see, so maybe it's just as well. My clients are quite genteel—most of them—and would hardly think of beating so well-favored a boy. Though I'm not sure you'd do in a bordello, Anjemalti—no, I'm certain of it—too much spirit. How old are you?"

"Nine years, Standard."

"Ah, yes, underaged…" She glanced over his head. "I'll give three full rounds of gold. My final price."

"Three rounds, mistress? But he's worth far more than that! Undergrown he is, yet you admit he is not ill-favored. Surely so well-traveled a lady as yourself knows of a person or two with more—sophisticated—inclinations…."

"I do not dicker," she said flatly. "My price is three rounds, which you take or you leave. I advise you to take it, myself, or cut the lad's throat and accept the loss."

Hesitation. "I accept the price of three full rounds of gold. Be warned, though, mistress—he has a brooding and murderous nature. Beating is what he understands best; I suggest your clients be made aware of it, that they do not endanger themselves by failing to keep him pliant."

The woman was standing, one hand still encircling Anjemalti's arm. With the other, she fished in her pouch, extracted three yellow coins, and tossed them, negligently.

"Fee paid," she said tonelessly, as Indemion snatched the money out of the air. She stepped away from the table, pulling Anjemalti with her, and brought him safely through the quiet bar and out into the port.

He woke, sweat-soaked; abandoned his bed and dragged on old, soft trousers and a faded shirt, not bothering with the lights until he was in his workshop. Here, he must have light, for he could not see well enough in the dark to do the intricate electronic tinkering.

He shook his head irritably as he sat at the bench. Edreth had found his 'assistant's' dark-seeing nothing short of wonderful, while Indemion Kristefyon had seen proof of inferiority in his nephew's shortened range of vision. And now this fanatic girl, crying out for anyone to hear that, blind as he was, the Tomorrow Log held his name.

"The Tomorrow Log!" He picked the wounded spider up; sat staring at it with unseeing eyes. The Tomorrow Log was a tale for children; a supposed prophecy, passed down from the First Captain. Even if it existed, the name of a sold-off and despised half-breed would hardly appear, attached with any honor.

"My name is Gem ser Edreth," he told the spider tautly. It was not so bad a name, nor had Edreth been so bad a master, merely wishing, as he had, to pass on his skills and understandings to a worthy successor. For the universe is wide and full of strange custom, so that even the profession of thief is on some worlds honorable. Always supposing, of course, that one worked for oneself, as Edreth had done, and took care to avoid entanglements—and the doing of favors.

Especially the doing of favors. And most especially favors for the like of the Vornet.

Gem opened the tiny mechanical thing carefully, probing inside with a power-pik barely thicker than a cat-whisker. Edreth had professed wonder at Gem's patience for such tasks, as well, but encouraged him to pursue the interest, saying that even the most successful of thieves might some time require a more mundane trade.

It occurred to Gem, in that far, objective bit of his mind not at this moment concerned with the ailments of mechanical spiders, that Henron had become a less-than-satisfactory base of late. The attentions of the Vornet alone would make departure prudent. Add the crazed Ship-girl—what was her name? Corbinye?—to the equation and prudence argued for even precipitous withdrawal. After all, *Lady Ro*, of which he owned a third, was in port; and *Dart* was due within a three-day.

Still, it went against one's pride to turn his back on mere difficulties. Corbinye, he had dispatched already. The Vornet was rather more problematic, but it would not do to become known as one who had run from them.

"Anjemalti Kristefyon is sold, dead and gone," he told the spider, resealing the cover and setting it on its many legs; "and Gem ser Edreth does not run from his enemies."

He touched the control pad on his wrist and the tiny insectoid obeyed the impulse, dancing as he directed.

CHAPTER FIVE

SHE WAS WAITING, wedged into a niche in the ornamental wall opposite his door, still and patient as any of the other statues.

Gem swore under his breath and strode straight across the court, with the intention of snatching her out of her shadow and administering a very sound shaking.

But, before he had gone four steps, she stepped out of the niche and raised her right hand, shoulder-high and open. "Good-day, Anjemalti."

"Gods scorn you for a fool!" He stopped just out of reach, in case the desire to shake her became overmastering; took a deep breath and exhaled it.

"How did you find this place?" he asked, quieter.

She looked at him out of astonished black eyes. "I am of the Crew. It was not difficult to trail you."

"Then it will not be difficult to find your way back. I have told you that I am not the one you seek; and I have told you to let me be. I *demand* that you cease this harassment and that you remove yourself from my attention." He leaned forward; snapped the last of it with all the power of command Edreth had taught him: "Leave me now!"

Consternation showed in the lean face; and confusion. She shifted in her shadow-pool, eyes narrowed slightly against the glare of First Noon, and gnawed her lip, but she neither left nor effaced herself, to Gem's dismay. Instead, she took a step toward him, and made as if to lay a hand upon his sleeve, though she did not quite touch him.

"Anjemalti," she said, in tones of gentle reason; "kinsman. I cannot know all your whys and wherefores, who have been away from us for so long. But it is foolish to deny your true name to me. I am of the Crew, in line for First, serving as Worldwalker, and Seeker for the Ship. I found the first trace of your uncle's mutiny; followed Sali Than Kermin to the ends of her route and persuaded her to say who had bought you."

She drew herself up. "A year and more I followed Edreth ser Janna, only to a find a dead man at the end of it, and that his apprentice was as skilled in disappearance as the master had been."

A pause, during which he returned her stare, stone-faced. "So," she said softly, "I know you, Anjemalti; and I know that I have found you. Whatever your schemes and business among Grounders, they are nothing, for your Ship needs you and you are called home."

"Damn your ship!" he cried and saw her flinch in horror, hand lifting to ward away the words.

"Damn your ship and damn your crew," Gem elaborated, pressing his advantage. "You know nothing of me, of my business, of my necessities, or my life. You have found Gem ser Edreth, who repudiates you and yours and forbids you to come near him! Come to me again and regret it…" He glared at her. "Do you believe that I mean what I say?"

"Yes, Anjemalti, I believe that." Still she stood there, staring at him out of enormous eyes.

"Then leave me!"

"The Tomorrow Log," Corbinye said then, as if all of his ranting had been mere pleasantry, "names the child of a Captain and a Grounder as the Captain who will bring the Ship out of the greatest danger we have faced since the Exodus itself. The danger is not just to *Gardenspot*, but to all the Ships and all the Crews. You are the one named to save us—"

"The Tomorrow Log is a tale for children—and for halfwits. It has nothing to do with me. Go!"

She stamped her foot, voice rising to a shout. "I have not sought you, world to world, year to year, to take 'nay' from an ill-tempered brat as my final orders!"

"A fine respect," Gem drawled, "to show for the Captain Hero." He snapped forward, put his face close to hers and spoke deliberately. "I am not yours. Go away."

So saying, he left her there, and she let him go, which upon reflection, did not make him entirely easy. He turned the matter over as he went from errand to errand, and made a note to speak to *Dart's* Captain Skot, when that ship came to port.

CHAPTER SIX

THE RESEARCH HAD gone slowly: he'd uncovered the breath of a possibility, nothing more, and Shilban in such a vile mood it was worth Gem's entire fortune, and the Vornet's as well, to disturb the scholar today.

Standing on the rotting verandah, he stared out over the city, rubbing the palm of his right hand down his thigh and frowning. Tomorrow. Tomorrow he would have the answer to the riddle of what protected Mordra El Theman's treasure so well. The day after, at the very latest, he would have an antidote—and damn Shilban's moods! Three days hence, the vase would be his and on its way off-world.

Gem nodded, discovered his hand still rubbing against his leg, and balled it into a fist. Third Noon was long past, and darkness was settling comfortably over the city below. He abruptly decided against going home. He would need to come back to Shilban's Library early tomorrow morning in any wise; it was senseless to add a trip from across the city and Down to the day's labors.

He crossed the verandah gingerly, sprang over the disintegrating steps and descended the slope toward the 'Ramp that would bear him down to UpTown.

Dinner covers removed by the efficient Phred, Gem leaned back in his chair and sipped an excellent brandy, languidly watching the ebb and flow of people within the Concourse. There were a good many tourists among the players; if he still picked pockets he would have done quite well this evening. Not that Edreth had sanctioned the picking of pockets as more than an exercise in versatility. He—and his apprentice— were of the elite, who stole art objects and valuables far beyond mere money or day-jewels.

Theirs was the glory and the greater gain, Edreth had said often enough; and, which he did not say, theirs was the greatest risk. A mere pickpocket might be fined, or lose a year of consciousness in the Blue House, while his body did service. A master thief, unlikely as it was that such would be apprehended, would lose his fortune, his name and quite likely his life, for Henron, at least, did not believe in rehabilitation of the persona, not with the demand for bodies so high. And so profitable.

Watching the players, he did not see them until they were upon him: an expensively dressed woman flanked by two men who wore vests, so the guns would not offend. But the guns were there, nonetheless; as apparent as Phred and the Concourse bouncer were absent.

Gem set his drink aside, rose and bowed as they came to his table, deeply and with profound respect. He straightened in time to see the surprise in the woman's eyes; smiled and showed her his empty hands in the age-old gesture of welcome.

"My lady. I am amazed and honored to see you."

Surprise had faded; the aquamarine eyes held speculation. "But you made sure that you would," she said, and her voice matched her person—lovely and expensive and very, very dangerous. "See me."

He made a show of astonishment. "I? How could I make sure of such a thing?"

"By ignoring my messages and confounding my messengers." She lifted a hand glittering with jewels; motioned. "May I sit?"

"If it pleases you," Gem said, though it far from pleased him. He watched as her gun-sworn pulled the chair out for her; and sat at the same instant she did, as an equal chieftain would, and affected not to see that the second gunman had raised his hand to his vest.

"May I offer you brandy, my lady?" he inquired courteously. "Wine?"

She lifted a finger and the man's hand dropped; smiled coolly at Gem. "Brandy would be pleasant. Thank you."

He raised his own hand and Phred was magically at his side, whisking away the half-empty snifter and replacing it with two, generously filled.

"You do not answer my charge, Master ser Edreth," said Saxony Belaconto, laying her bejeweled hands flat upon the table and fixing him with those alluring eyes.

He gazed back, his own hands relaxed and in sight. "What should I answer, lady? Your messengers approached me twice. In each instance I gave them a message to take back to you. If they failed of this, then I can only suggest—with all courtesy—that you must look to the quality of your employees." He dropped his eyes momentarily; brought them back to hers.

"As for confounding your messenger—she was overzealous, to my mind, and required a lesson. You note that she came back to you intact."

"I did note that, yes." She raised her glass; sipped delicately. "The message I received was that you refused my commission."

"It was never so harshly phrased as that, my lady."

"But that was the essence of the message," she pursued, watching him closely.

"Yes," Gem agreed, tasting the brandy carefully.

"I would be interested in learning why." She held up a hand, forestalling the explanation. "It was perhaps not explained to you: I return favors lavishly. You would not be the poorer for assisting me."

"I never doubted it," he told her, and sighed lightly. "My master left me several life-rules, all of which have served me well; all of which have sound reason and the experience of a long and fruitful life behind them. One of these rules was to never do favors." He gazed ingeniously into her eyes.

"Lady, I am desolate that I may not assist you. As I suggested to your gun-sworn, there are several of my profession on Henron; several more on Zelta. There is no reason to expect that they embrace the same life-rules as I."

"You were mentioned to me as the best," Saxony Belaconto said; "and the task I have in mind would challenge even the best, I think." She looked at him; he smiled and shook his head.

"Two hundred thousand qua," she said softly, and lifted her glass to drink.

The sum was large; fully twice his own liquid assets, here on Henron. The thought disturbed him, though, of course the Vornet would be able to command such information from any data bank. What disturbed him more was that she apparently thought the cash the full extent of his resources.

"A handsome repayment for even a challenging favor. I regret—"

"Four hundred thousand qua."

"Lady," he said, as gently as was possible. "There is no sum of money that can buy my assistance. I am my own man and no one else commands me. This suits me very well. I have no wish to offend you or your masters, I merely wish to be left to live my life as I would."

"I see." She raised her glass and drank again. "Passable. Allow me, though, Master ser Edreth, to send you some from my own cellar."

"My thanks to you, lady, but—no."

She laughed suddenly, as gaily as any girl, and reached across to touch his hand. "By not even so much as a bottle of brandy! Very well, then, sir."

She rose, and he did, and she beckoned to her bodyguard as he bowed. "Good evening, lady."

"Good evening, Master ser Edreth, and thank you for your hospitality. No doubt we shall speak again."

"I would welcome the opportunity," he lied politely; and she laughed again and left him.

CHAPTER SEVEN

THE BED SHIFTED slightly and Gem woke, watching through half-closed eyes as the roomgirl pulled on her robe and finger-combed her hair. She was pleasant enough to look at, and knew her trade, though he had made rough use of her skill, with unease over the Vornet foremost in his mind.

She finished setting her hair into order and made sure of the robe's fastening, full mouth puckered in concentration. He had a sudden, unlikely urge to ask her name, to apologize for his inattention last evening; but she had turned by then, and slipped out the door, so the impulse died and the worries resumed.

Rolling over onto his back, he stared at the pastel ceiling and tried to impose order on his thoughts. Only after a problem was logically arranged, Edreth had taught him, could it be fully seen and solved.

Of first concern was the Vornet. That Saxony Belaconto, chief of the Vornet's section leaders, should herself seek out a mere freelance thief was unprecedented. More in keeping with her office to simply dispatch a half-dozen gun-sworn and have him brought to her. Instead, she had come to him, acquiesced to the fiction of equality, and sought to *persuade him* to serve her. And the fee she offered! So very generous—and so quickly doubled.

"Stars and ships, what can she want?"

No answer to his whisper from the ceiling. Gem closed his eyes. Whatever she wanted, it was no concern of his, for he would not be the one to steal it for her.

Yet—that not-so-veiled threat, promising another meeting.

Anxiously, he considered his condition—no kin, that might be used as hostages; no close associates of any kind, now that Edreth was gone. It was true that the Vornet might freeze his accounts, but only a small percentage of his money was banked on Henron, and cash was easily replaced. There was nothing, really, that Saxony Belaconto could use as a lever to move Gem ser Edreth.

Except himself.

He opened his eyes and stared at the ceiling. Drugs existed; pain existed; and disease. The Vornet no doubt employed experts in the application of each. Saxony Belaconto had asked; had condescended to his skill and come herself to reason with him. The next step must be force, for what she wanted she would have; he had seen that in her eyes.

Breathing a trifle ragged because of the sudden constriction of his chest, he slid out of bed and went into the shower, clearing his mind; trying to count the moves and figure the timing of the thing. For he still had need of Shilban and his wonderful Library, which was the reason he had chosen Henron as a base in the first wise.

The Vornet would allow him a day to reconsider what he had heard last night, he thought, rinsing soap absently from pale gold hair; and that day he would spend with Shilban, gaining the knowledge necessary to defeat the demon in El Theman's vase. Tonight, he would slip the vase free, and be waiting for Captain Skot and *Dart* tomorrow dawn. The ship would serve as a sanctuary even the Vornet could not breach. Mayhap he could even show Skot sufficient cause to lift early, though he didn't count on that.

The shower cycled to cold and he gasped, suddenly and surprisingly longing for a sight of Linzer Skot's sharp-featured, daredevil face.

"Everything by the numbers," he told himself sternly, as the shower turned itself off and the dryer began to glow. "Retreat may be wise, but you will retreat in good order, one move at a time."

CHAPTER EIGHT

WOULD HE NEVER come home?

Corbinye stirred in the wall-niche, went through the Hemvil sequence to ease her cramped muscles and wondered for the eighth time whether she should leave her post across from Anjemalti's house and seek him UpTown.

As seven times before, she decided to stay where she was. It was so late, a mere hour from Primus Watch, which the Grounders called First Dawn—surely he was even now coming down the outer walk, and would turn the corner in a moment.

But the moment passed, and a handful of others, and still he did not come.

To pass the time, she began to plan what she might say to him. It was true that he had infuriated her with his stubbornness and—she allowed herself to know it—terrified her by crying out "Damn the Ship!" as if he were merely a couthless Grounder. But there was some justice in what he did, if one only gave a little thought to how matters must look to him. Sold, made into a thief by a Grounder of the same trade, abandoned, he must think, by Ship and Crew; he enters adulthood, at last his own master—and comes Corbinye Faztherot, her head so full of the Tomorrow Log and Ship's need that she takes no time to speak from the heart, kin-to-kin, and tell him how he had been missed, and grieved over, and sought after.

She stumbled here in her thoughts, because it was equally true that she had the barest memory of him—a fuzzy vision of a playmate half-a-head shorter than she, inexplicably clumsy in the dim halls and ductways that were the kingdom of children aboard *Gardenspot*, but very merry for all that, and given to laughter.

It was him laughing that she best remembered, so the lash of his anger now was more keenly felt. She nodded to herself in the wall-niche and resolved to take care with him this time, and show grace for his hurts.

She froze, ears catching again the slight scrape of boot heel upon walkstone.

At last! she thought and leaned forward—and froze, trusting that their poor Grounder eyes would not see her, though her hair must shine like a beacon in the dark, even to them.

For it was not Anjemalti, but a man and a woman—bulky, as Grounders often are, and moving with a care that screamed of stealth and the intent of deeds best not performed.

They passed, neither glancing aside, and Corbinye ducked into deeper shadow, watching them down the court.

Straight up to Anjemalti's door they went, as if they had a right to be there. The woman bent, probing with an instrument so light-gaudy that Corbinye winced in the distance, and strained to see through the multicolored glare. The man grunted audibly, fiddling with the darker machine he carried—and Anjemalti's door swung open to admit them.

Corbinye hesitated a heartbeat. Then, silent as a shadow, with all the stealth of Worldwalker and Seeker, she slipped down the court and followed them inside.

"Look at 'em fly!" Remee hissed, dancing back as the volt-meter crackled and sparked and fused. She swept a handful of fragile electronic spiders to the floor, laughing as they scrambled for safety; stamping them to bits under her boots. Chel was systematically smashing the instruments, and Remee left the rubble of spiders and began ripping cables loose and yanking various gauges and electronic junk off the wall.

She dropped a particularly delicate something on the floor and kicked it to bits, destruction-drunk and loving it.

The woman was on her before she could yell, slamming her head hard against the wall and putting a vicious elbow into her throat. The padding saved her life, but the blow was wicked enough to send her retching to her knees.

By the time she had groped the infraglasses back onto her face, Chel was swinging his bar at the woman—two-handed, so quick Remee heard it whistle through the air as she anticipated the soggy mess it would make of the woman's head—

Except the woman's head was no longer where it had been a heartbeat before. She dove for the floor, landed on her hands and continued the roll, space boots in a line with Chel's face.

He ducked at the last second, bringing the bar around to block the blow—and lost it as the woman twisted and kicked, impossibly sideways, and was back on her feet, blade out, half-crouched in a way that said she knew the worst of knife-fighting.

Chel dove, even as Remee yelled and launched herself clumsily at the woman's knees.

Corbinye leapt, used the momentum of the leap to twist—painfully slow in this gravity, though she knew the move as well as the sound of her own heartbeat—hit the floor with both hands, rolled and came up with the jack bar in one hand and the knife in the other.

The man hesitated; the woman licked her lips.

Corbinye grinned, beckoned with the knife; tested the weight of the bar. "Can it be you Grounders do not wish to die?"

"Look—" started the man, and Corbinye let the grin go, slashed air with the bar and yelled, with all the command of one born to be First.

"You motley pair of roaches! How dare you come into my cousin's house, destroy his works—you should die for that alone! But I feel pity for you, in your stupidity." She paused, filled her lungs to capacity and spent it in a roar. "GET OUT!"

They got out, running and stumbling as if the dark-seeing glasses they wore were insufficient against the comfortable dimness that pervaded Anjemalti's house. Corbinye tracked them by ear; slipped through the outer rooms to the door— in time to see both intruders turning the corner from the court to the thoroughfare.

Corbinye shook her head. "So, cousin," she whispered to the lightening gloom, "you had some cause to stay away last night."

She slipped her knife out of sight and stepped into the court, taking care to lock the door behind her. Frowning, she considered what she knew of his habits and haunts, before carefully going down the court and out into the thorough-fare, across DownTown and into UpTown, to find him.

CHAPTER NINE

ITS NAME, ACCORDING to the dusty gramarye he'd ferreted out from a low shelf of moldering bound books, was *Sarialdan*, and it was a demon of most puissant power, which answered to no known spell or amulet of protection.

Shilban, finally run to ground in the topmost study, stared grumpily at the page thrust under his nose; and then pointed that same nose sharply at Gem.

"What're ye into now?"

Gem grinned. "I could do you a disservice and answer."

"More like not," sniffed the scholar, and shook his frail head. "Fearstone's nothing to play with, young master. Find a safer toy."

"But this one's found me," Gem murmured, laying the book precariously atop the littered desk and hitching a hip onto the windowsill. "Nearly cost me my life—and it did cost me the job. What if everyone starts importing this Fearstone to guard their belongings? I'll be out of business."

"Adopt some other trade in a trice," the old man stated, pulling the gramarye onto his lap and frowning down at the crumbling page. "Doubtless as harebrained as this." He sighed.

"No need to bother yourself. Rare person who can stand to be in the same room with the stuff. Rarer still to be able to pick it up. Small reason to believe people will leave off nice, comfortable electronic alarms and such to go with something as chancy as Fearstone." Shilban carefully turned the page.

"The book says there is no antidote," Gem murmured, anxious not to let the old scholar lose himself too far in the volume. "But you just said that some people are more sensitive than others. That some people can hold the stone in their hands?"

"Well, of course they can. Why shouldn't they?" said Shilban querulously.

"Because the effects, when the stone is held, are quite devastating," Gem snapped and Shilban cackled.

"Ah-ah, the young master doesn't like being bested! But there you are—some people are great cowards; others haven't got the sense to fear. *Sarialdan* isn't alive, it's just a dumb transmitter. All it does is transmit fear, boy. Just fear." He closed the book and put it haphazardly atop a stack of random volumes.

"Just fear." Gem stared; slipped to his feet and fished a gold round out of his pocket. "Shilban."

The old man looked up, more than half back into the book he had been studying when Gem had found him. His eyes lighted on the round incuriously.

Gem took his hand, pressed the coin into his palm, closed the fingers tightly around it. "For you—and my thanks, Scholar, for all your aid."

"That's all right, lad," the old man muttered, fingers still tight about the coin. "I'll be seeing you, then." He bent his head over the book again.

"Perhaps you will," Gem said, though he was certain the other did not hear. "But I don't really think so."

Quietly, as if his steps could have disturbed the other's study, Gem slipped through the room and ghosted down the stairs.

Only fear.

He walked along the rotting streets of OldTown, wrestling with his thoughts, imposing structure.

Sarialdan transmitted fear. To best it, he need only acknowledge those things that he feared and recall that these terrors could not themselves cause his downfall.

He turned a corner, going from shade into brightness; his eyes adjusting instantaneously to keep his vision sharp.

He feared…He feared?

Death, of course: The lack of breath in the lungs; sightlessness; lack of consciousness forever—or consciousness, knowing oneself dead. Equally horrible. Equally unstoppable. Except on Henron, where the Blue House provided bodies to those who were dying. For a price.

Gem stopped, staring sightlessly across an overgrown park-square.

He feared the Blue House.

To lose his life in the Blue House, while his body served another…He shivered in the warm sunlight—and shivered again at the next thought:

To lose consciousness—and awaken in another body, looking out from behind a face whose expressions he did not know, to be imprisoned by a heartbeat never his own; to learn how to walk again, to run, to eat, to talk—

His hands were cold; his breathing accelerated; forehead slightly damp. He forced a laugh and shook himself, turning resolutely down a side street. Edreth had once told him that a master thief's greatest asset and greatest enemy was the intensity of his imagination.

Only fear.

Something scraped behind him and he spun, fear abruptly replaced by dead calm as the sorl-knife slid into his hand and his body melted into the crouch.

Corbinye stood two arm's-lengths away, back curled in a half-bow; palms up and out and showing empty. She was looking at a point near his boots.

He glanced down, saw the mangled remains of his spider; saw her knife beside it, sheathed.

He looked up and his face was cold, the knife still steady in his hand. Corbinye approved the speed with which he had adopted the fighting crouch, and the soundless smoothness with which he came both ready and armed.

She did not so much approve that particular look on his face, as if the tiny robot was kin she had laid at his feet; as if her knife, freely offered, meant just less than nothing. She raised her head and looked at him, eye to eye.

Eyes among the Crew were black or, more seldom, amber. Anjemalti's eyes were blue, which color lent them even more chill. Corbinye began to think that she had reasoned wrongly; that he would not even allow her—

"Five Words," he snapped and she sighed. Mercy, then, though meager, when the Captain might grant Five, Ten or Twenty Words of formal defense from a Crewmember before passing judgment.

Still, five words were better than none. Corbinye went to one knee, as befitted a supplicant, and raised her face to his.

"Housebreakers," she said firmly; "dispatched."

Almost, she thought a glimmer of humor ran through those chilly eyes; at least his knife went away and he stood up tall.

"Elaborate."

She shrugged and stood. "Two people—a man and a woman—came down the court to your house in the hour just before First Dawn. They used an instrument of some kind on the door, entered and began to destroy." She moved a hand toward the shattered robot. "They began in your workshop."

"So." The eyes were much less chill, though not nearly warm. "You said—dispatched. Dead?"

"No, Anjemalti. I did not know who they were. I do not know the Grounders' laws. I frightened them away, then locked the door and came to find you with the news."

"Locked the door…" He bent and carefully scooped up the broken spider; took up her knife as an afterthought and extended it, hilt first.

She took it with a slight bow. "My thanks."

"My thanks to you," he said absently, most of his attention centered, it seemed, on what he held.

She watched him for a handful of minutes.

"You know who did this," she said, certain without knowing why.

"Yes…" Still absent, as though he answered some thought of his own rather than her voice. As she watched, he shook himself, looked at her intently, and said, quite firmly, "Yes."

"Well, then, if they're less troublesome dead, why do we not grant them the gift?" She grinned. "Little enough challenge for us two, cousin."

He stared at her, lithe and wolfish before him, with the stark light of First Noon making a halo of her hair, her eyes great and black under arching brows. A comely and capable young woman, single-minded, deadly, as the Crew ever was.

"Corbinye," he began, and then hesitated, because it seemed that he had only this moment seen her, only this heartbeat understood that he named a person, as solid and as alive as he himself.

"Corbinye, you do not want to be part of this," he managed, and stopped this time because she laughed.

"Anjemalti, I am already part of it. Did I not frighten them away and threaten them with mayhem?"

He shook his head. "Those people were hirelings—the hands and muscle of a great and powerful lady. Of themselves, they are nothing, except that one does not make the mistake of cutting off this lady's hands."

Corbinye tipped her head. "You are feuding with this other Captain, Anjemalti? If so, then you have need of my service—for *you* have no hirelings, do you, that you might send to her place in order to exact payment in kind?"

"I'm not a captain, girl—I'm a thief! And Saxony Belaconto is a chieftain of the Vornet. An unequal contest, I assure you." He saw the puzzlement in her face and answered it. "The lady desires me to steal something for her. Urgently."

"And she sends people to break your tools and destroy your homeplace to persuade you?" She shook her head in clear disbelief. "It's a madwoman, Anjemalti; disregard her."

For the first time she heard him laugh, though it was a sharp and bitter thing.

"She tried kinder persuasions first and I denied her. Now, she seeks to remind me of her strength." His shoulders sagged suddenly and his fingers closed tightly around the broken spider. "I had thought I had a day…"

"A day?" Corbinye glanced up at the sky, ran the equation to transfer sun position into Shiptime and shook her head again. "Do you dice with comets, too?"

This time the laugh was sweeter. "Grant me grace: My master is barely two years dead, and I do not wish to sell myself to another."

"In that case, cousin, you must put yourself out of this madwoman's way. My ship awaits—we can lift within the hour."

Too large a wager, and a clumsy cast, besides. Corbinye silently cursed herself, as his easiness fled and his eyes grew colder.

"I have my own resources, thank you." He hesitated; thawed a fraction. "I owe you much, for the rescue of my house, and for the warning you bring. Payment is returned in kind: Go down to your ship and leave here. Lift within the hour."

"Anjemalti—"

"Corbinye." He came forward, laid his hand upon her arm and looked directly into her eyes. "Corbinye, the Vornet is too massive an opponent—even for you—and there is scant honor in fighting them. The captain you came to find died twenty Standards ago. You have done a service for Gem ser

Edreth, who is a thief, but honorable enough, in his way. Take thanks for the service and get yourself gone from the danger." The grip on her arm tightened; vanished. "*Do* it."

She hesitated; touched his sleeve. "At least your kiss."

The blue eyes were frozen; the controlled voice nearly a shout. "I am not your captain!"

"We are kin!" she insisted and dared to lean a little closer. "Besides, I find you pleasing. What harm a kiss?"

But he had backed away with a headshake, so that play was ill-made, too. Though she wondered, as she watched him leave, whether it had been a play at all.

CHAPTER TEN

DETAINED, the 'gram read; DINNER AND DANCING NEXT WEEK? LS.

And so much for the purpose that had brought him to the beam office. He crumpled the 'gram and tossed it into the waste chute. If Linzer and *Dart* were 'detained' until next week, there was no power that Gem ser Edreth knew of that would fetch them one heartbeat sooner.

A glance at the shipboard told him what he already knew: *Lady Ro* had lifted that morning; no other ship with which he had influence was in port. Idly, he wondered which was Corbinye's; and put speculation firmly aside.

He stepped out into the cool dusk of Third Noon and filled his lungs with damp air.

"Damn."

Well, Linzer had been late once before—with very good cause, as it had turned out, and not to his blame that Edreth had died of the delay. It was now up to Edreth's apprentice to see that he did not die of this new delay.

Obviously, it was not prudent to return to his house, though he grieved for the spiders abandoned there. A pair rode in his pockets, always; and new tools were easily acquired. It would also be foolish to try to draw money from his account, though his purse was distressingly flat.

So then, first order of business—money. Second, a place to stay for a few days. Third, to while the time before *Dart* gained port, another try at Mordra El Theman's vase. Yes, and perhaps a word in Shilban's ear, as well, that he might take what precautions he would against the Vornet.

"A what!" Saxony Belaconto stared at Chel, who quailed before the disbelief and anger in her eyes. From his station at the door, Vylar grinned and admired Saxony's ass. Quite a nice one it was, too, and very energetic in bed.

"But—A woman, Ms. Belaconto," Remee was insisting. "Looked like the thief, a little—blond hair sticking out all over her head, and eyes like—like—" she fumbled and Chel took it up.

"Glowed," he said, succinctly. "Her eyes glowed in the dark. Like a cat."

"You two—idiots," Saxony grated, with, Vylar thought, astonishing restraint, "want me to believe that Gem ser Edreth, who has never brought so much as a songbird to his house, is keeping a knife-wielding floozy—"

"Cousin," Chel corrected.

Saxony's eyes narrowed dangerously. "What did you say?"

"Said she was his cousin," Chel elaborated and turned to his partner. "You remember, Rem—called us roaches, and wanted to know who the hell we thought we were, coming into her cousin's house and busting up his stuff."

"That's right." Remee nodded. "Thought she looked like him."

"The lady," murmured Vylar, "seems to be an accurate judge of character, at least."

Saxony's eyes scraped over him once before returning to the bullteam. "You'll know her again, this cousin?"

"Yes, Ms. Belaconto," Remee said, with an uncharacteristic lack of enthusiasm. Vylar frowned: Rem was always ready for a scrap; apparently the knife-wielding floozy had made an impression.

"I'd know her," Chel said, Chel-like, and likely thinking no more about it than that.

Saxony nodded, walked over to the window and stared out, no doubt considering this sudden cousin. No doubt thinking that at last here was the handle on the thief, when they'd all been convinced he was smooth as blastglass.

"Vylar."

He straightened, with just the hint of a heel-click. "Ms. Belaconto."

"Bring her." She turned from the window; waved a hand at the bullteam. "Take them and as many others as you need. Use whatever force you must. But I want that woman and I want her now." She smiled, and Vylar felt cold feet run down his spine. "Imagine, Gem ser Edreth has a cousin."

She lost him in UpTown among the thronging Grounders, and took herself over to a park, to sit in the sun and think it out.

Corbinye was fond of parks: This one, with the fountain splashing and glittering and surrounded by weedy flowers, reminded her of the Conservatory from which *Gardenspot* took its name. She perched on the back of a bench, put her feet on the seat and sighed.

"A fine, foolish botch you've made of it," she grumbled to herself, pitching a bit of quartz into the fountain. Though, in justice to herself, there was nothing different she could have done. Honor did not allow her to stand by and watch while Grounder criminals ripped apart the homeplace of *any* of the Crew. That they dared use their destructive arts against the Captain's own home—

She sighed again and threw a second pebble angrily into the spray. "Not that he acts as much like a Captain as that…" Yet still, he was of the Ship, blood and bone, and the very stubbornness and independence that currently frustrated her proved his lineage more surely than any gene map.

A breath of wind dashed fountain-spray into her face and she reached up to push the hair out of her face. Over-long, the stuff was: nearly the length of four of her fingers, held together. Anjemalti wore his hair Grounder-style, down to the shoulder and caught back with a ribbon, which she found oddly pleasing. Her own she was used to having cropped close to her head in the way of the Crew.

She stood abruptly, casting the rest of the quartz-bits in a scintillant handful. Always it came back to that! The Crew and Anjemalti. Anjemalti and the Crew. Consistently he had denied his heritage; sought to drive her away—even now, he sent her from his enemies, whom they should meet shoulder-to-shoulder.

He had damned the Ship.

And yet—the Tomorrow Log. She herself had read the entry, written on real paper, ancient ink-marks faded, but still legible. She had borne witness to the execution of Indemion Kristefyon, though the death of a Captain was not for everyone to see. She had tracked a name and a prophecy through years and numberless deceits to her goal.

Only to find her goal an attractive young man with nothing of the god about him, and his own business to attend to.

If only the Log had been more specific! But she only knew that the offspring of the Captain Who Died Beforetime would bring the Ship from some terrible danger, to safety and a greater future.

Little enough to offer, even to one not raised as a Grounder, and bitter, besides.

Corbinye flung off across the park. She paused at the edge of a carpet of grass with the sun beating down upon her head, watching a group of children playing a game involving a ball and a great deal of rushing about and shouting.

Abruptly, she shivered, remembering the misshapen little body; the grave gentleness of the Medic as he explained it to her, while the birth-drug still lent some cushion to the pain—"Too deformed to live. It's a mercy; and he will be sent on his way with due honor, as a member of the Crew should be."

The ball escaped its gaggle of playmates; came bouncing raggedly across the grass, one small person in pursuit. Corbinye scooped the sphere up and held it out, smiling. The girl hesitated, small eyes stretched to their limit. Then her face cleared; she smiled and dove forward to snatch the ball away. "Thank you, lady!" she called, already on her way back to her mates.

"You are welcome, child," Corbinye said softly and shook her head. "If only Anjemalti were so easily won."

He moved within the crowded Third Evening, groomed to a fault, pale hair tied smoothly back with a ribbon that matched both the blue of his eyes and that of his wide-sleeved shirt. Jewels winked between his hands, at wrist and throat—enough to proclaim him a person of means; too few to draw the eyes and interest of the curious.

He spiraled through the crowd, occasionally leaving it to place a wager or take a bit of wine at a casino or bar. If anyone noted his partiality for very crowded spaces, that person would no doubt also note his youth, and subscribe the choice of crowds to the youthful lust for experience.

In time, his spiraling path took him near the less-favored, less-crowded emporiums of pleasure, and he slipped down a side-way, keeping pace with the shadowed shadow of himself. He came at length to a dim doorway and paused for a moment to look about and to listen.

Silence. Emptiness in all directions. He laid his hand upon the door and was admitted almost at once.

An hour later, a clerk in the last hotel between UpTown and Old looked up from her desk and frowned. "Well?"

The young man smiled apologetically and smoothed slim, ringless hands down his faded and carefully-patched brown tunic. "I need a room for tonight—for as many as two nights," he said meekly. "If—?"

The clerk's frown darkened, though, really, there was nothing to frown at—merely a shabby and no doubt respectable boy, his fair hair tied neatly back with a fraying blue ribbon and his boots in need of polish.

"We require cash in advance," she said. "If you want two nights, you pay for two nights. If you pay for two nights and only want one, you don't get any money back. Understand?"

"I understand," he answered and took a tentative step forward. "Do you have a room?"

She gave him a sharp look. "Just you?"

"Just me, mistress," he said gravely and she snorted.

"All right, then. One qua covers both nights."

He produced the coin from a flat and much-scuffed leather purse, and laid it on the counter, though his hand showed a tendency to linger in a way that the clerk knew all too well. She sighed, frown fading.

"What's your name?"

"Mel Boryonda."

She tapped in the information. "Address?"

He looked confused and a little abashed and she sighed again, typed in "Visitor", brought up the grid and handed him the card.

"Third floor, room sixteen. The lift's broken, but there's stairs right beside it. Put the card in the doorslot red side up to let you in, yellow side up to lock you in. No visitors, no food in the room, no pets. All understood?"

"Yes, mistress." He slipped the card from her fingers and bowed, slightly and stiffly, as if such courtesy was new to him. The clerk smiled, a little. "We're right on the edge of OldTown here," she told him, though she usually didn't bother, "and that's not such a great neighborhood. Best thing might be for you to put off any errands you've got until First Morning."

He bowed again, still stiffly, and subjected the keycard to serious scrutiny. "Red to open, yellow to seal."

"Right."

"Good night, then, mistress." And he was gone, boot heels clicking on the concrete floor.

He was not at Kayje's Concourse; he was not at Milbrun's Tavern; he was not at Three-of-a-Kind.

The Curiosity Shop was full to the doors; the registrar an older man with hungry eyes. Five qua bought a look at his log—Anjemalti was not inside.

One by one, she went to the places he frequented and came at last to the edge of UpTown and stood staring at the scant lights below. A man and a woman lurched past, linked by arms about each other's waist. Corbinye tensed as the man brushed her arm, smelled the liquor on his breath and let them go without comment.

It was possible that he had returned to his house. He was of Captain's lineage, after all, and common wisdom only one in the constellation of factors he must consider. How if he sought to decoy this other Captain into a trap? How if he chose to demonstrate that her show of strength was beneath his notice? To force her to reevaluate her position? Was it not true, should Anjemalti behave as if he had the entire Crew at his back, that this other Captain might wonder, and reconsider—and possibly withdraw?

Such things were not unknown. Corbinye had read the Logs as part of her schooling; and it seemed to her that many of the struggles between the great Captains of the past were merely games of fabrication and nerve, with the Captain whose nerve failed first yielding to the terms of the other.

Very possible, these things recalled, that Anjemalti had returned to his homeplace, Corbinye conceded. It only remained for her to determine how best to serve him in this play.

Were *I* the other Captain, she thought, leaning elbows on the rail and frowning at the city below; and thought I knew my enemy to be alone, I might risk the trap; the slender chance of a hundred armed crewmen awaiting their Captain's word. Yes, she thought, remembering the tenor of the rival Captain's crew members; yes, I might well take that chance. And move to crush him.

It was if a hand closed round her chest, then, squeezing heart and lungs, so that one pounded and the other labored. Corbinye straightened, licking her lips, remembering Indemion Kristefyon's face as he took The Knife from the First Mate's hand; the proud, unrepentant eyes as he reversed it for the stroke, so full of life it seemed he could never die.

But he had, bare moments later, by his own hand and The Knife, as even a rogue Captain might die, re-joining the Crew by the act, and buried, with honor, as one of their own.

Of a certainty, Anjemalti had gone home, too proud to take his cousin's aid, to try some mad ploy against a Captain who kept rogues and wanton destroyers among her crew.

Deliberately, she started down the 'Ramp, swearing under her breath, and did not hear the footsteps pacing her until she was halfway to the street.

She slowed, and the steps behind slowed, as well; she increased her pace, and they increased. Corbinye swore again; and abruptly grinned. If it was footpads, intent on overtaking her at street-level, they were about to partake of a new experience. The ill-lit street was all to her advantage, and her skill with the sorl-knife was legend, even among the deadly fighters of the Crew. The delay chafed, of course, but it need not be so long a delay as that.

So thinking, she leapt forward, running the last meters to the flat; charged into the deeper shadows and spun, knife out, to face the two clattering to catch her.

The woman was familiar—one of the destroyers she had routed from Anjemalti's house—and only moderately dangerous. But her mate in this endeavor was another matter entirely. Lean, supple, and canny, he dropped into a crouch, ready to take a charge, but offering no immediate threat. Corbinye slipped back a step, keeping him in her eye: No sudden rush at *this* one, who looked to know the business as well as she did. She damned the delay once more, then brought all of her attention to the current circumstance.

"We don't want to hurt you," the man said unexpectedly, and Corbinye grinned, moving the knife in invitation.

He moved his head in an abbreviated shake. "Saxony Belaconto wants to see you. Nothing to—"

"Saxony Belaconto may see me in hell," Corbinye told him, "whether you chose to fight or tuck your tail under and crawl home to lick her boots."

The woman grunted at that and made a move—quickly controlled as Corbinye glanced her way. The man grinned, but neither moved closer nor stepped back.

"Just a little chat, miss, that's all," he said, persuasively, though she still did not credit him a coward. "There's no need for any of us to bleed over it. Put the knife away and walk with us and—"

She heard it then, the reason for his talkativeness: Two sets of footsteps were moving softly toward them from her right; another set from her left. Corbinye jumped, scored a glancing kick off the woman's head; snapped into a roll and came up, knife leading, lunging for his throat.

He danced away, though her blade drew blood from an unwary forearm, and kicked, knife-gleam in his hand as he spun back. There was no time for finesse; no time for the subtleties of an honorable fight, with his compatriots bearing down upon them. Corbinye feinted, twisted, slipped—and threw as she leaned in to take the advantage, lodging her knife in his throat.

From the woman she had stunned, a keen of sheer hatred. Corbinye ripped her blade free, snatched the other out of slack fingers, reversed it and threw, setting the blade in the woman's chest as she ran for the 'Ramp.

Behind her, shouts and thundering footsteps; the whine and clatter of something thrown and fallen short. Corbinye followed the 'Ramp's twist, glanced up and saw her doom standing at the entrance, holding a pipe in his hand.

She checked minutely; cried out with sudden pain as something bit deep into her thigh; yanked it free and whirled, so that she faced them with two weapons ready, and her eyes gleaming murder.

The first never hesitated, but engaged at once, the second playing backup and slicing a path for the third to get behind as the one with the pipe came down to join in.

But even at that, it took longer and was more expensive than they expected. Just before the end Chel went with a dagger in his eye and Kris screamed and swung the pipe harder than he might, again and even again, though it was over by then, and Corbinye lay in a slick red puddle on the 'Ramp.

CHAPTER ELEVEN

IT WAS RAINING in OldTown.

The shabby young man in the brown tunic lifted his face and let the rain run into his ears and soak his hair. Almost, he laughed, remembering the first time he had been out in rain, screaming at Edreth to turn the sprinkler off and his master laughing. And, later, giving him books and his very own reader, so he learned about clouds and condensation rates and atmospheric conditions and weather.

The Library was lit bright against the gloom; the large, cracked window in front still shuttered. Gem frowned, then shrugged. No reason for Shilban to open the shutters to overcast sky and rain, after all. Better to stay inside, cocooned in the butter-yellow light of many lamps, and the warmth of wood burning on the crumbling hearth.

Gem went lightly up the chancy stairs, twisted the ancient knob and pushed the door wide.

Stared for—a heartbeat? an eternity?—as the young man struck the old man and screamed into his face, "Where is he?"

Shilban shook his head, raised it and said, quite clearly, "I don't know."

The man holding him shook him cruelly, but the one who had put the question only shrugged and sighed. He went to an overflowing shelf, pulled a book free at random and walked over to the fireplace. He showed the book to Shilban, then casually tossed it into the fire.

The old man screamed, writhed, and suddenly slumped in his captor's arms.

At the door, Gem screamed and hurled forward, knife out.

The questioner fell, and the man who held Shilban, before Carmen brought the dart-gun up and shot him in the throat.

CHAPTER TWELVE

PAIN, DISORIENTATION AND a smell of blood, far up in the nose.

Eyes quivered, resisted, finally came open—to darkness, horrifying and utter.

Throat cramped, but would not let the words through; as the body lay, stone-like, apart, and would not move.

"Easy, easy, there." The voice was kind; the hand upon one's forehead gentle. "I'm going to give you a shot to make you sleep," the voice said, and there were other small sounds, and a prick of pain.

"There, now," the voice said; "everything's going to be fine."

Tight muscles at last allowed a word. "Where?"

The kind hand smoothed one's forehead as the drug began its work, distancing the distant body. "The Blue House," the voice whispered. "Everything's going to be fine…"

CHAPTER THIRTEEN

THE BORTHO-LORANIA UNIT for Egotranslation offers a wide range of service to both individual and municipal clients.

For the individual, there is the transplant service, which makes suffering in an old, diseased or wounded body unnecessary. Healthy bodies are available from a diverse pool of age and ethnic groups, as well as a wide range of type. Persons considering a change of corporal residency are encouraged to take the tour and view prospective bodies. A Resurrective Therapist is also in residence to answer your questions and assist you in coming to closure with any anxiety you may have in undertaking such a change.

There are also a select group of bodies available for temporary use. Inquiries should be directed to the Office of Resurrective Therapy, which will coordinate details with the Department of Justice.

If you have any questions regarding the operation or system of the Bortho-Lorania Unit, please do not hesitate to contact our Public Relations Department.

The Bortho-Lorania Unit for Egotranslation is accredited jointly by the Hospital of Life Sciences, Bannger, and the Renfrew System Department of Justice, and is a publicly-held corporation.

—Excerpted from Pamphlet BLUEPR-66
"Is Translation for You?"

CHAPTER FOURTEEN

*"WELL?" ASKED EDRETH sharply, looking up from his book with a
frown.*

*Wordlessly, he held the ancient firearm out, light gleaming off cop-
per insets and mahogany grip. Barely, he was able to control the shaking
of his hands, the expression of his face, so that no sign of exultation
was apparent. A master thief, Edreth had taught him, was one who
went about things pragmatically, and, afterwards, might feel satisfaction
for a job executed according to his own high standards. Only a fool, or a
novice, allowed celebration to mar the pure business of stealing.*

*And yet—he had done it! Taken the precious thing out of its case
under the guard's very eyes, in a roomful of milling people, circumventing
the central alarm—all, all, all himself.*

Edreth glanced at the gun, raised his brows and repeated. "Well?"

*"I've brought it, master," he said, fighting to keep his cracking
voice even. "I took it as you said to, during peak hours, and left the
central system intact."*

*"I see." Edreth deigned to take the thing then, and study it, and
rub his hand along the worn satin wood. "Very well." He held the gun
out, grip first.*

"Now, put it back."

"Put it back!" He gasped, voice cracking twice.

*Edreth raised his brows and Gem reluctantly took the beautiful
old thing and slipped it out of sight.*

"Yes, master," he said, and silently sighed.

*Back at the museum, he twisted the knob in a door cracked and driz-
zling paint chips; pushed it open and stepped gingerly over the rotting
threshold—to stop in mingled shock and terror as the young man struck
the older and shouted, "Where is he?"*

*"I don't know," the old man said, and was shaken brutally by the
one who held him, arms pinned behind, while the questioner merely*

shrugged and went to a shelf, extracted a book, displayed it and tossed it into the flames.

"No!" He leapt across the room, knife out, but Shilban was hanging limp and slack-faced and a thrust killed the questioner and a slash across the throat accounted for the other and—

"Shilban?" More a hiss than a word—the best that swollen tongue and cracked lips could do.

The dream receded, leaving him a reality shot with various aches, of which pounding head and ringing ears were the worst. Thirst was a misery that accelerated toward agony as he came more fully aware.

Where? he wondered.

He was lying on his stomach on a soft surface; and his mistreated ears could detect no sound, beyond the hum of the filtering system. He pried his eyes open; ran dry tongue over sticky lips and tasted salt.

Bare inches from his nose was a mug, painted with a design of white flowers on a field of blue—handmade, his automatic appraisal went, but not intrinsically valuable. He concentrated, moved an arm that was dead weight alone, without muscle or sensation; forced it to place its fingers around the mug and lift it.

Raised his head—and drank.

There was a bitter tang to the water, but he drained the mug and allowed his head to thump onto the mattress. Slack fingers still braceleting the cup, he closed his eyes and listened to the chime of his ears, and the beat of his heart.

"Wake up!"

The command was emphasized by a whack across his rump and Gem gasped, twisted, hand with cup rising for the throw—and froze, as the man with the bitter eyes leveled a gun at him.

"Try it," he said softly, finger taut on the trigger. "Just give me an excuse, okay?"

"No," Gem rasped. The man grunted, disappointment showing, and motioned with the gun.

"Up you go—nice and easy—hands where I can see them, okay?"

He slid to his feet, nice and easy, and stood with his hands at chest level, open and palm-out, facing his captor.

"Turn around," the man said; "out the door and left. Try to run and you're meat, got it? Just like Birl and Julen."

Wordlessly, with exquisite gentleness, Gem turned and walked toward the door, which opened at his approach, and turned left down the hallway. Behind him, the gunman's boots squeaked.

"Hold it!"

Gem obeyed, glancing quickly around. To the left a blank white wall. To the right, a door indistinguishable from the last six they had passed. The gunman stepped forward, weapon trained on the center of Gem's chest, and laid his hand against the plate.

The door slid aside and he gestured with the gun. "Inside."

Inside was real wooden flooring, and a handwoven rug in rusts and browns and cream centered before a teak-wood desk as large as a single-man spacecraft. The walls were white, here hanging an abstract painting, there a rope-braided tapestry. Bookshelves held pottery totems, bits of unfinished gem and carvings. Gem's hands itched, his thief's judgment estimating and evaluating.

"Here he is, Ms. Belaconto."

Estimation crashed to a halt. He turned gently toward the window and bowed.

"Lady."

"Gem ser Edreth." She strolled toward him across yet another handmade rug, aquamarine eyes wide in a face that betrayed somewhat of tension. "I hope your accommodations were not overly unpleasant."

"I had very little opportunity to study them," he said as she stopped before him.

"Then all's well." She glanced beyond his shoulder. "You may go, Carmen."

"Ms. Belaconto—"

"I said that you may go, Carmen," Steel glinted in the perfect voice before she smiled and inclined her head. "Thank you."

"Yes, Ms. Belaconto." A whisper of sound, which may have been his bow, and a bit of boot-squeak before the door whispered open—snicked shut.

"Well." She smiled, slightly and unconvincingly, and gestured toward the chairs set near the window. "I beg you, sir, seat yourself and be comfortable."

He cleared his throat softly. "Lady, I ask why you have brought me here."

"Why, to continue our conversation," she said; "but there is no reason for us to be uncomfortable while we speak. Please, sir—sit down."

There was command in that and his body almost betrayed him by obeying. He shook his head sharply. "The conversation we parted on was finished; though I might ask you how it happens that your gun-sworn were harrying a grandfather in OldTown?"

There was a slight pause before she turned and walked a few paces away from him, toward the rug and facing chairs. "They were there at my order," she said flatly; "to discover what had become of Gem ser Edreth." Another pause, which he did nothing to fill; then, softly, baiting him:

"You do not ask what became of the old man."

He bowed. "I had hoped that the hospitality you had shown me you had also extended to him."

"Then you're a fool," she snapped, eyes glittering; "he's dead."

Grief, sudden and crushing—and as quickly, outrage, that she should order it; that she should gloat of it and use it like a knife, to cut and weaken him.

She smiled. "You will do as I say, Gem ser Edreth, and you will do it with courtesy and care."

"Because you murder my friend and savage my house?" He snapped forward two paces; saw her hand slip into her pocket and stopped, grinning. "A gun, lady? Shoot me and all's for nothing—as it is now! Shall I obey a madwoman, who kills for no cause? You destroy before you threaten; and—"

"Your cousin."

He froze, staring; saw the outline of hand in pocket tense, as if she gripped the gun in earnest.

"Your cousin," she repeated. "Corbinye Faztherot."

He took a deep breath. "She is not in this."

She smiled, and gently shook her head. "Your cousin is in the Blue House."

Fury jerked him forward; the gun in her hand stopped him, and his thoughts were for Corbinye, who was strong and full of life and in it because she had threatened a madwoman's minions. Corbinye, with her own mad obsession, and her youth and her off-handed courage.

The Blue House—ship and stars! What a fine price Corbinye's body would bring!

"There is nothing left for you to destroy, then, Saxony Belaconto," he heard himself say from worlds away, "saving only myself."

"The bitch is alive!" she snapped, finger tight on the trigger of her gun. "She should be dead—I lost two top fighters to her and—a captain. All beyond recall! But your cousin we brought to the Blue House, though she was two breaths away from her death. We paid the price—and she lives."

He stood utterly still, looking at her and thinking how many tricks were yet possible; and how unlikely it was that Corbinye's new body in any way approached the perfection of her original.

"Because we have shown this mercy—gone to this expense—for your cousin," Saxony Belaconto was saying, very softly, "you will do precisely as you are told. Fail in any way and she gains yet a third body—as old and decrepit and ugly and painful as can be acquired." She lowered the gun, slowly, but did not yet slip it away. "Do you understand me, Gem ser Edreth?"

"I will see her."

She laughed, sweet and horrifying as a girl. "But, of course! Take the evening—assure yourself that the Vornet is generous, even to its enemies. And return to me at Second Noon tomorrow, so that I may give you the details of your task." She waved a hand. "You may go."

He did so, omitting the bow.

CHAPTER FIFTEEN

THE WALLS WERE covered with red-and-gold flowers, printed on a reflective foil background. There were tubs of flowers flanking the receptionist, flooding the waiting room with their odor, and an empty bud vase on his desk. He nodded as he scanned the patient list and looked up at Gem with a smile.

"Corbinye Faztherot. Yes, sir. Room 14-86. Our Ms. Jancy will escort you. Just a moment while I let her know you're here." He touched a key on his console. Gem wandered across the room, wincing away from the gaudy wallpaper and the sharp-edged light, and stared out the window.

The Blue House was on a mezzanine level—MidTown, according to the local government—equally handy to Up and DownTown; within sight of the Port. Gem stared at the familiar constellation of DownTown. No reason, now, to bide away from his house—mere instinct had sent him to an UpTown hotel to shower and change into clothes more expected of a family affluent enough to pay the body-fee.

"Master ser Edreth?" The woman who asked it was petite and sprightly and smiling. He bowed and lightly brushed her outstretched hand with the tips of his fingers.

"I'm Coral Jancy," she said, smile never dimming. "You're here to see your cousin, I'm told. Right this way."

He followed her past the receptionist and the tubs of flowers; through a door and into a blessedly dim hallway.

"Have you been here before?" his guide asked him, smiling up into his face. "Visited a friend, perhaps, or another member of your family who had undergone translation?"

He shook his head. "No."

"Well, then," she said cheerily, "don't be disappointed if your cousin seems a little disoriented, or takes a little while to recognize you. It's perfectly natural. The procedure is perfectly safe, but it *is* radical and there is a progression of natural and necessary adjustments that the patient must go through on her way to complete synergy."

"Yes," said Gem, trying to breathe evenly, though the smell of flowers was overpowering.

"Now, in your cousin's case," Ms. Jancy continued, "we were quite, quite fortunate. Of course, we always try to match body-type as closely as possible in emergency cases, to minimize any further shock to the patient, you know."

"Of course," Gem echoed, as they turned into a wider hallway and paused before a bank of lifts.

Ms. Jancy pressed a button; stepped into the lift, Gem at her heels. "Fourteen," she said into the speaker, and the doors slid shut.

"I'm sure you know that young bodies in good health are difficult to come by," she said, smiling back at Gem, "but in this case, it happens that we had just finished preparing a host—a female quite near your cousin's age, I'd say; approximately the same height and coloring. Facial features—well, that's a little harder for me to say, considering the shape she was in—but your cousin was a handsome girl, I'd imagine."

She paused, apparently awaiting some response. Gem cleared his throat. "Quite handsome, yes."

Ms. Jancy nodded happily. "I'm sure she'll be quite pleased with the new host. A suicide, of course." She touched his sleeve soothingly. "Nothing violent! And no residual drugs—the procedure mandates a complete flush of the host body before translation."

The lift door opened then, and he followed her out into a cheery yellow hall. The reek of flowers nearly choked him.

"Here we are!" Ms. Jancy laid her hand on a door bearing the legend "86" and it slid open. "There's a small antechamber, and refreshments in the refrigerator. Beyond is your cousin's bedroom." Again, she touched his sleeve. "Remember, she's newly translated, and might be a bit disoriented yet; give her time to recall you. If she falls asleep, please don't wake her. Sleep is very important at this stage of the process. All right?"

"All right," said Gem numbly and her smile became even brighter.

"Have a nice visit, now. Call the desk when you're ready to go—there's a phone in the anteroom." She touched his sleeve once more and went lightly down the hall.

Gem stepped into Suite 86, his stomach full of stone, and the door slid shut behind him, closing away the stink of flowers.

The walls were pale blue; the thick carpet sapphire. There was a recliner, a refrigerator/bar combo, a walldesk and chair. The walldesk held a computer screen and a voice-phone.

There was a velvet curtain across the door into the next room. Gem lifted it aside with icy fingers and stepped into sapphire dimness.

The body shrouded by the silky blue blanket was long, though not as long as it might have been, nor nearly so angular. The hair was a torrent of deep yellow, swirling over a shoal of jewel-colored pillows.

The face—the face was a delight of smooth honey skin molding high, sweet cheekbones and rounded chin. A face to haunt dreams, to break hearts, to inspire poetry.

But never, never, never her own.

Horror buckled his knees and he knelt, staring at her, fingers twisting in the blue blanket as he breathed her name.

"Corbinye?"

Slim brows contracted over velvet-lashed eyes. "Who is that?" Soft, resonant, flexible—a singer's voice.

He cleared his throat. "Gem."

"Anjemalti!" Exultation and terror in that expressive voice. The thick lashes flickered, snapped open to reveal black eyes, overlarge, by Grounder standards, moist and half-crazed. She struggled, got a hand free of the blanket and groped toward him. "Anjemalti."

Almost, he failed of raising his hand to take hers; was astonished at the warmth and softness of her flesh. "Gently," he said, remembering the cautions he had been given. "Gently, Corbinye. Do not tire yourself."

She did not seem to hear him; her fingers dug into his hand; her eyes wide and unfocused. "Anjemalti, where am I? What has happened? They come—they say things—they drug me to sleep—I cannot walk; I can barely raise a hand! And my eyes—my eyes…"

Madness, of the kind that came when one knew oneself to be desperately ill. So had Edreth been, in the last few days. Gem squeezed the warm hand in his and made to lie it back upon the coverlet.

"Be easy, Corbinye; all—"

"Do not tell me that all is well!" she cried, fingers tightening. "Tell me what has happened!"

He hesitated, and suddenly her fingers went slack; the lashes drooped over her eyes. "Anjemalti—" and even her voice had lost its vigor—"By any god you own to—I beg you to tell me the truth."

He felt the shape of the hand he held; looked at the lovely, alien face and cleared his throat.

"You were in a fight," he began and felt her shudder.

"I recall it."

"Yes." He touched tongue to dry lips. "You were badly hurt, Corbinye, and your eyes—you were given new eyes."

They opened, staring toward his voice in what must seem to her to be utter darkness.

"New eyes," she repeated, dread softening toward understanding. "A transplant?"

"New eyes," Gem repeated and found the courage to raise his other hand and touch her honey cheek. "And also an entirely new body."

She neither cried out, nor recoiled, nor even wept, but was merely silent for a time, staring hard into her darkness.

"Anjemalti," she said finally; "one does not go drunk to comfort kin."

"No," he agreed.

She drew a deep breath. "A new body?"

"You were dying," he told her, struggling to keep his voice free of horror. "You had been so badly beaten there was no chance of healing your hurts." He hesitated, but she made no sound. "There is technology—they transferred you—your personality, your memories, your *self*—into a healthy, whole body…" He stumbled to a halt and knelt there staring at her until she sighed and asked, with a sort of strained calm:

"Can you see me?"

"Yes," he said, biting off the "of course."

"And I cannot see you," she mused. "You tell me you see this new body."

"Yes," he said again and felt her fingers tighten on his.

"Anjemalti, turn on the light."

"Corbinye—" his voice choked out and he felt himself trembling, knowing what she would demand next; knowing what he would demand, in her place.

"They cannot hide me from myself forever!" she cried, half coming up off the pillows. She fell back as if her strength failed then and her hand went limp in his. "Anjemalti—"

"Yes." He laid her hand down and lurched to his feet, found the switch and brought the lights up until he saw the distended pupils begin to shrink and, unasked, went over to the dresser.

She was staring at her own hand when he came back to kneel at the bedside and terror was beginning to show in her face.

"Corbinye?"

She looked at him; lifted her hand with grinding effort and lightly touched his cheek, as he had just touched hers.

"Hold the mirror for me, cousin."

Wordless, he brought it up; watched her trace the winging brows, touch the rounded chin and stare into her own eyes. The tears, when they came, came silently, sliding unabated beneath her lashes, when at last she closed her eyes.

Gem set the glass aside, took her hand between both of his and tried to rub warmth into fingers gone damp and chill.

"Corbinye—"

"Do not call me that!" She turned her face away, breast heaving.

"It is your name!" he snapped, holding to her hand in new terror, lest she deny the body she found herself in and will her death upon her.

"I am dead!" she cried, echoing his thought, and he cried out, "Live!" so that she turned her face to him again, eyes pulled wide in wonder.

He held her eyes with his; repeated it with every nuance of command possible: "*Live*, Corbinye!" And, then, because it smacked of magic, said that way: "Please."

Almost, she smiled. And then the door in the room beyond whisked open and a brisk voice was saying, "Here, here, here! What's this, lights on! You, sir, whatever can you be thinking of! This young lady needs her rest and you—What!" The nurse bent and straightened, holding the mirror out in accusation.

"Really, sir."

"She asked to see," said Gem. "She had to see, sometime."

"And would have seen, in due time," the nurse snapped, touching a stud on her belt. "I'll have to ask you to leave; it's time for Corbinye to have a nap."

The hand he held had stiffened; from the other room came the sound of the door opening once more.

"Come along, sir," the nurse said sharply. "You've done enough damage for one day."

"Anjemalti," Corbinye's voice was a thready whisper. "Anjemalti, do not leave me here."

"I must." He laid her hand down. "You require aid—assistance in learning. I will come again to see you." He hesitated. "May I have your kiss?"

It was a trap, of course, enclosing them both. He saw her understand that, through the layers of terror and grief; saw still the indecision.

"Cousin," he said; and, "please."

"My kiss," she agreed, weakly. "Come back for me, cousin."

"Of course." He bent and laid his lips against hers, very lightly; touched her cheek and rose. Sidestepping the nurse, he found Coral Jancy waiting for him in the anteroom, frowning and tapping her foot.

Her displeasure was so great that she said nothing to him during the long trip to the front door; and never smiled at all.

CHAPTER SIXTEEN

"THE OBJECT IS called the Bindalche Trident." Saxony Belaconto sat behind the teak-wood desk, hands folded on the satiny surface, aquamarine eyes wary and arrogant.

Gem, sitting on a wooden chair more aesthetically than physically pleasing, said nothing, though he allowed his face to express polite interest.

"The Trident," she continued after a moment, "is currently in the possession of Jarge Menlin, where it has been for the past eighteen months. It is against the Vornet's interest that he remain any longer as caretaker."

Gem shrugged. "It appears you need a sharpshooter, lady; not a thief."

She frowned; the light from the window showed lines in her face which had not been there two days before.

"Jarge Menlin is an influential man," she said; "and an occasionally useful one. The Vornet prefers to allow him to live."

"Lacking only the Bindalche Trident."

Her frown deepened. "Do not bait me, Master ser Edreth. Did you visit your cousin?"

"I did."

"Then you know the stakes."

He said nothing, and after a moment she continued her tale.

"The Trident will be in my hands no later than First Dawn, Obret eighteenth."

Seven days! He did not allow dismay to show in either face or voice.

"I will need certain information," he said to her, coolly, hearing Edreth behind every word. "I require a description of the object—length, mass, configuration—a sketch, holograph or photo would aid the task considerably. I require details regarding the layout of the house, most especially the room where the Trident is kept. I require a timetable, describing Jarge Menlin's routine, if he has one; and also a detailed description of all alarms, guards and house residents."

She nodded. "The Vornet can provide these things. But I will mention to you, Master ser Edreth, that there is no certainty that Menlin keeps the Trident in his house."

Of course not. "A compilation, also, of places he frequents, offices or residences away from his main house." He considered. "Ships, if he owns or part-owns any; warehouse space; mechanic's shed."

Again, her nod. "These will be provided, as well. Is there more?"

"Yes," he heard himself say, with vast astonishment. "I will have your agreement that you will release my kin to me at the same moment I put the Trident in your hand. You will cease to remember that either of us exists and you will call upon me for no further service."

She looked amused. "Of course, you cousin is yours to take, as soon as our agreement is fulfilled. She's of no use to me."

Gem leaned forward. "And the rest?"

"The rest?" Her amusement grew. "The Vornet claims service from whomever will serve them best, Master ser Edreth. It may happen we will need a thief again."

He stared at her for a long moment, until some of the laughter left her eyes and the lines settled again in her face.

"Do not bait me, Saxony Belaconto," he said softly, wondering how he dared it. "You may find the stakes not to your liking."

Unease now in the handsome eyes. She put her hands flat upon the desktop and stood. He rose at the same instant.

"You are dismissed," she said, sharply. "The information you have requested will be brought to your home this evening."

"Thank you," he said gently, recalling Corbinye, lying alone in the dark; and turned and walked away.

CHAPTER SEVENTEEN

SHE LAY FOR a long time, eyes straining against the blackness, ears stretched for any sound.

Satisfied at last that the room was empty, she pushed the blanket away, curled round on her side, slid her legs over the edge of the bed and lay for a moment, panting.

Sternly, she squirmed into a sitting position, got her feet solidly under her and pushed herself upright.

The first attempt was hopeless—and the second—her knees buckled before they ever straightened, and she bounced on the edge of the bed, teeth drawing blood from her lower lip.

On the fifth try, she was standing, trembling in every limb, gasping as if she had just completed a Class Ten sequence. She waited until the trembling eased somewhat before sliding her right foot forward and cautiously drawing the left after; and then again; and then a third time, which bought her disaster.

In her mind, Corbinye flung her arms out to break the fall; in actuality, she slapped face-first into the carpet, and lay swearing into the nap until the sound of the lilting stranger's voice wrapped around the familiar phrases silenced her.

Grimly, she got to her knees; tried from there to gain her feet and, when she fell again, began to crawl.

She found the wall by running her head into it, and clawed her way upright, feeling about for the light switch. By luck, she located the knob immediately, and twisted it until it would go no further, flooding the room with light.

Then, she stood, quaking, braced against the wall, staring at the room and all there was in it, while the tears ran her face and splashed on her breasts.

Startled, she looked down at herself; raised soft stranger-hands to cup golden breasts fuller than hers had been, even in pregnancy. Cautiously, for by her reckoning the nurse was due soon, and she dared not risk another fall; Corbinye craned to see the rest of this stupid lump of a body, with its milk-toast muscles and lack of reaction.

Breasts—hopelessly huge—a slim torso flaring to rounded hips; long slender legs; shapely feet. She moved a hand, cross-body; felt of her upper arm—and was agreeably surprised to find muscle there, after all; firm under the velvet skin. Wishing for the lost mirror, she ran her hand across the flat belly; down the tight waist; over the firm backside—and felt a flicker of hope. Not the body of a fighter, no. Certainly not the body she had worked and trained so hard. But one that had known some sort of work; so Corbinye was left a legacy of basic fitness upon which to build.

Abruptly, she wondered about the woman who had been here before her—what sort of work she had done; why she had died. And then the door to the outer room whisked open and wonder fled.

Corbinye straightened away from the wall; holding knees and back straight by force of will alone.

The nurse flicked the curtain aside, hand continuing across the wall toward the switch before she realized that the room was already lit.

"What—" she began and then froze, eyes on the empty bed.

"Good-day to you," Corbinye said politely, and the nurse jumped a foot, hand lifting to her throat.

"How did you get over here?" she demanded.

Corbinye stared at her. "How do adult persons normally cross the room?" Carefully, she inclined her head toward the needle the other woman held. "I do not want that."

The nurse had recovered her countenance, if not her courage. "It's time for your nap."

"I am not in the least tired," Corbinye lied; "and I require no drugs to induce sleep. What I do require is clothing;

and a full-length mirror; and a pitcher of water." She paused. "And some cheese."

The nurse eyed her in fascination. "You're hungry?"

"You have my requirements," Corbinye said coldly. "See to them."

The nurse glanced away, slid forward half-a-step, thumbing the trip on the needle.

"If you try to put that into me," Corbinye said conversationally, "I will break your arm."

The nurse licked her lips; apparently thought better of her act of valor and stepped carefully backward, keeping her eyes on Corbinye. Reaching behind, she clawed the curtain out of her way and ducked into the other room.

After a moment, Corbinye heard the door open, and then shut.

CHAPTER EIGHTEEN

GEM STOOD IN the wreckage of his workroom, straddling the voltmeter, one hip braced against the tool bench, fingers tapping the tiny buttons on the wrist telltale.

There had been fourteen. He had two alive in his pocket, and the mangled corpse Corbinye had brought him. Eleven were yet unaccounted for.

At his feet—a rustle, a shift of small debris—and two spiders struggled into the open; gained his boots, and then his trouser-leg; began the long climb to safety.

There was a stir from the far ceiling-corner. Then, slowly riding the payline down to the floor, came a spider, slightly larger than the first two; chip eyes glowing dark purple. Gem grinned. Number Eleven, genius among his kind, was working his way home.

From behind him, a sudden scrabbling, and he glanced at the table top to see Numbers Six and Twelve marching purposefully forward as Number Four—Eleven's twin brother—emerged from the protection of a smashed lamp and scurried to join them.

Gem waited while his companions gained his person by their various routes; touched the telltale again, and waited.

No more tiny robots came to answer that summons. Gem sighed deeply, and shook his head. Eight remaining. And only by the grace of sheerest luck were Numbers Four and Eleven among them.

He devoted three minutes to cursing the Vornet and Saxony Belaconto in terms Edreth would have deplored and Corbinye applauded. Then, spiders sitting on his shoulder and clutching his hair, he rolled up his sleeves and began to put order back into his place.

Well into the night, order restored, with Number Fifteen half-assembled on the worktable, there came the chime of the outside annunciator.

Gem looked up from his work, blinking.

The chime sounded again, and he sighed, pushed away from the table and made his way to the door, surefooted in the dark.

The street was empty when he opened the door. On the threshold was a package wrapped in thick buff paper and tied with a silver cord.

Gem bent to pick the thing up—and checked as a spider launched itself, trailing a silken parachute, and landed on the silver cord, eyes glittering amethyst.

Quickly, Number Eleven circumnavigated the package and returned to the cord, as the telltale on the man's wrist beeped three times.

"All safe," murmured Gem and extended his hand to the robot, which climbed aboard and scurried up his arm, shoulderward. "Thank you," Gem added, picking up the package and shutting the door.

Jarge Menlin had been a courier, carrying messages, currency and other necessities for various Vornet chieftains and even a few "respectable" businesses. Sometimes, his contracts took him off-planet—there was a list of the pilots and ships he most often employed on these trips—and sometimes an off-planet customer would specify Jarge for a certain job. He was known for being discreet, competent and—unusual for one in his line of work—painstakingly honest with his customer.

The picture, Gem thought, scanning quickly through the dossier provided by the Vornet, was of a man successful at his trade, and perhaps even rising toward a sort of chieftainhood of his own. Forty was old for a courier, yet

Jarge Menlin had achieved that age and showed no sign of faltering in the disfavor of the powerful.

Eighteen months ago, Jarge Menlin vanished.

It was thought at first, of course, that he was merely traveling on behalf of some client or another. But time passed, and people began remarking that Jarge had never been gone so long before. The Vornet used other couriers, some of whom fell by the wayside, to be replaced by still others.

A year gone, Jarge Menlin returned, bought a house in the fashionable part of UpTown, bought a warehouse at the port and leased a hotpad in the portion of the Yards reserved for deep-space vessels. He refused all commissions for courier work (And how, wondered Gem, had he made that stick?), renewed his acquaintances among Henron's freelance druglords and several months later astonished them all by offering hesernym in bulk from a seemingly unending supply.

There followed here a detailed layout of Menlin's house, with alarm-schemes and several time-studies, and a brief notation about a bodyguard. Gem put those aside for later study and picked up the next page.

The Bindalche, he quickly learned, were a loose affiliation of barbarians occupying three worlds in the Spangiln System. The queen-world was Bindal, and it was here—and only here—that the *tremillan* flowers from which hesernym is extracted grew.

Previous attempts to deal with the Bindalche had resulted in ambassadorial massacre; attempts to duplicate the hesernym affect artificially simply failed. For the fifty years since its discovery, hesernym had remained the emperor of drugs—virtually unobtainable; staggeringly expensive when available at all.

Until Jarge Menlin, thought Gem, flipping through several sheets for a description of the Bindalche Trident.

There was better—clipped to the last page was a flatphoto. Gem frowned. The Bindalche Trident was roughly six feet long; seemingly hewn from wood, set all around with pebbles and shells and, and—he groped along the table top, found the loupe and screwed it into place.

Circuitry. Bits and blasted fragments of circuit-wires were set into the irregular surface, whorling artistically around the shells, nuts, transistors, capacitors and jewels. Gem took the glass out of his eye and flipped the pages back.

The Bindalche Trident, according to the Vornet's information, was an artifact of power. It had not been observed functioning in any manner; it did not seem to generate or gather energy. However, all Bindalche revered Trident and Trident-Bearer, for reasons the Vornet had either been unable to discover or was disinclined to share. Most important, from the point of view of the reporter, was the fact that, as an act of reverence, the Bearer was tithed in hesernym.

In as much hesernym, it appeared, as he wanted.

Gem laid the last sheet down, tamped the edges and tied the pages together with the silver cord. Absently, he picked up the whisker-tool and bent over the emerging Number Fifteen, face blank in concentration.

Two hours later, with Second Dawn lighting every corner of the kitchen, Gem fixed himself a cup of tea and watched the new spider cavort and spin and finally climb dizzily up a sleeve and into a shirt pocket.

Gem sipped his tea, considering the information he had—and the information he did not have. Saxony Belaconto *wanted* the Bindalche Trident, thus it followed that she had provided the most complete information at her disposal. And, where it dealt with Jarge Menlin and his effects, this was substantial.

Where he sensed a lack was within the body of information regarding the Trident itself. It had the *feel* of an object powerful in its own right. Many of the so-called "magical" items cataloged in Shilban's library had the same feeling of presence; of the most powerful, the aura most often described was that almost of *sentience*.

Gem shivered and drank his tea slowly, while intuition spun its web of what-if, and thief's necessity uneasily sorted the data, over and over. And, in the end, found it insufficient.

Grimly, knowing it had to be done, for the debt he owed Corbinye, if not for his own life and body; Gem left his house to travel cross town and Up; and up one level more, to OldTown and Shilban's Library.

CHAPTER NINETEEN

THE INTERCOM BUZZED and Saxony Belaconto looked up with a frown.

"Well?" she demanded.

"I'm sorry to disturb you, Ms. Belaconto," her secretary said hurriedly, "but I have Dr. Walney on the line. He says it's urgent."

The director of the Blue House. Her frown deepened. "Put him through."

"Yes, ma'am," her secretary murmured; and Fel Walney's deep voice rumbled nervously through the speaker.

"Ms. Belaconto?"

"Dr. Walney," she returned calmly. "What can I do for you today?"

"Morning, ma'am! Morning! Terribly sorry to bother you and all that—know how busy you must be. Thing is, my records indicate that you are the person responsible for Corbinye Faztherot." His voice trailed off on an unmistakable query-note.

"That's right." She hesitated. "Has something happened to her?"

"Oh, nonono—nothing like that, ma'am! It's just that she seems to be doing—aah—much better than anticipated, and—aah—is putting a little strain on the staff. Regulations, you understand, ma'am, and, after all, we do have a planned procedure—and, well, it just seems best to us that you come and—aah—perhaps bring her home. We'll be happy to detach a nurse, of course—"

"Dr. Walney."

Silence, then a creak, which may have been him shifting in his chair. "Ma'am?"

"I have a contract with your Center, sir. It specifically includes domiciliary care and physical therapy for my—ward—until she is fit to re-enter the world. Am I to understand that Ms. Faztherot is, at this early day, fit to re-enter the world?"

"No, ma'am." He cleared his throat. "That is, not exactly."

"I would be delighted," she said dangerously, "to learn what it is I *am* to understand."

"Certainly." More throat clearing. "Ms. Faztherot is an astonishing young woman. She—not only is she several days ahead of the average progress expected of a newly-translated person, but she appears to be making significant progress in areas we have no expertise to measure."

"Indeed." She sighed, fingers tapping on the highly unsatisfactory profit report she had been reviewing. "Could you be more specific?"

"Yes, yes, certainly. I—she…" A sigh and another chair-creak. "Normally, a new-translation would drink a little water on the third day; work on eye-hand coordination, sitting up in bed—perhaps even sitting with the legs dangling—between the third and fifth days. Somewhere during those few days, the client will complain of hunger and be given small amounts of gelatin and soup, working toward solid foods. A few cases have been reported where, on the fifth day, the client was able to walk across the room and into the antechamber, sit in the chair and then walk back to bed. That is, I submit, remarkably quick progress and very, very rare."

"And I am to understand that Ms. Faztherot is progressing more rapidly than this?"

"She is eating cheese, bread and also vegetables." Dr. Walney's voice suddenly did not sound nervous at all. "She not only walks, but she exercises. We had thought at first that she was doing dance exercises, and there was some speculation among the staff. The body's previous resident had been something of an artist of the dance… At any rate, Dr. Mowker tells me that these exercises are not dance moves at all, but something he recognizes from his service in the Marines." He faltered and Saxony Belaconto found she was sitting very still, staring at the intercom.

"Well?" she snapped.

"Dr. Mowker," the man said diffidently, "seems to feel that Ms. Faztherot is practicing—well, assassin's moves. She seems—quite dedicated, and there is a clear progress being made. She pursues shifts of two hours—exercise and rest. During her rest periods, she works on eye-hand coordination and fine precision." He cleared his throat yet again.

"She's threatened several of my staff members, Ms. Belaconto, and refuses both drugs and the assistance of the physical therapists. The Resurrection Therapist won't go near her at all."

"I will come and speak with her," she heard her own voice say.

"Ma'am?"

"I said," she snapped, "that I will come and give Ms. Faztherot a lesson in manners, since she seems to require one. In the meantime, you and your center will fulfill your contract with me, Dr. Walney. Do I make myself clear?"

There was clear reluctance in his voice. "Yes, Ms. Belaconto. I—thank you. When can we expect to see you?"

She tapped her fingers once upon the report, recalled the shine of murder in Gem ser Edreth's eyes, and pushed her chair away from the desk.

"I'll come at once," she said, and cut the connection.

The antechamber was lit with the light of many lamps, set all around the wall, so there were no shadows anywhere. Strewn about were pieces of clothing, some buttoned and zipped and sealed, others gaping open, as well as bits of knotted and braided string, twists of wire, and several different keyboards.

In the midst of all the clutter and glare, sitting facing the vanity's large oval mirror, was a girl of exquisite loveliness, dressed in loose tunic and pants, bare feet crossed neatly under the upholstered bench. As Saxony stepped into the room, the girl's ebony eyes found and tracked her in the mirror.

Three days translated, by the gods! Saxony stared at her, unwillingly recalling the painfully slow relearning that had characterized her own translation, eight years ago.

"I am Saxony Belaconto," she said, all the hauteur and assurance of a Vornet leader ringing in her voice.

The delicate brows rose as a slim hand fumbled for a moment among the oddments atop the vanity and closed upon a comb. She raised the comb and brought it deliberately down the length of hair shimmering over her shoulder.

"Are you," she said, and used the comb again.

"I am." Saxony moved forward a bit, just to the edge of the mirror's range. "Has your cousin told you about me?"

Corbinye carefully divided her hair into three portions, laid the comb down and began to weave a braid.

"You are a Grounder captain," she said, off-handedly. "You deal destruction and demand service of freemen." She raised her eyes to the mirror and Saxony found her gaze caught and held. "They say that you are my patron here."

"They say correctly," she said, breaking that oddly compelling gaze and moving out of the mirror's influence.

"Then," said Corbinye, minding her braid, "it is you I must thank for this body I find myself within, for it was your henchmen beat my own so badly it could not be healed."

"You are," Saxony suggested, "grateful."

Corbinye turned her head; stared at her out of depthless black eyes for the space of three heartbeats.

"Beatings inspire no gratitude, Saxony Belaconto."

"And yet you should be grateful," Saxony persisted. "For life is sweet, and the body you seem to scorn is seemly."

Corbinye snorted. "Am I a courtesan? And while life may be sweet, you hold mine hostage, which I find bitter indeed." She finished the braid and found a bit of ribbon on the vanity top. It took her two tries to pick it up. "You use me to compel Anjemalti to do what you wish. Better I had died than I ever shame Ship and Crew by placing the Captain in danger."

"Touching," Saxony said, coming forward; "and enlightening, as well. Who would have thought a barbarian had such a high notion of honor?"

Corbinye tied the ribbon around the braid-tail and looked up, black eyes fearless, no expression at all on the smooth, lovely face.

"Listen to me, barbarian," Saxony said, low and vicious. "You will stop threatening the staff of this place. You will do as you are told. When the time has come, you will be brought to my house, where you will continue to do precisely what you are told. If you do not do these things," she finished, "I will kill your cousin."

The big eyes widened. "Has he already done what you demanded of him?"

Saxony straightened. "Did I say when I would kill him?"

"I see," said Corbinye, and tossed her braid behind her back. "Enlightening. Who would have thought that even a Grounder captain would hold no notion of honor at all?"

Saxony's hand rose even as Corbinye turned her face away and began to tidy the objects on the vanity. Saxony clenched her hand and put it into her pocket.

"I will cease to terrify the Grounders charged with my care," Corbinye said softly. "And when I come to you I shall behave as befits a guest." She raised her head. "I will continue to exercise and work and refine this body. It is I who must live here, and I have certain requirements. Also, it is necessary that I have the proper measure of my limitations and strengths."

"Very well." Saxony stepped back; turned to go.

"Saxony Belaconto!"

She turned back. "What is it?"

"The man you call Gem ser Edreth is not without resources, Saxony Belaconto—do not think that you feud with some crewless rogue captain." She stood, easily, gracefully. "A word in your ear." She smiled. "From gratitude."

"See that you mind your manners," Saxony snapped, and Corbinye inclined her head.

"You have my word."

"Keep it." She whirled on her heel, went out the door and with a snarl collected the bodyguard she had left just outside. Three days translated—and gods knew how dangerous! And it was imperative she be kept alive, or Gem ser Edreth would have no leash at all.

It was becoming increasingly more important that Gem ser Edreth be tightly leashed, indeed.

CHAPTER TWENTY

HE WOKE WITH sun glaring in his face; cheek resting on a mildewed page, arms flung haphazardly across a vast drift of books. He inhaled sharply—choked and began to sneeze on the ambient dust—and jerked upright, wincing at his back's protest.

The sneezing abated and he rubbed at his streaming eyes with grimy fingers, blinking at the glowing desk lamp and the row of respectful spiders sitting along its rim.

Slowly, careful of cramped legs and spine, he eased out of the rickety chair and stretched; checked his wrist and bit off a curse.

Nearly six hours wasted in sleep while he was no wiser regarding the Trident than he had been when he had slipped into the Library twelve hours ago and had been relieved both to find the place standing unmolested and that someone had disposed of Shilban's body.

"No Blue House for you, lucky old man," Gem whispered, and shook himself sharply, lest he indulge in another bout of swearing directed at Saxony Belaconto and her tribe of murderers.

No Blue House for the scholar—and no help for Gem, who had some skill as a researcher, but none to match Shilban's genius, and who was armed with a puzzle that was like to be his downfall. And Corbinye's, as well.

Wearily, he sat back in the chair, ignoring his stomach's growling, and pulled the crumbling volume he'd fallen asleep over into the pool of light beneath the patient spiders.

"And in the beginning was the Father and the Sister and the Brother and each held a mighty instrument of power." The passage was faded, cracking, splotched with mildew. Gem squinted and reached up to adjust the lamp.

"Time wore wearily on. The Brother and the Sister copulated and their union produced children, who became the Five Telios of the Bindalche.

"More time passed, and the Father and the Brother and the Sister decided to test the might of their weapons, each against the other, to see who was the greatest of the three. The contest raged for years, as the Telios measure time, and laced the sky with lightnings, broke mountains, sundered valleys, boiled and loosed the seas.

"The Brother fell first, his Spear of Light shattered by the Father's Sword, and in giving up its magic, destroyed the Brother, though he was a god.

"Then the Father joined battle with the Sister—Sword against Trident—and the skies opened and rained rock down upon the wondering Telios, while strange winds blew from all directions at once, and snow fell, blinding, while the sun burned the land to dust."

Gem frowned, rubbed at his forehead and carefully lifted the fraying page to turn it.

"After season upon season of striving against each other, the Father at last cornered the Sister in a cul-de-sac of heaven and raised his sword to sever the Trident and prove himself most powerful.

"But the Sister brought the Trident up and stared at the Father, remembering that the Father had slain her Brother and her Lover and, in an anger so great the seas roared and the ground buckled, she thrust hard and true and impaled the Father upon the Trident's prongs.

"The Father screamed and flamed and died, Sword rupturing as he went. Likewise, the Sister screamed, and threw the Trident from her in loathing before she turned her thought upon herself and followed Brother and Father into unlife."

"Nice family," Gem mumbled and knuckled his eyes before turning the page again.

"The Trident fell among the Telios, who gathered 'round, but did not dare lay hands upon it. The great chiefs of the Bindalche came and fasted and dreamed beside it and in their dreams it was told that the Trident was the guardian and the master of the Bindalche, children of the Brother and the Sister, grandchildren of the Father; and that the deeds of the Trident are inextricably bound up in the deeds of the Bindalche and in the deeds of those the Trident chooses.

"For, lo, the Trident does chose its own pathway, for the glory of its Children, and one shall be appointed by the Telios to walk three steps behind and mark well the Trident's choices."

What? Gem read that bit again, trying to ignore the cramping of his belly—in fear? in hunger?

"And the Trident shall go where the Trident shall go, according to its own need and desire and the duty of he who walks behind shall be to watch and remember rightly until such time as his memory becomes the memory of the Telios and another is called to follow the Trident's choice."

"Bodyguard," Gem whispered, leaning back in the chair and staring, unseeing at the motionless row of spiders. "Jarge Menlin comes home with the Trident and a body-guard—who is no bodyguard at all, but the Trident's memory." He snorted. "The Trident's operator, more likely!" He recalled the bits of technology fused to the Trident's skin—and the ugly little myth hinted that the Trident *was* technology of some alien sort....

"Gods of fools and children." He closed his eyes.

After a time, he opened them again, gathered his spiders up, straightened the desk and turned out the light. On his way down the stairs, he caught a glimpse of himself in the mirrored ceiling—rumpled, grimy, hair dusty and straggling out of the ribbon, a smear of gray book dust on his cheek, another across his forehead.

On the verandah, he paused to order his thoughts. First, a shower, clean clothes. Breakfast. Then, a stop at the Blue House, to check on Corbinye's progress *before* he spoke with Saxony Belaconto.

CHAPTER TWENTY-ONE

SHE SAT BEHIND the desk and stared at him as he came down the room; a tallish and slender young man dressed in quiet elegance, from the glittering hand-rings to the cunning, spider-shaped brooch pinned over his heart, the very picture of civilized sophistication. Which appearance, she had learned from his cousin just recently, could be very misleading.

"Well, Master ser Edreth."

"No," he said coldly, stopping and fixing her in those large and remarkable eyes; "not well, lady."

"I'm distressed to hear you say it," she drawled. "In what humble way may the Vornet assist you?"

He glanced at his wrist, then back up to her face. "By allowing me to visit my cousin." He waited, and when she did nothing more than lift her eyebrows, added: "The Blue House turned me away, saying that my name had been struck from the Visitor's Roster—and that it was at your instruction."

"Surely, Master ser Edreth, I am not such a fool as to grant you unlimited time to visit your so-lovely cousin while you have a job to do for me." She paused. "Quite a challenging job, I do believe, and one that should, in all fairness, command your entire attention. Time enough for lust and familial remembrances when the job is through."

Impossibly, the large eyes widened; he glanced at his wrist again and bowed, slightly and ironically. "Indeed, as you point out, a very challenging job. And one that grows more challenging by the hour. I had originally thought to come here, not on behalf of my cousin, but to discover whether there was anything else that the Vornet was hiding from me?"

She stiffened. "And what does that mean?"

"Why, only that the Vornet left it to me to discover that the artifact it desires in fact is contained in two packages, rather than one." Another quick glance at his wrist.

"A minor problem," she drawled, relaxing slightly, "for an artist such as yourself, sir."

"Hardly." The eyes were sapphire cold. "I am not a kidnapper, lady."

Deliberately, she pushed the chair back and stood, making no effort to mask her displeasure.

"You will explain yourself and then you will be gone about your business, Master ser Edreth. I do not exist for your amusement or your convenience. I remind you a second time that you have a commission to fulfill and that time is a precious commodity."

He shrugged, markedly uncowed by her display. "It is merely that it astounds me," he said, and the irony in his voice crackled along her nerves, so that she longed to slap his face, or to call in a bullteam and have him hurt more fully, "that the researchers of the Vornet, who must be among the best in the business of garnering information, should have missed the fact of the Trident's operator."

"Operator." She blinked at him. "Jarge Menlin controls the Trident."

"Not so," he corrected sharply. "The Trident currently resides with Jarge Menlin and the Bindalche tithe him because of it. But the important person—the Trident's operator—is the one your report dismisses as a mere bodyguard. Without this man, the Trident is merely an interesting pre-tech art object." He glanced at his wrist; back to her face. "I repeat: I am not a kidnapper."

She thought, and he glanced at his wrist yet again, so that she snapped at him to have done. "You were the one who forced this interview, Master ser Edreth! Leave over looking at your watch!"

He started; bowed. "Certainly, lady."

She frowned. "Shall I detach one of my own to go with you and deal with the operator's persuasion?"

He laughed, and the spider on his tunic seemed to blink its purple eyes.

"Those you employ seem clumsy in the extreme, lady. If an equal may say it to you. I merely wish you to be apprised of the case; to inquire whether there is anything else the Vornet knows that it has not told me; and to inform you that the deadline runs a fair possibility of not being met, in light of this complication."

She went cold; drew herself stiffly up. "The deadline is not negotiable, Master ser Edreth. Do not speak to me of complications. You refuse the Vornet's assistance. The Trident and whatever must attend it to make it whole will be here in this room no later than First Dawn, Obret eighteenth." She stared at him intently. "Understand me: If these things are not in this room by one minute after Dawn's chime, your cousin is forfeit."

"I understand you, lady." He bowed, with a show at least of respect. "I leave you now, with permission."

"Go," she said curtly, and watched him walk, all graceful, across the room and out the door. When the door closed, she sat down, hard; and covered her face with her hands.

Gem went down the hall and was let out into the dimming Second Noon by an armed guard. He went down the steps into the street, well pleased with himself and with Number Eleven, riding so bravely on his tunic.

Mapped, analyzed and recorded by spider senses were each bug, telltale and alarm node in Saxony Belaconto's private office. Gem grinned as he turned his steps toward MidTown.

Such information was very, very valuable.

CHAPTER TWENTY-TWO

"WHAT ARE YOU doing here?"

The one who demanded it was thin and small and sharp: a sliver-knife of a woman, with an ill-natured, sallow face. The tag on her shirt read "Aide".

Corbinye looked down on her—necessary, even from this body's diminished height—and lifted a shoulder.

"I am walking to the observation port," she said mildly. "The nurse had said it was in this direction."

"You're not allowed to walk the halls by yourself!" the little woman snapped. "Patients must be accompanied by a nurse or a therapist, and you must go at your assigned time. You can't just go to the sun room whenever you feel like it!" Suspicion sharpened her face further. "How did you get out of your room?"

"The door was open," said Corbinye. And so it had been, though briefly, as the nurse, he of the happily unobservant nature, had quit the room. The halls had been quite empty, due to the lateness of the hour; and she had begun to believe in escape.

All for naught, now; hopes broken on this grudging blade of a woman. Corbinye inclined her head, feeling the weariness etched into her bones and the beginning of deep muscle tremor, as will happen, when one has pushed oneself past sense and strength.

"I'll go back to my room," she murmured; "and ask my nurse to bring me, tomorrow."

"*I'll* take you back to your suite," the aide snarled, and Corbinye silently cursed her and the gene pool from which she'd been spawned. "What's your room number?"

Corbinye sighed. "Fourteen eighty-six."

The ruin of her hopes was nearly worth the opportunity to behold the expression on the little woman's face. "*Fourteen*?" she squeaked.

"Indeed, yes," Corbinye said solemnly; "fourteen."

"This is the *ninth* floor." Confusion blurred the sharp-featured face for an instant, and was replaced by determination. "What's your name?" she demanded.

"Corbinye Faztherot."

The aide thumbed a stud on her belt-comm, rapped out a request for room number verification on Corbinye Faztherot, and frowned quite blackly when a tinny voice told her, "Fourteen eighty-six."

"Patient found wandering on Floor Nine," she snarled. "Send a chair and a team."

"Indeed," Corbinye protested untruthfully, "I can walk back to my rooms. It's the merest step."

"Shut up!" the aide shouted, goaded past the limits of her patience.

Corbinye shut up and they waited, glaring silently at each other, for the arrival of the chair.

When they had gone, she got out of bed and went out into the antechamber in her sleeping-gown. The door would, of course, be locked. She tried it anyway, then went around the room, turning on the lamps.

This done, she sat down before the mirror and began to unbraid her hair, slanting sidelong glances at her reflection as she did. The face of the woman in the mirror held a certain fascination, though she had long since stopped looking for clues of Corbinye Faztherot in the high cheeks and smooth skin; or in the black, black eyes.

Tonight, a glimmer caught her half-glance, so that she looked up fully at the mirror—and saw the spider hanging there.

No ordinary spider, such as might be found in even the most pristine of Grounder homes. This was rather a large spider—perhaps the size of her new fist—and its eyes gleamed a friendly and interested yellow.

Corbinye drew a short breath—barely more than a dry sob against the tightness of her throat. The next went better, and she said, very softly, "Anjemalti?"

There was no answer, save that the spider shifted a bit and slid down-mirror, trailing a line of fine black silk.

Corbinye sighed and picked up her comb, sternly forcing trembling fingers to yield to her will and perform their function, weary or no. She glanced up again as she pulled comb through extravagant Grounder-length hair, and saw the spider cutting capers across smooth glass, describing spirals and lunges and—

GEM SENDS GREETING the black silk spelled. **AND ASKS IF YOU ARE WELL**

She stared, comb frozen; recalled herself and completed the stroke.

CORBINYE the spider spun. **COUSIN**

"I am well," she whispered, wondering how he could hear her; wondering if he could see her. "I exercise, Anjemalti; and grow strong."

THE VORNET REVOKES MY RIGHT TO VISIT the silken letters spelled. **EXERCISE   GROW STRONG BE BIDDABLE   I WILL COME FOR YOU**

"Saxony Belaconto says that she will kill you, cousin."

The spider described an arc, dropped down and wrote **SHE MAY TRY**

Corbinye grinned, and the woman in the mirror for a moment gleamed wolfish, before she sobered and asked the spider, "When will you come?"

TWO DAYS the spider spun out; and then, much more slowly **TRUST ME**

"I trust you," she murmured and suddenly closed her eyes, as fear and loneliness held him up before her mind's eye: young and comely and graceful, with his Grounder hair and his face that was the face of the Crew. She swallowed hard and hoped that he could not see her, and be ashamed for the weakness of her tears.

"I trust you," she whispered again and opened her eyes.

The spider had dropped even lower on the mirror. **THIS IS NUMBER FIFTEEN WHO WILL STAY WITH YOU BE WISE   GROW STRONG**

"Yes."

COURAGE CORBINYE The silken letters conveyed not reprimand, but compassion and she felt her heart ease somewhat, that he was not, after all, ashamed of her.

I GO NOW

"Take good care, Anjemalti," she said softly.

The spider spun at the end of its lifeline; then danced back along the word-webs, swallowing its own silk until the mirror was empty except for the reflection of the exotic Grounder woman, patiently combing her hair.

Number Fifteen swung down to the vanity and picked its dainty way across the littered top. Corbinye lowered her comb to watch, and shivered as spider-claws minced across her hand, to her sleeve, and thence downward, until Number Fifteen slipped into the pocket of her gown.

Sternly, she raised the comb and finished dressing her hair for the night. Then she rose and went methodically around the room, turning off all the lights except for one. She tried the door again and went into the bedroom to lie down.

She closed her eyes and tried to will the body into relaxation, though tension sang through her, and longing, and a bone-deep weariness that pitched the mind past exhaustion and into hyperawareness. As she lay there struggling to impose a seemly discipline, she heard a scrabbling nearby and opened her eyes.

There, brave in the wash of the light from the room beyond, golden eyes glowing valiantly, Number Fifteen stood upon her pillow, guarding her rest.

Smiling, Corbinye closed her eyes. And, very shortly, slept.

CHAPTER TWENTY-THREE

IT WAS NOT in his house; nor was it in the warehouse at the port; nor at the fashionable UpTown office.

It was not in his mistress' lavish river-view apartment; it was not on the premises of any of the eight businesses of which he was part owner.

Gem ordered a cup of strong tea and stared out the window of the cafe, wondering for the nine hundredth time in six days where in the name of all demons Jarge Menlin kept the Bindalche Trident.

Six days gone. He had until First Dawn tomorrow to discover the thing, steal it and bring it safely to Saxony Belaconto. That she would then allow Corbinye and himself to depart peacefully he did not expect; yet it was impossible to form further plans until he had the Trident in hand.

And if the Trident did not come to hand? He shook his head and sipped the hot beverage. He had no doubt he could steal Corbinye from the Blue House; little doubt that Linzer Skot would hold *Dart* in readiness, once he claimed the message waiting for him at the port.

But he felt utterly certain that Saxony Belaconto would hunt them with her last breath and hold them up as an example of what became of those who dared to thwart the Vornet.

Out of the office building across the street came a fleshy, half-bald man in clothes too fashionable for him. Gem put aside his cup and slipped out of the cafe to follow Jarge Menlin, wherever he might go.

He went all over UpTown; visited each of the eight businesses of which he was a partner; stopped briefly at Iliam's, rather longer at Korson's Jewelers; and no time at all, really, at the Flower Basket. Gem fidgeted and thought about the mistress' legendary temper and her passion for a certain exotic blossom; and cursed Jarge Menlin, the Five Telios of the Bindalche and the Vornet, in no particular order.

Jarge Menlin came out of the Flower Basket, turned right through the thickening crowds of Second Noon, and went with uncharacteristic vigor toward the River DownRamp.

At River Plaza, he hailed a cab and Gem swore and broke into a run. His elbow caught Menlin in the middle of his back as he began to bend to the cab, nearly overbalancing him. Gem grabbed the older man's arm, spouting apologies, brushing at the expensive clothing—

"Enough!" Menlin roared, one large hand flashing out toward Gem's throat. "Try to pick my pockets, will you?"

Gem danced back a pace, empty hands out and up, an expression of well-meaning vacuity on his face.

"No, then, sir, I was only meaning to help, since my clumsiness almost tumbled your honor straight onto your head! As to picking your pockets, sir—I'm not half clever enough to be a thief. Check and see if it's not so!"

Frowning, Menlin patted his pockets; pulled out a wallet and slid it back away; did the same with a flat velvet jeweler's box and a folder of keycards.

"All right, then," he said irritably; "but watch yourself. There's some not as easy-going as I am, who'd shoot you and *then* count their change."

"Your honor, I know it," Gem assured him fervently. "My sincerest thanks for your good humor and your advice." He bowed, backing away slightly as he did. "Fortune keep your honor and may blessed circumstances surround you."

Menlin had turned his back before this pleasantry was half-done and climbed into the cab, snarling directions into the driver's speaker. Gem stood on the walkway, watching the little blue-and-gray vehicle zip down the road and 'round the first bend. Then he ran out into the road and commandeered a cab for himself.

The blip was strong and steady. Gem directed the cab in an unhurried murmur, eyes on the wrist readout. Number Six, certainly the humblest and least complex of spiders, clung to his target and broadcast his simple message over and over with a tenacity that commanded his master's love.

The signal stilled; began to move again, much more slowly.

"Stop here," Gem murmured to the cab and slid a coin into the meterbox as the door cycled open.

On the walk, he spun slowly around to get his bearings. Just so. Three blocks from the Port; very near the warehouse district, yet not quite among them. A neighborhood of sullen shops and shabby offices, street and sidewalk bare of traffic at barely past Second Noon.

A glance at the readout told him that, two blocks southwest, Jarge Menlin was walking at a hurried pace. Gem smiled to himself and ambled along, looking into dusty shop windows and trusting to Number Six.

CHAPTER TWENTY-FOUR

"CORBINYE FAZTHEROT?"

She deliberately speared the last morsel of breakfast, chewed and swallowed before looking up at him, and frowning.

"Yes."

He was scowling; thick brows pulled together and down, cheeks furrowed and fleshy mouth turned down. His fingers quivered, ever so slightly, no doubt yearning for the grips of the weapons riding on his hips.

"Saxony Belaconto sends for you," he snarled. "You will come with me."

Corbinye inclined her head. "Very well. Await me in the hall."

The brows lowered further, and the fingers of his right hand, at least, found solace 'round a gun-grip. "I can pump you full of tranquilizer and carry you out, or you can walk out on your own two feet," he growled. "But you're going and you're going now!"

Corbinye came to her feet with perhaps a quarter of her old speed, hands slapping the breakfast table, pitiable muscles tensing for action.

"I will go when I am prepared to go and not an instant sooner," she said coldly. "Try me at your peril, Grounder."

The brows were somewhat less definite. Corbinye pushed her advantage.

"Does your mistress go from council room to council room all mussed from sleep, like a whore?"

This argument held some force, she saw from his face. She called up the Command voice and pointed at the door. "Await me in the hall!"

He started, even beginning a salute before he caught himself; stiffened and marched out the door.

Shoulders abruptly sagging, Corbinye looked around at the prison room that suddenly seemed like sanctuary. After a moment, she went to take a shower.

Some while later, dressed in dark trousers and boots and a scarlet shirt with blousing sleeves; hair braided with a length of ribbon exactly matching the shirt, Corbinye looked at Number Fifteen, watching patiently from his perch on the mirror's edge.

"Anjemalti?" she said, very softly. "Cousin?"

Number Fifteen blinked golden eyes and relapsed into stillness.

Sighing, Corbinye stood and held out a hand. The spider came readily into her palm, claws mincing; she brought it nearer, peering, as if she could see through the golden eyes and down along the invisible lines that kept it tied to Anjemalti...

She shook her head at her own folly, and gently put the spider in her pocket. Of the other objects in the room, she took only the flat folder containing her IDs, credit chits and cash. Slipping it into her other pocket, she went to the door and laid her hand against the plate.

As never before, it slid open, and she stepped out into a hallway crowded with armed guards.

Corbinye stopped, sought and found he of the scowling brows and pointed. "You. What is the meaning of this?"

He started, stared around him as if only now seeing the mob of his mates, and looked back at her, brows twitching.

"Ms. Belaconto sent us to get you." He grinned, gap-toothed. "Maybe she wanted to be sure you didn't get any ideas about going solo, huh?"

Corbinye stared at him coldly. "Saxony Belaconto has my word that I will behave as befits a guest. She might as easily have sent her grandmother to show me the way, and let you free for—other endeavors." She shrugged, eloquent of resigned outrage. "Why do we tarry? I had thought I was to come to your captain immediately."

Thus recalled to a sense of his duty, he barked orders and the rest of the crew formed themselves into a square around her, guns very apparent, and marched her out of the Blue House and into a waiting car.

CHAPTER TWENTY-FIVE

THE FAT MAN came, as he always did, red-faced and breathing hard, shoving open the door as if it were man's place alone, and not also the abode of that which was not man.

Witness for the Telios sighed and wondered in his private heart what it was that Shlorba's Smiter wished of the fat man. Certainly, it was not reverence; though Witness-memory taught him that a thirst for reverence had not in the past been characteristic of the Smiter. Yet, those Chosen of the past had had a certain—boldness—in common; a certainty of purpose, no matter that each purpose had been as different from the other as each grain of sand was different from its brothers. Witness for the Telios, in his private heart, believed that Shlorba's Smiter found this boldness—exhilarating.

The fat man was not bold. He came as if compelled to the Smiter's Center, smelling of liquor and women and flowers; laid his hand upon the grip and muttered his name as if any moment his bones would give up their duty and there would be nothing left of the fat man at all, excepting a smear of pudding on the floor.

As part of his duties as Witness, he had studied the fat man's society and culture and as much of the fat man himself as it was possible to do, to thus give context and perspective to the Memory. It annoyed him, in his private heart, that an Epoch that had so much potential—the Smiter sets forth from the Bindalche, forsooth! and rises into the stars to clutch who knows what new and terrible magics to itself—should wither into boredom in the fat man's soft, scented hands.

The fat man had turned from the Smiter and was standing now before him, hand clenched, the stink of liquor on his breath. Witness for the Telios sighed and stood, awaiting the inevitable. At first, he had not understood the fat man's insistence on asking these questions, on seeking assurance, as if he were a boy untried rather than an adult, Tried and Named and Tested. Study had provided him with certain answers. Within the fat man's culture, there was neither Testing nor Trying, and one might go from womb to pyre bearing only the milk-name given at birth. In a sense then was the fat man a boy untried, laboring under the milky influence of an infant-name. Witness for the Telios endeavored to keep this truth before his heart's eye in all their dealings.

"Is all well with you?" inquired the fat man, wrinkles around his moist brown eyes.

"All is well," replied Witness, with the gentleness one reserved for children, reminding his heart that the question was meant kindly and not as the deadly insult it must have been, asked between men.

The fat man nodded. "And—that?" He gestured toward the Smiter. "Does it require anything? Is it—content?"

"I am Witness for the Telios," Witness said, as he always did; "you are the one Chosen."

"Yes, of course," muttered the fat man, as *he* always did, with his eyes dropping and darting tiny sharp glances around the room. He pulled himself upright, with a boy's brittle bravado, and nodded his head sharply.

"Until next time, then. You know how to get in touch with me, if anything should happen."

This was merely a nonsense phrase, a pleasantry, or so Witness thought. For what could it mean, "if anything should happen?" when everything within the Thought of the gods—fat men, the Bindalche, Shlorba's Smiter, and every Witness the Telios had brought to the Smiter—was caught forever in a state of event? How could it be that something *not* happen? But, there, it was merely the milky thinking of a child. And who could expect more, from one denied the Trial and the Naming?

Witness for the Telios bowed, since the fat man had in the past understood this to signal agreement, and then had gone away.

Today, however, he hesitated.

"No one else has been here, have they? Asking questions? Trying to buy the Trident? Have they?"

There was fear in the moist eyes. Witness brought his hand up in the gesture of Truthtelling. "No one."

The fat man stared, long and hard, finally nodded his head and moved to the door. "All right then. But you keep an eye out, all right? It'll go bad with you, if somebody steals that thing from under your nose."

Mere sound, signifying nothing. Witness bowed and the fat man slipped out the door, looking both ways with a stealth clumsy enough to make a fond father laugh.

Sighing, Witness turned back to the larger room, eyes straying to the magnificence of the Smiter, reposing in its Center. He checked for a moment, and his private heart rose, singing, in his breast.

Crouched upon Shlorba's Smiter, Mighty Weapon of the Mightiest Warrior, Destroyer of God; and undisturbed by any of the magics that warded lesser creatures and left their small husks in a litter on the floor beneath the Center, was a spider.

Witness for the Telios walked slowly backward across the room, eyes on the Smiter and on the spider sitting there, so bold. So bold.

The back of his knees touched the study-chair, and he sat, prepared to Witness all.

CHAPTER TWENTY-SIX

THE ROOM WAS below ground level, windowless and large. Whether it was in UpTown, DownTown, near the Port or by the river Corbinye prayed Number Fifteen knew, for the only certainty she held was that they remained upon Henron.

The car windows had been opaqued; and the driver had exerted some ingenuity to confuse her sense of direction, so that they drove for more than an hour, east and west, north and south. When they finally came to rest, he of the scowling brows made a sign to another of the troop, who snapped forward in the crowded passenger bay and pinned Corbinye's arms to her side. She gritted her teeth and made no struggle against this indignity, though she nearly cried out when the blindfold came down over her eyes.

Sightless, she was dragged along by both arms, led stumbling up three short steps and quick-marched down a long expanse of carpeting. There was a brief, downward ride in a lift, another march, this time over a floor that rang with their footsteps—tile or stone, Corbinye thought—and the hiss of a door mechanism.

Her guards pushed her then, and the body failed her, so she crashed to her knees upon plush and cried out even as her hand came up and tore the blinders away.

Uninterrupted white walls; carpeting like a field of snow, stretching away in all directions. Pale blue chair; white lacquer desk; silver reading lamp on a white wood table. A silver tray holding four blue mugs painted with dainty white flowers, and a crystal decanter.

Pillows—pale blue, rose, dark white—heaped like barrows above the snow.

Corbinye came slowly to her feet, caught a glimmer of movement from the corner of the eye and spun.

The other woman spun, as well, dropping cleanly enough into the crouch; flipping the long braid behind her back with a head-jerk as her hand dropped toward right boot-top and the knife she no doubt wore there. A competent opponent, but slow, and handicapped doubly—once, by heavy Grounder bones; twice, by the very voluptuousness of her figure.

The black eyes were opened wide, betraying concern; yet the face showed cool determination. Well enough.

It was only then that she recognized the clothes, the braid, the face—and snapped erect, went a dozen steps forward, reached out and touched her own mirrored hand, cool and very smooth.

"Aiiee…" she breathed and let her hand drop away. Number Fifteen stirred in her pocket, spider claws pricking skin comfortingly through fabric. She made as if to bring him out; checked at the slight sound and spun once more, this time toward the door.

Saxony Belaconto came with none to guard her, a plain silver band held in one hand. At the room's center, she stopped and bowed, very slightly.

"Corbinye Faztherot. I trust I find you well?"

"Well," she said uncompromisingly.

Amusement showed in the aquamarine eyes. "I hear from my captain that the escort I sent you was deemed insulting. Accept my apologies, for I did not intend it so."

"No," said Corbinye; "you merely did not believe that a barbarian could keep her word." She shifted. "Where is my cousin?"

Exquisite eyebrows rose. "About the business for which he was hired, I do most sincerely hope." She smiled, coldly. "And you must hope so, as well, for if he does not come to me with the item I have commissioned by tomorrow, First Dawn, your life is forfeit."

Corbinye frowned. "You tie us both with the same cord, Saxony Belaconto—I to die if he does not do as you wish; he to die if I do not."

"Are the knots undone?" The other shook her head, and held out the hand with the silver circlet. "Enough pleasantries. I have brought you this, which you are required to place upon your wrist. Do so now, and do not remove it."

She hesitated and Saxony Belaconto laughed and threw, lightly, but with enough accuracy so Corbinye was forced to fling a hand up and catch the thing to prevent it striking her face.

"Look." Saxony Belaconto had pulled one of her sleeves up, displaying the dull sheen of a bracelet very like the one Corbinye held.

"The main computer tracks all members of my household via these links. Any organic life in the house which is unlinked, the computer believes to be an enemy. And disposes of accordingly." She shoved her sleeve down. "It also registers pulse, blood chemistry, respiration—so we may be assured of your continued good health. Put the bracelet on and remove it for nothing while you are a guest here. Do you understand?"

"I understand." She slipped it over her hand, pushed— and the circlet sealed firmly around her wrist.

"Good." Saxony Belaconto turned to go. "The bedroom is through that door. You will find clothing in the dressing room; a shower and other facilities just beyond. Meals will be served here when the rest of the house dines." Her hand on the doorplate, she turned back, her smile like the thrust of an ice-knife. "I hope your stay here is extremely comfortable. Forgive me, that I cannot visit longer, but times are very busy, just now." Then she was gone.

Corbinye went over to the door and laid her hand against the plating, hissing in surprise at the slight electric shock. She went back through the white room and into the bedroom, which was all shades of gray and black, with a blood-red cover for the bed. Cautiously, she slipped Number Fifteen from her pocket and sat on the edge of the bed for a long time with the spider cupped in her hand, looking deep into its golden eyes.

CHAPTER TWENTY-SEVEN

THE DOOR OPENED, gently as a prayer. The spider on the Smiter and Witness in the chair turned their eyes toward the slowly-widening portal. Witness, at least, held his breath.

Barely had he chided himself for this breach of duty and regained the proper distance from his heart than the door stopped its movement and a person slipped into the room.

Stealthy he was, and silent as a shadow's shadow; yet he moved with surety, with no trembling fingers or fumbled movements in the heartbeat he required to close the door and seal it.

He turned, with purpose though without haste, and looked about him—studying the place, so it seemed to Witness, and perhaps tasting of the power. His eyes—enormous and blue in a face as austere as a chief's—touched Witness; stayed for a moment; moved on. Only when he had surveyed the room entire did he go forward—quietly, calmly—to stand before the Smiter.

One slim hand beckoned the bold little spider, which jumped, scurried up the arm and vanished beneath the collar of the plain white shirt. The Seeker then stood, head bent, studying the bracelet on his right wrist. After a short time of this, he reached into a pocket, pulled out a stubby black rod, took it between both hands and stretched it until it was a slender black stick. This he passed back and forth over the Smiter, coming closer and ever closer—so close that Witness felt his private heart begin to fail—and then pulled back, nodding as he squashed the stick back into rod and returned it to his pocket.

From the left sleeve came yet another spider, larger than the first, eyes vividly purple. It spun itself a silken lifeline down and, still spinning, commenced to cover the Smiter's area—over, under; over, under—in fine black silk.

The Seeker divided his attention between his wristlet and the spider's progress; nodded once more and glanced over his shoulder.

"The evening is cool and rather damp," he said neutrally, as a man may speak to a man. Witness for the Telios inclined his head.

"I hear you, O Seeker, and give thanks for the news you share."

Thin golden brows arched above those luminous, large eyes. "Just so." He returned his attention to the Smiter and the changes being wrought there.

The spider completed its last circuit and jumped to its master's hand, trailing thread behind. It paused for a moment on the man's palm, cut the silken strand and vanished beneath a sleeve-cuff.

The Seeker took the strand and carefully attached it to one of the many studs upon his bracelet; touched three others in rapid sequence—

Witness for the Telios hurled to his feet, so far forgetting duty that his heart's cry escaped his lips, and the Seeker turned, mild surprise on his grave, cool face.

"Yes?"

Witness took breath—and another—sternly chastising his private heart even as he stepped away from events, turning knowledge of the moment over to eyes and memory.

The Seeker frowned slightly; glanced over at his handi-work and then back.

"You are disturbed," he said gently, though in a tone that acknowledged such things occurred, even to those Tested and Tried. "I mean no—disrespect—to the Goddess or to her Instrument. You may tell me if I have offended."

A direct request for information could be answered— must be answered! Witness felt his private heart ease as he raised his arms in the sign of Answering Truly.

"Offense in the past has been shown by lightnings, by earth-tremor, by loss of breath and the stopping of the heart of the offender."

The Seeker glanced down at his slender self; glanced over at the blurred space of air where Shlorba's Smiter had, until a moment ago, lain; and looked back at Witness for the Telios.

"I assume offense has not been taken," he said dryly, glancing at his wrist. "It is time to be gone."

So saying, he turned and bent; the rectangle of blurred air rose in his hand and, as he stopped by the door to undo the seals, leaned against his side.

Witness for the Telios went softly to the Place where the Smiter had been; satisfied his eyes and his hands and his private heart that the place was now merely a place, and turned to follow Shlorba's Smiter, wherever and however it might go.

CHAPTER TWENTY-EIGHT

THE SEEKER MOVED through the darkness like a lyr-cat, passing silently down the court and up a set of shallow steps. At the top, he paused to do certain things, and the door slid open before him.

He stepped within, Witness coming after.

It was less dark inside, though nowhere near light. The Seeker walked on, past the scant furnishings, through a short hall and down a long flight of stairs, bearing Shlorba's Smiter invisibly in his right hand.

As his feet touched the carpet of the room below, he called out "Light!" and light there was, illuminating every corner of a place full to overflowing with devices, instruments, keyboards and others of the diverse tools used by those who were not Bindalche.

Witness for the Telios felt his feet slow as his private heart took in this treasure-house of knowledge, near quivering in its desire; then he sternly picked up the pace, following the Seeker and the Smiter across the room to the far wall.

This was uniformly gray and set with a mosaic of tiny lights, dials, and key-studs. The Seeker stopped before the wall, rested the blurred air that was the Smiter against his hip and worked carefully at his wristlet.

The blurring writhed abruptly—and there all at once was the Smiter itself, all wrapped in spider silk, leaning nonchalant against the Seeker's side.

"Ah…" the Seeker murmured, and reached to touch certain keys in that mosaic before him. Carefully, then, he laid the Smiter before the wall and took the single strand of silk that had recently been attached to his bracelet and knotted it about a gray metal protrusion.

Shlorba's Smiter blurred out of existence once more.

The Seeker turned from the wall and Witness for the Telios was before him, fingers touching eye-corners, then temples, in the ages-old request.

Large eyes regarded him calmly with no flicker of understanding in their cool blue depths. Witness composed himself for speech.

"It is necessary that I understand what I have Witnessed," he said, crossing his arms over his chest; "for the Memory to rightly serve the ones who Witness after."

Understanding dawned, and a certain thoughtfulness crossed the chiefly face. He turned and gestured toward the Place that hid the Smiter.

"The computer is scrambling the light waves in the Trident's immediate area, making it difficult for human eyes to see. A limited ruse, but effective enough in the dark. If we had passed through a scanner-beam, the Trident would have been—noticed—immediately."

Witness considered. "I understand that machines have eyes which see more deeply in some instances than the eyes of men," he acknowledged, recalling his study of the fat man's culture. "In what manner does the spider silk serve?"

"As a conductor for the computer's energy."

So. The silk was the road by which the machine's thought traveled, to the confounding of the Seeker's enemies. It was well. Witness lowered his arms.

"I thank you, O Seeker. The Witnessing is made more full by your words."

Humor glimmered through the blue eyes, though the face did not warm. He bowed slightly. "I am delighted to assist." He straightened and gestured about him. "These things are not to be touched—here…here…here. You may sit on the carpet, on yon stool, or on the edge of that table. Later, if your duty permits, I will show you where food is to be found."

Witness felt his private heart sing hosanna as he copied

the other's bow. Better, O twelves better! than the fat man was this young slim Seeker, with his cool face and knowing eyes! Almost, Witness allowed words of well-wishing to cross his lips, and was unaccountably dismayed that his duty did not permit him to speak so to this one.

"If you have no further questions…?" The Seeker waited a courteous moment, then nodded and turned away, moving smooth and sure through the wilderness of devices to a certain keyboard and screen. He hitched a hip onto the stool set before these, one foot hooked behind a rung, the other braced stoutly against the floor, reached forward and flipped switches.

The screen glowed cream, blue lines multiplying there like crystals in a salt-storm. Witness saw the Seeker frown, touch keys; nod.

"So, then…"

More keys touched by clever fingers—the blue lines shifted, reformed into arcane patterns of words and numerals. The Seeker snapped a toggle from left to right and the screen shimmered then steadied into a gridwork of absolutely equal squares, stretching to infinity.

Deliberately, the Seeker's fingers played the keys, drawing letters within the grid. Paused. Played again, briefly.

"Anjemalti?" The woman's voice was bright, fevered; gladness sheathing fear like gold over lead. "They have brought me to her house."

The keys clicked. I KNOW, Witness read in the screen.

"Yes," the woman said, slowly; "I suppose that you do." There was a pause. Then, rapidly, as fear overtook all: "Anjemalti—do not come here. She means to kill you, whether you fulfill her task or no. My ship is on Hotpad Sixteen—*Hyacinth*. She's a sweet ship, cousin, I swear to you—equal and better to any! Palm-sealed to my ID, but certainly you can contrive—"

CORBINYE, the Seeker wrote across the screen. COUSIN DO NOT

"Anjemalti, it is to throw your life away! Surely honor cannot compel you to deal as an equal with a rogue Grounder! There is nothing for you to gain by completing—"

YOUR LIFE the letters danced into the gridwork IS MORE PRECIOUS THAN THIEFS HONOR

"I am half-dead in any case!" the woman's voice cried and the Seeker shouted, "No!" as his fingers flew over the keys.

NO NO NO LIVE CORBINYE TRUST ME IT WILL BE WELL   YOU MUST LIVE CORBINYE SWEAR IT

Silence.

CORBINYE SWEAR TO ME THAT YOU WILL LIVE

"Corbinye?" the Seeker murmured and leaned forward, eyes piercing, as if he would make of the grid-covered screen a window into whatever place the woman was kept prisoner.

"I swear that I will try to live, Anjemalti." Infinite shades of sadness echoed in her voice. "I beg you will do the same."

I AM NOT A SUICIDE he assured her. ONE MORE NIGHT CORBINYE   HAVE COURAGE

"Take care, cousin. Remember *Hyacinth*, should madness pass."

The Seeker smiled slightly, hands flickering over the keys.

THE CREW WERE EVER SINGLE MINDED

The pause this time was charged with something undefined and powerful. "So we are," the woman agreed. "Ship and stars guide you, Anjemalti."

SHIP AND STARS CORBINYE

The grid went dark.

The young Seeker sat a moment, shoulders sagging. Then he straightened and rose, bustling here and there among his instruments and devices.

Witness for the Telios sat carefully on the edge of the table, dividing his attention between the Smiter, invisibly asleep, the restless Seeker, and the wonder of his private heart.

CHAPTER TWENTY-NINE

THE SPIDER CEASED spinning, blinked its golden eyes twice and began to backtrack over the white rug, swallowing black silk words.

Corbinye whirled, going from knees to feet in a vicious snap. The woman in the mirror performed the move with grace, body eloquent of snarling, efficient energy. Corbinye glowered at her, strode forward three heavy, Grounder strides—and spat.

"Dirt-grubber!" she shouted, watching pink, and then red, mantle the fair cheeks, as the black eyes widened in a parody of true, Crew eyes. "Worthless, heavy, bundle of meat! No muscle, no speed, no finesse—you make me sick!" She caught her rage, grappled with it as if with a live thing, no little dismayed at its strength.

The woman in the mirror was crying, soundless and steady; the jutting cheekbones gleamed with the tears that ran over them, to drip, unheeded, from the soft chin.

Abruptly, Corbinye's rage died away, leaving only an ache of pity. That, and the chill, many-toothed terror that gnawed, day and night, at her belly. She sighed and reached up to rub the tears away.

"Very well," she told the woman in the mirror, with utmost gentleness, "the Third Sequence, from the top; treble speed."

Obediently, the woman in the mirror adopted the stance and began the moves, Corbinye echoing her in every muscle.

CHAPTER THIRTY

WITH STEALTH AND in utter silence, he slipped down the darkened hallway to the door he sought. Gently, he brought the specially-etched glove from his tunic and laid it, palm-flat, against the lock-plate.

The door sighed gustily as it opened, and Gem crouched, ears straining to catch the slightest hint of unrest from the household slumbering about him.

Silence in all parts of the house. The telltale on his wrist showed no surge of energy, as from the triggering of a remote alarm. The room itself was dark, slightly cool, smelling less musty than on his previous visit. Gem slid the infraglasses over his eyes and stepped across the threshold.

Number Four made a circuit of the case, transmitted the all-clear and jumped to Gem's sleeve as he leaned to raise the lid.

Mordra El Theman's greatest treasure shone, grail-like, before him. Gem bent forward and picked it up.

Revulsion erupted as his heartbeat spiked in terror.

Carefully, he up-ended the urn and spilled *Sarialdan* into his palm.

Horror filled his throat with bile; fed imagined cries of discovery to his ears.

Hands determinedly steady, he set the urn precisely back in its place, brought the case-lid down and stared at what he held in his palm: an ugly, irregular lump of brown stone, its surface broken here and there with sullen green crystals. Gem slipped it into his hip pocket; felt it lodge next to his body like an enemy's knife.

He took a moment to close his eyes and recite the charm he had found in Shilban's library, wishing he could believe that the fear had lessened, then grimly reviewed the next steps of the operation in painstaking detail.

Satisfied, he went silently and swiftly across the room and slipped into the hallway, sealing the door behind him.

Four steps only had he taken, back the way he had come, when the alarm screamed to life.

No subtlety here; merely a wish to terrify the intruder, confuse him with sound and with strobing light, so that he bolted, mindless, easy prey for the police.

Gem whirled, took in the octagonal grid of an olfactory sensor set just above his head and flattened against the wall, terror a live thing, clawing his mind to shreds; felt the shudder in the wood at his back that was feet, running in the upstairs hall; heard the shriek of other sirens under the alarm's din and knew the police had arrived.

They would expect him to run for the nearest exit. A map of El Theman's house unfolded before his mind's eye, showing the nearest escape behind him—end of the hall and left, through the kitchen and out. Straight into the arms of the police.

Gem jumped forward, running silent on his toes, skidded into a side hall just as he heard two of the wakened household reach the main foyer; dodged into the butler's closet and slammed, panting, into the service lift. Shaking, he punched buttons and the lift went—up.

Up. Past the second floor sleeping rooms; past the third floor exercise rooms and studies; up.

To the ballroom.

He nearly fell out of the lift; sent it back down, with instructions to park at the second floor, and ran across the imported wooden floor, the Fearstone burning against his leg. Through the glass dome the early morning stars blazed like a fever-dream of diamonds.

Heedless of alarms, he burst through the archway into the rooftop pleasure-garden, charged through a swatch of gold-and-blue flowers planted in the shape of El Theman's badge to the perimeter wall.

He located the door after a moment's search, artfully hidden behind a lamonchi shrub, leaned over the lock and pulled out a power pick.

There was no question of stealth; he made only the most minimal attempt to shield his tampering from the main household computer and stepped through when the door popped open a heartbeat later, not even bothering to close it behind him.

There was wind, prowling the ledge like a hunter-cat, damp and smelling of the River, eight stories below. Gem huddled close to the wall, moving carefully to the left, concentrating on the count, letting his body deal with the niceties of balance. There was no room, presently, for fear.

Forty-two. He finished his count and went to his knees with exquisite care, reaching over the side, fingers scrabbling against stone siding—and found the lattice-work.

He hesitated, fingers twined around that slender escape, and looked out and down. Directly below, between the fifth and sixth floors, a thick utility wire joined the lattice-work. The utility wire connected with an insulated glass pole, two blocks distant and barely discernible in the mist. With luck, he would be able to descend the pole to the street and make his way home unmolested. First Dawn and his appointment with Saxony Belaconto was still four hours away. Luck…

She means to kill you, Anjemalti, Corbinye's voice was startlingly clear in his memory. *My ship is on Hotpad Sixteen, should madness pass…*

He closed his eyes; opened them and swung out, fear reduced to a mere leaden ache in his gut. Luck or no luck, it was inconceivable that he fail.

He slid the last few feet to the ground, muscles quivering in exhaustion, mouth dry, even fear drained away, at last. Three hours to First Dawn.

He stepped away from the pole, thinking only that he must hurry; that he must on no account chance missing that meeting with the Vornet. He didn't see the cop at all until she burst out of the bushes to the right of the utility pole, gun out as she shouted her location into her belt-comm.

Gem spun around and ran.

CHAPTER THIRTY-ONE

THE SEEKER HAD been gone for some time.

Witness for the Telios climbed the stairs from the Center, turned left down the hall and went into the kitchen to refill his mug with cold tea. The tiny window over the sink glowed with the clear gray light of pre-dawn. The Seeker had been away the whole night through.

Sipping his tea, Witness went back down to the Center and the dazzling clutter of the Seeker's devices.

Anjemalti, the woman had called him. Witness tasted the sound, liking the weight of it in his mouth. Anjemalti, she had called him, and begged him, for his life, to stay away.

Witness sat on the edge of the table, eyes straying from the shimmering Place where the Smiter rested, to the base of the stairs down which the Seeker must come, did he return at all.

To the woman's plea had Anjemalti the Seeker responded with both cool determination and blazing passion. Witness found himself well-pleased by this, for the greatest chiefs— and the greatest of the Smiter's Chosen—had each held fire and ice in their natures, side-by-side and equal.

Abovestairs—a creak, a step. Witness composed himself to See and to Recall, shutting his private heart and all its likes and desires away from the instant of the event.

In the next instant the Seeker was with him, skittering haphazard down the stairs, hair flying, grim lines etching a face gone from young to old in a single night. He ran to a desk along the sidewall, jerked open a drawer and scrabbled out an enameled box. Feverishly, he upended it, spilling out several rings, glittering stones and other small items of power; and rummaged ruthlessly again through the drawer, removing at last a strip of embroidered linen, and a pillow of white velvet.

Less hasty now, the Seeker placed the pillow into the totem-box, then fished in his pocket and withdrew a thing.

Witness drew closer, the better to See and Recall; noted as well the glamour that clung to the Seeker now, a chill reaching into the private heart and to the marrow of the bones, not unlike that doom pervading the Trial, when the soul was separated from the heart, to be read and judged.

The Seeker's fingers withdrew from the totem-box and Witness peered over his shoulder. Flat green crystals glared balefully from their prison of rock, brown as mud against the salt-white purity of the pillow, emanating a cold that teared the eyes and called forth the faces of one's dead. Witness for the Telios felt his private heart shrink in awe; knew that he hovered on the brink of an Action as had not been Witnessed in twelve twelves of lifetimes.

Reverently, he stepped back, that the Seeker might tuck the 'broidred cloth about the stone, and gently close the box.

Feverish again, Anjemalti the Seeker moved among his devices, flipping this switch, turning that knob, calling this and that instrument to life. At last, he went to the computer-wall and with exquisite care detached the spider silk from the machine stud and attached the strand once more to his wristlet. With a look of sadness in the large, fey eyes, he stared around the room, then reached again to the master machine, slid back a panel and flipped five toggles, sharply.

Standing away, he looked at Witness. "Do you pray?"

An inappropriate question, asked as it must be of the private heart. Yet the magic surrounding this Chief of Seekers was not to be denied. Witness met eyes with eyes.

"I pray, Anjemalti. Men might."

"So," a soft exhalation. The fey eyes sharpened. "And do you fight?"

Witness did not lower his gaze. "A man may fight. A Witness first strives to See and Recall."

The eyes left him as the Seeker pointed. "There is a knife in that drawer. It is yours, if you wish it."

So saying, he went across the room, his stride smooth and quick, as if the weight of Shlorba's Smiter were nothing. He paused but briefly at the desk, to take up the totem-box and slip it into his pocket. Then he was gone like a wraith up the stairs.

Witness for the Telios hesitated one beat of his private heart before crossing to a certain drawer and pulling it open. The knife slid easily into his boot-top, and the prayer he murmured on his way up the stairs was the one that hunters pray, just as they begin the hunt.

CHAPTER THIRTY-TWO

SHE WAS WAITING for them, straight-backed and haughty, the scarlet shirt a flame in the cold white room, Number Fifteen crouched hidden in her pocket.

The spider shifted as she fell in between her guards, claws pricking her thigh through the thin lining. Resolutely, Corbinye kept the pace, hoping that the stranger's face she wore was as blank as she willed it. Was Anjemalti the source of his creature's restiveness? Was he trying to send her one last message of hope? Or did he wish her to do some special, vital thing—now too late to be described?

Or had madness passed, after all, and Number Fifteen been called home?

Fear dried her mouth and the ever-present terror in her belly growled and stretched and bared its fangs. Corbinye marched on with the dignity befitting one both Worldwalker and Seeker for the Crew, between the two murderers come to escort her to her death.

Saxony Belaconto sat behind a desk of real wood, hands folded on its gleaming surface, aquamarine eyes glitteringly bright. Corbinye stood between her guards and met that feverish stare unflinchingly, determined not to show awe in the face of such arrogant display of wealth. The desk alone was worth a ship's ransom; the carpet she stood on barely less. It occurred to her for the first time to wonder precisely how expensive this new body she wore was.

There was a flicker of movement on the edge of Corbinye's vision, and a voice.

"So, this is the barbarian I've heard so much about, eh?" He came to stand beside Belaconto's chair, a bull-shouldered, powerfully built Grounder: dark hair, dark mustache; dark, old eyes in a boyish, unlined face.

"The very same." Saxony Belaconto's voice was wary, respectful. Corbinye studied the man with new interest; saw his smile and very nearly shivered.

"How long?" The man demanded, reaching among the few pieces of bric-a-brac on the desk top and selecting a knife. Corbinye could not contain the gasp; the tensing of desirous muscles—and the man smiled again.

"Seven days translated," Belaconto told him, still in that chillingly courteous voice. "And she moves as if it were her birth-body."

"Does she indeed." The man toyed idly with her blade; tested its edge; held it balanced; flipped it up and caught it, showily, by the worn grip. Corbinye's palm itched for the feel of it and she schooled her face to blankness. "So, barbarian, you want this, do you?"

"It is mine," she said flatly.

"But you didn't have the strength to keep it, did you? Eh? That's why it's here—the Vornet took it from you."

Corbinye smiled, wolfish, nodding toward the other woman. "Ask Saxony Belaconto the price of that taking."

The young, cruel face went white; the knife rose, flipped, and fell toward his hand as her guards dropped hurriedly back and he shouted, "If you want it, catch it, bitch!"

It came, a barely seen blur, thrown for a shoulder wound, not for the kill. Corbinye sidestepped, twisted— and watched amazed as the soft, stranger's hand plucked the blade out of the air as it went by, fingers curving lovingly around the hilt.

She saluted him, mockingly, touching finger guard to heart before thrusting the blade through her belt and dropping her arms once more to her side.

"My thanks."

Saxony Belaconto gave one short, harsh shout of laughter and raised her hand.

"You are my guest until your cousin claims you, Corbinye Faztherot."

"I know it," she answered quietly, despite the desperate pounding of her heart; "and a courteous guest in a courteous house keeps her weapon in her belt, bonded by her word."

"Exactly," Belaconto agreed, slanting malicious aquamarine eyes at the man.

He was glowering, arms crossed over his chest. "Seven days translated!"

"You may check the records from the Blue House." Saxony Belaconto still spoke softly, but yet not as warily as she had. Corbinye glanced at her—and looked sharply away, stomach churning, certain that it would ease Saxony Belaconto's life enormously, should Corbinye Faztherot kill this man.

Across the room, a clock whirred, clicked and sang three notes.

The door behind her opened and she whirled in time to see a woman step within and bow nervously, eyes darting from Corbinye to the guards to the desk. She cleared her throat, pushing her sleeves back so that the house bracelet gleamed for an instant before she folded her hands firmly together.

"Gem ser Edreth is here, Ms. Belaconto."

CHAPTER THIRTY-THREE

"Bɪᴅ Mᴀsᴛᴇʀ sᴇʀ Edreth rest himself in the antecham-ber," Saxony Belaconto said calmly. "I will be ready for him soon."

The woman by the door hesitated. "He has another man with him, Ms. Belaconto. The ID net could not supply a name."

"Then bid both rest," she snapped and the woman bowed hastily and ducked out the door.

"Our guests should be arriving shortly." A slender fore-finger singled out the guards. "Bring the table. Place it against my desk. Four chairs." She stood. "Corbinye Faztherot."

"Saxony Belaconto."

"You are standing in an awkward place. Come with me, so that you may be placed more suitably."

Corbinye wavered momentarily, caught the glitter of black eyes, watching her in malice, and walked around the desk, shoulders defiantly squared.

They stopped seven paces behind the desk, where the room widened into a small foyer. There was a door in the far wall, hidden from the larger room before the desk. The walls were white, unadorned; there were no priceless carpets on the wooden floor.

Saxony Belaconto paused, glanced back at the desk and nodded. "Your cousin will be able to see you and hear you, but you will not be in the way." The jewel-bright eyes sharp-ened. "Be wise, Corbinye Faztherot."

"As wise as may be," Corbinye agreed, and the other laughed sharply.

"Chimi!" she called.

"Ms. Belaconto?"

"Guard Ms. Faztherot, please. Carmen will assist you in a moment—ah! Our guests!"

Saxony Belaconto walked to the hidden door and laid her hand against the plate just as the chime sounded a second time.

An old woman stumped into the room, hair white and thinning, shirt hanging loose from bony shoulders. At her back came a tall, dark-haired girl, face smooth with first youth, eyes wary and calculating, gun holstered efficiently on her hip.

"Jenfir Chung. Thank you for coming so promptly."

The old woman sniffed and peered up into Belaconto's face. "You knew I'd come." The sharp old eyes ran over the younger woman's figure, came back to the flawless face. "Not bad, for a woman pushing ninety." She stumped on past, bodyguard at her shoulder. Corbinye earned one glance from each; a dismissal from both—and the door chimed again.

A short, slender man of undetermined age, conservatively dressed, mild-faced and vague-eyed. He bowed to Saxony Belaconto.

"Nar Veldonis," she murmured, unexpectedly respectful. "Thank you for honoring my house."

"Quite," he murmured absently, and waved a hand toward the hulking bald man at his back. "You won't mind Michael, will you? He's no trouble." He moved on without waiting for an answer.

Carmen hurried around the desk and took his place to the right and just behind Corbinye, hissing for her ears alone, "Try anything at all, bitch, and you're meat, understand?"

She pretended not to hear, eyes on Saxony Belaconto, who was checking her watch and glancing nervously down-room.

"Where's Janns?" the old woman demanded from the table. "I don't have much time left, and I don't relish squandering the balance waiting for that rattlepate."

"Another moment and I'm certain he'll be here," Belaconto said calmly.

"Man has the least distance to travel and can't be on time…" The old eyes lit on the bull-shouldered man lounging on the corner of Belaconto's desk. "Well, Harcourt, what the hell are you doing here? *I* understood this was a Z-level meeting."

"Keldren aspires," Belaconto said softly and the old woman cackled.

"I think—" began Keldren Harcourt, hotly, but Nar Veldonis raised a hand.

"No, I beg that you don't."

The door chimed once more.

This man was big, red-faced, hard-bodied. He came alone, with a gun holstered under his left arm. "Damn' city's crawling with cops," he snarled. "News on the scanner that there's a 'crime wave'. Some damn' amateur." He snorted disgust and brushed past Belaconto's greeting, striding around the desk and dropping into the single vacant chair.

"Jenfir, Nar." He glared at Keldren Harcourt. "Shit."

"Thank you all for coming," Saxony Belaconto said, moving leisurely back to her desk. She folded her hands on the polished wood. "My man will be bringing the item in just a moment, if you will indulge me with just a bit more patience."

Corbinye pricked her ears. What man was this? Was it not arranged—she barely contained the outraged gasp. This upstart Grounder claimed *Anjemalti* as her crewman? Dishonor even to hear it said! How—

"Easy, bitch," Carmen breathed from behind her. "You don't want to get wasted before your boyfriend's here to see it…"

She swallowed, willing the body to relax; at the desk, Saxony Belaconto touched a stud and sat back.

The receptionist was afraid.

He was not afraid. No one could say that he was afraid. He was calm—see? Hands folded just so upon the knee; heartbeat steady and unhurried, pounding in his ears. He breathed—in…out. There was nothing to fear. And he was not afraid.

He had a plan. Edreth had drilled him, over and over: Make a plan. Review the plan until you know it like you know your own heartbeat, pounding clear and unhurried in your ears.

Gem reviewed his plan. Take the Trident and the stone into the office, where Saxony Belaconto and perhaps a guard or two awaited him. Corbinye would be there. A watcher— no doubt a watcher, but he had prepared for that. Even now was Number Twelve crouching by the proper set of circuits, awaiting the pulse that would destroy spider and sensor, together. Gem recalled that he was grieved over such a use of the spider, but that its death was called for. In the plan.

The plan: Into the office, the Trident laid on the desk— sweetly and gently, he must address her. She must see that he was not afraid. He would explain that Witness was essential to the Trident. Would pull out the box holding *Sarialdan* and place it in her hand, explaining that this object enhanced the power of the Trident. And while she was overcome with ter-ror—in the diversion of her fear—Corbinye and he would flee. Straight to *Dart* and Linzer Skot and safety and blessed— peace.

The receptionist spilled a cup of tea over her keyboard and scrambled to mop up, towel and fingers trembling. She was afraid.

He was not afraid.

"Ms. Belaconto will see you now." The receptionist's voice shook with her terror. Gem inclined his head and came unhurriedly to his feet. He grasped the invisible Trident firmly in hands that did not shake and went leisurely to the door, across the threshold—

And nearly cried aloud in mingled frustration and confusion. He stood just inside the door, clenching the Trident against his side, plan shattered to countless shards of useless planning, Witness' breath cold on the back of his neck.

A sea of faces; a wilderness of eyes—He took a deep breath, denying hysteria; summoning those cool powers of observation that were a master thief's greatest asset.

Faces, indeed. Nine in all. Of them, he found and named Saxony Belaconto, Carmen, and—yes—Corbinye, brave in her scarlet shirt. Between them, six persons, and she standing with a guard on either side.

Saxony Belaconto's eyes were jewel-bright daggers; her face hovering on the edge of displeasure.

He bowed.

"Master ser Edreth." The voice suggested mollification. "Please come forward. You *have* brought the item?"

People. Who were these people? Gem straightened.

"I had not expected so large an audience, lady."

The old woman wheezed a laugh. "Wants introductions, does he? Cocky bastard." She tapped herself on the chest. "Jenfir Chung." A scrawny finger jabbed at the man next to her. "Nar Veldonis." Another jab, in the direction of the balding man. "Filbar Janns." She grinned, showing perfect teeth. "Satisfied?"

Gem took another breath, mind racing heartbeat. Four Vornet chieftains ruled Henron between them. And all four were gathered in this room. Now. To see Gem ser Edreth deliver the Bindalche Trident—into Saxony Belaconto's hands? Was she to become chiefest of the chiefs? Or was this gathering to ensure that *none* gained ascendancy over the others?

"I thank you, lady," he said to the old woman. "But it appears the introduction slighted one."

She laughed again, like metal across glass. "Don't let Harcourt worry you, boy. I'd judge you his match any day—

as long as you're careful not to turn your back on him."

"I—" began the squat, black-eyed man, and was cut off by the bald one.

"Play with the courier later," he growled. "I want to *see* this thing." He snorted. "Hesernym, right? And all we got to do is sit back and collect it." He snapped thick fingers. "Come on, ganef, show us the lolly."

The insult bit sharp. Gem stiffened, caught himself and looked to Saxony Belaconto, awaiting her word.

She smiled tightly and waved him near, though there was a bit of a waver to her usually graceful gesture. "Display the trident for us, Master ser Edreth. On the table, please."

He approached, stopped and let his invisible burden slide down until it rested, butt-end against the carpet, and leaning athwart his hip. "Corbinye!"

She stirred in her scarlet shirt, flipped the braid behind her back with a jerk of the head. Braid? He tried to recall if she had had a braid, before, then let the puzzlement go.

"Anjemalti!"

He strained to see her clearly, but there were shifting mists before his eyes. He wondered if he were going blind and shook that thought away, too.

"Are you well, Corbinye?"

"Anjemalti, I am." Her voice resonated with countless levels of meaning. He strained to decipher none of them, but looked instead at Saxony Belaconto.

"I suggest that my cousin might await me outside," he said mildly, careful of her dignity, here among her peers.

She laughed. "For shame, Master ser Edreth! Do you not want her to see the apex of all this striving? She's as much involved as you or I or any other here! She has a right to be see!" She turned her head slightly. "Don't you, Corbinye Faztherot?"

"In my judgment, yes."

Saxony Belaconto laughed again, though the face she turned back to Gem was paler than usual. "So very careful, your family." The laughter faded. "The Trident, Master ser Edreth. Quickly."

The Trident. Yes, certainly, that was part of the plan—to give her the Trident and then the Fearstone and be rid of the gods-blasted things—He bent his head and worked at the wristlet, carefully unwinding the slippery silk from the power stud. He recalled, as if from another life, that he had once thought the Trident to have been technology, and he almost laughed, though a mad alien stood at his back and his cousin stared black-eyed from across a sea of enemies.

Technology! And all this while it had the current running through it and showed no signs of life at all. Perhaps he should have asked the Witness—the silk came loose at last and the Trident shimmered into being.

"What's it wrapped in?" demanded Jenfir Chung.

"The thief's trying to pull something," snapped Harcourt.

Nar Veldonis waved a languid hand as Gem glanced at Saxony Belaconto.

"Conductive wire," he said to her wild eyes. "It is only a moment to unwrap it, lady, so that you and the—honored—may see the thing complete."

"Unwrap it," she ordered, a rasping edge on the expensive voice. Behind her, Corbinye shifted; stilled.

Gem obeyed, patiently unscrolling the line until it was all coiled in his hand and the Trident stood free. He lifted it then and placed it gently upon the table, frowning at the whine in his ears and the continued mistiness of his sight, which insisted that, here and there among the blasted and hopeless ancient circuitry, the Trident was beginning to...*glow*.

"*That's* a hesernym mine?" The bald man lolled back in his chair, unimpressed. Jenfir Chung laughed.

"You young ones always judge competence by beauty,"

she said. "Get you in deep trouble, someday." She tipped her head, like an evil, yellow-eyed old bird. "Me, I think it looks just as it ought."

Gem stirred, pulled his eyes from the intermittent glow of the Trident and raised them to look at Saxony Belaconto.

"There is something more," he said, in a voice that rang false in his own ears.

She frowned, the aquamarine eyes showing some white around the edges. "More? You are overzealous, Master ser Edreth; I commissioned only the Trident." The eyes flicked beyond him for an instant, and Gem felt the Witness stiffen. "And the operator, of course."

"Another—component," Gem insisted; "a connection discovered—by accident." He laid his hand against his pocket, careful that the gesture showed no threat. "By your leave, lady…"

"By my leave, is it?" She moved her eyes again, captured the bull-necked man. "Keldren, Master ser Edreth has something in his pocket that he wishes me to have. Do me the kindness of fetching it here."

The man sneered, and Gem wondered how he dared it, came up from his perch on the table edge and walked down the room, promising mayhem with every swaggering step.

The palm he held out was ridged with callus, the fingers thick and strong. "All right, thief, let's have it."

Gem looked into the cold face, deep into the eyes, to the strain and the cruelty and the rabid self-interest within. He tasted the man's tension like lemoned salt, smelled the copper-stink of desperation, and smiled.

Slowly, he reached into his pocket, keeping each finger-move smooth and unassuming. Slowly, he fished the jewel box from its nesting-place and brought it, reverently, forth. Tenderly, he worked the catch, and laid the cover-cloth back.

With fingers that betrayed nothing more than thief's competence, he took the Fearstone up and placed it, all gentleness, in Keldren Harcourt's palm.

He screamed, did Harcourt, fingers convulsing into a fist. He spun back to the gather-table and screamed once more, shrill and despairing, before lunging straight at Nar Veldonis.

It was then that the Bindalche Trident exploded into light.

CHAPTER THIRTY-FOUR

HARCOURT TOOK WHAT Anjemalti gave him, shrieked like a man in mortal pain, and dove clumsily for Nar Veldonis.

He had covered barely half the necessary distance before the bodyguard pulled his weapon and fired. Corbinye saw the blood-flower bloom on Harcourt's shirt front, but the impetus of his terror carried him forward two more steps before death kissed his soul and he fell, the jewel spilling from his hand.

Chimi the guard cried out and leapt to his mistress' side, Carmen half-a-stride behind. Saxony Belaconto herself was standing, ordering Veldonis to control his man, while Jenfir Chung's gun-sworn came to her feet, weapon out, eyes beyond wary in a face gone gray with terror.

Down the room, Anjemalti staggered, hand before his eyes, as if shielding them. The stranger at his back reached out a steadying hand, all the while staring at the object that lay, forgotten, in the center of the table.

The guards had unlimbered their weapons, all attention down-room, Corbinye Faztherot mist and ash to memories apparently addled by the prevailing fear. At the table, Filbar Janns lurched suddenly upward, gun swinging out—

Corbinye slid three steps to the right, saw Anjemalti waver again and heard the one with him cry aloud in a tongue strange and exultant.

The lights flared, flickered. The house bracelet dropped from Corbinye's wrist and the door to the outer hallway sagged suddenly open. Someone screamed and Filbar Janns fired his gun as Anjemalti leapt forward.

Anjemalti fell. The lights flared one time more, then failed altogether.

Almost, Corbinye screamed. Training, or pride, kept her voice still; horror goaded her into a run through the blackness. She slammed into a body, snarled and pushed forward, heading for Anjemalti's last position, refusing to think that she might overrun him in the darkness, or that he was dead.

There were more screams from the blinded Grounders and Belaconto's voice, etched in hysteria, crying out for light.

Light of a sort miraculously came forth, grayish and weakly as it was, not quite enough to show her Jenfir Chung's body before she fell across it, and slammed painfully to her knees.

"Anjemalti!" she cried—and then she saw him, golden hair glowing in the weak light, an ominous splash of darkness across the whiteness of his sleeve.

She crawled to him, touched his face, pulled that lush grounder-length hair. "Anjemalti!"

His eyes opened.

Relief blurred what meager sight she had. She dashed a hand across her eyes and tugged at his undamaged arm. "Cousin, let us go. Quickly."

He licked his lips, struggled to get his knees under him. "The Trident."

"What?" She stared into his face as best she could, renewed her grip upon his arm. "Anjemalti, let it be! Give Saxony Belaconto joy of it! Come—"

"The Trident," he repeated, and she heard, with sinking heart, the note of command in his voice. She dropped his arm.

"Stay you here," she told him. "I'll fetch it."

It was grueling, though not overly dangerous. The remaining Grounders were deployed about the room, huddled in safe places from which now and then a shot would wing. Corbinye snatched the Trident from the table and crawled back, finding him not quite where she had left him, half risen to his knees, hand hovering over something on the floor.

"Anjemalti, I have it," she hissed. "*Will* you come?"

"Yes." His hand swooped, captured, and slipped the captive something into his pocket, then he shambled to his feet, heedless, it seemed, of the possibility of bullets, and ran for the door.

Cursing, Corbinye followed.

The empty halls were lit by emergency dims, and the pace Anjemalti set through them tried her pitiful new body to the strain-point, and then beyond. Her world shrank to these necessities—to stay moving, to keep him in sight, to hold to the accursed Trident, to not, to never, fall.

The door onto the street gaped open, spilling the gray light of First Dawn into the foyer. Anjemalti stepped through to the street and waved his hand at a cab.

It wasn't until the machine had pulled over and opened its door to admit them that Corbinye realized that the stranger who had accompanied Anjemalti to the conference room was standing at her shoulder.

"Leave us," she snarled at him. "Take your freedom as gift and run!"

He gave her back no answer, eyes and face so unremittingly bland that she thought for an instant he was blind. Then reddish lashes quivered in a faint blink and the face altered somewhat.

"I am Witness for the Telios," he said, voice as bland as eyes. "I travel on the whim of the Smiter."

"He comes with us," gasped Anjemalti, half-falling into the open cab. "Corbinye…"

"Yes." Very plain where duty lay, with the Captain injured and half-swooning within sight of his enemy's stronghold. She slid beside him, cramming the damned Trident in crosswise and ungainly, barely leaving room for Witness to fit his broad shoulders.

The cab's door descended and there was an inquiring *thweep* from the autopilot, then a scratchy "Destination sir or madam. This unit requires instruction."

"Anjemalti, where do you take us?" But the swoon had overtaken him and in the dome-light she saw the sleeve dyed crimson to the wrist.

"The spaceport," she told the robot, sternly overriding the body's instinct to cry. "Hotpad Sixteen. With all speed, if you please."

"This unit is programmed to obey all local limits. This unit's key is known to appropriate local municipalities." There was a whir of catching tape; then: "Spaceport processed as destination. Sub-address Hotpad Sixteen. Verification sought."

"Verified," Corbinye snapped, and very nearly the body had its way with its stupid tears as the cab gently pulled out and merged with the light dawn traffic.

She reached instead to try and work with the sodden sleeve, thinking to see how bad the wound was, for surely it had not been bleeding as heavily as that before—

Anjemalti stirred, coming half out of his faint. "Let be," he muttered.

"It bleeds, cousin. I thought to bind it at least until—"

"Linzer will have a kit," he mumbled, words slurring badly. He stirred yet further, eyes slitting open, though she doubted they focused on any one of them there. "The spaceport," he said, with painful distinctness.

"The cab takes us there even now."

Restlessness left him at that, as well as strength. He had barely croaked out a "Good" than his body went limp against the cushions and he was lost to all sense.

Corbinye shifted, abrading the back of her hand on one or another of the bits of broken garbage littering the hilt of the Trident. She bit back a curse and pointed at Witness.

"You! Are you keeper of this thing?"

There was a slight pause, as if her words had to travel some little distance to reach that place where he was himself.

"I am Witness for the Telios," he said eventually, in his colorless voice.

"So you had said. I ask if that means you are guardian of this object."

The response came more quickly this time, as if she had somewhat engaged his interest.

"Shlorba's Smiter guards itself best," he said.

Corbinye curbed her temper with an effort. "Then to whom does it belong?"

"To itself," replied Witness. He paused, then gave fuller answer, since these were worthy questions, and some that the Telios asked among themselves. "Some say also, to events, or to the Sister, even to the Chief who currently it favors. Others say that indeed the Smiter is holy because it may alter the event in which all the rest of what is finds itself enmeshed."

Anjemalti's cousin turned her face to the Trident for a moment's study out of quick, fierce eyes. Witness found his secret heart approved her—a warrior of purity, who would carry what the Chief commanded without desiring it for her own. Such things were written, and some few Remembered, but to have found such a one here, where he had so lately despaired of the fat man, sang of the potential for vast change in the state of what is.

"How is it," began Corbinye—and the cab shuddered once, violently enough to throw Anjemalti against her and Witness against the door, and slammed to a halt.

A glance out the window showed a narrow street lined with shabby houses, several with broken windows, sealed with battered doors.

"This is not the spaceport!" Corbinye cried. "Taxi! Proceed upon your coordinates!"

"This unit is forbidden to continue," the mechanical voice announced. "This unit's key is known to appropriate local municipalities. This unit—"

"Law force." She spun, gripped her unconscious cousin by his good arm and shook. "Anjemalti, be aware! The cab is stopped and the police approach!"

He made no reply and she gasped, shifting around again in the cramped confines of the cab without realizing how close that gasp had sounded to a sob.

The robot's central system was easily identified by the leaden shield protecting it. Corbinye grunted and pitched half over the low divider, finding the shielded wires by touch, laboriously following them toward the main console, willing the stupid Grounder hands to taste each nuance of shape and size and smoothness and—the break in smoothness.

"Yes…" she hissed. She worked her knife around, ignoring the growing sounds of sirens, patiently got the blade where it would do the most good and, one hand on the hilt and the other palm cradling the tip, pulled with all the body's force.

The stupid wire stretched, withstood—and snapped with a suddenness that sent her toppling back as sparks crackled and the console flared—and all the doors flew open.

"Out!" she shouted at Witness, and thrust the Trident into his startled hands, turning to get a grip on Anjemalti and haul him free.

Haul him she did, but his weight overbore her, who had once been able to lift double her mass and hold it for a count of five. She toppled to the gritty walkway, he sprawling atop her, and the sirens sounded perilously close.

Out of nowhere came hands, square and hard and competent, lifting Anjemalti as if he were the veriest babe. Corbinye scrambled to her feet as Witness settled Anjemalti across his shoulder with matter-of-fact ease. He glanced up and used his chin to indicate the thing leaning against the cab's fender.

"It is forbidden that one set to Witness should touch the Smiter."

"Your pardon, I'm certain." Almost the impulse to leave the damned thing overmastered her, then reason returned: How, after all, could she convey Anjemalti to safety, if the one who was able to carry him stayed to watch the Trident?

She snatched the thing up, took a moment to decide that the sirens bore in from the north, and set off to the south, Witness following after.

An odorous alley crossed the main way and she took it, though it jogged off parallel to the port. It might, she thought half-wildly, be defensible, should it come to that. She gasped a laugh and leaned suddenly against a stretch of splintering fence.

"Defensible, certainly!" she cried aloud, dismayed by the edge of hysteria in her own voice. "With a bladed knife and a half-rotted relic for weapons!"

"I have a knife, O Warrior," the Witness said from beside her; "and some knowledge of the lore."

She turned to study him. "Do you? And is one set to witness permitted to fight?"

"A man may fight," he said solemnly, and a grin abruptly split his sober face. "But a dead man may not Witness."

She laughed, still hearing the hysteria there and feeling her heart battering against her ribs. "Spoken like a Crewman! We may yet make the spaceport, with such a will! Let us—"

A siren wailed distressingly near at hand. At the further alley-end a police car pulled up, and stopped.

Corbinye swore and leapt forward, running as fast as the weak body would allow toward the top of the alley and perhaps a chance at another strike for the port and *Hyacinth*. Behind her, she heard Witness, moving not so quickly as she thought he might, having a care, no doubt, for Anjemalti, draped unconscious across one broad shoulder.

At the top of the alley, a car slid into view, annihilating the hope of the street beyond. Corbinye slammed to a halt, a wordless wail escaping her. Defensible...

"Morela! Quickly, Morela, come in!"

She turned, saw the fevered eyes, the thin hand holding wide a gate in the scabrous fence and plunged within, Witness on her heels.

CHAPTER THIRTY-FIVE

BEYOND THE GATE was garden. Corbinye caught a blurring glance of bright blooms against lavish green before her sleeve was caught in a wire-thin hand and she was bustled through another archway and into dimness.

"Close the door," directed the stranger and Corbinye heard the catch work, saw Witness standing just within the tiny foyer, Anjemalti dangling from his shoulder like a dead man.

"Ship's mercy!" Corbinye spun toward their host. "Grace…" she hesitated; deciphered the nuance half-shielded by dark hair, thinness and a certain fevered, burning energy— "madam. My cousin is wounded and requires aid…."

The dark eyes widened, shifted to take in the hale man and the wounded. "This way." The tug on Corbinye's sleeve was renewed and she followed its command, waving her hand at Witness to come.

The tunnel-like entranceway gave to spacious brightness. Corbinye glanced up to the skylights, looked at the wall which had been replaced entirely with glass, saw the easel set to catch the light—*so*—and here and there a screen, cutting what might be an alcove or another room off from the main studio.

"Behind the red screen is a couch, antiseptic and gauze in the chest beside it," said the stranger. "I'll opaque the windows, disconnect the bell…" She hurried away and Corbinye turned with Witness toward the red screen.

Anjemalti groaned when they laid him down, but made no sound when Corbinye cut the sleeve and bared the wound.

Witness brought medicines and lint from the chest and the stranger came bustling back, bearing a pan of water. She set it next to where Corbinye knelt beside the couch and stepped back.

"The cops are going down the alley, ringing bells," she said in her harsh, high-tension way. "I pulled the plug on mine and shut down the windows. They know the signs of vacancy."

Corbinye spared one glance at the flushed face. "Will they enter regardless, knowing you are not home?"

Teeth flashed briefly. "One of the few advantages of being related to the Board of Directors. The cops will leave me strictly alone, never fear."

The wound daubed clean, Corbinye spread antiseptic lavishly, then wrapped the whole tightly with gauze. It would do, she reckoned, and knew a sudden, aching desire for *Hyacinth* and the medical unit there.

Carefully, she got to her feet and made shift to settle Anjemalti more comfortably against the cushions. Witness reached to help and she let him take over that task while she pulled the coverlet from the couch-back and shook it wide.

She had bent to cover him when a certain gleam caught her eye, nestled between his hip and the worn upholstery.

"Here, what's this?" She reached, found her wrist captured by Witness' big hand.

"It is the gem that drove the Harcourt mad," he said. "The gem Anjemalti had intended for the bandit chief." He loosed her hand and leaned over, patting the unconscious man's pockets. "The totem box is gone." He straightened.

"Anjemalti had taken care to enclose this stone with all proper respect, which is the wisest course with magical things. It might perhaps be given a place to live, but I do not believe it should be left out in the air where it might freely partake of events."

"Enclose?" Corbinye frowned, recalling all too clearly Harcourt's scream and sudden madness. She tucked her fingers into her belt, having no wish to touch such a thing.

Unexpectedly, their host came forward, leaned close to study the stone before shrugging bony shoulders. "Just a moment," she said brusquely and bustled away.

She returned in something less than a moment by Corbinye's reckoning, holding a small metal urn with a stopper attached to it by a copper cord and a pair of wooden tongs. Briskly, she bent, captured the stone with the tongs and deposited it in the urn. She pushed the stopper firmly into place with the heel of her hand and handed the sealed bottle to Corbinye.

"There. That'll keep it out of mischief." Another show of teeth, in what was possibly the best of her smiles. "A genuine djinn's bottle, the merchant who sold it to me swore. If it was powerful enough to hold a djinn, it'll certainly do for an ugly rock."

Corbinye blinked. "My thanks to you. For all your kindness."

The face shadowed, as if the words blighted, rather than eased, and the too-bright eyes sought the floor. "You know I'd do anything for you, Morela." The eyes flashed back, searing Corbinye with their passion. "Anything."

Corbinye hesitated, drew breath and looked directly into that gaze.

"You believe you know me."

"Believe!" The voice conveyed astonishment. "As if you could ever be mistaken!"

"And yet," Corbinye persisted, with unCrewlike gentleness, *"you* have mistaken, if not the body, then the person who now resides within it." The other woman's eyes took on a tinge of distress; the face betrayed confusion.

"You have heard, perhaps," Corbinye said softly, "of a place called The Blue House?"

Distress conquered confusion; and half a moment later had erupted into fury. "He *dared!* To punish her for one of his made-up slights, I'll swear! To make her heel, as if she ever would. To make her—it's insupportable, horrible! He won't win this one…" The eyes had turned calculating, hard. She looked back at Corbinye. "What is your deadline?"

"I beg your pardon?"

"Your deadline! How long a time did you buy in her body? A month? Two?...*Six*?"

Corbinye's head reeled. Had the Grounder gone mad in her grief, or—?

"You mistake the case yet again," she said, and this time the coolness the Crew reserved for Grounders was evident in the rich, stranger's voice. "I am Corbinye Faztherot, who should be dead, except that—someone—bought a newly-dead body and had me placed within it, to become, as you see..."

"NO! I don't believe it! Morela—*dead*? Even he wouldn't dare—" She jammed her fist into her mouth, stared wildly from Corbinye to Witness to Anjemalti, unconscious upon the couch, turned and quit the alcove at something very near a run.

Corbinye felt herself flick forward, controlled the hasty reaction and deliberately closed her eyes, taking breath after deep breath: The Eelvinc Maneuver, designed to impose calmness, reestablish tempo and inner balance.

"Died and reborn," the chant came softly from behind. "She who was not is become She Who Is. Death's Warrior steps into event, and takes oath to serve the Smiter's Chosen."

She spun, staring for one long minute at Witness, standing there with his arms outstretched, beatitude in his eyes.

"Blessed be," he sang. "Shlorba's Smiter stirs and the stars and the plants and the mountainsides are full with expectation."

"Oh, Ship's grace, man, have sense!" She flashed a glance at Anjemalti, still caught in the depths of his swoon. "The only expectation we can have is that girl will immediately have the police or the Vornet upon us—or both! Much good to your Smiter then!"

"The Smiter shakes event, and event of necessity responds," Witness stated, eyes half-glazed, as if he had drunk overdeeply of one of the Head Engineer's more potent distillations. "What shall gainsay the Smiter, the Chosen and the Champion of Death?"

"What, indeed?" Corbinye returned, with calculated insouciance. "Saving only the Vornet, the cops or Anjemalti dying of his wound."

The Witness smiled at whatever glassy vision he gazed at, and slowly lowered his arms. "Anjemalti shall not die," he announced.

"You set my mind at rest," Corbinye told him, but apparently his was not a nature receptive of sarcasm. He chose a corner of the alcove for himself and settled cross-legged to the carpet, eyes dreaming upon the Trident, lying where she had left it before the medicine trunk.

"I go to find our host and beg her not to be precipitate," Corbinye said, without much hope that he was attending her. "Do me the favor of minding my cousin, and of calling me if he wakes."

A long moment passed before he raised his eyes, clear and sane-seeming, to her face. "Warrior," he said calmly, "I shall."

"See that you do," she snapped, all out of patience with his ways, and stomped off to find the owner of the house.

CHAPTER THIRTY-SIX

BUT THEIR HOST was not so easy to find as that.

Corbinye warily checked behind the three remaining screens and found no more sign of the woman than was evident in the open studio-room. Baffled, she took up a stance in the middle of the room and began to slowly revolve on the balls of her feet.

The door was set flush to the westermost wall, painted an identical off-white. Only the shine of the palm-plate betrayed it.

"So." She walked silently across the smooth stone floor. Standing slightly askance, so that any mischance waiting behind the door might miss her with its first shot, she laid her palm against the plate.

The door swung open, silent on grav-pins. If mischance waited beyond, it was wily and well-used to the game.

Hating to trust so important a move to the ill-trained and ungainly Grounder body, Corbinye swung into the room, poised to leap, should mischance at last show itself.

The room was very small. Spotlights illuminated each of the paintings hanging on the four white walls. A carpet of silvered blue covered the floorstones.

In the center of the carpet sat the owner of the house, salt tracks glistening on her cheeks, eyes hot with something beyond even madness.

Corbinye shifted weight with utmost care, sinking flat-footed into the soft pile, hands deliberately limp, dangling from strengthless wrists.

The woman on the carpet laughed. "No," she said, "you're nothing like her at all, are you? She moved—she moved as if every step were an—*experience*: a poem. You move as if every step has a *purpose*..." She shuddered and hid her face.

Corbinye considered her. "And how else should it be, when one is Worldwalker and an unwary step might bring the Ship to grief?"

The other woman only shuddered again, and waved an agitated hand about her, indicating, perhaps, the paintings. Her face she still held hidden.

Corbinye glanced at the painting directly across; arrested, she stared, and took three unnoticed steps along the rug.

The woman in the portrait gazed back serenely, her great black eyes soft and distant as she executed some weirdly sensual dance step, breasts thrust against the filmy stuff barely covering them, long yellow hair hanging unbound and shining down her back.

The painting to the right showed her seated, clad in costly brocades, bent forward with outstretched hand and beatific face to the children clustered at her feet. The next painting showed her nude, yet some way inviolate, as if her skin were all the garment she ever needed. The next had her dancing again, fully clad and as wanton as any spacebar hussy.

"She was a dancer at Jiatlin's Playhouse—a storyteller. A singer," the voice of the other woman wavered, cracked. "Everyone loved her. She could have had the protection of any of a dozen of the most influential…She could have—but there was Qaffir and what claim he held over her she would never tell me! He abused her, made her crawl, stole from her—and she never…"

All at once she moved, springing awkwardly to her feet, and threw her arms wide, as if to embrace all the painted women at once. "You see why I cannot believe she is dead!" she cried, and without awaiting an answer, spun to face Corbinye fully.

"Tell me!" she demanded. "Did he kill her? I'll hurt him, if he dared it—hurt him like he hurt her…"

"Forgive me if I say that seems unlikely," Corbinye said, meaning no cruelty, but with her eye full of the other's awkward, passion-driven movements. The woman recoiled.

"You doubt my love," she said bitterly.

"Indeed I do not," returned Corbinye. "But love has very little to do with the matter, the beloved now being dead. And while revenge is certainly yours to claim, if you find the one who deprived you of your friend, revenge is most efficiently carried out in a cooler state of mind, without temper, or hatred—or fear."

The glance that went across her face very nearly scathed. "You sound very sure of yourself!"

"I have had some experience of revenge—and related matters. A Worldwalker must know defense, offense—must judge the utility of either—to deal successfully for the Ship among Grounders." She tipped her head, making no effort to trick the other's eye. "What is your name?"

Consternation showed, followed by an ironic bow. "Theo." It seemed she was on the verge of saying more—and was cut off untimely by the pounding.

Corbinye spun, willing the body into a crouch. She was two steps nearer the door when Theo cried "Wait!" and lunged forward to grab her sleeve.

It was well that the body she wore was not her own. As it was the slap the Grounder woman received sent her crashing to one knee, hand covering her cheek—but the other hand yet amazingly gripping Corbinye's sleeve, while the undamaged eye glared, undaunted.

"Wait!" she repeated, with less volume, but more urgency because of it.

The pounding ceased abruptly, and voices could be heard, indistinct as to words, but clearly arguing. They rose and fell for very nearly a minute, then a third voice joined in, and shortly thereafter came the sound of footsteps, marching away.

"There must be a new cop on the beat—one who doesn't know the signs," said Theo. "That happens sometimes, but the older ones always put them straight." She fingered her cheek, wincing. "You didn't have to hit me so hard!"

"But I hardly hit you at all," said Corbinye, with a mildness she was far from feeling. "You would do well to learn not to snatch at me, mistress!"

The clear eye widened, the lips parting while some sort of notion altered the grief riding in her face. She might indeed have said something, but a shadow came then across the open door and Witness put his head carefully within.

"I find you, O Warrior," he said in his flat, colorless way. "Anjemalti the Seeker awakes." He closed his eyes, opened them, and went away.

"Praise the Ship!" breathed Corbinye. Abruptly, she remembered the woman beside her, and turned to offer aid in standing.

This Theo disdained, snapping to her feet in all her fevered clumsiness. "Go see your cousin," she said, without much grace. "I've got work to do."

Something even there gave Corbinye pause, but the searching glance she sent at the other's face uncovered nothing more than unease, and that same bare-controlled passion.

"I thank you," she said softly and made the bow, graceful, as a guest should, and went out of the room and across the studio, to the place where Anjemalti lay.

CHAPTER THIRTY-SEVEN

THERE WAS A scent of apricots; and there was pain, burning the length of the right arm, down to the fingers' tips.

Otherwise, there was sound—the pounding that had wakened him; various small creaks and nearby rustlings that doubtless came from the nurse employed to watch over him. In a moment—or two—he would open his eyes and show himself cogent.

Damn' fool thing to do, he told himself, muzzily. Edreth will likely break the other arm for you—and none ever more deserving.

The rustling became proximate, jarring him loose of memory. The sweet scent intensified just as he recalled that Edreth had never scolded him for that particular piece of mischief at all.

Gem opened his eyes and stared in new befuddlement at the lovely face so near his own.

Brilliant ebon eyes clouded and the face removed somewhat, as if she sat back upon her heels.

"Anjemalti?" The voice thrilled, igniting fires Edreth had been very careful to bank. "It is Corbinye, cousin. The Witness had said that you were awake."

"Corbinye…" His voice cracked and he passed a dry tongue painfully over fevered lips.

"There, you do wake! A moment…" She stretched a long scarlet-clad arm and brought back to him a sweetly steaming tea bowl. "Drink…there. Your wits are with you, are they? For I don't scruple to tell you, cousin, we are in the damnedest coil!"

"Are we?" He struggled and she put the bowl aside, reaching to help him sit. Between them, they got his feet on the floor, and he took a moment to close his eyes and review several potent curses while the fire flared in his arm and his senses spun.

Opening his eyes, he discovered Witness cross-legged in a corner and bent his head in respectful greeting. "How fares the Trident?"

"Very well, Anjemalti. Events shake and the Witnessing hovers on the edge of astonishment."

Corbinye laughed. "His notion of a revel," she said, and Witness turned his eyes to her.

"That which is, is all there may be, O Warrior. To alter event is holy work."

She moved her shoulders and glanced back at her cousin. "It's madder even than most Grounders, cousin, but it appears to be disposed toward us kindly."

"So I should hope." Near memory had returned and he stared about him, taking in the couch, the chest, the red screen and stone floor. "What place is this? I had thought the spaceport, *Dart...*"

"We were making for the spaceport when the lawgivers overrode the taxicab's imperative. Nothing to do but leave the curst thing and run, with you bleeding and limp as a corpse! Witness carried you and I bore the Trident—but we should have still fallen, cousin, except that we were rescued by one who is—was— a...friend of the person—she who had first worn this body."

Gem frowned and looked at her sharply. "Who?"

"Who?" Corbinye blinked. "Why, she calls herself Theo, cousin. And there is a room in this house hung with nothing but paintings of—of Morela, her name had been, who was dancer and storyteller at Jiatlin's theater and possessed of a lover named Qaffir, whom the Theo suspects of murdering her."

He shook his head. "The Blue House had her a suicide."

"That will doubtless ease the Theo's heart," Corbinye returned tartly and saw his brows quirk together before he lifted a shoulder in dismissal.

"Whether it does or not is no concern of ours. Our tasks are to gain, first, the spaceport, and then *Dart*. After Linzer has us out of here—"

"Why depend upon a trading ship and an alien pilot when there is *Hyacinth* set to welcome you—aye, and a pilot of the Crew to lift her!" She hesitated as a near-blasphemous thought struck, and looked at him cautiously. "Do you pilot, cousin?"

Humor glinted far back in the blue eyes. "I thought you supposed me the Captain?" He shifted, perhaps to ease the arm, and the humor faded away. "I can pilot, don't fear it. And as for why I at least intend to make for *Dart*—I hold half-share in the ship and Linzer Skot is my partner, my—co-captain...My friend."

He stirred again and sighed. "You might do as you choose, of course. We are quit of any debts between us. Take *Hyacinth* and return to your Ship. Tell them that the Tomorrow Log lied and that the hero-Captain does not exist."

"Yes, certainly," she said, feeling the bite of sarcasm on her tongue. "I shall misinform my elders, give the lie to the First Captain, and also doom the Ship." She sighed, abruptly very tired, and glanced down at the slender hands folded upon her knee. Dread struck her all at once and she looked back up at him.

"Truth told, cousin, I am in need of you." She held up the elegant stranger's hand, noting that it quivered, just a little. "*Hyacinth* is palm-sealed, but this is not the palm that sealed her."

He stared at the hand, flicked his gaze to her face.

"So, there remains debt," he said, flatly. "Very well. I require a description of the locking mechanism, as well as the ship-interface program. I will unseal your ship for you, but then, by all the gods alive and dead, Corbinye, we are quit!"

The words surprised, cut deep, so that the tears welled and spilled over—she, who was Worldwalker! She raised a hand, spread-fingered before her face, and any of the Crew would have read in that a request to avert their eyes.

Anjemalti instead moved forward, as if to touch her, and froze of a sudden, breath hissing between his teeth. "Corbinye…"

"It is nothing," she said rapidly, struggling to impose her will over the foolish, shameful tears. "The body is yet weak, Anjemalti—pay no heed." She gulped and lowered her head, since still he did not look away. "As for this other—we are kin. There is no debt-counting between us. If you choose to aid me, I welcome it, for it is true that I see no way to enter my ship save by such aid. If you…If you do not care to do so…"

A hand had closed most gently around her wrist, and she glanced up in startlement, to meet his serious eyes.

"Forgive me, Corbinye," he said, softly. "I spoke with neither grace nor understanding. Honor me and say you will forget it."

Gladness flooded, as shockingly sudden as the tears, and she smiled at him. "It is already forgot! It was ill of me not to have considered your wound…"

"Or my long sojourn among rag-mannered Grounders," he said, with a twist of bitterness in his voice as he sat carefully back. "Let us have done making excuses for me and consider—" A shadow passed over his face. "Where is the Fearstone?"

She frowned. "The—?"

"Fearstone." He held out his hand, first finger and thumb marking size. "About thus, brown, with green crystals."

"Oh." She reached again, rummaging among the objects littering the chest-top, and eventually put a small metal urn in his hands. "Theo said the pot had once held a djinn and so was up to the mischief of a mere rock." She sighed. "What is a djinn, cousin?"

"A spirit composed of equal parts malice and magic," he said, though absently. "As a race, they seem to spend a fair time locked away in bottles." One-handed, he fretted at the stopper and Corbinye bit her lip on protest.

"Let be, Anjemalti," Witness said surprisingly, causing them both to start. "The stone is within the jar. Both the Warrior and I saw it placed there." He glanced up, eyes gleaming. "Unless you sense cusp, and we are called to work once more?"

Almost, it seemed Anjemalti smiled. Certainly, he had done with worrying the stopper and inclined his head with utmost gravity.

"Not just yet, I think," he said, as calmly as if the mad alien made perfect sense; "though perhaps soon."

"Soon?" Corbinye stared at him. "How is the arm, Anjemalti? For if it is well enough and you feel your senses rooted, we should make all haste to *Hyacinth* and a proper medical unit. The lawgivers are doubtless gone by now..."

"The cops left some time ago," Theo announced from the entrance, her eyes hot and the energy shimmering around her. "But you can't leave yet." She smiled and Gem felt his blood chill, for she was certainly far from sane.

"I'm afraid you may mistake matters," he told her gently. "My friends and I have urgent business. I understand that you have aided us remarkably, and I am prepared to compensate you for your trouble..."

"My trouble," she repeated and smiled again, shaking her head. "There's no trouble," she said. "Or there won't be, soon. Qaffir is coming to see me. And when he does, Morela will kill him."

CHAPTER THIRTY-EIGHT

"No, THAT I will not!" Corbinye cried, and came all at once to her feet. "Do your own murders, mistress—you have no hold on me!"

Theo looked at her quite calmly. "You were running from the cops," she said. "I can call them, if you'd rather."

The slim shoulders seemed to lose some of their starch under the brave crimson shirt, and Gem cleared his throat, drawing the mad woman's attention.

"You perhaps are not aware that the Blue House records show your friend took her own life."

Theo shrugged with magnificent unconcern. "Qaffir drove her to it, then. She would never have done such a thing if he hadn't been brutal to her."

"Possibly true," Gem acknowledged, just as Edreth might have done, playing his words like chessmen. "However, we have no knowledge of either your friend or her lover. To demand that one of us kill a person of whom we were until just a moment ago unaware…"

"She wears Morela's body!" Theo cried, pointing at Corbinye. "She has a—a moral obligation!"

"Nonsense," said Gem crisply. "You know as well as I that obligation follows the living person—the one who has undergone translation. The body's debts are written off." He looked at her sternly. "You *know* this, mistress, if you've lived only six months on Henron."

"I've lived here my whole life," she said flatly. "My uncle sits on the Board of Directors. Morela gave that woman life. There is debt." She looked straight into Gem's eyes, the fire somewhat abated, but sanity nowhere evident. "Do I call the cops, master? Or do I call my uncle? *You* might bring a profit to the House, and the other man's not so ill."

Gem swallowed. "Call either and you forfeit your friend twice."

Theo shook her head. "No, I'd protect Morela. Of course I would. I love her."

"Then there's no more to be said," Corbinye announced suddenly. "Certainly I shall dispense with this difficulty, Mistress Theo. What is the life of a Grounder to me?"

The thin face lit. "Ah, you do understand! He must be punished, you see it now, don't you?"

"Completely," said Corbinye, and Gem looked at her in foreboding. "He must be made to pay for his iniquities, and you must find your peace."

"Yes," said Theo, and Witness shifted in his corner, taking both eyes and heart from the presence of the Smiter, to stare long and hard at Death's Own Warrior.

Qaffir was to come at Second Dusk.

By First, Anjemalti had rested and then awoken to a fresh shirt and a sup of watered wine, at which he chafed, saying he was no invalid. Corbinye had not argued the point, merely placing the cup firmly in his strong hand and asking, "Are you able to use the sorl-knife, cousin?"

He glared at her. "I thought it was you who specialized in murder."

"Anjemalti, do not bait me!" she snapped and opened her mouth to go on before apparently heeding some wiser instinct. "I require information," she said mildly. "Of your kindness. Are you able to use the sorl-knife in protection of yourself?"

He eyed her warily and had somewhat of the wine. "Yes."

"Good." She turned to Witness. "You are able to fight, should it come to such?"

"Warrior, I am. And how shall the Smiter go?"

She frowned. "Demons take the thing! I—"

"Strong evidence exists," Gem interrupted, "that this is in fact the case. I can carry the Smiter, if Witness can guard my back."

"Done!" cried Witness and sat back in consternation, appalled by the boldness of his secret heart.

The Seeker pretended to see nothing amiss, so chiefly was his grace. "Well enough," he allowed and turned to Death's Warrior. "For what battle do we gird ourselves, cousin? Is Qaffir expected with an army?"

"As you said," she answered coldly, "murder is my enterprise. I have no wish to smirch your honor. However, if it should come about that you are threatened, then it comforts me to know you well-guarded." She turned her face away. "The Captain's safety is paramount, Anjemalti. You are aware of this."

There was silence, stretching. Witness settled back to taste in full the nuance, for a Chief may be best known by the manner in which he treats his warriors.

"I bring you trouble in double-measure, cousin." Face and voice were of the mildest, though the eyes showed fire. "I remind you again that I am no captain, but a thief—sold off and despised for the fault of carrying Grounder genes. It astonishes me that my uncle did not strike my name from the Roll."

"Indemion Kristefyon is dead," she said, as though to a child. "He died by his own hand, redeeming honor after confessing treachery. He was gracious, Anjemalti: a great-hearted Captain who served the ship well. Wrongful action has been nullified by righteous. Surely, alive and strong, you can match his greatness."

Gem sighed. "Corbinye, were you born knowing the duties of Worldwalker? Did you come all at once into your skill, with neither teacher nor sparring partner?"

She blinked. "Of course not. One was chosen as most likely among the agemates. One was schooled and drilled and shaped for duty, according to The Protocols."

"Ah. While I lost my mentor at age eight, was sold off and Shipless at age nine, and apprentice to a master thief by age ten." He leaned close, holding her eyes with his. "Tell me what my training fits me for—cousin."

She drew a deep breath, crimson shirt stretching over rising breasts. "Your name is written in the Tomorrow Log, Anjemalti. I have seen it with my own eyes."

"What if the Tomorrow Log is mistaken?"

She stared, astonishment writ plain across the lovely face. "How could the Tomorrow Log lie?"

The Crew, thought Gem, suddenly, almost despairingly: so deadly—and so childlike. "Corbinye," he said softly, "I don't even know how the Tomorrow Log can *be*. How could the First Captain have known the name of a halfling born three hundred years after the time of her death?"

"Ah." She looked comforted at that and reached to take his hand, which tingled at her touch. "These are great Mysteries, cousin. We are taught to merely believe, but it goes hard against the grain, I know, when in all other things we are taught to question and reason and deal only in fact. We—all of your agemates—have raised these questions. All, except you, cousin, have had their questions put to rest, after they have seen the Tomorrow Log, touched it, and read a page with their own eyes."

"So you counsel me to have faith in my—fate."

His bitterness was lost on her. She squeezed his hand and dropped it. "Exactly so, Anjemalti. When we are back with the Ship, then your doubts may be satisfied, and you will be easy."

Gem sighed, closed his eyes—and gave it up for the moment. There were, after all, matters pressing them more closely.

"How will you deal with Qaffir, Corbinye? You should not endanger yourself in—"

She stood, cutting him off. "As we have already decided," she said coolly; "that matter belongs to me. I go now to prepare myself." She glided past him, slipped through the curtain and was gone.

CHAPTER THIRTY-NINE

"WELL, THEO? WHAT is this urgent matter?"

The man's voice was insolent; the man himself a beauty. Corbinye stared at the marvel of him, felt her face heat and was glad of the sheltering curtain through which she peered.

Grounders, in Corbinye's training—and, truth, within her experience—were slow, graceless and despicable. This Qaffir was none of that. He moved with the fluidity of one bred to low-grav. His skin was dark, as if tanned after the manner of those who kept the engine-rooms or worked within the Garden. His eyes were not large, but they were black, flashing with intelligence, darting quick glances here and there about the room, making inventory of all.

"Well, Theo?" he said again, and this time the arrogance carried an edge of dismissing amusement. He shook his long, unbound hair back and folded his arms across his chest, eyebrow cocked in disdain. "Well?"

Theo glared into his beauty, face rigid with loathing.

"I can't find Morela," she said sullenly. "I thought you might know where she is—take a message to her."

"I take a message to Morela?" The second brow rose as well and the dark face took on a cast of malignant surprise. "Really, what a diverting notion! But, do you know—I'm unable to oblige you."

Theo made no reply, saving that her glare may have become more loathful. Qaffir appeared to notice nothing out of the way, however. Behind the curtain, Corbinye began to tremble.

Qaffir leaned a little forward, his voice almost caressing, "Don't you want to know why I can't oblige you, little freak?"

"One of your distempers, I expect," Theo returned with surprising aplomb. "You never could bear it that I loved her— or that she loved me in return."

He laughed at that, flinging his head back, so that the cloud of his hair swirled about his shoulders. Corbinye wiped damp palms down the side of her trousers and began a simple breathing exercise. In the room beyond, Qaffir laughed once more and Corbinye gasped, concentration shattered.

"Even Morela," the man was telling Theo, "wasn't foolish enough to love *you*. But we digress! The riddle was this: 'Why will noble Qaffir not take Theo's message to the lovely and delectable Morela, queen of a thousand hearts, stupid sow and slut?'" He tipped his head, cruelty glinting from those dark, intelligent eyes.

"I have the answer," he said softly and leaned down, putting his lips, loverlike, next to Theo's ear. "Because," he murmured, though still clearly enough for Corbinye to hear; "the bitch is dead."

"No!" shouted Theo and leapt back, which moved Qaffir to more laughter.

"Oh, but yes!" He assured her with utmost glee. "Dead and no doubt rotted by this time—think of that, little freak! Her face fallen in, her hair out in clumps…" He paused, as if struck by a thought. "But I forget that you are a painter! Morela has been your subject in all of her estates. Of course you would wish to paint her in this, as well. How selfish I have been! I will send straightaway and have the cadaver brought to you! You must forgive my shortsightedness—"

"Morela!" Theo cried out, meaning herself, but Corbinye was frozen where she stood, stomach churning, hands sweating, knife thrust, useless, through her belt.

"Morela!" mimicked Qaffir, shrilly, and Corbinye felt herself jerked forward one step, as if he held the reel-end of a harpoon buried into her soul.

"Morela," he screamed again, taunting Theo, and Corbinye's body jerked forward one more step, through the curtain and into the room.

Qaffir's eyes widened as his laughter abruptly cut off. Theo dodged sideways, face aglow with blood lust, lips half-parted, showing teeth.

Corbinye stood entirely still, except for the shivering she felt in her limbs and prayed that neither could see.

"Well," said Qaffir. "It appears I am—misinformed." He smiled in full malice. Quailing, Corbinye made a concerted effort and willed her hand toward her knife, though she doubted she could follow through with the throw.

"Morela!" Theo cried. "Kill him!"

"*Kill* me?" demanded the man, in apparent delight. "Oh, but Morela would never kill *me*, little freak. Far more likely that she would kill herself. Which is what she did, you know—and very artfully."

He moved forward a step and the craven body had not even the strength to step backward in balance. Laughing low in his throat, he extended a smooth, scented hand and stroked the backs of his fingers down the side of her face. Desire heated Corbinye's belly, salted with terror.

"The Blue House had the keeping of her," Qaffir murmured, running his fingers across her lips. He pulled lightly on the lower and they parted, as if for a kiss. He smiled. "There's someone else living in Morela's body, but that someone else heeds me as she did, little freak. Is this not fascinating?" Still smiling, he cupped Corbinye's chin in steel fingers, tipped her face up and sidewise until her neck ached and then leisurely, tauntingly, bent and kissed her.

The desire flared, and Corbinye hung, near senseless with terror, barely heeding as he moved closer, crushing her body painfully to his, wrapping fingers in her braid and pulling her head even further back as he bit at her lips and moved his mouth down, nuzzling the arch of her throat, mouthing a breast—

A wordless shriek interrupted him—Corbinye staggered and fell to the floor as he abruptly let her go, though she retained enough sense to fall into a ball and roll. She fetched up near the curtain and there she lay, unable to rise to her feet, watching Qaffir try to pry Theo from his back.

"*I'll* kill you!" the little woman wailed, skinny, paint-spattered hands clawing at his throat. "Bastard! Murderer! Kill the only pure and beautiful thing either of us has ever known—"

Qaffir spun and shook. He roared, yanked fruitlessly at the choking hands and hurled himself backward against a wall.

Astonishingly, Theo hung on, though it seemed to Corbinye that her hold slid a little.

So it must have seemed to Qaffir, as well. He renewed his grip and stood utterly still in the center of the room, all his strength focused on wrenching those skinny, desperate hands apart.

From Theo, a cry, half-savage, half-despairing. Qaffir bared his teeth, mustered a last spurt of power and flung the little woman from his back.

She fell with a grunt, twisted and scrambled sideways, too slow to avoid the kick that smashed into her ribs, breaking bone with an audible crack.

"No!" The cry wrenched itself from Corbinye's throat, and she was somehow standing, hand snatching at her knife, while still the body shook and fought her and Theo's keening ran like acid along nerves already stretched beyond sense.

Qaffir spun. "No? I'll 'no' you, bitch. I'll—" He took a stride forward, another, pointing at the blade in her hand. "What's this? A weapon? Do you actually think you can kill me?"

Corbinye held onto the knife, held to the proper stance like her last hope of salvation, and knew the body would not—would never—obey her in this. Then she looked into his eyes and knew that she was dead.

Qaffir laughed, stepped within striking distance, paused a moment, all exposed, then laughed again, reached forth and grabbed the blade.

She twisted, turning the knife with a will, slicing palm and finger-flesh and he screamed, the other fist swinging out of nowhere toward her head, her dodge limited by the desperate need to hold onto the knife—

"Gaah!"

The descending fist struck her temple a glancing blow as the fingers loosed the knife blade and Qaffir crashed to his knees, eyes glazed and blood running, thinly, from the corner of his mouth. A sorl-knife the very twin of her own protruded from the base of his throat.

A moment he knelt before her, as if in worship, or contrition, then all his muscles gave loose at once and he fell forward upon his face.

Anjemalti was past her in the next instant, kicking the body to its back, wrenching the blade free and cleaning it with two rapid passes over the fine shirt front. He thrust the knife away, spared a glance at Theo, curled around her hurt and moaning, then swept back the way he had come, grabbing Corbinye's arm and jerking her with him.

In the foyer he dropped her to take up the Trident, gathered the silent Witness with a nod and finally favored her with a word.

"Can you keep the pace?"

Corbinye drew breath, put her knife in its place and met his eyes, which were cold beyond ice.

"Anjemalti," she said, and so far had she sunk in her own esteem that she was amazed to hear her voice firm; "I can."

"Good," he returned, and, jerking open the door, walked out into the alleyway.

CHAPTER FORTY

THE CAB DROPPED them at the spaceport gate, speeding away with neither coin nor memory of the fare, by grace of Anjemalti's spiders. Corbinye stood poised on the balls of her feet, hair pricking along her nape, straining through senses still oddly fogged, trying to sort normal port bustle from possible threat.

"*Dart* will be on a hotpad," Anjemalti said, and was off, weaving through the various tractors and high-lows as if he had no enemies within system, much less on world, the Trident cradled against him and Witness at his back. Biting her lip, Corbinye followed.

Ostensibly, all was as it should be, and Anjemalti's head-long march no bravado. Yet the hackles would not settle along her neck and the soft, betraying fingers twitched, yearning for the knife she would not draw.

At the edge of the hotpads the traffic thinned and became sparse—except for the crowd of vehicles clustered tight around Pad Eleven.

Corbinye flung forward, meaning to snatch him back from danger, but he had already seen, already checked and side-stepped and disappeared into the shadow of a cargoslide. Corbinye sought the shadow a heartbeat later and found both Witness and Anjemalti craning there, studying the vehicles and their meaning, in a silence more dreadful than any cursing.

"Grav beams," Anjemalti said flatly; "screen grips and catapults."

"Cousin?" She slipped to his side. In the darkness, she sensed his head move; saw the shine of his eyes, looking down at her.

"*Dart* is pinned. Linzer..."

"*Dart* is pinned," she agreed with rapid patience, as if he were one of the nursery. "But *Hyacinth* is not."

Large eyes widened further and she felt him pull away from her in the dark. "You council me to abandon my friend to his troubles—*cousin*? And if I had followed such advice an hour ago?"

"Am I honorless *and* stupid?" she cried, sliced to the quick and caring less that she might be heard by enemies than he despise her. "How will you free your friend in your present state, Anjemalti? Send spiders, one at a time, to disable the machinery? Brandish that thrice-damned piece of metal and demand to be let within? How will you let your friend know he is liberated, shout through the hull?" She heard the rising note in her voice and took an abrupt breath.

"*Hyacinth* has guns," she finished, flatly and in undertone. "Guns—and a comm."

Silence for a slow count to seven; then a long, soft exhale and a blink of the glowing eyes.

"Pad Sixteen, I think you said?" His voice was as flat as hers had been.

"Pad Sixteen," she agreed, and dared to lay a hand on his arm. "This way."

Luck had placed *Hyacinth's* hatch a half-turn away from *Dart*, and all the busyness surrounding her. Corbinye waved Witness to a post where he could observe that action and cry warning, should some part of it take interest in *Hyacinth*.

Anjemalti was already bent over the lock, frowning at the palm plate. Something moved beneath his collar and came into sight on his shoulder, heading purposefully down his arm, purple eyes glowing.

Corbinye held her breath as the spider marched across the back of Anjemalti's hand, over the single bridging finger and vanished behind the lockplate.

Straightening, Gem flashed her a look, noting the flush mantling her cheeks.

"Number Eleven," he said, with more gruffness than he intended. "Fifteen's elder brother." He pushed the sleeve back from the telltale. "We should have a configuration in few moments." He glanced over again, trying not to see how the red shirt molded to her breasts. "Where's the Witness?"

"Watching *Dart's* trouble, in case it has mind to become ours," she said, taking a breath that tightened the fabric alluringly. She looked up. "Your friend's difficulties are legion, Anjemalti. *Hyacinth* is yours, but she is not a battlewagon."

And for one of the Crew, Gem knew, a ship was life itself, whether it be shuttle or Greatship.

"Did you register your weapons with the Port Master?" he asked, knowing in his deepest heart what the answer to that was.

Corbinye blinked. "I?" She laid her hand briefly against the well-kept, ancient hull. "An M-class jumpshuttle, Anjemalti. Who mounts guns on such?"

Only the Crew, thought Gem, and his quick grin carried all a Crewman's feral humor.

The telltale on his wrist chimed.

"Ah."

The data was unexpectedly complex and he took several minutes to sort it through, aware of a vibration against his shoulder, where the Trident leaned, and a tightening of concentration to his left, where Corbinye was schooling herself sternly to patience.

He looked over at her.

"Number Eleven requires assistance. Number Fifteen is somewhat larger—a bit more intelligent. If I may have his service back from you?" He barely waited for her nod; had turned back to the telltale before desolation bloomed in her eyes.

Obedient to the telltale's summons, Number Fifteen climbed out of her pocket and into Anjemalti's palm. Corbinye swallowed against the hard lump in her throat, beseeching the gods not to let the body shame her again with its too-ready tears. Cry over the loss of a mechanical toy, no matter how clever? Why, she bid fair to become as unstable—

As Anjemalti, she thought suddenly, remembering his face as she laid the ruined spider before him on that day, the last she was to spend as herself…

Behind her, a noise, louder than the unending whine of the grav-beam generator.

The body spun; Corbinye controlled its forward dash, and crept toward the sound.

She arrived at the sentry's post in time to see Witness kill the first guard with a knife thrust through the throat. She was just a heartbeat too slow to catch the second, who was racing back toward *Dart*. Already one of the attackwagons was breaking formation, turning its ugly nose toward *Hyacinth*.

Cursing, she grabbed Witness and dragged him back with her.

"Anjemalti, we are discovered! The guard calls for aid and a tank moves to attend us!"

One glance he spared her, from ice-blue eyes, then bent again to the lock, fingers tapping at his wristlet.

Behind, the sound of treads across hardtop and the more distant sob of a siren.

"They came upon me without warning," Witness declared, gently disengaging his arm. "One drew his weapon—without even a hail! A man may protect himself against hunters of men."

"Indeed he may," Corbinye agreed with ready sarcasm. "And a quick man may slay two enemies in the time a sluggard kills one."

Witness turned his head, stolid face showing slight amaze. "The other did not draw, O Warrior. He ran when he understood he faced a man."

"Very proper in him, I'm sure," she snapped, as the treadwork drew closer and the siren was joined by another. "Anjemalti…"

The spiders clung to his collar, and he laid his palm against the lock with the assurance of a man expecting admittance.

Nothing happened.

The twin sirens had been joined by a third, this one much closer.

Anjemalti laid his hand against the plate again.

Again, nothing happened.

The closest siren wailed into the causeway. Corbinye heard tires squeal against blast paving as the driver forced the turn and then the scream was heading straight toward them.

Behind, the tread-sound had been overlain by the puff of the attackwagon's motor and the blather of radio static.

"Damn you!" Anjemalti's low-voiced curse was charged with fury. He gripped the Trident where it leaned against his shoulder and stared at the lockplate as if his glare alone would force it.

"Open, damn you!"

There was a flare, as of a energy bolt, a *whomp* of sound felt in the chest rather than heard, and a stink of ozone in the air.

Corbinye cried out, simultaneously slamming back against the hull and spinning toward the rear, thinking only that the attackwagon had fired the moment it was in range and that two knives and an antique Trident were worse than useless against—

"Glory and praise! The Smiter lives!" Witness grabbed her arm and turned her back, toward the lockplate and Anjemalti. "Look, thou, O Warrior, and rejoice!"

Snarling, she allowed herself to be turned—and blinked once at the gaping hatch before she looked to Anjemalti.

He met her eyes, his own seeming slightly dazed. "Edreth had—always said—that I must contrive to control—my temper."

"It would seem potent," she agreed unsteadily and became alive again to the other sounds, especially those of the closing police car, and leapt forward. "Inside!"

Anjemalti went first, pitching the Trident before him and rolling in clumsily, careful of the wounded arm.

Corbinye went next, and landed running. She pushed past Anjemalti, smacked the toggle to release the inner lock and pelted down the hall toward the command center.

She hit the chair and opened the board in one motion, barely aware that he had found the co-pilot's seat and was unsealing the ship's Eyes. She was herself busy with screen readings and a demand for damage report on the forced hatch. She touched the red toggle almost as a by-the-way and in a moment heard Anjemalti murmur, "Weapons armed."

"So," she acknowledged and let a little breath hiss between her teeth in relief as ship's stats reported the hatch sealed and spaceworthy. "That's a remarkable toy you possess, cousin."

"None of mine, and all of the Bindalche's," he said. "I'm sworn to return the thing to them at earliest—There's *Dart* on Three. I'm searching a clean comm line..."

"Go through Weapons for a scramble and transmit direct," she told him and he nodded, fingers flying over the keys.

"Anjemalti," Witness said suddenly over their heads, "the Smiter lies alone in the inner hatch."

"It needs remain there for the present, friend," Gem said, as the buzz of an open comm line filled the cabin. "It is my deepest hope that the Goddess is not angered."

There was a sound from where he stood behind them—almost it seemed to be a laugh. "No, Anjemalti," he said. "I think the Goddess is not angered at all."

"Good," he said absently, and then, more forcefully: "Linzer. It's Gem."

"About damn' time," Skot's voice was as laconic as ever. "This your idea of a party, ser Edreth?"

Gem grinned. "What do they want?"

"You, so the gentle who's been haranguing me for the past two hours says. I told her I didn't have you, but she seemed inclined to doubt it. Wanted me to open the door and let a search party in." He snorted. "Mama Skot's youngest ain't that big a fool."

"I thought you were the eldest," Gem said, fingers playing over the keys. He sent an image to Corbinye's main screen, saw her read it and begin to ply the weapons keys.

"This ain't the time to argue lineage. You fixing this mess or am I?"

Gem tipped his head, reading over the rather distressful situation surrounding *Dart*. By comparison, their own ring of one attackwagon and three armored cop cars were mere decoration.

"Can you fix it?" he asked Skot.

"I can broadbeam a piloting lesson about what happens to an energy field generated by, say, gravbeams, when the object enclosed by the field suddenly goes hyperspatial and kick in the engines for emphasis. Ought to give 'em something to scramble for." He clicked his tongue against the roof of his mouth, a characteristic sound that told Gem Linzer was more worried than he allowed. "These are cops, kiddo. They ain't gonna risk their lives over physics."

"Maybe…" Corbinye had done with the weapons keys and was gently easing the engine feed up. Gem nodded at the schematic she'd sent to his screen, heard her murmur, "We have attempted contact, Anjemalti—from the 'wagon. I feign deafness."

"Sounds too risky," he said to Skot. "What if we draw their attention away for a moment? Can you lift?"

There was a slight pause. "You done here? 'Cause if I lift straight, without a flight plan and with the local gendarmes peeved, there ain't a bribe big enough to clear *Dart's* name for landing here again. Ever."

"I'm done," Gem said quietly, tripping the appropriate toggles. "We're on Pad Sixteen, your starboard. We will provide a diversion. At the first opportunity, lift. We'll be right behind you."

Another pause, slightly longer than the first. "Got you sighted. Rendezvous?"

"Three months, on Cheyenne?"

"Gotcha. Let's get outta here."

"Diversion starting in sixty seconds. Luck to you, Linzer."

"Luck to you, son. Out."

Gem hit the first switch.

The volley went over the beamrigs. One flare hit the tip of a catapult tower; a second smacked into a cop car.

The broadcom roared confusion and the screens showed a very gratifying milling about, as the big engines tried to come around to face this new threat.

Gem hit the second switch.

The closest beamrig exploded, followed by the second and one of the smaller attackwagons. Radio noise was replaced for an instant by stunned silence as Corbinye threw the engine slide all the way to the top and smacked the lift-warning bell.

The cop cars and wagon hanging onto *Hyacinth's* skirts scrambled backward, ship's stats showed readiness to lift—and Gem threw the third switch.

"Eee-HAH!" yelled Linzer across the beam and in the screen *Dart* hurtled upward, adding a few shots of her own to the melee as Corbinye yelled at Witness to grab on and sent *Hyacinth* climbing after, through the puny lightnings that the groundwagons hurled.

"All RIGHT!" Linzer yelled. "Smooth as taffy candy! Best escape I've ever been—"

In the screen, *Dart* blew apart.

CHAPTER FORTY-ONE

HE CHOSE DARKNESS, did the young Chief, perhaps the better to meditate upon the faces of his dead. That there were several of these, Witness knew, for Anjemalti had sought out Shlorba's Smiter, as was proper and fitting, and laid his hand upon the leather-bound grip and whispered, "Linzer. Shilban. Edreth." And one more, so faintly said that Witness had to trust to the echo from the walls to aid his ears—"Mother."

He had borne the Smiter away then, out of the hallway where it had lain while he and Death's Warrior had been about the business of escape. But he did not carry it with him wholly into darkness. Rather, he leaned it athwart the door of the room in which he meditated, as a lesser man might lay his sword across his tent-flap, ensuring privacy.

Given such duty, the Smiter lay, seemingly quiescent, though Witness, from his watching-post in the dim passway, felt an emanation his secret heart named "amusement."

The chamber which held the Chief Anjemalti was quiet; the Smiter dozed. Almost, Witness dozed. He caught himself on the edge of sleeping and sternly disciplined his mind, setting about the task of ordering the events of the past day, shaping all into Memory.

Elsewhere within the star sailing ship were clangs and clatters: Death's Warrior about some task or another, he supposed, and wove her more firmly into the Memory.

It was surely a most puissant sign, the Witness thought as the Memory spun within him, that event should have cast up, at this time of the Bindalche's shame, such a Chief, assisted by so astonishing a champion. That the Smiter was pleased with these gifts was patent. That it quivered and responded to the young Chief's touch as a maiden to the hands of her lover, was a joy, vindicating the Memories of the oldest Witnesses. Memories that even some of the Telios had whispered were but legend.

More clankings came from the depths of the star-sailer. Witness smiled, in keeping with his secret heart's amusement. So busy, Death's Warrior. So busy—and a puzzle of herself.

For it was plain that this Warrior, who claimed in a voice translucent with truth to have died and been reborn, was most vibrantly alive. In the past, so said the old Memories, when a chief had desired service from a champion who had untimely died, the Smiter had partaken of event and reshaped a part of the fabric of time, so that the fallen rose and did the bidding of the chief, and lay down again when duty was done.

But those, Memory insisted, had been dead. Dead, they had risen, and, dead, had obeyed most dreadful need. The hearts of such did not beat, Memory taught; and the flesh had continued to rot as, blind and breathless, they waded into battle, swords held in nerveless fingers, dealing death, sowing madness.

In the dimness of the passway, Witness shivered with the old Memories. Shivered and pushed them away, though duty said he should rather hold them close and be instructed. Instead, he replaced the vision of the ancient risen with a picture of Anjemalti's warrior—young and comely, with voice and breath and heart all strong; quick as a flash-strike; silent as a hunter—

The lights came on in the passage.

Witness blinked in the sudden glare, and blinked again at Death's Warrior, standing over him, hands on hips and red shirt shining.

"Is the intensity uncomfortable?" she demanded in abrupt grace.

Witness glanced about, allowing his eyes time to adjust, then looked back up. "The light is welcome, O Warrior. I thank you for the gift."

She shrugged. "With three blind crew it's madness to miser power." She pinned him with her great black eyes. "Where is Anjemalti?"

The Witness used his chin to point, and she pivoted on a heel, frowning at the Smiter that blocked her way.

"Well…" She shrugged once more. "There's food, if you're wanting any, and cabins enough so you needn't sleep in the hall."

"My thanks for your care," Witness said, for so he perceived that it was. "I am Witness for the Telios."

"So you do keep reminding one, from time to random time," Corbinye returned, and sighed. "Where do you think it can go? Out the door for a stroll?"

He considered that carefully. "Within the nature of event," he achieved after a moment within Memory, "all things are possible."

She snorted and made a wry face. "So it seems, upon reflection. Don't let duty starve you."

"Warrior," he returned, "I will not."

He thought that she would go, but she tarried a moment longer, a frown marring the comely face.

"My name is Corbinye Faztherot," she said, flatly. "I am Worldwalker and Seeker for the Ship *Gardenspot*. It is my duty to go among Grounders and to deal with them when needful, for the good of the Ship. I speak the trade tongue and Universal, as well as several dialects. I am a pilot and a navigator. I have heard Grounders say that my duties among them earn me the title 'assassin.'" She glanced down; fingered the shining red sleeve.

"Red is the color of the weapons board," she said, and finally did turn and walk away, silent on the metal floor.

Witness let loose the breath he had been holding, settled himself straighter against the wall, fixed his eyes upon the Smiter and let the information she had given—and a gracious, godly gift it was!—let the information fill him and his secret heart and wash over into Memory entire, illuminating what it might.

After a while, Gem had slept, slipping from half-crazed mourning into fevered dreams where he saw *Dart* exploding again and again and somewhere in the midst of it Edreth scolding him for lack of forethought—"A thief must be one step ahead of his opponent. Plan! And then follow the plan! Improvisation is for amateurs."

"I didn't know," he said miserably. "How could I think they would have found *Dart*?"

"How could you have thought they would not?" Edreth's voice answered him. "How many times have I told you to court invisibility? How many times have I told you to remain aloof of everyone, to do no favors, to avoid power and the wielders of power! Alone, you are invincible!"

"But," Gem protested, around the anguish and the dream-sight of *Dart* exploding, "but *you* weren't alone, master. You had me. And Linzer…"

"My errors, child," Edreth's voice seemed abruptly weary. "Do yourself service, and don't repeat them."

"Master—"

"Anjemalti?" The woman's voice was sweet, low and tentative. A roomgirl? But he never gave such his name; and certainly not *that* name.

"Anjemalti," insistent now, and accompanied by a gentle touch to his shoulder. "Cousin, awaken. Your wound wants tending."

Cousin. He opened his eyes and snarled upright, taking savage satisfaction in the startlement on her face and the slight shrinking back.

She recovered herself instantly and glared down at him. "You require the attentions of the med unit, which awaits you. You require food, which is available and nutritious."

"It would seem," he commented nastily, "that I also required sleep."

"Two hours should be sufficient to the tasks of healing and eating, after which you may sleep until we raise Ship and damned to you!"

Her anger hurt. He cast about for something conciliatory to say, then tipped his head, the better to hear the echo of Edreth's voice: "Aloof…"

Gem stood, ignoring the protest of the arm, and glared, savoring his height. "Very well. A session with your medical unit would be welcome. Also some food. Of your kindness. But reconcile yourself, Corbinye. I do not go to your Ship."

She matched him glare for glare, lovely mouth set, eyes blackly cold. "You will go where the pilot takes you," she said flatly, and Gem laughed.

"I thought I was the Captain Who Must Be Obeyed?"

"I think you're an overgrown brat," she snapped, turning on her heel. "And an ill-mannered one, at that."

He grabbed her arm, more harshly than he had intended, and spun her toward him, ducking an instant before her fist would have struck his cheek.

"Quick," he commented, seeing her exercise control and resentfully bring herself to rest. "But you were not nearly so quick with Qaffir."

Her pale cheeks flamed. "Taunt me, Anjemalti, do. Childish pranks amuse me."

"So?" He made one step toward her, checked himself and drew a deep breath, mindful of the arm's throbbing. Reason told him that this was not the course to plot with her, however much Edreth might have counseled the wisdom of aloofness. Gem had turned his back on that advice too many days ago. The consequences proceeding from that choice were now what must be dealt with.

He bowed, very slightly, and tried to make his face less forbidding. He saw an echoing softness in Corbinye's face, though the eyes stayed wary.

"What happened of Qaffir, Corbinye?"

She moved her shoulders. "The one before me—Morela—had been slave to the Qaffir," she said slowly. "When he spoke, the body obeyed him, whether I wished or no." She shrugged again. "Are such things usual, Anjemalti, among those who return from the Blue House?"

He hesitated, hearing the note of half-sick yearning in her voice, the wish for something that would explain her failure, that would restore her assurance of herself.

Pity. Edreth would weep with despair, and he saw the hash his 'prentice had made of life, when he'd been left safe, with rules that worked to live by. Pity, and horror. For this he had wrought, to take one of the proudest of the Crew, imprison her in a hated Grounder body, and make her doubtful of her every instinct. Gem licked his lips.

"I had not heard of the effect," he said. "But the Blue House is not something I studied—in depth."

"Ah." Just perceptibly, her shoulders sagged, eyes showing infinite distress in the moment before she turned again toward the door. "Let us get you to the med unit, Anjemalti. The arm must pain you."

Filled with pity, and a revulsion of self, Gem followed.

CHAPTER FORTY-TWO

ANJEMALTI CAME SLOWLY from the med unit's maw, pale and gingerly of movement, as if the arm chafed him still. Corbinye felt a surge of pity and turned her face away, lest he see it in her eyes and scorn her.

He must not, she thought, pouring tea with studied, unshaking precision, he must not be brought to the point of an order. Ships and stars, what shall I do, if he orders me elsewhere, for some Grounder necessity? He is the Captain and I am sworn to his service; to die, if he speaks the word. And yet he must go to the Ship, whether he wills it or no...

"Cousin," she said, by way of greeting, and put the tea down by his hand. "Sit, do, and tell me what you will have to eat."

At least he sat, though he did not immediately speak, looking instead deep into the depths of his cup, as if he would read all of his future in the darkling depths. When he did glance up, long minutes later, it was to address Witness, who sat to one side, eyes dreaming on the ugly Trident where it leaned against the wall.

"Have you an interpretation of the Smiter's will, given the pattern of recent events?"

Witness blinked his slow, sleeper's blink and focused his red-brown eyes on Anjemalti.

"I am Witness for the Telios," he said in his eventual way. "Prediction is not mine."

"Assuredly it is not," said Gem briskly. "But I was under the impression that you were able to match current patterns to remembered patterns and make that information available to those whom the Goddess currently honors."

"Oh," said Witness and was quiet for a time, so that Corbinye finally despaired of them both, punched high-protein hot rations from the board and thumped a bowl of the resulting gruel in front of each.

"At least feed the body," she snapped at Anjemalti and thrust a spoon into his hand.

Witness opened his eyes when she smacked the spoon beside his bowl and locked his gaze with hers. "My thanks, Corbinye Faztherot," he said, and smiled.

She turned to the board, showing him her back, and took her time about her own selection. "Thank me by eating the damned stuff."

"Yes," said Witness, still soft-spoken and gracious; then, to Anjemalti: "It was said, even among the Telios, who should have known better, that the Smiter was deep into sleep. Some said that the Smiter would never awaken, that it was, as would be said of men, dead."

"But," said Gem, "that does not seem to be the case, given the scene in Saxony Belaconto's office and the burst of power that opened the ship's hatch."

"It is perhaps true that the Smiter *had* slept," said Witness, picking up his spoon and filling it carefully. "It is perhaps true that it perpetuated a hoax upon event, pretending to sleep while it spun its influence beyond the ken of the Bindalche and even of the Telios, so that the fat man finally came and took it away, to a place where a strong Seeker would come forth."

Gem spooned up a portion of gruel. "Are the Bindalche so weak?"

"The Bindalche are confined to the Spangiln, Anjemalti. We bide under the protection of The Combine, which insures our ships do not carry the stardrive. Nor are our people allowed to swear service to citizens of The Combine."

Corbinye turned from the foodboard, pivoting silently on one heel, eyes on Witness' face. "The Combine?" she said, very softly.

"Yes, Corbinye Faztherot. Have you knowledge of it?"

"Knowledge of it?" she repeated, and turned a stricken face to Gem. "Anjemalti, it's a child."

"More likely full adult." He put the spoonful of gruel in his mouth and wrinkled his nose. "This is not very good, you know, cousin."

"Compliment my cooking with troopers bearing down from all directions! Anjemalti, did you hear what he said? Interdicted by The Combine! And yet here he sits—do you think they will not have missed him?"

"An excellent point," Gem conceded and had a sip of tea. "How is it that you came away from Spangiln System, friend, when it is so closely guarded?"

"I am Witness for the Telios," he said, as, Corbinye thought crossly, they might have known he would; "I go where the Smiter goes, to observe and to remember."

"Assuredly. So the Smiter hid you from the watchers The Combine had put into place?"

Witness wrinkled his brow and took a moment or two to stare into the depths of his ration-bowl, perhaps communing with the nutrients there. When he finally did look up, Corbinye thought his face showed rather more animation than it was wont.

"I do not think that it was necessary for the Smiter to alter event in this instance, Anjemalti. Certainly the Memory reveals no such magic. I think it was rather that the fat man used his own devices to come as he had gone, invisible and silent to those who watch our borders."

"That's sensible," Anjemalti said, looking at her and nodding. "Jarge Menlin was a Vornet courier of high repute. He employed the best pilots and the best ships. Running a Combine blockade would have posed no major difficulties."

"Except if any go looking for him—or for that damned—*device*! How if—"

"Warrior, none shall. The Smiter makes its own way, as the officers of The Combine have found in the past, to their sorrow. As for myself, who counts the grains of sand, or the rocks within the riverbed? I am Witness for the Telios, and I follow the path the Smiter forges through event and space and time. None of The Combine knows my face—how could they? And if any seek me by name, why, my name is safely upon Bindal, and so the servants of the Telios will testify."

She stared at him, lips parted as if she would any instant speak, for several moments. Finally, she turned away and punched buttons on the foodboard, savage in her silence. "If it is not a child, Anjemalti," she said at last, back to them. "It is mad."

"Possible, but not proven," he returned and ate another spoonful of gruel before pushing the bowl away. He considered the Witness. "The Smiter did not—alter event—while it stayed within Jarge Menlin's keeping?"

There was another of his longish pauses. Corbinye sat and began to eat, wolfish in her sudden hunger, striving to ignore the terror in her gut. The Combine, by all the gods of space! And there it sat, blank-faced and calm as, as a *cow*. His name safe at home, forsooth! And Anjemalti no more sensible than—

"I believe not," Witness said. "There was no manifestation of power as had been Remembered from the past."

"And these present occurrences?" Anjemalti said. "The display in Belaconto's office; the power that forced the hatch?"

"These are consistent with memories of the Smiter's past actions in the realm of event," said Witness, and hesitated.

Anjemalti's eyes sharpened. "There is something else that you may tell us regarding the Smiter's glorious past?"

"An—oddity—Anjemalti. It—it seems that the Memories which match the Smiter's current mode of entry into event—they are very old. As if the Smiter *had* been resting, and has now awoken with renewed vigor, as in the times of the greatest Memories. They have almost the flavor of the Memories wherein the Smiter brought the ships of the Bindalche's enemy down from the skies, in the time of the Chief Ral Ean Te."

Hyacinth stuttered and things seemed to slide a little out of focus for a moment, then the gyros kicked in and reality steadied once more.

Corbinye held her breath, neither daring to look up or to a side. From the corner of her eye, she saw Anjemalti raise his cup, then put it down.

"Corbinye."

Still she dared not raise her eyes and kept her face bent toward her bowl, like a child discovered in wrongdoing. "Anjemalti."

"That was secondary transition, was it not?"

"Secondary transition, yes." Gods, gods, let him not...

"I wonder if you might share with me, cousin, an overview of our itinerary."

Mild as milk—and able to flash into fury in a heartbeat, if he in anywise resembled his uncle. Corbinye called on her courage and raised her face to look squarely into his eyes, as befitted a Worldwalker addressing her Captain.

"Anjemalti, since we had first met, it was my avowed purpose to return you to the Ship. I have made no secrets of this; I have asked you enough times to accompany me of your own heart. Had your—had your friend been in need of succor, then most assuredly I should have targeted Cheyenne." She drew a breath and kept her eyes steady on his, which were blue and unreadable. "Since that was not the case, and in the absence of orders from the Captain, I set course for *Gardenspot*."

"In the absence of orders from the Captain," Gem repeated softly, and sighed. He was tired, suddenly; bone weary and lethargic. Corbinye's duplicity—no, he reminded himself: her single-minded adherence to her duty—failed to raise even a spark of annoyance in him. He sipped lukewarm tea and pushed back from the table.

"So, then," he said, and noted how relief loosened the muscles around her eyes, around her mouth. "We to *Gardenspot,* as predicted by the First Captain." He stood. "Witness should find The Tomorrow Log fascinating."

He took up the Trident before he walked out, leaving half a cup of tea and nearly all his rations behind.

"Now where to?" Corbinye cried, loud enough for him to hear, except that he chose not to.

"Perhaps to meditate," said Witness, rising as well and heading for the door. "Anjemalti the Chief has plans to make, now that he is certain of the Smiter's favor."

"And you?" she snarled. "Where are you going that you can't even finish your rations?"

"I am Witness for the Telios," he said, and stepped into the hallway an instant before a bowl of cold gruel hit the wall where his head had been.

CHAPTER FORTY-THREE

THE CABIN HE had chosen for his own smelled faintly of flowers and the bed he had rumpled showed signs of having once been lovingly ordered. The locker, obedient to a tweak from Number Fifteen, opened to display a Spartan wardrobe of trousers and shirts, all meticulously clean, several carefully patched—all sized to fit a Corbinye who was no more. Gem stared at them, dry-mouthed and heart-stopped, for several frozen seconds, before shutting the door and turning away to sit on the bed.

He pulled the Trident across his lap and bent his head to study the whirls and whys of the old, alien circuitry. Absently, he patted his pocket and pulled out the little urn that held the Fearstone. He laid that aside and groped in the pocket again, barely looking up from the Trident long enough to screw the loupe into his eye.

It was there: Blasted bits of wiring; broken transistors; the remains of capacitors—Yet all was not destruction, he saw as he bent closer. Here and there whole systems remained coherent, connected. And who was to say whether the nuts, shells and gemstones were not also part of a system or systems, independent of or integrated with the bits of system he very nearly recognized?

He put his attention on one seemingly whole system of wires, tracing the route through the rubble, noting where it made connection with a capacitor, where it crossed another system of wires, where it wound tightly, over and under, a faceted gem, where—

Gem sat back and pulled the loupe from his eye.

"How long has it been since the Smiter was damaged?" he asked, not bothering to turn, knowing that the other would be standing near, attentive to all.

"There are several Memories which show that the Smiter did—overreach event, Anjemalti. One of those was during the time of Chief Ral Ean Te, who brought the ships of the Bindalche's enemy—"

"Down from the skies," Gem finished, and twisted 'round on the bed so that he could see Witness where he sat in the doorway. "Was that the most recent time?"

Witness blinked.

"The most recent Memory of the Smiter's overreaching dates from the War Against The Combine, where Seeker-to-be-Chosen Vin Ean Li called upon the powers residing within her secret heart to join with the powers of the Smiter to blast the minions of foulness and destroy their unholy dam, which was a blasphemy upon the world and a hardship to the Bindalche, who live in the world."

Gem waited, then, when it seemed no more information was forthcoming, asked, "And did she succeed, Seeker Vin Ean Li?"

"Alas," said Witness, "but she did not, which is the reason the Bindalche find themselves shackled and contained to the home worlds. But it was a glorious striving, Anjemalti, full of rage and righteousness and worthy of any of the great Chiefs of the past. Many of The Combine's men went mad and drowned themselves before event cast forth its net and the Smiter was caught."

"How?" Gem asked. And, when Witness only looked at him with those sleepy, unexpressive eyes: "How was the Smiter caught?"

"By treachery, so teach the Telios. Event is not to be trusted, Anjemalti; recall it."

"Be certain that I shall," Gem returned. "But what was the physical experience of the Smiter's capture like? Was there no Witness—"

"Assuredly there was," this Witness said, almost sharply. "A glow was Witnessed, about both Smiter and Seeker, as will happen when the greater magics are wrought." His voice had taken on a cadence of ritual, and his eyes were full closed. "But this intensified and moved through the spectrum to violet, where it hung, pulsing. On the field, there was felt a great dismay of the spirit, so that several of the younger warriors among the Bindalche dropped their weapons. Some wept openly, with neither shame nor thought of shame. Screams came from among those who served the evil Combine, and at least one there turned her weapon upon herself, while more cast their weapons away and flung themselves into the trapped waters, which already were choked with dead.

"The Seeker stood apart, limned in light, the Smiter raised in beautiful defiance above her head, tines pointed at the enemy of the Bindalche. She gave voice to the war cry and in that moment the light contracted and terror crushed the hearts of all upon the field. None could look upon the Seeker; many shielded their faces from the sudden blast of heat. There was a high, keening cry, followed by a small popping sound and the field was released from terror.

"Where the Seeker Vin Ean Li had been, there was glassed sand. The Smiter lay quiet beside the spot." Witness opened his eyes.

"What happened then?" Gem whispered.

Witness sighed and shook his head, wearily. "There was a rout, Anjemalti, though it shames me to say it. The Bindalche ran and The Combine pursued and eventually were victorious. One from the rank of warriors was bold enough to lift the Smiter and run with it to the Telios, who replaced it within its Center. That one was not a Seeker, you understand, but the Smiter relishes boldness. He carried the marks of the Goddess' favor, burned into palms of both hands, until his death." He sighed again.

"Vin Ean Li was the last of the great Seekers. Her death ended an epoch."

"How long ago?" demanded Gem.

Witness frowned. "Forty of your standardized years, Anjemalti, as closely as I am able to cipher."

"Forty years." Gem closed his eyes, rubbed them and blinked at the Smiter, quiescent across his lap. "And now it wakens. Why?"

Witness did not answer.

Gem sat looking at the Smiter, thinking that wiring could be replaced; thinking that electronics could be rebuilt, reorganized, empowered. Thinking that—

"A great dismay of the spirit..." he murmured, and reached for the Fearstone's urn.

He paused with his hand on the stopper, staring intently at the wall, Witness thought. Or perhaps beyond the wall, to the place only Chiefs and gods can see.

Slowly, Gem set aside the sealed urn. Then, movements growing ever more precise, he laid the Trident across the bed, and began to touch various studs on his wristlet.

Spiders streamed from his sleeves, from beneath his collar, from within his pockets, from under his hair. Eyes of purple, yellow and green glowed as they approached the Smiter and scrambled up among the various protrusions and took position.

Each of the nine was given a section to walk and map and probe. Each was required to report every finding, every detail, no matter how minute. Gem fiddled with the wristcomp, dumping backup systems ruthlessly, to make room for the incoming data. Then he walked over to the doorway and sat down by the Witness.

"Will you wake the Smiter to fullness, Anjemalti?" asked that one.

Gem glanced sideways, humor glinting. "Are you allowed to ask such things?"

"Information offered from those who knowingly challenge event can only enhance the Witnessing, thus enlarging the Memory," returned Witness, deadpan as always. He met Gem's eyes. "You ask of me, do you not?"

"Most assuredly I do," Gem said, surprised at his own sudden laugh. "And likely to ask more of you, since Corbinye has set us for her ship—and nothing but trouble to come of it, either." He sighed and waved a hand at the Trident, or at the spiders, so busy and so bold.

"It distresses me to see a device ill-used and badly kept. The thing was meant to do something, after all. Why should it not be returned to a state wherein it may function according to its design?"

"Have you powerful enemies, Anjemalti?"

He started, then shook his head. "It would seem so. The Vornet—it must have been a Vornet warwagon, hidden among the port vehicles, that blasted *Dart* out of the sky. The port has nothing like that mobile. And if the Vornet chooses to follow us off-planet…" He moved his shoulders, as if to throw off the worry plain on his face.

"Corbinye took us into primary transition quickly. I doubt any could have traced her coords. Even if they had, extrapolating destination from preliminary transition is—" He stopped, turned to stare, wide-eyed at Witness.

"Why did the Bindalche tithe Jarge Menlin in hesernym?"

"Anjemalti, it was what he asked of them. The Bindalche are sworn to serve the Seeker of the Smiter in whatever manner such Seeker demands. In return, the Seeker and the Smiter work to alter event to the benefit of the Bindalche."

"Saxony Belaconto wanted the Trident so she could control the hesernym trade," Gem nearly whispered. "It's the only reason she ever wanted it—the only reason she thinks *anyone* would want it."

"Then she will gather her minions to her and set forth immediately for Spangiln and for Bindal," said Witness, calmly. "She and hers will face you and Corbinye Faztheroth, Death's

Warrior, and the Smiter, which you have sworn to restore to glory." He smiled then. It was the first time Gem had seen him smile—slow and sweet. Childlike. "It will be a Memory to outshine all Memories, Anjemalti. The Bindalche will recall you in the Rolls of the Chiefs forever."

CHAPTER FORTY-FOUR

"BACK-UP SYSTEM SIX?" Corbinye blinked at him in bafflement. "It is what it says it is, Anjemalti—the backup for Ship System Six, should there be failure."

Gem stifled his burst of annoyance. "Certainly. But my question, cousin, is: How vital is this system to the safety of ship, crew and passengers? What is the effect if System Six should fail, and there be no backup to immediately take over its function?"

She frowned and leaned a hip against the panel-ledge, arms crossed under her breasts. "Effect on safety of personnel, should there be no backup of System Six, is minimal," she said finally, speaking slowly and distinctly, as if he were a child—or a half-wit. "System Six is itself a redundant protocol, responsible for powering outer hatches, docking lights, hold environment and pallets. It is most likely to be used when the ship is on a coldpad and there is cargo to unload. Otherwise, MainComp orders those functions." She shrugged.

"So the backup for that system is unlikely to missed, even if there should be failure," Gem concluded. "Good." He began to ply his wristband.

Corbinye watched with trepidation as the spiders scrambled down Anjemalti's trouser-legs and started purposefully toward her.

"Perhaps you should rethink your strategy," she said. "This is a sealed bank."

"Ah," he returned, not even looking up from his wrist.

The first spider, smaller than Number Fifteen and green-eyed, reached her boot, detoured around and vanished through the seam where wall met floor.

"How…" she breathed and then gasped as a second spider—larger, with its eyes glowing violet, also vanished behind the panel.

"Anjemalti!" she cried sharply, to capture his attention. "What are you doing to my ship?"

He did glance up at that, with a glint of grim humor that she mistrusted. "But I thought that I was the Captain, and that the Ship and all ships dependent upon the Ship, and all the Crew, belonged to the care of the Captain."

"But *I* pilot this ship! How if you render it incapable? How if you damage a primary system? What—"

"By cannibalizing the backup of a redundant system? After I was assured by the ship's pilot that no danger would maintain, should this specific system fail?" His shrugged. "Be easy, Corbinye. I may find nothing I need."

"May—" Movement by her boot drew her eye and she pounced, slapping her cupped hand over what marched, amber-eyed and courageous, in the wake of his fellows. "No!"

Gem froze, fingers hovering over the wrist-comm, and all the spiders froze as well, those within the panel as well as those without.

"Corbinye—"

"No!" she repeated, in no calmer tone, and straightened, holding her hand cupped against her breast, spider eyes gleaming yellow through her fingers.

"You shall not require it of him!" She cried and her eyes were damp, her face fevered. "After his courage and his loyalty you shall not force him into warfare with my ship, Anjemalti, and that I do swear!"

Gem stood with his fingers poised over the studs that would enable Number Fifteen to free itself, to clamber down and across the floor and enter the working behind the panel. He looked at Corbinye, who met his eyes plainly, though she trembled—he saw it. He thought of her as she had been, laying the ruined spider before him, and her knife; bending the knee and asking Captain's Mercy...

"Very well," he said softly. "He is yours, Corbinye. I had not thought the matter through."

Her face relaxed somewhat, though she still kept her fingers caged about the spider. Gem bent back to his bracelet and started the spiders marching once more—all of those that remained his own.

In the end, the panel yielded wiring, and various electronic bits and bothers. Gem loaded his booty into a collapsible crate, checked the tally of spiders—eight with him, one elsewhere— stood and brushed at the knees of his trousers.

Corbinye had long since taken herself to another portion of the ship—perhaps even to the bridge; he resisted the temptation to query Number Fifteen regarding exact location. Instead, he hefted the box and bore it away down the hall, toward his cabin and Shlorba's Smiter.

The Smiter was where he had left it, across the bed in the dim room. From his post in the doorway, Witness glanced up, eyes focusing slowly into reality.

"Anjemalti," he said, by way, Gem supposed, of greeting.

"Witness for the Telios," he responded, and stepped over the threshold, placing the crate carefully in the middle of the limited floor space.

He fetched the Trident and the Fearstone's urn from the bed and sat, clumsily cross-legged, beside the crate before unfolding the printout he had coaxed from *Hyacinth's* antiquated system.

"What is that, Anjemalti?" Witness had drawn closer; sat facing him across the crate.

Gem turned the paper so the other could see the diagram and the microprinted lists of specifications. "The schematic," he said tiredly, "for the Smiter."

Witness for the Telios frowned. "You believe that Shlorba's Smiter is a—*machine*?"

Gem rubbed his forehead and tried to focus on the tiny print. "I think," he said, only half minding what he said, "that there are many sorts of devices, with many governing protocols, in the universe. To call something a *machine* is to limit its destiny. Form follows function, after all. This is a device which was designed with a specific purpose in mind. At one time, it fulfilled that purpose. It took damage and no longer functions. Logic would indicate that repair of the damage would allow it to function once again."

There was silence from the Witness, which was welcome. Gem bent close to the schematic, marking out the places where the original wiring was gone; hesitated a moment and glanced at the bounty Back-up System Six had provided.

"I intend," he said to the Witness, "to rewire the entire system, then repair the other damage. These places—" he held up the schematic again and touched the spots with his finger "—would seem to have once housed gemstones. Have you any Memory that would tell me what stones these were?"

The brown eyes filmed over, as if, Gem thought, the man had an inner eyelid, like a lizard. A minute passed, then two. Gem sighed and returned to the schematic. After a time, he put it aside and touched the wristcomp, ordering the tireless spiders out, and set Numbers Six and Twelve to the task of stripping complicated, ship-system wire down to simple pairs. Number Eleven and Fourteen he set to cleaning out the blasted receptors and transmitters along the Smiter's surface. Then he reached for the urn.

He had barely worked the stopper loose when Witness spoke.

"Atop the middle tine of the Smiter was seated the Soulstone, which purpose was to look upon the souls of the Bindalche's enemies and drink dry those who were unworthy. The Soulstone is an artifact of great power—a mover of event in its own force. It is to be recalled as an ally of the Smiter, collaborating in the acceptance or rejection of a Seeker and in the unending struggle to command event."

He opened his eyes, wide, and Gem saw how the sweat ran the man's dark face. "That was a far Recalling, Anjemalti. Of the others, I find nothing, save a general Memory, not quite as old as that concerning the Soulstone, which indicates that the enhancer gems must be faceted according to a pattern I am now able to draw, should you require. No other specifications were Memorized."

"And the—Soulstone," Gem demanded, hating the need that forced him to drive the other. "Were there specifications for shaping it?"

Almost, it seemed Witness would laugh. "One might as well shape the Smiter, Anjemalti. It is its own power, so Memory tells us. Who dares impose his own form upon such?"

"Who, indeed?" murmured Gem, looking at the charred spot above the Trident's middle tine.

The Soulstone had been somewhat larger than Mordra El Theman's thief-catcher, and the brass clasps that had held it in place had melted half away. The fittings that had held the two lesser stones were merely broken.

Well, thought Gem, there will be other things that will hold it just as securely. Epoxy, perhaps, or—He yawned, suddenly and hugely, abruptly aware of crushing exhaustion. He glanced down at his own hands, and was mildly surprised to see them shaking.

He looked at Witness. "Before I undertake such an exacting task, I will sleep. I hope it will not offend if I counsel the same for you."

"I see the path you point me, Anjemalti, and trust my skill to bring me game."

Whatever that meant, Gem thought, and got shakily to his feet, walked the two steps to the bed and fell across it, sight blurring and mind showing him nothing but a swirl of random colors.

Drowned in color, Gem slept, and dreamed of picking flowers and of Corbinye, laughing.

CHAPTER FORTY-FIVE

FOR A TIME, she sat in the pilot's chair. Merely sat, the spider quiescent on her knee, amber eyes sage and bright. And after a time of sitting, she dozed and dreamed of the child that had not lived, the child of her body. Her dead body. And she dreamed of the child she had been, and that Anjemalti had been, and the games they had played with the others in the dark corridors of the Ship, where the air smelled as it should and every bend and twist of hallway was known, gene-deep, and there was nothing to fear in all the beloved expanse of the Ship, where everyone was cousin, or closer, and each depended wholly upon the other.

Fear lived among the Grounders—blind, incomprehensible half-humans. Fear, and treachery, for there were always those who wished to entrap the Ship, to gain the freedom of the Crew for their own, to roam from star to star, as real humans did, rather than continue as animals, grubbing dirt from birth to dying-time.

And yet, the Ship required repair, from time to time; required such things as only Grounders, dirt-grubbers and half-human as they were, had the way of manufacturing. For the Ships—she had read it in the Log of the Eighty-Fifth Captain, who was called Mad Endriatta—the Ships had never been made to be used as the Crew chose to use them, decade upon century, with no touching down, or taking on of passengers, or exchange of persons with friendly colonies.

Captain Endriatta was offered the Knife for her blasphemy, and she did redeem herself, before Ship and Crew; her First Mate followed by seconds, killed by his grief. In the dream, it was vivid—real—as if she had seen it all with her own eyes.

Corbinye stirred in the pilot's chair, came awake and glanced at the trip-clock. Fifteen hours yet until the end of transition. If the gods smiled, *Gardenspot* would be within hailing distance when *Hyacinth* hit normal space. She stretched her cramped body and smiled ruefully at Number Fifteen.

"A sorry thing," she said, "when the pilot must sleep in her chair." She sighed and offered the spider her palm. It came willingly, as always, tiny claws mincing across her flesh, and she wondered anew at Anjemalti's skill.

"Well," she said, and stood up, stretching cramped muscles. It had been too long since she had put the body through its paces. Very bad, should she lose discipline now, just when she had been approaching a degree of competence. She caught sight of her face—high-cheeked and lovely—in the darkened screens and froze, staring. She felt a slight weight, moving up her sleeve: Number Fifteen, climbing. "I had forgot," she whispered, raising a hand to cup the dewy cheek, then shook herself.

"I am Corbinye Faztherot," she said, firm and loud in the quiet of the ship, "of the Crew of the Ship *Gardenspot,* who owes duty to the First Mate, and to the Captain-to-be. I am Worldwalker, and Seeker, and Speaker-to-Grounders. I have passed the tests and the trials. I have borne a child for the Ship. None can negate my actions, and my actions have been always honorable and just."

The spider reached her shoulder, skittered beneath her collar and held on. Corbinye sighed, and turned away from the screens and the busy boards.

"I am tired," she said, perhaps to the spider, perhaps only to herself. Briefly, she wondered what Anjemalti was about— then set the thought aside. Anjemalti despised her—how often had she seen it in his eyes? Best leave that alone, to wither and to die, and not to think on the comeliness of him. Best to regard him as the Captain, who must be obeyed. After he was safely with the Ship.

"Hai…" she went down the companionway, heading for the cabin that was intended for the second pilot, though she never ran with such. She hesitated at the galley door, then stepped in, banging her hip against the table before she remembered the light, and poured herself a half-glass of Viktrian Brandy—Grounder stuff, and excellent of its kind. Better, Corbinye thought, putting the bottle back into its hatch, than any distillations the Crew produced.

Carrying the glass with her, the spider a comfort tucked beneath her collar, she went down the hall and let herself into the tiny cabin.

She woke some untold time later, sat up and rubbed her neck. Apparently, the new body had not the tolerance for Viktrian grape that her old one had. She blinked blearily at the pillow, where Number Fifteen stood patient guard, and grimaced.

"A cold shower, I think. And a workout. Then a hot shower, clean clothes…" That brought her up—Her clothes were in the cabin Anjemalti had made his own—and would hardly fit her new shape, in anywise. "Very well, then," she said and stood up briskly enough to send a flare of pain through her head. "We shall wash these clothes." And hope, she added silently, that the ancient cleaner unit was equal to the task.

An hour later, exercised, showered and in clothes from which the worst grime had been removed, she went down the companionway. The galley showed signs of having been used— tea had been brewed and journeybread withdrawn from the food bank. After putting the brandy glass to be washed, she withdrew tea and journeybread herself and carried the meal with her to the bridge.

Seven hours until transition into normal space. Corbinye ran such checks as were needed and leaned back in her chair, dusting the last crumbs of journeybread from her fingers.

"All's well with the ship," she murmured, though she had never been prone to speaking aloud to herself—before. She moved her shoulders and felt the friendly weight of Number Fifteen just within her collar. Mere politeness, after all, to speak to one's visitor, and explain the signs and portents of the day. She shook her head. "I begin to sound as mad as this Witness of Anjemalti's."

With which thought, she came out of the chair and picked up her mug. "Best see what madness the two of them have wrought this while," she said to Number Fifteen. "For it's as if they are children—too much silence foretells disaster."

The room that had been hers smelled metallic and damp and there was a sweetish stink, as perhaps of patch adhesive, which had overloaded the air-cleaning system and simply hung, like a putrid mist.

She paused in the doorway, hip against the jamb, and looked at the two of them: Witness cross-legged and intent upon the bed, leaning vulturelike over the floor where Anjemalti knelt amid a blizzard of parts, wire and stripped insulation, papers and spiders. His hair was twisted into a knot at the back of his head, held with wire skewers, his sleeves were rolled to the elbow and his hands were delicately—so very carefully—probing here and there among the junk that littered the surface of his damned Trident. At his knee was a pot of epoxy and in a half-ring around him were the spiders, varicolored eyes no less intent than the Witness' own.

Corbinye sighed and had a sip of lukewarm tea. Anjemalti reached among the litter on the floor and drew forth a flash of deep, glittering red—a ruby, Corbinye thought, and deliberately did not think that he might have gotten it from the weapons tuning kit, though she made no doubt he had.

Carefully, he matched the stone with a place upon the shaft of the Trident, and touched the epoxy brush to the surface. Even more carefully, he turned the stone in his fingers, orienting it to some lodestar only he could see, and pushed it firmly into the glue.

On the bed, Witness let go a deep, shuddering sigh. Neither he nor Anjemalti looked up.

Once more, Anjemalti reached among the trash surrounding him and pulled out the urn in which Theo had imprisoned the brown and green stone an age or so ago. He worked the stopper and spilled the stone free.

It flared as it hit Anjemalti's palm, washing the room in baleful green light. Corbinye came straight upright in the doorway, a scream of sheer terror cramping her throat. Witness raised a hand and drew a series of patterns in the air before his face, minding neither the sweat that mantled his forehead nor the tears that spilled from his eyes.

Only Anjemalti seemed unaffected. He picked the stone up between thumb and forefinger; turned it this way, that way; laid it against a spot centered above the Trident's tines.

Green lightnings sparked about the room and distant thunder rumbled. Several of the other stones on the Trident flashed, sparked; ghostlight flickered along the wiring.

Anjemalti plucked the stone from its resting place and dabbed the spot with epoxy. Setting brush and pot aside, he glanced up at Witness.

"This may end all Memory, friend."

"I think not, Anjemalti," returned the other, eyes never leaving the Trident. "You are a Chief of many powers. A Seeker of astonishing boldness."

"And thus the Goddess will love me," Anjemalti said ruefully. "We shall see." He pushed the stone firmly into the adhesive.

The ship disappeared in a sheet of green thunder and Corbinye fell away and down and into the noise and the fire and the terror. Beyond it all she heard someone singing crazed hosanna and someone else crying her name.

"Corbinye!" Her name once more, snapped like an order, and accompanied by a sharp slap to the cheek. Not an order, then, for none of the Crew would dare to strike her. They knew her, so they did, and knew what she would not brook.

"Corbinye!" Again, voice crackling on the edge of familiarity. She opened her eyes, more out of a desire to see the fool who so ardently wished his arm broken than because the tone commanded her.

"So." Anjemalti's face, grime-streaked and stark, hung over hers, almost near enough to kiss. So like him, she thought wearily, to choose a blow instead.

"So," she managed in turn, and tried to right herself, only to be pinned where she lay by astonishingly gentle hands on her shoulders.

"Rest a moment, Corbinye. You struck your head—and lucky you didn't slice it open. It was enough to stun, though—"

"My ship," she cut him off brusquely as memory returned. "What has that damned thing done to my ship, Anjemalti?" She struggled, the hands lifted away and she sat up, though her ears rang with the effort of it and her vision swam.

"The ship appears unharmed," he said, amazingly mild.

"Have you been to the bridge?" she snarled. "Have you run systems checks? That—*monster*—swallows my ship and you tell me it *seems* unharmed? I'll tell you plain—*cousin*—it's my opinion that my ship isn't all it's swallowed!"

His cheeks flamed scarlet and his mouth tightened ominously. "And just what is that plain speaking meant to say?"

"Only that it's gained possession of your mind; made its own existence paramount, so that you risk Ship and Captain and—aye!—*Crew* to aid it. Damn the Ship, you dared to tell me, Anjemalti—recall it? Well, I say, damn that fool stick! Space it and have done; cease toying with destiny—you have destiny! You have folk who need you, who wait on your arrival! Seven hours until you're home—"

"Home." His mouth was hard, and his eyes. He turned his head and spoke over his shoulder. "You hear my cousin, friend? She claims that the Smiter has eaten both her ship and myself."

"It is not Recalled that the Smiter has ever eaten any but enemies, Anjemalti; though Chiefs and Seekers have fallen valorously, striving with it to bend event." There was a slight pause while Corbinye strained to see him around Anjemalti's shoulders, and failed.

"As for the ship—it is all around us. That the Smiter did taste of it seems certain. Newly wakened to fullness, it would require information regarding its location within the state of event. That the Smiter has swallowed ships is Remembered. Witnessing does not support the theory that this ship has been swallowed."

Anjemalti looked at her, eyes sapphire-bright, sapphire-hard. "Satisfied?"

"Oh, certainly!" she cried, rolling away from him and coming to her feet, despite all the body's protest. "I shall take the word of a madman who claims memories a thousand years old that my ship is intact and that—" she pointed at the Trident, quiescent now among the litter, ringed around with spiders "—is my best friend, second only to my Captain in commanding my trust! My heart is eased, Anjemalti—behold my calmness, my tranquillity. In seven hours, you are home and I wash my hands of you both!" She turned toward the hall, foot clinking against the fallen teacup.

"Corbinye Faztherot?" Witness was looking at her from bright brown eyes.

"What madness now?" she snapped.

"Only that the Memories I may draw upon are much older than a mere thousand of your standardized years," he said mildly. "I thought it meet that you should know it."

She closed her eyes; drew breath for the gods only knew what retort.

"Saxony Belaconto is most likely even now on course for Bindal," said Anjemalti.

She opened her eyes wide at him. "No concern of mine where the bitch goes, so long as she fails to come alongside the Ship."

"She will terrorize the Bindalche," Anjemalti persisted, as if it had something to do with her—or with him. "She'll kill for hesernym, enslave who might not die—"

"You forget The Combine," she said sweetly; "Bindal is well-protected."

He brushed that aside with an impatient hand, snapped to his feet and stood over her, face and eyes intent. "We must go to Bindal," he said, slow and excruciatingly calm. "We must return the Smiter and the Witness to the Telios. A Seeker will come forth from the ranks of the Bindalche. The Smiter is rewired—functioning as it should. With it the Seeker and the Bindalche will be able to repel the Vornet." He paused, then repeated. "We must go to Bindal."

Corbinye sighed. "Well, and if you must, Anjemalti, who am I to tell you nay? I only do my duty, as given me by Acting Captain and First Mate Mael Faztherot. That duty is to bring her Captain-to-be Anjemalti Kristefyon, so that his Crew may know him and he may be about the business for which he was foretold." She shrugged and decided against bending to retrieve the cup. All were lost, should she swoon again...

"And if I require you to give over command of this ship to me?"

"As much as it must grieve me to disobey the Captain-to-be, he is not as yet the Captain-in-fact," she said, though her heart wept for the lie.

His face was tight, but he asked the question anyway, voice deadly soft. "And if I take command of this ship?"

"Alas," she said, her own voice as soft, and meeting his eyes most straightly. "I have anticipated you, I fear, cousin. The board is geared for my hand only; Navigation requires a set response to an imposed list of queries. If my hand fails and even one question is answered incorrectly, this ship dies." She gestured, encompassing Witness, spiders, Trident—himself. "And all within it."

"My duty shall be dispatched with honor," she said, though she wanted only to weep at the look of his face. "It has always been so, and with all else that has changed for me, this will not."

Silence, except for the rattling hum of the air scrubbers, valiantly striving against the odor of epoxy and fear. Corbinye licked her lips. "Seven hours, Anjemalti."

"Seven hours, Corbinye," he returned, dead-voiced, and showed her his back.

Swallowing hard against nausea and dizziness, she went out of the cabin and down the hall, feeling nothing but ashes where her heart should be, and no joy at all that she had won the bluff.

She went and sat in the pilot's chair to wait the hours out, and if she cried while she sat there, none knew it, for even Number Fifteen did not come near.

CHAPTER FORTY-SIX

GARDENSPOT, FIFTH TO be commissioned of a Class of 36 GenerationShips designed, patented and built by Doctor Sir Albee K. Messenger of GriffithPod L5, Father of the Crew, hung in viewscreens six through nine.

Corbinye allowed herself a moment of self-congratulation. "Pretty piloting indeed," she murmured approvingly, and felt a quiver as Number Fifteen stirred beneath her collar. She ran the board-checks and flipped open the hailing frequency. Although still too distant for rational conversation, they would have read her ID by now, and news of Anjemalti's presence must be published as soon—

"Tight piloting," Anjemalti's voice was in her ear a bare instant before he hit the second's chair. She glanced over at him, noting that he had bathed and cleaned his clothing and perhaps even rested. His shining hair was tied neatly back with a strip of ribbon. The side of his face was what he showed her, so she could not read him that way; his eyes were all on the screens.

"Thanks to you, for your praise," Corbinye said softly; still he did not look at her, but only stared at the Ship.

Well, she thought suddenly, and why should he not? Nine years old when last he saw so brave a sight. Let it fill his heart now and recall to him the magnificence of his heritage. Let him be made proud, who had forgotten so much of what it was to be Crew. Let him weep with the glory of it and with the joy of—

"In hard need of repair, isn't she?" Anjemalti murmured, with no hint of awe in his voice.

Corbinye started, raked a glance at the screens and spun back to him. "What's meant by that?"

He blinked as if startled by her vehemence and flicked his own glance at the screens before shrugging. "I meant no offense—and it is difficult to tell without full magnification. But just from what I see here—that scar in the fifth quad where something's been ripped free of the hull—not recently. Solars are missing, and the master vane in the third quad seems out of true…"

Corbinye opened her mouth—and closed it, for how could she rebut the truth? She bent to the board and ran the full check series again, although there was no need.

"I see its glory," she said, hearing the sullen note in her voice and wishing it were gone. "Its past splendor. It is home, Anjemalti, though the past years have not been—kind—to us. There have not been so many contracts with the Grounders, and, we have, after all, our own troubles with The Combine, that thinks all of space belongs to it, to police and to say who goes where and who may not enter at all." She sighed.

"Truth told, to many of the Crew less contact with Grounders seemed not a bad thing, but a good."

He frowned. "There is no Ship's treasury?"

"Oh—aye," she said slowly, uncomfortable discussing these things, which should be told him by Acting Captain Faztherot. "But gold is—cheap—many places, Anjemalti. And such gemstones as we have are of military grade. We work, for whatever coin is current, or in trade for repair. For a time, we had work as a freighter—goods, mostly, from this world's warehouse to that. And we hauled ore, time and enough. But, the work is less plentiful of late. I—the reasons are complex, Anjemalti, and best told you by the Acting Captain."

"Reasons such as there are faster ships to be had, and crewhands who are less xenophobic," he said. "And captains who will speak with ground-traders without insisting upon an interpreter."

She licked her lips. "We are the Crew. We have our ways."

"As do others. Inquire of the Witness."

The radio spat and from the static came a voice.

"Ho, the ship! Name yourself and state your business!"

Corbinye started, half-choked and snapped the toggle to the left.

"Name myself, shall I, when the Ship has pulled my ID these fifteen minutes and more? Who do you think it will be, Veln Kristefyon? Space vampires? And where is your mother?"

"Navigation," the imp gave back, unholy glee overriding even the static. "Dolfiata took a burn when the second comp gave out and he's in sick bay, wrapped in jelly and cursing like a Grounder, Jelbi says. Half the techs on-shift are in Navigation, doing repairs, Mother and Acting Captain Faztherot are piloting and they said for me to man the mike and warn everyone away." There was a slight giggle—interference, Corbinye thought, though it could as well have been Veln.

"Should I warn you away, cousin Corbinye?"

"You would do better to clear me for marriage and pipe down to Acting Captain Faztherot that Captain-to-be Anjemalti Kristefyon is returned to the Ship."

The silence was longer this time, as if her announcement had stilled even Veln's chatter, though she had never previously known him to quiet for anything but sleep.

"Veln Kristefyon?" Anjemalti murmured next to her and she glanced over to find him still staring at the screens.

"The child of Indemion Kristefyon and Siprian Telshovet," she said. "He will have—nine or ten Standard Years, I believe. Perhaps eleven. I have been away—some time."

"Yes," said Anjemalti.

"*Gardenspot* to outrider ship *Hyacinth*." This transmission was nearly clear; the woman's voice crisp and no-nonsense. "We have you tracked and identified. Expect you will adjust course and local velocity to marry the Ship at thirty-two hundred hours, targeting Level Two, Bay One. Transmitting orientation data."

Corbinye's board beeped and she shunted the information to NavComp.

"Received." She hesitated. "Reporting the presence, in addition to Captain-to-be Kristefyon and myself, of a male person."

"Designation?"

"Grounder—" she closed her mouth before "barbarian" escaped; glanced at Anjemalti, who was watching *her* now, rather than the screens. "He calls himself Witness for the Telios."

"Claim upon the Ship?"

Anjemalti shifted; stilled himself. Corbinye drew a breath. "He travels with the Captain-to-be."

"So." A space of mere crackling, then: "The Ship shall receive him."

"Noble of the Ship," Anjemalti murmured. Corbinye shot him a quelling look, though his voice had not been loud enough to penetrate the static.

"Please inform the Captain-to-be of our great joy in his return," the radio instructed. "Ending official transmission. Corbinye?"

"Mother?"

"Are you well?"

She hesitated, looked down at the soft hands, that moved with incongruous briskness across the board. She tipped her head and felt the braid pull and swing, was aware of the weight of her breasts. She thought the thought and one of the soft hands flicked the send toggle.

"I am well."

"You sound—unlike yourself," Mael Faztherot said, penetrating all.

"It has been some years—and the connection is poor."

"So it is. Until docking then, daughter."

"Mother…"

The transmission light went dark.

She sat, frozen, staring at the darkened stud and trying to think...

"Corbinye." Anjemalti, that. She spared him a look.

"There are accommodations to make in preparation for docking," he said neutrally. "I would make them myself, except that you indicated the board might find my touch—repellent."

"Yes," she said, and forced the soft stranger's hands to move, matching her equations with those sent from the Ship. It was duty, after all. The same duty that had sent her away from home and safety, among Grounders on a dozen worlds and eventually into the Blue House. Duty was all that was left. And she would dispatch her duty with honor, until such time as even duty were denied her.

CHAPTER FORTY-SEVEN

DOCKING WAS ACHIEVED, among various moanings and creakings offered up by the Ship's mechanism. At the end of it, Corbinye sat in the pilot's seat, hands cold and sweaty, and stared at the board, seeing this telltale, then that, then that, go from green to yellow, as *Gardenspot* took over *Hyacinth's* functions, one by careful one.

Finally, the entire board glowed amber. Yet she sat, staring at the lights until they blurred into one light, glowing like a small sun. Soon, now.

"Corbinye?"

Anjemalti, again, returned from wherever he had taken himself off to, when he was satisfied that the docking maneuver was well in hand. She sighed and closed her eyes against the blurred brightness of the board lights.

"Corbinye." Stubbornness sounding there, and a note of command. She sighed, spun the chair and opened her eyes.

He stood in the doorway, the Trident in one hand and a repair beacon in the other. Witness for the Telios could be glimpsed over his right shoulder.

"Is docking complete?"

"We are at one with the Ship," she told him, hearing the weariness resonate in the voice that was not hers. She swept a hand at the board. "Married, and at peace."

"Cleared for entrance?"

"Oh—aye." She stood, frowned at the beacon. "Why bring that?"

"My recollection is that, save for the Garden, the Ship is dark, and my eyes have always been weak. Allow me to indulge myself with the means to look plainly upon the faces of my Crew."

Dark. She had not considered. The Ship to her had never been dark. She nodded. "Let us proceed, then, cousin."

She popped the hatch and swung out first, entering a darkness so absolute that she cried aloud and thrust her hands before her and all but fell. Fingers closed around her wrist, digging into her flesh, and a voice snapped from somewhere over her head to be *still,* and she was let go, but there was nothing to see, though her eyes strained until the darkness bled rainbows—

Light, glorious and golden, wavery with weakened batteries, timorously bathed the bay.

"Much better," Anjemalti commented, and dropped lightly to the decking, Witness for the Telios coming immediately after, bearing the second of *Hyacinth's* lanterns.

"Now." Anjemalti held his beacon high and frowned a moment at the ring of Crew faces confronting him. "Ah." He went forward, carrying the Trident with him, and paused before a worn-faced woman, slightly taller than the rest, and slightly thinner.

"I expect you must be my Aunt Mael—at least, I called you that, didn't I? My mother's best friend."

"So I was," Mael Faztherot allowed. "And hope to be her son's, as well." She hesitated. It is the blue eyes, Corbinye thought, or that he looks so Grounder…

"I doubt you'll find much of her in my face," Anjemalti said gently. "My uncle had always said I looked as my father."

"Not entirely true," said Mael. "Though I recall his eyes were blue… His name was Jova Flanry. I will show you where it is written in the Log."

"That would be kindness," Anjemalti returned and Corbinye wondered at his soft-spokenness, he who had damned both Ship and Crew.

He glanced around the ring of faces once more. "I am afraid that no one else—"

"You don't know me, *do* you?" An imp stepped out of the crowd, hair spiky and clothing crumpled. Anjemalti looked down at him.

"Veln Kristefyon," he said softly, and sketched a bow, still holding fast to Trident and light. "Cousin."

The imp blinked, taken off-stride, then made a recover by pointing at the beacon. "Why do you need that?"

"Because my eyes are poor," Anjemalti said. "Learn grace of other's failings."

The boy blinked again, and opened his mouth to blurt who knew what other outrage. A woman reached out and gripped his shoulder. "Veln."

He subsided and Anjemalti turned his attention to the woman. "Siprian Telshovet?"

"The same." she returned composedly, though her face betrayed anxiety, and the fingers that gripped the boy showed white knuckles. "Navigation Chief."

He nodded, caught her eyes. "My vendetta died with my uncle. Your record with me is as clean as the boy's."

Relief flooded her face, and her grip on the boy loosened, but only slightly. "I hear you—Captain."

"Is he the Captain?" demanded the irrepressible Veln and the question rustled the circle of Crew, but no one gave him answer. He pulled away from his mother's hands. "Where's cousin Corbinye?" he cried and Anjemalti stared down at him while Corbinye felt her heart stutter and her body soak with sudden sweat. She licked her lips.

"Here," she croaked, and stiffened as a dozen pair of Crew eyes focused on her.

I will not flinch, she told herself. I will not cry. I will not beg. I am Corbinye Faztherot, Worldwalker and Seeker for the—

"That is not my daughter," said Mael Faztherot.

In the rest of the bay, there was silence, broken abruptly by Veln, who ran across to where she stood, lock-kneed and short of breath, and stared up into her face.

"Cousin Corbinye?" His own face was creased with distress and she longed to hug him, to reassure him.

"Yes," she whispered, then cleared her throat. "Yes, Veln."

He bit his lip, reached out a tentative hand and touched the braid, where it hung across her shoulder. "You look—" his eyes were double their normal size, and awash with tears. "You look—*different*."

"I am different," she told him, and the voice was firm this time, falling naturally into the rhythm of the tale. "I was— beaten by thieves—and my old body—died. But on Henron there is a place called the Blue House, where they take the memories and the—soul—of one person and transfer those into a body empty of memories; riven of soul." She raised her eyes from the boy's face and looked to her mother, who stood, stone-faced and silent.

"I am Corbinye Faztherot," she said, urgently, and hated herself for begging. "In everything but the body—"

She stopped and dropped her head, grinding her teeth to deny the tears that welled, despite her will. More words were useless and worse than that.

Mael Faztherot had turned her back.

"Is this," Anjemalti inquired in the tone of false lightness he used when he wished to mortify his hearer, "how the Crew rewards loyalty? Is this the gratitude won by pursuing duty to death and beyond it? I am instructed, Acting Captain."

Corbinye looked up, breath-caught. Mael Faztherot's face was rigid; lips pale.

"I had been concerned," Anjemalti continued, still in that lightsome tone, "that my past would dishonor the Crew, since I was raised and trained a thief. I am relieved to find that these fears—"

"Anjemalti!" Corbinye cried, hands up in front of her, fingers snaking about themselves in some alien gesture of distress. "Anjemalti, do not!"

He turned to look at her, eyes fey in the flickering yellow light. "All you have done for them—your duty dispatched in every particular. And you ask me not to chide them, Corbinye? You ask me to bear insult the like of which no Grounder—or thief, either—would bear?"

"They mean no insult to you," she said hastily. "You are welcomed. Anjemalti, it is nothing."

"Nothing?" He stared. "Corbinye—"

"It is nothing," Mael Faztherot announced forcefully. "It is a matter of Crew's Judgment—Captain Kristefyon. Nothing with which you need concern yourself. Nothing—administrative. I will be pleased to instruct you in these matters. The logs are complete; AdminComp shall be put at your disposal. It grieves me that this matter should distort your view of us, who have been away from home so long. We are indeed delighted to have you returned to us, and ready to step into your rightful place." She glanced around at the sober, worn faces. Here and there, one nodded, and there was a soft, "Aye, be welcome, Captain."

"There is no need to keep you standing about in the dock," she finished briskly, gathering two—Zandora and Eil, it was, Corbinye saw—with her eye and she went forward and made to take Anjemalti's arm.

He stepped back, gracefully avoiding her and instead placed the beacon into her outstretched hand. "Kind of you, ma'am. Though I am afraid this unit will require a recharge soon. As I said, my eyes are poor, and those of my associates—"

"Certainly, we understand the difficulty," Mael said. "Recharging the beacon will be no problem. We might even bring some sections of the ship up to twilighting, if you command. I can show you the schematics..." Talking so, she turned him and the others fell in around, so that he must needs go with them, and Witness, as well—though that one did pause a moment to set his beacon gently upon the floor.

Corbinye gritted her teeth and visualized the thought-patterns for forbearance and patience with adversity. Zandora came and stood by her right side. Eil grabbed her left arm, deliberately rough. Testing her.

She stared into his face. "I know the way. Cousin."

She did not expect the slap and Zandora grabbed her so she could not dodge it.

"I'm no kin to you, Grounder-bitch! Think you can steal our ways and kill our kin and feed us some crazed tale about transferring souls and have us give you the keys to the Ship?" He spat this time, and Zandora still held her so she couldn't wipe the cheek clean. She held the zens before her mind's eye and kept her muscles loose.

Eil grinned and reached and wrapped the braid around his fist. He yanked, turning and marching briskly off in the instant that Zandora released her.

She stayed afoot, having no taste for being dragged three levels on her face. She stayed afoot, and she did not cry.

But she had to run to keep up with him. All the way to the brig.

CHAPTER FORTY-EIGHT

"OF COURSE," SAID Acting Captain Faztherot, "there will be a period of readjustment, while AdminComp is keyed to yourself and the rest of Ship's systems are brought onto line. In a dozen shifts you should have most systems under your command."

"A dozen shifts?" murmured Gem, doing the conversion in his head and being careful not to frown. A Standard week to assign and activate a password? Even several passwords, coupled with an ultimate override, should not take more than an hour or two. Why, he could do it himself in less than—

"When the Ship accepts you," Mael Faztherot said sharply; "it accepts you blood and bone. Captain and Ship are one being; sharing soul." She looked at him closely. "Surely your mother spoke of these things to you?"

"My mother," Gem reminded her softly, "died when I was eight years old. And afterwards my uncle spoke to me only to taunt me. I regret the circumstances which have caused these lamentable gaps in my education."

"Certainly, certainly." Corbinye's mother gave back in a hasty embarrassment her daughter would have scorned. "The Logs are at your disposal and these mysteries are fully addressed within. As for this other…" She turned and tapped a series into the administrative computer's keypad, a pad so old, Gem saw, that the hard plastic keys were worn smooth, its symbols pounded into oblivion by generation upon generation of fingers….

"We will require a complete gene-reading, which will be submitted to the medical computer for verification. Once verified, the data is transferred to Captain's comp—administration—which informs all of its systems and subsystems. Administration runs the Ship entire, and it must keep up with its duties even as it acknowledges a new Captain. Hence the time-lag." She glanced sideways at him.

"I have heard that Grounders have discovered the way of building multifunctional computing machines, which may solve countless problems at lightspeed, as well as maintain primary system tasks. This is very well for Grounders, but the Crew has well-served by this comp and we see no need to upgrade."

She turned to look at him fully and he read both pride and anxiety in her face. "But I need not tell you," she said, "how it is to be Crew."

"I may require reminding from time to time," Gem said carefully. "Recall that most of my years have been spent among Grounders and that I am used to certain—ahh—amenities."

"It is certainly the Captain's privilege," Mael Faztherot said stiffly, turning her face aside, "to provide amenities, should he judge the Ship requires them." She shook her head sharply.

"In the meantime," she said, coming to her feet and beckoning him brusquely to his. "We must have you to sick bay, so that the tests may be run and your initiation begun! This way. If you please, Captain."

The gene tests were astonishingly easy, the sick bay up to date and gleaming in a way wholly at variance with what he had thus far seen of the Ship.

Afterward, there were meetings with this section chief and with that—though no inspections to be made; they were careful of that. He kept the Trident in his hand the whole time, and Witness perforce came behind, but every inquiry of Corbinye was cut off, derailed, ignored.

Finally, he pled weariness, which was nearly true, and Mael Faztherot showed him to a spacious cabin, where one wall slid aside to let in the light and the odors of the Garden, and the furnishings were real wood and in good repair and the coverings on the bed were costly and sweet-smelling.

"Thank you," Gem said, by way of dismissal. "This will do very well."

Yet Mael Faztherot hesitated. "I know you are weary— and with every cause! But I would not be behind in any courtesy. Captain. Is there one from among us that I might send to you? Certainly, a roster will be made, as proper. But for this night, if one had caught your eye—"

He blinked, remembered to keep his face bland. "I thank you for the thought, but I am most truly tired and would hardly be able to do my part. After the roster is made…"

"Certainly," she said again, and nodded at the Witness. "I shall see your servant comfortably bedded."

"No need," Gem said calmly. "He is accustomed to sleeping athwart the door, and I don't like to disappoint him."

She looked at him suspiciously. "You have no need of such protections here, on your Ship and among your Crew."

"But my friend is used to certain conditions and it is only courtesy to bow to them." He returned her gaze, eye for eye, finding it much easier than it ever had been with Corbinye.

She broke contact first, bowing stiffly. "Very well. If the Captain will instruct me as to the hour of his waking—"

"Let me call you when I wake," he cut her off. "I am exceedingly tired and still recovering from the effects of a wound. Best I get whatever rest my body demands, rather than undertake my new duties half-exhausted."

Another bow, stiffer, if possible, than the first. "The Captain is wise. I am at his disposal at whatever hour. He need only press 'one' on the commboard." She pointed at the wall unit, with its numbered keypad and archaic earcup.

Gem nodded. "I am in your debt, Acting Captain," he said, and saw her face ease somewhat. "Good-shift."

"Good-shift, Captain," she returned and was finally gone.

Witness went and sat on the floor, back pressed firmly against the door. Gem eyed him before going and laying the Trident carefully across the bed.

"Insulted, Witness for the Telios?"

"Indeed not, Anjemalti. One's own heart can but marvel at the wisdom you display." He settled himself more firmly against the door. "It seems to me that you are newly a man—barely beyond the Testing. And yet you are as canny as one with years of the hunt behind you." He smiled his sweet, predator's smile.

"I speak from my own heart, understand—as a friend and a brother of the hunt. You yourself addressed me thus."

"And so no insult is given," Gem concluded and stretched, hands over head and back arched; tensing every muscle and relaxing all at once. "But you are mistaken in me. I fear my testing is just commenced."

There was a sound, slight in the quiet room; as if a sudden stream were gurgling over hidden rocks.

Slow with amazement, Gem turned around.

The Witness was laughing.

"A jest worthy of a man," he said finally, raising a hand to wipe at his eyes.

Gem sat carefully on the bed. "You must, of course, be the judge," he managed, then, back hunched against the open wall and any watchers in the garden below, he pulled his sleeve back from his wristlet and began playing his fingers across the tiny studs.

Spiders began to appear, scurrying here and there upon their magical missions.

Witness for the Telios leaned back against the door, well-pleased with the current shape of event.

It was dark.

It had always been dark. And cold. And stale of air. There had never been anything else.

Corbinye stretched high on her toes, trying to ease both the cramping of the arms chained above her head and the pain of her abundant bruises. Zandora and Eil had been no more gentle than they should have been and her returning three or a dozen responses to their tenderness had elicited even sterner measures.

The blood had long since dried, stiffening the hair that covered her scraped and battered face. The red shirt they had torn from her—sacrilege that a Grounder be clad so!—and slapped and abused her breasts. Grounder-cow, they'd called her. But that hadn't been the worst.

The dark was the worst—and they'd known it. Taunted her with her blindness, made noise in the dark so that she missed her strike again and again and was put on her face after all, eating metal, while the boots and the fists pounded her into unconsciousness.

To waken in chains. Alone. In the dark.

The tears burned her cheeks; she barely noticed them. Beaten by two of the Crew's ruffians, who were fit only for bullwork, who Corbinye Faztherot had bested effortlessly in every childhood trial. Hung up like meat, to drip blood and stare uselessly into the blackness, until such time as she was sent for, filthy, raving spectacle as she would no doubt be, to be stared at and vilified by the Crew entire before the final push into the Garden's composting unit and the tenderizers finished her.

No burial in the stars for Grounders. Return to the dirt was fitting for those.

Corbinye closed her eyes, or opened them. It barely mattered which.

Except that, in the darkness, there was light.

Tiny, amber spots of light, a mile or an inch across the infinite blackness, which disappeared and reappeared, one after the other—and then began to move.

She licked swollen lips and tried to call out, but the lovely storyteller's voice was broken to bits; dust in the back of her bruised throat.

Voiceless, she hung, watching the constant amber eyes grow larger until finally they reached her boot and she felt spider claws take hold of cloth and begin to climb.

She tried to hang still; to not dislodge the tiny climber: Number Fifteen. Her last friend. She tried to hang still, but back, arm and shoulder muscles spasmed at once, so that she twisted in agony and tried to push higher on her toes to ease them and the legs went, and she howled with the shattered remains of the dancer's voice and bucked against chains, hitting her head a solid whack against the wall and sending herself back into unconsciousness.

CHAPTER FORTY-NINE

THERE WAS LIGHT where she woke. Light and the smell of growing things; even a breeze and what might have been water-sounds. There were voices—elsewhere; softness covered her body. She lay as if upon a cloud. Floating, there was no pain.

Carefully, in the astonishing absence of agony, she tried to remember who she was.

For the instant, it eluded her, and it made no matter that it did. The ease of her body was enough—she could be anyone, any age, any name. There was no pain. And light was benediction, all around.

In the light, she saw the trees and flowers beyond the edge of the cloud she floated upon. Closer looking diminished the cloud to a bed, silken covers shrouding her legs. Atop the silk lay a long, elegant hand, soft and pleasingly made, with pearly nails and golden skin. She flexed the fingers of the hand, establishing that it was hers, and lay back, deeply satisfied. She was a person who possessed a hand. It was enough.

"Corbinye Faztherot," a voice murmured near her head. "Do you wake now?"

She took her time replying, considering the nuance—a man's voice, gently respectful; and it named her. Corbinye Faztherot. She felt something shiver, deep within her painless lethargy. Corbinye Faztherot. She turned her head.

The man was broad-shouldered and boxy; powerfully formed and not unpleasing. She wondered if he were a bed-partner, then lost the thought as he spoke to her again.

"Corbinye Faztherot. Do your dreams still hold you?"

"I am awake," she said, hearing how the languor lent depth to her slow, silken voice.

"That is well," said the man, brown eyes frowning. He leaned close, so that she could smell the scent of him. "Do you know me?"

"Shall I know you?" she returned, luxuriating in the power of her voice, that made the simple question into invitation. Something flickered across the man's face. It may have been annoyance.

"You are still lost in the drug-dreams," he announced, and abruptly went away.

Well, she thought, closing her eyes and nestling deeper into the soft bed, let him go. There are others.

"Corbinye." This voice was also male, accompanied by a touch to her shoulder. She opened her eyes and stared into his—blue, wide, beautiful. Something else shivered within her inner fog. Shivered and broke through.

"Anjemalti?"

Relief showed in the eyes; there was a rearranging of the bed as he sat on the edge. "You're waking," he said. "That's good. Witness told me you'd lost your wits forever."

"Lost my wits…" They were fast returning, so that she looked around her, at the Atrium below, and the luxurious room; at Anjemalti himself—and forgetfulness fled, to be replaced by horror.

"You meddled with Crew's Judgment!" she cried and twisted against the prisoning softness.

His face froze. "Your pardon, madam, but I saved your life."

"Again!" She managed to sit up, never minding that the coverlet fell away from her shoulder. Never minding anything but the enormity of his action.

"Anjemalti, listen to me, as you love your life." Her voice was low, throbbing with urgency. "You must give me to the Crew—plead ignorance of our ways—a child would hardly have seen Crew's Judgment—who could expect you to know? Return me, become known to the Ship, fulfill your destiny. It is your duty, what you were made for—" She reached, blindly, hardly knowing her own intent, and felt her hand captured in his.

"Corbinye…" His face held a mix of emotion, of which she read exasperation and worry and stubbornness. "If it were possible to return you to the Crew, they would kill you, would they not? The medic gave me to understand that you are at the very least an interloper—a Grounder who has stolen Crew secrets—and at the very worst exactly what you claim to be—Crew in a Grounder body. A monster. Either way, you're only fit for the most horrible of deaths." Astonishingly, humor glinted.

"Saxony Belaconto's investment all laid to waste? Pity on your enemies, cousin."

She laughed, deep and throaty, head tipped back so that she felt the hair sweep her shoulder blades. "Gods forbid I should be so graceless!" She sobered abruptly, caught by his other words. "What medic was this?"

Anjemalti shrugged. "Tornbel, did he call himself? I think that was the name."

She stared at him. "You had Tornbel to physick a Grounder? Anjemalti—"

"Well," he said judiciously, "I fear he required some persuasion, and even after tried to trick me—as if I can't tell one med unit from another." He shook his head and sighed. "I finally had enough and left him webbed to the operating table while we finished the repair on you." His eye moved then, flickering down and coming back up to her face, reflecting satisfaction.

"I think we did quite a good job, considering the shape you were in when we found you." His face shifted again, showing anger. "Who was responsible for that, I wonder?"

She stared at him dumbly, lips half-parted.

"Crew's Judgment," he cried, suddenly savage. "You were thrown to the dogs by your own mother, to be torn and worried to bits; harried to death—"

"It was half-done," she said then, soft-voiced with the truth. "Anjemalti. It—"

"Half-done!" He pulled his hand from hers, snapping to his feet and staring down at her. She saw him close his eyes and take a deliberate breath. "More than half-done," he said, calmer. "The internal injuries—" He opened his eyes and offered a wavering smile. "This body is not so tough as your Crew body, cousin. Forgive me."

"No offense," she said absently, looking down at the perfectly-formed, perfectly-smooth hand. She had landed some blows—there should be scratches, bruised knuckles—she looked back at him. "I am still in—in Morela's body?"

He met her gaze fully. "There is no Blue House here, Corbinye. But the medical units are quite up-to-date. Amazing. I congratulated Tornbel on his instruments, but he was less than gracious. A very rude man."

She felt laughter rising again; managed to make it nothing more than a twitch of the lips. "I am sorry you did not find him congenial."

"Oh, no fault of yours." Anjemalti waved a hand. "But we've established that your wits are with you. And since I am not, after all my efforts, inclined to return you to the mob to be tortured and murdered, I wonder if I might prevail upon you to join my bridge-crew. I don't scruple to tell you that I need a mate such as you, who is familiar with the byways of this damned warren."

Horror rose again and she sat straight, the coverlet falling into her lap. "Anjemalti, what have you done?"

"Done?" His eyebrows rose. "Nothing more than was being done, at the Ship's own slow pace. The acting captain assured me that I would be made known to the Ship and given access to all administrative data banks. But she is a busy woman, cousin, as I am sure you know, and her best time for completion of the ID was nearly a Standard week." He shrugged.

"Well, you appreciate, after having come so far, and being the Captain-who-was-foretold, I could hardly wait so long to be made one with my Ship. In short," he glanced to the right, then looked back at her, "all life functions are presently being controlled through this suite. Acting Captain Faztherot is quite upset."

"Anjemalti…"

"You see why I need you," he said briskly. "And now I must excuse myself. There are clothes." He went across to the chest and pulled out dark slacks, a white shirt like his own—Administration's colors. He laid them over the edge of the bed.

"Tornbel was especially furious over the color of your shirt, cousin. Apparently he feels red doesn't suit you. Come to the next room when you're ready."

And he was gone that quickly, striding across the costly rug and vanishing through the door, leaving her to stare at the white shirt and finally put out a hand to take it up.

CHAPTER FIFTY

THE TRIDENT OF the Bindalche leaned against the wall, its rubies winking in the blare of light.

Corbinye had cringed on the threshold, beholding that light, while the part of her that had been in training for First relentlessly tallied the expense, speculating which subsystems were shut down entirely, that their power might bleed here, unrecoverable, generating nothing but...light.

The waste barely concerned her now: The screen Anjemalti had called up held more potent horrors.

Life support systems for the Ship entire—air, gravity, light, humidity, temp—were now fed through this tiny subordinate screen in an antechamber of the Captain's Rooms.

"Why life support?" she demanded after her first panicked scrolling; after she had gathered enough wits to run a check and pull out a detailed map of his meddlings.

"It was most vulnerable," Anjemalti said, shrugging. "And, once subverted, the most easily defensible." He looked at her closely. "I needed to make a protection for you, until such time as you woke and directed me to return you to your death. I needed to show them that I was not without resources—that they mistook the case entirely, if they supposed me a witling—or still nine years old."

"But—life support." She stared at the fortifications he had erected. "How long has this held?"

"In its present form, a Ship's day," he said. "They have at it from time to time and modifications are required. Tedious. But, again, my play was for time—time for you to heal; time for them to learn a little about my mettle. It was my intention that the lessons learned would open the way for—more equitable dealing, with Acting Captain and with Crew."

"They will never forgive you," she whispered. "Anjemalti, you held their lives hostage to the life of a Grounder. They will hate you."

He looked half-amused. "Oh, come now. There's been no meddling with the backups—"

"The backups are not to be trusted," she said, hating the truth even as she spoke it. "On many levels. One wrong move and you could kill the Ship—out of ignorance or out of malice. How can they forget that?" She shook her head and slid down in the chair, stretching her legs out before her, eyes still on the screen. "Have you spoken to my—to Acting Captain Faztherot?"

"Several times. She has gone from promising me amnesty and my place aboard Ship, to advising me to add spin to the Garden and hurl myself to my death."

She looked up. "She did not offer you the Knife?"

"I doubt I'm worthy of it," he said, appearing nearly cheerful in the admission.

Corbinye closed her eyes. "Anjemalti, you are not Crew."

"I did try to tell you that," he said mildly. "Several times."

"So you did." She sighed. "What's to do?"

"An excellent question. We are here, where none of us are welcome. Two of us at least have pressing need to be elsewhere, and it seems better for everyone's health if all of us were gone quickly." He put his chin into the cup of his hand and rested his elbow on a knee. "What chance they'll give us *Hyacinth* and let us go?"

"No score on that throw," she returned. "Truth told, I see no clean way out of the coil—and to suicide by hurling yourself to the floor of the Garden is no honor, Anjemalti, and unworthy of you."

Startlement showed briefly in his eyes, hidden by an ironic seated bow. "My—"

"Rogue Captain Anjemalti Kristefyon!" demanded the comlink perched precariously atop the screen. Anjemalti grinned, though Corbinye could detect no humor in that snarling voice.

"You see what I put up with," he murmured and punched the button atop the link. "Now what?" he inquired of it.

"You will surrender to the Crew the bitch-Grounder in your keeping. You will place yourself and your servant into the custody of Acting Captain Faztherot. You will do these things immediately."

"Surely we've had this conversation?" Anjemalti said plaintively and Corbinye very barely stopped herself from laughing.

Their communicant was less amused. "You are a danger to yourself and to your Crew. It is clear that your Grounder genes have caused you to become demented. The Acting Captain will determine whether it is possible for you to comprehend honor and, if so, will aid you in its attainment. Your name will be written in the Captain's Roster and future Crews will respect your memory." There was a hesitation.

"No blame is attached to your infirmity. It is understood that this is the fault of Grounder genes. We are taught that Grounders are mad—and have seen ample evidence of this."

"So instead of blaming me for putting the Ship in danger, we'll blame my mother, who ignored wisdom," Anjemalti said, suddenly tart. "Very good. To whom am I speaking—Siprian?"

Another hesitation before a less assured, "Yes."

"Very good," he said again. "Siprian, how many children have you?"

"I—childre—? Well," she stammered into sense, "there is Veln…"

"Yes—only Veln? A woman your age, with your abilities and rank—surely you were allowed another child?"

"But she was born—twisted, Cap—Sir. Many of them are…Corbinye's was…" Silence.

Anjemalti cocked his head, as if he could see the woman on the other end of the link. "And how many playmates has Veln, to run with him through the back corridors and explore the ductways?"

"I—two, Cap—Sir. But Timin is lame and not much able in the ducts."

"So—"

"So," a new voice snapped over the link. "Will you surrender, Anjemalti Kristefyon, or will you force your Crew to rip you from your hiding hole?"

"Acting Captain Faztherot," said Anjemalti. "I was just discussing that with my staff. Perhaps we could come to an accommodation."

"Accommodation." Flatly unemotional.

"No dishonor attached to that, is there? You bargain with Grounders as a matter of course—or did, within my lifetime. Surely you recall the way of it?"

The comlink buzzed slightly, but from Mael Faztherot there was no reply.

"No?" said Anjemalti lightly. "Then I will refresh your memory. You provide something that I desire, in return for obtaining something you desire from me. For instance, in this case, you desire me to relinquish control of the life support systems of this vessel and to be gone—permanently. I, on the other hand, am also possessed of a desire to be gone, and find that the care of the life support system grows tedious."

"It would seem that our goals in this—accommodation—are remarkably alike," commented the comlink.

"Ah, you see that! Excellent. Then you will also see that it is to everyone's advantage for the Ship to relinquish *Hyacinth* in full working order so that I, my first mate and my…historian may leave. In return for this, I shall give over control of the life support system and promise never to return to the Ship. My crew will promise likewise."

"An accommodation with some charm to it," said the comlink and Corbinye sat up straight, voiceless in disbelief. "Let us consider whether it covers all points. For it is the Crew's right to dispose of the Grounder woman in—" Over the link's drone came a new sound, slight, quickly muffled, emanating from the ceiling.

"The ducts." Corbinye was on her feet in one smooth motion, chair falling backward with a *thump* as she grabbed his arm, her eyes tracking the sound across the ceiling. "Anjemalti, they are coming through the ducts."

Startlement flicked across his face, then he was up, sweeping the comlink to the floor, spinning to snatch up the Trident. "The Garden, quickly."

But they were there—a line of lean wolf-figures, just within the shadow of the perimeter trees. Anjemalti exhaled a curse.

"The hallway, I suppose?" He glanced down at Corbinye. "Or is there more honor in being trapped like a rat?"

"The hallway," she said, around the hammering of her heart. "They will be there, too, but we must to the open someway. If they drop gas cylinders…"

He looked up at the ceiling, noisy now, as if those who climbed knew their mission was discovered and only haste counted.

"The hallway," he agreed. "Now."

To her amazement, the door slid open to his hand. He stepped through first, and then she, and finally Witness, bearing a torch, his eyes glowing like river agates.

They got as far as the Engineering Corridor, three short halls from the Captain's Rooms. And they were met by no mere ragtag group of subCrew but by Mael Faztherot and Siprian Telshovet and Ardornel Clevryon and three of the mid-rank, all bearing arms. Three of those arms took sight on Anjemalti, who bowed, with no little irony.

"Acting Captain Faztherot. How nice to see you again."

"Rogue Captain Kristefyon. Surrender your weapon and you will be escorted back to your rooms."

"You are kind, ma'am, but in that case I would fear the fate of my companions."

She bowed formally. "Of course. And it is certainly right and honorable that you be allowed to cut the throat of your own servant. We are not barbarians." She flicked a glance at the guards. "Escort Rogue Captain Kristefyon and his servant to the Captain's suite."

Gem sighed. "An incomplete solution, ma'am—forgive me for saying so. The lady you do not acknowledge as Corbinye Faztherot is also my companion and I will not leave her to the mercies of your Crew. Who *are* barbarians."

Mael Faztherot paled under her tan. "As I told you before, Rogue Captain, that—"

"Is not my concern," he finished for her. "But I feel—most strongly—that it *is*—and you might just as well address me as Gem, or Master ser Edreth, you know. 'Rogue Captain' is neither accurate nor flattering."

"That is a Grounder name," Ardornel Clevryon said, flat-voiced with loathing.

"Indeed it is," Gem returned. "And a Grounder is what I am. A Grounder in a Crew body, which must be as blasphemous as one of the Crew wearing a Grounder body—no matter what duty forced upon her." He brought the Trident around and wrapped his hands about it, just behind the branching; leaned forward so that one tine lay against his cheek and looked into Mael Faztherot's eyes.

"What did you expect?" he asked her softly. "*You cast me out.* Made me dead to the Ship. Breathing dead, *I was sold*—to a Grounder, who cared for me and taught me; gave me a life and a name. Who shall I honor as my kin? Whose ways should I chose to follow? Is it sense to exalt the Crew that abandoned me, or to bide by the teaching of Edreth ser Janna, who named me son as he lay dying?"

"Son to a Grounder!" snarled Ardornel Clevryon.

Gem looked at him in mild, sarcastic, surprise. "Son to two Grounders, sir," he said sweetly. "Surely you were aboard Ship when I was born?"

It was too great an insult to be borne. Ardornel snatched at his sidearm, firing even as the Mael Faztherot's arm swept down to prevent the shot.

Corbinye leapt, all her thought to knock Anjemalti aside—and slammed into him, gasping as his arm came hard around her waist and she heard the pellet whine by one ear and strike something close by the other with a resounding *clunk!* and barely had time to understand that one of the guards had also fired, when the energy bolt struck the Trident, which fizzed blue for an instant and then subsided.

Anjemalti's arm loosened and she stepped back, staring at the pellet which was stuck fast to the Trident, just beside the largest ruby. There was silence in the hallway.

"FOOLS and CHILDREN of fools!" The voice reverberated off the metal walls, the floor, the ceiling.

Corbinye craned to see the speaker, and froze in amaze as Witness stepped forward, both arms upraised, the glow from the torch making reddish halos around his head.

"Have you not read your own histories? Have you not meditated upon the prophecies of your Great Ones? There! Written in your own logs is the story, plain enough for a child to cipher—and you call yourselves hunters and made-men! Fools!"

Corbinye drew breath and looked around her, wondering which of them would draw first, and shoot Witness down. But all seemed transfixed, staring at the apparition of him.

"IS IT NOT WRITTEN," demanded the Witness, "that there shall return unto the Ship a Captain, who will lead the Crew back into greatness? Is it not written?"

Astonishingly, there was a mutter of assent from Ardornel.

"Yes," the Witness reiterated, "it IS written. Look about you, blind ones! Is this greatness? Your ship dies around you, backup systems are suspect, there is not sufficient energy for light and forward power both. EVEN THE GARDEN IS DYING! The garden is dying, blind ones, do you hear me? You, who were given the holy task of bringing the green things to the stars—you are failing."

He lowered his arms. "Event throws to you salvation, in the form of the Captain who was foretold—and you strive to kill him! You strive to slay his handmaiden, his partner in the war against event! And even then you behave as children, rather than honorable foes. What would have occurred, should either of those missiles gone wide of the mark?" He turned and pointed at the wall, which also served as the back of the Engineering computer.

"What lies behind this wall?"

There was a stillness among the Crew. Siprian's face was gray.

"You did not think," the Witness concluded, with great sadness. "Well for you, thoughtless ones, that Shlorba's Smiter saw fit to save this Ship, and ate both projectile and energy." He turned abruptly to face Anjemalti and swung his arms out and back, head swinging toward his knees in a sweeping, bird-like bow.

"All hail to Anjemalti the Seeker, Trident Bearer, Chief of the Bindalche, Foretold of the Crew! Best to heed him, and boldly walk in his footsteps, O you who have been blind! Follow him, and do his bidding—or die in the dark between the stars, with the stink of rotting leaves choking you."

"Oh," Anjemalti breathed. "Wonderful."

It was Mael Faztherot who moved first; who drew her weapon and held it in two hands. She stared into Anjemalti's face for what seemed a lifetime to Corbinye, tensed to throw herself into the bolt when it was fired.

But Mael Faztherot did not fire her gun. Instead she bent and laid it with her sorl-blade at Anjemalti's feet before going, awkwardly, to one knee.

"Captain," she said, voice rough with emotion. "Your Crew is ready to be led."

CHAPTER FIFTY-ONE

THAT IT HELD atmosphere proved both the existence of gods and their beneficence. That it sheltered life of any kind was an unlikelihood on the magnitude of miracle. That the life it sheltered still wore more-or-less standard human form and was only slightly insane was either benediction or curse.

Gem leaned carefully back in the rickety command chair and rubbed his eyes. His stomach growled and his back ached, unsubtle reminders of the hours he had spent hunched over the keyboards, forcing information from the ancient, unwilling MainComp.

He should go soon, he thought, half-muzzily. Corbinye would be worried.

He sighed. If only a quarter of the Crew wanted their new Captain dead and rendered to fertilizer, fully one hundred percent felt that fate should be meted immediately to the "Grounder-bitch." No one was sane on this issue, not even Siprian, whom he found in that state most often.

The sum of her vast unpopularity was that Corbinye must stay within the confines of the Captain's Rooms, which were spider-guarded and warded with other engines he and she had devised together. She monitored the construction of the Arachnids from there, which gave her purpose, but Gem could feel her raging frustration as if it were his own.

"Anjemalti," Witness said quietly. "One comes."

"Delightful," Gem returned and came abruptly to his feet, stretching high on his toes, fingers straining toward the metal ceiling. The annunciator sounded as he finished stretching and he snapped down the toggle that opened the door, at the same time laying his hand on the Trident and bringing it up.

The man who stood, hesitant, in the door was short, for Crew, thin even among his slender mates. His hair was more gray than blond; his face tanned into leather, with deep grooves around the eyes. His lips held a firm, straight line, and Gem thought it would take much to make him unseal them, and speak.

But speak he did, quietly, eyes as sane as Crew eyes ever were. "Captain?"

Gem nodded. "The same. And yourself? You're from Engineering?" Engineers were often tanned thus, he had learned—the damned, deteriorating shields...

"No, sir—Atrium," the man said, taking no offense that he had not been recalled. "I'm Finchet. The Gardener."

"Ah." Gem nodded again and sank back into his seat, laying the Trident to hand. "Finchet the Gardener. Enter, please. No use letting the draft in." One of Edreth's phrases, meaningless here. But Finchet's firm mouth bent upward, just a trifle, as he stepped inside and the door slid closed behind him.

He stood at rest, hands clasped loosely behind his back, legs wide. Gem let the silence grow, until he felt Finchet had had sufficient opportunity for study, then he spoke.

"Is there something I can do for you?"

The man considered that, head tipped a little to one side. "Might be you can," he allowed eventually. "Heard from Nav you'd set us a course. Heard from—starwind—you was thoughtful of setting us down."

"Starwind, is it?" Gem considered the gardener gravely. "And you came to relate these rumors to me?"

"Nothing like," Finchet returned. "Figured you'd do as you would with rumor—ignore it, most like, and steer your course. Your mother's way. Uncle's way, too. You'll have noticed that."

"Indeed I have," Gem said. "Why did you come, then?"

Finchet jerked his chin at Witness, sitting quietly in the shadows. "Talk to him says the garden's dying. Never leaves you, so I come tin-side. Hate to. But he says the garden's dying and I'm Gardener. I got my charge. I read the Book. Garden don't die on *me*, begging Captain's grace. Figured man who can see death through all that green, when I can't, who's lived under leaf since weaning—figured that man might tell how to save it, or at least say what's gone wrong."

Clearly this was the longest speech Finchet had made in some time. He shifted a little, bracing his legs, and took a deep breath.

"Well…" Gem started, but—

"You have lost crops," Witness intoned, in his colorless, carrying voice. "Whole species have died out, over the years and years of your wanderings. It is written in the logs. Many no longer seed. Most are altered from what they were. These things are also written. As to the cause of the error…" He paused, looking off into the nothing, as he was wont, until Gem, who was accustomed to it, felt his nerves stretched to screaming.

But Finchet seemed entirely disposed to wait for as long as it took Witness to see his answer and return to convey it.

But when Witness finally did return, it was with a question.

"You have read the old logs?"

"Me?" Finchet seemed genuinely surprised. "Stars love you, man, I'm no Admin. I got the Book, and the notes from the ones before. There's truth in your saying—we've lost variety. But we was meant to lose some variety—or if not meant, it wasn't misexpected. Book says that plain. Old notes kept track of what died. If that's what you're on with, it's true, but not worrisome, see it? But you said the Garden was *dying*. Right now dying—and that's my concern, because I'm Gardener and it's my place to keep green, green."

"A joyous burden," said Witness gravely. "But you have information without perspective—event has seeded you with false complaisance. You feel that nothing shall alter, because nothing has altered. This is a trap. The Garden dies because it does not thrive. The Garden will continue to die until event has been altered."

Finchet frowned, and the silence stretched around him while he struggled to understand. Gem felt a flash of sympathy and was aware again of the passing of time. Corbinye would be—

"I don't doubt you spoke deep, friend. But I'm not Admin, or Tech. Just the Gardener. Might you could take some time from the Captain's side and walk in the green with me? Point out what's wrong. That's what I understand best."

Witness was silent with a finality Gem recognized. He stirred, stood. Finchet looked up, wariness showing on his face.

"No offense meant, Captain. Just trying to do—"

"Your duty," Gem finished gently. "As we all are. The Captain's Rooms overlook the Atrium. Is it possible that the two of you could survey things from the balcony there?"

"Try it, if he's willing," said Finchet without hesitation.

Witness bowed his head and rose. "I will do my best, Gardener. Anjemalti—"

"Yes." He fixed the man with a stern eye. "My rooms and the things or persons you find within my rooms are there by my desire and will. I'll brook no interference from you. Understood?"

Finchet nodded without surprise. "Understood."

"Good," said Gem. "Let's go."

There was reason to suspect the shielded line to the control room, and she misliked calling him where anyone might hear. The less the Crew were reminded of her existence, the longer she would live.

Not that she expected to live to see Spangiln System, much less the groundfall Anjemalti planned upon Bindal. But she intended to live as long as she could, and foolishly calling attention to herself was not consistent with that goal.

The best thing, she decided, was to deploy one of the completed Arachnids, thus reminding Anjemalti of the time at the same moment she reassured herself of his safety.

For the Captain was not safe from his crew, Corbinye thought, not for the first grim time. There were those who would have him dead in an instant—and Mael Faztherot, too, if she sought to protect him.

Chafing at her powerlessness, she called up the grid, located the Arachnid closest to Ship's core and ordered it to the control room immediately. She watched it back toward the cross duct that led to its goal, orient and move off more swiftly. It sent a projected time of arrival—six minutes. Corbinye gritted her teeth and mustered what little patience she could bring to the wait.

The Arachnid had reported four minutes to goal when the door to the Captain's Rooms sounded three rhymed notes. Corbinye flashed to her feet and was half-way across the room before the door opened.

Anjemalti led the way, and Witness brought up the rear. Corbinye froze at the sight of the man in the center.

He turned his head as if he felt her scrutiny and paused just over the door-line, surveying her out of wrinkle-prisoned eyes. She endured it, blank-faced and stiff-shouldered, heart hammering in anticipation of a rejection more hurtful than even her mother's—

Finchet nodded, held out a callused hand in welcome. "Corbinye. Heard about it. Bad luck."

Relief almost brought her to her knees. She mastered herself in time; lifted a hand in returning welcome. "Uncle. Duty done."

"There's that," he allowed. "Come to view the trees. Listen if this fellow can tell me what's dying and what's to be done." He jerked a head at Witness, half-turned and looked back. "You stay vigilant. You get trouble, come to the trees."

Tears threatened to overflow. "Thank you, Uncle," she whispered.

"Nothing to it," he returned Finchet-like, and sent an amused glance to where Anjemalti stood, watchfully holding the Trident. "Not that I think Marjella Kristefyon's son can't keep you safe."

"High praise," murmured Anjemalti and Finchet gave one of his rare smiles.

"Just fact."

Anjemalti returned the smile and gestured with the Trident. "Shall we to the balcony?"

"That tree there, with the jagged branch, you see? And those yellow blooms at the edge. There are clear descriptions of those within the old logs and it seems to me that these are changed out of those descriptions." Witness looked over to where Anjemalti stood, gazing bland-faced across the greenery. Death's Warrior stood at his shoulder, and her gaze did not range so far. Witness felt True Speaking rising in him and locked his tongue, though not before the first word escaped.

"Anjemalti."

"Hmm?" Anjemalti glanced over, eyes sharpening somewhat. "The logs can be made available to you, Gardener, so that you may compare these descriptions yourself. Will that be helpful?"

"Helpful?" Finchet frowned. "Give me a starting point, leastways. If I know for sure how they've altered, then maybe the Book can tell me the fix." He nodded, almost a bow. "Take it kindly, Captain."

"Only doing my duty," Anjemalti returned sweetly, and the Gardener smiled again.

"That's right," he said approvingly. "Might be the best thing for you to have a copy of the Book. Not the usual way. No need for the Captain to know the Gardener's duty. Except times are changing, as your friend here says. Changing too fast for some, might be. And you the one foretold, written down in the Tomorrow Log. Saw it with my own eyes—years ago, when your mother was still thinking we could troth. What's good for the heart isn't always good for the Ship. Saw that in the end. Saw other things. Took that pilot to bed and made a baby with him. Sensible man. Spent a deal of time under leaf. We talked. Nobody else but Marjella would have him near. I missed him, when he left us."

Anjemalti was very still, his eyes hard on the old man's face. "You knew my father?"

Finchet nodded. "Sensible man," he repeated and returned the gaze that threatened to burn through him. "Don't see him in you, truth told. Only the eyes." He paused, looking into those eyes, and turned his away, to stare over the Garden. "Might be the eyes is enough."

"Might be," said Anjemalti softly. "You'll give me a copy of your Book, then?"

"Send the electronic copy to Captain's private line as soon as I get back below. You want the Book itself, you need to get yourself down to the Garden and take it up off the shelf. Corbinye knows my line code. For the log copies."

"I'll make the transfer now," she said, moving away from Anjemalti, though her eyes lingered on the side of his face like caressing fingers. "Particulars?"

"Send all," Witness suggested, "so that he may find his own trail to truth."

Anjemalti looked at her. "Can you do that?"

She nodded, avoiding his eyes. "Of course." She turned to go—

And almost fell over the knee-high, eight-legged, steel-shelled Arachnid, its lantern eyes glowing orange.

Corbinye cursed, caught herself and sidestepped. Finchet gurgled and went for his knife, belatedly recalling the Captain's warning.

"It's only an Arachnid," said that same Captain, mildly, leaning against his gaudy trident.

Finchet sighed. "Certain that it is, begging Captain's grace. And its purpose?"

"We use them to clean the ducts," Corbinye said. "And to do spot repair." She grinned. "They only look that way because we made them out of scrap, Uncle. And they have to be bigger than the others because of the equipment they carry."

"Others?" said Finchet, then showed his palm. "Never mind, girl."

She laughed, and Witness marked how Anjemalti's eyes were led by that sound.

"All right, Uncle," she said, and her voice was very nearly merry. "I'll just make those file transfers then, shall I?"

With that she was gone and the Gardener and Anjemalti bent together over the Arachnid, exploring of this and the other.

Witness leaned back in his corner and considered the Speaking he had not allowed across his tongue and wondered in his secret heart what it was Shlorba's Smiter planned to bring against event.

CHAPTER FIFTY-TWO

"Leave the Ship?" Mael Faztherot stared at him, eyes wider even than Crew eyes usually are.

Gem regarded her with amusement. "It can be done."

"Of course it can," she said sternly. "The question is: Why should we leave? We are the Crew."

He bit back a sharp retort, mindful of the Witness, sitting quiet in his corner.

"Indeed you are the Crew. And unless you relish being Crew of a Ship largely derelict, it may be time for you to become something else."

"We were commanded never to abandon the Ship," she stated flatly and folded her arms across her chest.

Gem considered her. "Now that," he said, matching her tone, "is a falsehood, as I am persuaded you know. The primary directives governing this ship at its launching included a very specific list of planetary conditions to be met before the Ship released passengers and Crew. The name of this Ship, so I learn from the First Log, is: *GenerationShip Five, Class One, Gardenspot.* Built by Dr. Albee K. Messenger and commissioned by the LawCouncil of GriffithPod. Built as a *colony ship,* to bear the L5's surplus citizens to a likely planet and set them down, to live—"

"To live as ground-grubbers?" Mael Faztherot burst out. "To live as animals? That I do not—will not!—believe! *We are the Crew!* The stars belong to us. We are free, why should we be tied to a sphere of dirt, subject to weather, disease, catastrophe and worse! Have you read the Logs? Have you seen the endless lists of planets desolated by war, by sunflare, by plague, pestilence, weather gone awry? Here we are safe from those things. Here we go on as we always have, secure, unfettered—"

"Why are the babies dying?" Gem snapped.

She stared at him, mouth half-open.

"Why?" he cried, unexpectedly savage. "Corbinye's baby was born 'twisted,' dying as it took its first breath. Siprian's daughter died of the same cause. The Log is an unending litany of infants born dead or dying, spontaneous abortions of children too deformed to be brought to term, name after name of those who are no longer fertile." He glared at her, where she stood frozen before him.

"Ten years," he said, every word distinct—a piece of the whole truth that she would grasp the instant she had heard all. "Ten years and how many children? Veln, Jelbi—and Timin, who is lame, and not much use in the ducts." He stared at her and came slowly to his feet, using the Trident as a lever.

"Where is your safety, Mael Faztherot?"

She swallowed hard; and it was to her credit that she did not give deck, but stayed where she was, well within a Trident-thrust.

"There are fewer children than before," she said, voice barely shaking. "There are misformed births. Infertility. A groundfall, denial of our heritage, will not mend these things. The Ship is old. If we must die, then let us die Crew."

He shook his head. "The Ship is killing you. The shields are rotten. Infrastructure precarious, at best. Entire primary systems are missing. Backups for the systems that remain might as well not exist. The Ship you cling to shreds even as you grasp it. Release your hold and reach for something else." He closed his eyes, opened them with a wrenching effort.

"Veln, Jelbi and Timin will be the last. Unless massive repairs are undertaken, the Ship may hold together another twenty years. May. Can you choose suicide for them, as well as for yourself?"

She licked her lips, but her eyes were steady on his. "We are the Crew," she said, with no hint of hysteria. "Bred for the stars, from stock which had been Grounder, five generations in *their* past. After these hundreds of years, how can we be Grounder?" She sat, looking as weary as he felt, and stared up at him.

"You ask if I can condemn them to die with a dying Ship. I ask if *you* can condemn them to die in an alien place, with dirt in their mouths and the laughter of enemies in their ears."

Too true, thought Gem suddenly, and the weariness seemed like to overwhelm him and leave him in a swoon at her feet. Too true, indeed. I would certainly have died, if not for Edreth, who was so desperate for an heir he took a mad barbarian to himself and tried with superhuman patience to make the barbarian sane.

He looked at Mael Faztherot, sitting slumped under the weight of her knowledge, leaned his cheek against the Trident's tine, felt the metal score his cheek and said, "Where are the others?"

She frowned. "Others?"

"The other GenerationShips out of GriffithPod. *Gardenspot* was fifth in a class of thirty-six. Where are the other Ships?"

"Surely it's in there?" She waved a hand at the computer bank, meaning the Logs encrypted and carried within. Then she slumped further in her chair and ran shaking fingers through her short hair. "No," she corrected herself. "All the Logs say is that we had lost contact with this one, with that. But we only knew eight others. How to be certain thirty-six were even built? Shall we return to GriffithPod to ask?"

But Gem had read of the fruitless search for GriffithPod a double century ago. He grinned at her, acknowledging the joke. "No need to bother them."

She gave a bark of laughter. "Not at this remove," she agreed, then sobered and shook her head. "Though it would be pleasant, if they could but build us another ship."

The words were like an electric jolt, coursing through his veins, igniting his mind. His fingers tightened until they were white-knuckled, gripping the Trident as if it alone could hold him against the force of the plan, the beautiful plan, unfolding with preternatural precision before his mind's eye.

"Captain?" Mael Faztherot was on her feet, hand out-stretched, a certain wariness on her face—he was aware of her, but the plan required all his attention, whispered as it seemed to be directly into his ear, whole, perfect, intensely beautiful. He listened and watched and a far part of him wondered, unheeded, just where the lines ran, between deception and salvation.

"Captain!" She came a step forward, purposefully—

"Touch him not!" commanded Witness from his corner. "Anjemalti the Seeker communes with the Smiter."

"Communes—?" asked Mael Faztherot, as well she might, and turned toward the Witness; Gem saw the hot words forming on her tongue. "Communes with—that? How—"

"A ship," Gem said and both Witness and First Mate turned to stare at him. "Another ship." He looked deep in the woman's eyes, his own hypnotic and blue. "Another ship can be had, Mael Faztherot. Is this the Crew to take it?"

"Take?" She fairly goggled. "We are not pirates."

"But The Combine is," he said, leaning toward her against the anchoring Trident. "I know where there is a ship—several ships! It needs only valor to win them. Keep the stars! Become a fleet! The Crew need not die. Fate can reverse itself. Expand the gene-pool, become fruitful…" He straightened.

"The Combine?" she said doubtfully.

"Why not?" He returned. "What right has The Combine to restrict the Ship's trade, ban it from certain systems—which it has done! The Combine owns good ships, fast ships. None so large as this, perhaps—but ships."

He had her. Her eyes gleamed and the corners of her mouth turned up in a rapacious smile. "Indeed they do. Indeed. Let me put it to the Crew. But I think they will be—interested."

"Good," said Gem and nodded her dismissal, which is how it happened that he failed to see the Witness smile.

CHAPTER FIFTY-THREE

IT WAS DAMP under the trees; dimly green, smelling of humus, live leaf and mint. Gem paused on the stone-lined pathway, closed his eyes and tipped his face up, as if there were sun above him, instead of tree-tips and, beyond, the pearlescent shine of the dome.

"That's right," Finchet said comfortably. "Forest is the best spot in all the Garden, ask me. Hundred Acre Wood, the Book names it. Taken from another, older book."

"Ah," Gem smiled; looked at the old gardener. "And is it a hundred acres?"

"Maybe half that in wood," Finchet answered. "There's the farm and the bogland and the paddy-field to make the rest up—hundred-twenty acres, so the Book says." He cocked an eyebrow. "Acre's a unit of measure—forty-three thousand, five hundred sixty square feet. Got a unit stick up the house, if you care to spec it."

Gem grinned. "I believe I'll reserve crawling over a hundred and twenty acres with a ruler for an afternoon when I'm a bit less pressed for time."

"Well enough," returned the Gardener and moved back onto the pathway, keeping his eye carefully away from the third member of their party, moving almost silent on its hideous long legs.

The path curved, rose slightly to go over a stream, ran along a field of fern, through an avenue of wide-girthed, ancient trees and finally into a clearing.

The clearing rose in a smooth sweep of silky grass, up to a cottage built of stone, its overhanging roof of green-painted wood, pierced at one end by a stone chimney. The door set into the stone front wall was arched and painted red, except for the pane of yellow glass set high inside it.

Gem stopped. Finchet stopped. The Arachnid stopped. After a moment, Gem sighed.

"Charmingly done, Gardener."

"Cozy, I admit it, and just what I'm used to, having lived here all my life. But don't be thinking it's my plan now, Captain. Gardener's cottage was set at GriffithPod, same as with the sheds 'round back and the utility buildings at the farm."

"I see," said Gem, and then said no more, merely looking at the cottage and the little glade and the tall trees all around, protective and comforting.

Finchet shifted a little, he who had the habit of stillness, and put out a hand to touch the Captain's sleeve. "Happen you'll wish to see the bank," he said diffidently.

Gem sighed, recalled to a sense of his duties and the critical shortness of time. "Doubtless you're right," he said, and set his feet on the cobbled path to the door.

He stepped aside and let Finchet open the door and lead the way within.

The cottage was one spacious room, furnished with hand-made wooden furniture, the few chairs made more inviting with pillows and roughly sewn cushions. Strings of wild garlic, onions, rosemary and parsley hung from the rafters; wood was neatly stacked by the hearth and a bright woven rug covered the worn stones there.

Under a large window was a table bearing a small comp and keyboard, several lamps, and a large, leather-bound volume.

Finchet walked over and laid his hand on this. "The Book," he said reverently, then moved on, waving Gem past the tidy bedstead to the far back of the room.

Set in the backmost wall was a control board and piloting screens, various telltales glowing amber among the mica-washed stones.

Gem sat carefully in one of the two standard-issue pilot's chairs, staring, great-eyed, at the board.

Finchet sat in the other chair and folded his hands on his lap.

Eventually, Gem bestirred himself and put aside the wonder of it, pushed the sleeve back and tapped certain commands into his wristcomp.

A spider, pretty and dainty as any found in the wood, minced down his arm and across his bridging hand, vanishing into the control board.

Finchet sighed. "Now, those," he said. "They're right handsome."

Gem sent him an amused glance. "But you don't find the others so pretty?"

"Not by half," Finchet said stoutly, though he couldn't help but look over his shoulder, to where the Arachnid loomed just behind the chairs, eyes like lanterns, claws like hedge-shears.

"They have their uses," Gem said. "And soon to have more, which is why we're building so many." He shook his head. "The mercy is that they're so very easy to build, compared to the smaller ones."

"Aye? But you'll be needing more of the little tykes, as well, to set this plan of yours moving."

Gem nodded. "A problem, given the scarcity of resources the Ship possesses. The only hope was to upgrade the juniormost—install enhanced chips, upload more complex programs." He touched several studs on his bracelet; looked up.

"The weak point in the plan is the small number of spiders we are able to field. I don't like to attach more than two Arachnids to an upgraded spider and even Number Fifteen can hardly be asked to control more than three, and fulfill his own tasks as well..."

He fiddled again with the studs at his wrist. "The control unit I'm building for Mael Faztherot will necessarily take up some of the details the spiders cannot attend to." He shook his head once more and looked up, sadness etching his face. "They were never meant for war, poor things."

Finchet was saved the necessity of responding to this by a muted chime. Gem bent to his wristcomp; nodded.

"As I thought, Gardener—entirely usable. If you will help me with the access panel, we will let the Arachnid within to do such cleaning and preventive work as may be necessary and I'll be on my way." He sent a bright glance at Finchet's face. "Unless you would prefer not to be left alone with the Arachnid?"

Finchet laughed. "Gods love you—I'd only rather not see it—I've no fear of it!" He sobered. "Beside that, the little tyke will be here, won't he, to supervise?"

Gem smiled and stood, heading for the access hatch set low in the corner of the wall. "Indeed he will, Gardener. No fear for that." He turned suddenly.

"You have the training, do you, Finchet? Who is your second?"

The old man bent to the hatch, twisting the holding nuts with strong fingers. "I've had the drills," he said calmly. "Practice them once a seven-shift since the day I came nine. As for co-pilot—I'll have young Veln, if you're willing. He's as close as I have to a 'prentice in these days when we're thin of children."

Together, they lifted the hatch aside and stood back to let the Arachnid enter the service tunnel. Gem nodded and turned to go.

"Veln it is," he said. "I'll send him to you now and have you keep him here, if there's room. Drill him—and start him on learning the Book."

"He's had some of that," said Finchet, walking with him to the door. "I'll move him more serious, if that's your wish. And there's plenty of room. Blanket roll in the closet there— Veln thinks it an adventure to sleep out on the grass."

Gem stepped into the glade and glanced around him, drawing in a deep breath of wood-tanged air. "Lucky Veln," he said softly and nodded to the old man. "Take good care."

"Yourself as well, lad," Finchet said, and stood at the door, watching, until the path turned and his Captain was lost from view.

CHAPTER FIFTY-FOUR

IT WAS A slow shift on the InRing.

Milt Jinkins sighed and stretched, leaning far back in the contoured chair. Before him the scan ran, tirelessly, endlessly, filling dials and screens with infinite bits of information, building a second-by-second picture of Spangiln System that invariably showed empty, empty, empty.

Not strictly true, Milt told himself, settling more comfortably in his chair. There were five more Combine blockade ships within sublight scan; a dozen more inside bounce-scan range; twice that within so-called "shouting distance." Though it did, Milt thought, get a tad tedious talking to the Outriders. Lagtime tended to make a hash out of any extended conversation, unless you were an old-timer and fluent in doubletalk.

Milt had only been riding blockade for a Standard Year. His partner, Ria, had been an Outrider for six times that long and before that, when she was Milt's age—but faster, so she said—a hyperspace pilot for The Combine. Ria spouted doubletalk effortlessly and had the trick of keeping two independent conversations going at the same time so ingrained that she spoke that way realtime, to Milt's initial confusion and frustration.

It was growing on him, though. Milt thought that in another six months he'd be good enough at doubletalk to try it out on the Outrider circuit. Maybe even—

"What the shit is that?" He demanded, eyes bugging at the forward screen in the instant before he slapped the warning toggle, opened up the spill-line and sent the image and the zany readings to the next ship in line. He had just zipped and fired the same information to the Big Ship, far beyond the Outriders' ring, when Ria hit the assistant's chair, fingers dancing over the comm keys, twitching, tuning—

searching. And all the while, her eyes were on the image in the forward screen.

"GenShip," she said, not looking at Milt. "Comm lines'll be old system. Saw another once. Radio, maybe. It was dead. This one, too—no."

No, Milt echoed silently. Static sputtered over their line, blaring as Ria missed the match, then astonishingly clear as she found it and locked.

"Attention, all hands," the woman's voice was cold, efficient. "This is not a drill. All Crew will prepare to abandon ship. Technical staff, initiate system shutdown. Pilots, engage lifeships. This is not a drill. Crew assigned to Level Seven will report to Bays One, Three, Five. This is not a drill. Level Six evacuation commences in fifteen minutes. Level Seven pilots signal readiness. All Crew, all Crew. This is not a—"

"Drill." Ria touched the tuner and skipped to the next band, this one a chaos of voices that reminded Milt of an Outrider conversation. "Techs," Ria said, and, "Sounds bad."

It did sound bad. Milt's half-trained ear picked out grim-sounding phrases: "...mother system down...lost contact...Engineering...main computer sluggish..." And, abruptly, one whole, telling sentence: "...power shunt, damn you! I want everything you've got on those Bay doors!"

Ria made adjustments; touched a speak-stud. "This is Combine Ship three-three-six in blockade of Spangiln System. This system is interdicted. Repeat, this system is under Combine interdiction. Touch down at your peril."

"I've peril enough!" That was the cold-voiced woman, shockingly plain. "We're abandoning Ship, Grounder, do you understand that? Talk to me of peril when my folk are safe."

Ria nodded, as if she'd expected nothing else, and twitched the dial again. The evacuation instructions murmured on as background, just loud enough to tweak attention, if an important phrase were spoken. Ria fiddled with the auxiliary line; pegged the techs and let that one run, too. Milt frowned. Could the woman really follow *that* many conversations at once?

"Well," said the woman, "we gave 'em their warning. You zipped a bag for the big ship?" That wasn't really a question, Milt knew, so he kept quiet, listening to her talk to herself.

"Outriders'll scan the lifepods; us'll scan the worlds." She leaned back in her chair and finally looked at him, the lines of her face snagging shadows. "Lot of salvage," she said, "in a GenShip."

Milt blinked at her. "Salvage?"

"Ours by right," said Ria; "shared equal with the rest of the InRing. Tapes'll show who saw her first. Might be us; I didn't hear any shadow chatter—" another old spacer's trick; one Milt felt uncomfortable believing in. "If we pegged her first, we get an extra share." She showed her teeth in a grin. "Kill fee."

"Salvage," he repeated, looking at the screen, seeing the sheer size of the ship, adding up the profit in the metal alone, not to mention whatever system components there were, weapons—He started.

"First pod's out!" he snapped; then, "Second! Third! I— those are *lifepods?* They're almost as big as us!"

"GenShips," said Ria wisely, twiddling various dials, picking up and losing the voices of pilots, calm and businesslike, talking coordinates and vector and relative mass.

"Looking to go out-system," Ria said. "Good. No trouble for us. Just wait 'til they're gone, then latch the ship, set our beacons…"

"What if it blows up?"

She looked at him pityingly. "You've got a grab-board," she said. "Ride it."

Irritably, he called up his remote-scans, broke a moment to acknowledge receipt of ancillary information from Syn, passed by voice-link from halfway 'round the InRing, then swore as the GenShip's codes kept breaking.

"GenShip codes'll be old," Ria said softly and he bit his lip to keep the swearing inside, went all the way down the scale to the edge of tech—and matched, all systems.

He was still riding the scanners when the second wave of lifepods broke loose and fled the mother ship, pilot voices reiterating transition coords and rendezvous points.

Just before the fourth wave went, he pulled out of the scan and leaned back, looked over to find Ria fielding skip-calls and voice-link.

"Aye," she said, to one of them, fingers flickering across the controls. "Coded and sent. Three-three-six out. Dez, we got another wave going out. Far as we scan, they're all for outsystem. My partner's on the grab-scan—Yeah? Okay. We trade when he finishes up. Five ticks. Out." She leaned back and grinned at him. "What find?"

Milt moved his shoulders. "Massive systems failure, as far as I can tell. Engines are banked. Life support's a mess. Shielding leaks. Something funny in the drives—like the translation engine went out."

"Old," said Ria, and grinned again. "We have salvage right Okayed by the big ship. Tapes show we get the kill fee. Dez wants to swap grab-scan data. Whenever you're ready."

"Sure," he said, and leaned back over the board.

CHAPTER FIFTY-FIVE

"WILL THEY TAKE the bait?" Corbinye demanded as *Hyacinth* tumbled free of the Ship.

Anjemalti glanced over from the co-pilot's chair. "A fortune in salvage, hanging, empty, before them?"

"Empty…" she sighed.

"Regrets, Corbinye?"

She toyed with the trajectory setting, frowned at the counter. "We're coming to the first mark," she said, instead of an answer, for the piloting took precedence. Anjemalti nodded and took over his end of the business and together they wove *Hyacinth* through the tricksy bit of piloting and skimmed her clean and sweet into the shadow of the third planet and out from Combine scrutiny.

"Unless," Corbinye muttered, "they have eyes to see through the planet image and pick us out…"

"And guns to blow us apart, or beams to capture us," Anjemalti finished mockingly. He glanced up as she turned the chair, and caught her eyes with his. "Needless worry. The Combine will not see us."

"You sound very certain. Do I believe The Combine blind, deaf and stupid?"

He shrugged. "Sufficient to believe in spiders. And Arachnids."

"And in Anjemalti," Corbinye said resignedly, "who always will be tinkering among the gadgets…"

Unexpectedly, he laughed, eyes bright with delight. "Finchet knows what to do?"

She looked sour. "So he says. If his Book is written by the same prescient who foretold yourself—"

"Then the universe looks to being changed in substance," he concluded, working with this and that on his side of the board. "Which brings us around to the Witness' view of things. Refreshing, when prophecies align."

"Well for you to say so," she said irritably. "Excepting only that the Tomorrow Log foretold you would return the Crew to greatness! Instead, we have the lifeboats spilling out in all direction; Grounders looking to take the Ship for salvage—" She bit her lip. "What is the Crew without a Ship, Anjemalti? What sort of Captain, foretold or elect, leaves his folk alone in such a venture, while he hares off to solve the problems of those who are no kin to him, who are Grounders—and mad beside!"

There was no laughter in the blue eyes now. "Madness, as Edreth taught me, is a relative term. If the Bindalche seem mad to the Crew, how much more demented must the Crew seem to the Bindalche? Ask the Witness. If you dare. As for aiding folk who are none of mine—who is? Edreth is dead. Shilban is dead. Linzer is dead." He closed his eyes in a grimace almost of pain and Corbinye bit her lip, found her hand stretching toward his and snatched it back.

"I have set things in motion—ill deeds have been spawned from my actions," Anjemalti said slowly. "I strive to amend that which I have put awry. The Trident is restored to potency. I will return it and the Witness to the Bindalche, who will then be able to choose a new champion and—gods willing—vanquish the Vornet." He opened his eyes, and Corbinye's heart quailed at the depth of weariness in them.

"Of the other—the Ship was killing the Crew, and they have been encouraged to leave—to gamble for life rather than bending their necks to death. What more would you have me do for the Crew, when I find them as strange and as mad as you find the Witness?"

She had no idea what she meant to answer him; only knew that she had begun to speak.

The bell rang, signaling the second mark, and they spun their chairs at the same moment, fingers snapping toggles, minds on the necessities of piloting, and all the words they spoke for some time had to do with that.

Witness for the Telios sat in the Smiter's Center, his eyes half-closed and dreamy, his secret heart quiescent, his mind ablaze with trance.

Into the trance *She* came—Slayer of God, Mother of the Bindalche, Trident Bearer—terrible and holy. With Her hands, She raised him up and carried him out, beyond the pitiful walls of metal. Out into the blackness of the void She bore him, the stars about Her feet like dust, Her body enclosing worlds. Onto one such world She set him and he stood upon the pinnacle of Brother Mountain and looked out over the world of his birth.

But it was not, after all, the world as he had left it, the world as he had always known it—withered, sand-dry, gasping. No. This land that stretched out from horizon to horizon was green and moist and wholesome, with the silvery threads of rivers, the mirroring of ponds and lakes, glittering here and there within the tapestry. The smell of growing things came into his nostrils and his mouth tasted of young leaf.

Witness for the Telios stared out over this green and luscious land and knew that he was seeing future, not Memory. He fell to his knees on the rocks of Brother Mountain and stretched out his arms to the sky.

Mother, he cried. *What has happened to my land?*

The Goddess laughed and the mountain trembled and Witness for the Telios was afraid.

Mother, he cried again. *I am commanded to Witness fully, to recall rightly. You yourself chose this work for me and took my name in surety. Is it meet that you laugh at my questions?*

IMPERTINENCE. Her voice went through his head like needles and he closed his eyes in agony. TELL MY PRESENT LOVER HE PLEASES ME WELL. TELL HIM: EVENT TREMBLES.

And that was all, except the searing blast of blackness and the sickening spin of stars and the scrape of metal as he plummeted through the ship's hull and smashed back into his body.

He lay flat on his back on the cold metal floor, lungs laboring, tasting sweat—or blood—on his lips, smelling the stink of his own fear. His private heart was wailing, there in its solitude, shamed to find such terror in one long named a man. He had pity on that man, now nameless, and brought up a Memory of an earlier Witness, one of those most revered by the Telios. Upon returning from a sojourn with the Goddess, that one had bit and clawed until it became necessary to forcibly restrain her from harming herself and others. She was thus restrained for a period of days, until the madness passed and she recalled herself and her duties.

To speak to the Goddess is no easy thing, Witness for the Telios told his private heart. *No shame can be attached to fear, when the very eldest of the Telios tremble and hide themselves from Her face.*

His secret heart somewhat soothed, Witness came stiffly to his feet. In its Center, Shlorba's Smiter gleamed and vibrated illusions of What If. Witness bowed before it, fingers touching eyes, ears, mouth, breast. He straightened, aching in every joint, and looked down at himself. The knees of his buckskins were muddy and scuffed, smeared with grass stains. The palms of his hands were scored, as if he had fallen, and caught himself against rock.

He bowed again to the Smiter. "Mother," he murmured and went back to his place of watching, where he sat and composed himself for duty.

CHAPTER FIFTY-SIX

IT WAS DIM in the grotto and Saxony Belaconto took a deep breath of warm air. The walk from the ship across the strip of baking earth had parched her; the hint of moisture within the grotto soothed abused nose and throat membranes.

She blinked several times to clear her vision, then turned her head to frown at the man beside her.

"You'd better be convincing this time."

The heat had not treated Jarge Menlin kindly. Nor had the Vornet, in the days he been in custody. Who could have known, Saxony Belaconto thought, not for the first time, that Jarge had such a skill at hiding? For more than a week he had eluded the Vornet's best efforts, while Saxony Belaconto's patience, already frayed, frazzled and finally tore.

When even the noisy capture of his overindulged mistress had failed to bring Jarge to heel, Belaconto had begun to believe him mastermind of an elaborate plot in which Gem ser Edreth was merely a pawn—a vehicle for the deliverance of her death.

Except that she had not died, though others had done so, and still others come close. It would have been enough, if Jarge had moved quickly, decisively—but the second, killing, blow did not come. Instead, Jarge went into hiding and Gem ser Edreth fled the planet, with Trident and operator and barbarian cousin.

And, eventually, Jarge Menlin was found.

"How the hell," he said now, "am I supposed to be convincing, when it's the Trident they want, and not me?" He mopped a dangerously red face with a soiled white kerchief and glared at her, small eyes half-mad with desperation. "Didn't you listen to what the chief said?" he demanded. "They don't care about me, or you, or the damn' thief. All they care about is the Trident and the guy who watches it."

"Then they will at least learn to care about me," she snapped, "and about the power of that ship out there."

Menlin sighed gustily and then hastily bowed, groaning with the effort it caused him.

The aged, sticklike figure in faded green robes did not bow. It merely stood in an attitude of patient attentiveness until Jarge Menlin had straightened once more.

"Good sun," it said then, its voice soft and sexless. "Who comes to the Grotto of the Telios?"

"Jarge Menlin," he said huskily and cleared his throat, "Trident-bearer. And Saxony Belaconto."

"Where is the Trident, O Seeker?" the Gatekeeper questioned, with neither mockery nor heat. As if, thought Saxony Belaconto, they had not stood here for three consecutive days, going through exactly the same routine.

"Safely kept," Jarge returned, as he always did. "Is it possible to speak with the Telios?"

"Many things are possible, O Seeker."

Jarge gritted his teeth. "I want to see the Telios," he said, voice suddenly harsh. "Now. No more fooling around."

This was a slight departure from the script. If the Gatekeeper noticed, it gave no sign; certainly it did not deviate from its own lines.

"I will carry your message within. Please await me."

What would follow now—based on the experience of the last three days—was the return of the Gatekeeper, regretting in monotone that the Seeker could not be conducted within. They would be invited to return when their petition had reached fullness. Whatever that meant.

Saxony Belaconto closed her eyes, thinking of the Vornet and all of those who waited upon it—uneasy allies all too ready to turn wolves, should the Vornet be seen to falter.

"We go through it," she said, barely recognizing her own voice. "Today, we don't take 'no' for an answer."

Menlin nodded and mopped at his face, which was no longer red, but gray. He licked his lips, as if he would say something.

The Gatekeeper reappeared.

"The Seeker and his companion will be seen," it announced without emphasis. "Follow my steps, if you will."

It took Saxony Belaconto a moment to understand that they were being admitted without a fight—and she nearly had to run to catch up with Menlin and the Gatekeeper.

The air grew cool, cooler—nearly cold. The Gatekeeper walked on and on, following a corridor of rock that twisted this way and that. After five minutes, Saxony stopped.

"Where are you taking us?" she demanded.

The Gatekeeper walked on, pace undisturbed. Jarge Menlin cleared his throat.

"I—please, umm. Gatekeeper. My—we wonder where you are taking us."

The sticklike figure turned around. "You asked to be seen and your request was granted. You are shown to the Chamber of Viewing."

"It seems a long way," Jarge persisted. "Do you need to walk so far, when you go to announce us?"

Almost the Gatekeeper smiled. It did raise its hands, tracing a complex sign in the air. "When one has grown old and understood much, there are other ways to go, aside walking. This way." It turned again and plodded off, Jarge Menlin following.

After a moment Saxony Belaconto followed, as well. Seething.

The Chamber of Viewing curved away into vastness, its roof and sidewalls shrouded black, center brilliant with torches.

The Gatekeeper left them in that center, standing on the cold stone floor, and vanished into shadow.

From the left, five figures filed out of the dark, each shrouded in green robes, hoods pulled up to conceal five faces, hands tucked deep into wide sleeves.

Silent, they came across the stone, lined up opposite Belaconto and Menlin and turned as one to face them. No word was spoken.

Jarge Menlin cleared his throat. "I am the one who came and took the Trident away. I am here to claim my tithe of hesernym, which the chief in the valley will not give me."

The figures rustled as if a strong breeze had blown through their ranks—steadied. Several heads turned, several pairs of eyes peered from hooded faces.

One of the figures stepped forward, turned its head so that its hidden eyes seemed to stare at Saxony Belaconto, then at Jarge Menlin. The figure turned and walked away, down room, to the edge of the torchlight...

"Let's go," hissed Menlin and went after, and Saxony Belaconto again followed, trying to ignore the prickling between her shoulder blades.

The hall bent twice in crazy succession, then opened into yet another room, this smallish. The chill air was warmed by a tiny fire in the pit at the room's center. The stone floor was soft with rugs and tapestries and pillows. There were several low tables here and there among the cushions; one held a samovar, another a tray of fruits, yet another, a jug and several glass beakers.

Their guide slid long hands free of copious sleeves and neatly laid the hood back about her shoulders. She looked gravely at Jarge Menlin and bowed, with astonishing reverence.

"Please," she said, "be seated."

Jarge did so, half-falling onto a pile of pillows. Saxony Belaconto settled more gracefully, keeping her legs coiled under her, ready for the springing of the trap.

"Refreshment?" the woman asked Jarge. "Tea, or wine? Fruits?"

Fruits. Saxony considered the tray; perfectly formed, perfectly colored apples and peaches—the mark of a hydroponic garden. Was there a hydroponic plant within this vast cavern, she wondered. How advanced were these Bindalche, anyway? Once, she had misjudged a person, a situation. Never again would she make the mistake she had made with Gem ser Edreth.

"Wine," Jarge was telling the woman and Saxony looked up to find the reddish eyes on her.

"Wine," she rasped and the woman bowed with serene courtesy. She moved to the table that held the jug and poured from it into two beakers. The first went to Jarge. The second came to Saxony Belaconto. This hostly commission dispatched, the woman sank gracefully to a cushion opposite and turned her grave, ageless face to Jarge.

"In the Room of Viewing it is not permitted to speak," she said. "The message the Gatekeeper delivered was that you wished to see the Telios, rather than you wished to speak to one of the Telios. No doubt an error in translation. Here you may be comfortable, and speak what is in your heart."

Jarge hastily swallowed a gulp of wine. "Umm—thank you. Not the Gatekeeper's fault—I believe I did ask to see the Telios—not a precise speaker. Apologies…" Saxony shifted on her cushion and his eyes were on her instantly, his damp and more than a little crazed.

"We've come," she prompted him, with awful patience, "about the tithe."

"Yes," he agreed breathlessly, "about the hesernym tithe." He looked back at the woman. "The chief in the valley refuses me my portion, even though I was the one claimed the Trident—you know that, you were there. All the Telios were there."

"Recalled," the woman said, "that you were Chosen of the Smiter. Recalled, that in your company the Smiter did take to the stars. Recalled, that you asked of us a certain number of the tremillan flowers." She folded her hands carefully in her lap and looked earnestly into his face. "All recalled, with honor and with respect, Jarge Menlin, Trident-Chosen."

"Well, that's fine," Jarge looked gratified and had another deep draught of the wine. The woman rose silently and refilled his beaker, then returned to her seat. Jarge swallowed more wine and leaned forward.

"Then you'll tell the chief down below to release the tithe to me and to my—associate—so we can get about our business."

"Ah." The woman looked over at Saxony, a world of pity in her eyes. She returned her gaze to Jarge. "Where is the Trident, Jarge Menlin? Where is the one who is Shlorba's Eyes and Memory?"

He cleared his throat. "In a safe place, both of them. It's a dangerous universe, you know, and I'm a man with—with enemies. Seemed best to just tuck them away safe, where no enemies could find them."

"I see," she said, still grave, still courteous. "But coming so, there is no assurance that the Smiter chooses still to be with you. It is possible, Jarge Menlin, always possible, that the Smiter has chosen another—no lack of honor to yourself."

"Chosen another—" he blinked and the woman bowed her head, then turned to speak to Saxony.

"This happens, of times. We will care for him, if you want it. If there is no other place where he will be kept with honor and with safety. To bear Shlorba's Smiter is a great thing, a heavy thing. It is not unknown that the loss of the burden makes the former Chosen foolish—as a child, and forgetful."

Saxony considered that, what little seemed to make sense. "You'll take care of Jarge?" she said, carefully. "And render him—honor?"

"Assuredly," the woman said, with a soft, sad smile.

"And," Saxony said cautiously, "the hesernym?"

The woman shook her head. "The hesernym was the tithe named by Shlorba's Chosen," she said softly, as one explaining an immutable force of the universe. "There is no tithe due those deserted of the Smiter. Only care is due them, and honor, and peace."

Saxony sipped the appallingly bad wine, considering, feeling Jarge's eyes on her, feeling his wordless shriek: *Don't leave me here! Don't—*

She sipped again, considering the weight of the gun beneath her arm, the timing…

The timing stank.

She forced a smile and nodded at the woman. "I appreciate your—help. Your clarification of my friend's status. I will have to consult with others—tell them what you have said. If I may come again, to tell you what has been decided?"

The woman bowed from her seat upon the cushion. "Come again two suns from now, at the same time. The gatekeeper will expect you." She rose, effortlessly, and bent to offer a hand to Jarge.

"Come now," she said softly, as if he were a biddable child. "It is time to go back out to your ship and attend the counsel of your friends." Jarge climbed to his feet and let her take the glass away from him and clap her hands together sharply, twice.

The Gatekeeper appeared in the stone archway.

"Show Jarge Menlin and his friend to the Supplicant's Gate," she directed and raised her hands to pull her hood into place.

"Yes," said the Gatekeeper, and, "Follow my steps."

And so they did, all the weary way up until they stood in the hot entranceway, blinking out into the afternoon sun.

CHAPTER FIFTY-SEVEN

THE LAST LIFEPOD had broken free of the GenShip and headed out-system. Data had been traded 'round the InRing, analyzed and, finally, accepted.

When the consensus was reached—when every pilot on the ring acknowledged the GenShip was empty—then Milt and Ria moved in to set the beacons.

"Why here?" Milt asked as they launched the first marker and watched it settle into sympathetic orbit around the big ship.

"Why here what?" Ria returned.

"Why abandon it here, where there's nothing except a Combine blockade and three interdicted worlds? What were they *doing* here?"

Ria shrugged, busy with the equation for the second launch. "GenShips go where they want," she said, speaking linearly for a change. "GenShip crews're star-scarred—crazier'n ore pilots. If they had a reason, it wasn't sensible—believe it. Might've just been on their way someplace else. GenShips're *old*. Limited ability for sustained translation."

"So they dropped out of hyperspace for a rest and then noticed that the ship was in bad shape—dammit, there's nothing redlined on this ship! Nothing they probably haven't known about for months!"

Ria locked in the equation. "Let 'er loose," she said and he did. The second beacon wobbled a bit and seemed to have trouble orienting.

Milt was reaching for the remote when he heard Ria inhale, air hissing through her teeth—"What the nub—?"

"It's breaking up!" he yelled, hands already moving across the board, sending them into a tumble away from the GenShip while he squealed a warning to Dez and the rest of the InRing and the board under his hands was showing red and Ria was taking care of that part, shunting systems and closing out nonessentials…

Above them, in the looming bulk of the GenShip, the bubble of what he had thought was an observation room continued to rock back and forth, sending cables and sheets of shielding spinning free. With one final, gargantuan heave, it broke completely free, sending a meteor-storm of ship-metal scattering toward the InRing.

Free, it fell. *Fell* toward Bindal, like a meteor itself.

Milt hit the magnification and swore, softly and with dis-belief. Beside him, Ria was quiet.

He zipped the image and hurled it at the Big Ship, half-hoping that one of the brass would tell him that there were no *trees* in that falling bubble…

They landed on a baked strip of rock some small distance from a huddle of dun-colored tents and scraggled trees. Corbinye rolled out last and stood between Anjemalti and Witness, squinting. She could feel the moisture being sucked out of her pores and the glare of the sun upon her unpro-tected head was fearful.

"Well…" Anjemalti murmured. "I think, my friend, that it is time for you to lead."

Witness raised his hand and drew one of his incompre-hensible patterns in the harsh air.

"Lead is what I may not do. It is for the Trident and the Bearer of the Trident to forge the way through event. It is mine merely to follow—and recall."

"A hard enough task," said Anjemalti, and coughed. He motioned toward the tents with the Trident. "What place is that?"

"The camp of Ven kelBatien Girisco—a young chief, scrupulous in her dealings. She bides near the Telios by choice and invitation rather than through transgression. An honor.

Her folk are gatherers. It is they who harvest the tremillan flowers and render it to hesernym."

"Flowers—" Corbinye looked around at the frying earth. "Hard to believe flowers grow here."

Witness looked at her gravely. "Before the Combine's sacrilege, the land was lush: Grain, fruit, game were plentiful. The land sobs for water now, and labors to put forth sufficient sustenance for the Bindalche, caretakers of the land. Event has moved the Combine into grievous error."

"The Combine needs no help," Corbinye told him, "to find grievous error. Or to rejoice in doing harm."

"I don't know about the rest of this ship's company," Anjemalti interrupted, "but I am being cooked. Before I become half-baked, I suggest a move toward yon village and perhaps a chat with the chief." He glanced at Corbinye. "The sooner we return the Trident, the sooner we may embrace air-cooling."

"And other business," she agreed, matching his stride toward the tents.

Witness came one step after, his private heart exultant in the return to the homeworld.

Long before they reached the tents, a woman had come from the center of them and stood waiting on the edge of their meager shade, hands held empty before her, buckskin-cased legs braced wide. Her shirt was open to the waist and her sweat-slicked belly was flat and hard; around her waist was a wide leather belt, hung with fobs and trinkets and bearing a sheathed knife. Black hair hung below her shoulders, with feathers and tremillan flowers braided into it.

Gem stopped some paces away, feeling how his own clothes clung damply to him, braced the end of the Trident against the ground, and bowed. "Do I address a Chief of the Bindalche?"

"I am Ven kelBatien Girisco, Chief of Tremillan Tribe, servant to the Telios." One sturdy brown hand rose from the belt and traced a sign in the air. "The Trident Bearer is seen and will be known. May Tremillan Tribe know his name? For the songs."

He hesitated. "Anjemalti Kristefyon," he said finally and waved at Witness and at Corbinye. "According to these."

She touched her ear. "It is heard. And according to you is the name—?" She met his gaze levelly, her eyes the color of sand. "It is understood that a man may own more than one name."

"Gem ser Edreth," he told her, compelled, someway, by those eyes.

Her hand came up, fingers closing, as if she caught the name he tossed to her. She brought her closed fist to her breast and opened the fingers wide. "My heart has heard yours," she said solemnly. "This, too, for the songs."

Gem opened his mouth to say—what? But there was no need, the chief's gaze had already moved beyond him.

"Shlorba's Eyes, I greet you," she said and looked to Corbinye without awaiting an answer.

"Beautiful lady, your name?"

Corbinye swallowed a painful ration of parched air. "Corbinye Faztherot, W—" She stopped and stared into the woman's eyes.

"I am a Chief of the Bindalche," the woman said. "Your name is safe with me."

"Alas, that my name has been untimely shortened."

The woman frowned.

"Death's Warrior," Witness intoned from his position behind Gem's shoulder, "walks at the Seeker's side."

"Ah." Barely more than a sigh. The chief laid palms flat over her breast, then held both hands out, palms up. "I have lived to see wonders. All honor to you, who takes up again the pain of life, and willingly relinquishes peace." She lowered her hands, face and eyes shining. "Shlorba send when death comes to me, she walks so fair as you."

Gem cleared his throat. "We thank you for your welcome," he said. "And are sorry to impose upon your hospitality." He moved the Trident slightly and the sandy eyes shifted to track the motion, then flicked back to his face.

"The Trident Bearer need only ask."

So, Gem thought. Now, if only the Trident Bearer knew quite *what* to ask. He licked his lips.

"One wishes to speak to a—teacher, perhaps. Someone wise in the ways of the Smiter, who might listen to what I say and aid me in decision."

"The Trident Bearer wishes to speak with one of the Telios." The chief nodded her head. "There is no easier thing." She turned and pointed across the blaze of the land.

"Yonder lies the Grotto of the Telios. You need only present yourself and your request to the Gatekeeper."

Gem shielded his eyes. "How far yonder?"

"An easy walk," she assured him, "except at midday."

"And it is currently what time of day?"

She looked surprised. "Going toward evening."

"Going toward evening," Gem repeated. "Good. Is there someone who might be given the task of guiding us to the Grotto?"

She laid her hand over her heart. "The Trident Bearer need only ask."

They got underway without any more asking, to Corbinye's short-lived relief.

The chief led them a twisting route among the tents, which spilled forth men who might have been the Witness' brothers, gaunt women and thin brown children. Eyes followed them, and whispers and louder voices, and Corbinye felt tension prickling between her shoulder blades, she who was the Captain's sworn protection. She strode on, keeping herself as often as possible between him and the tent-folk, fingers itching for her knife.

The chief led them down another sandy street, made thinner by the folk gathered there. Corbinye gritted her teeth and dared to sigh relief, just as one of the stocky males surged into the way, facing Anjemalti with a look on his face that only could be madness.

Her knife was in her hand and she had thrown herself forward, crying aloud—"Hold!"

"Hold!" An echo from the chief and Corbinye kept herself from the thrust, though the knife shone killing-bright in the wicked sun.

"Hold," Anjemalti murmured behind her, and she felt his fingers on her shoulder. "Be at ease, cousin."

He stepped forward, even with her, all but touching noses with the Grounder. He planted the end of the Trident in the rock-hard ground and leaned slightly forward, blue eyes contemplating the madman—

—Who reached out a callused paw and stroked Anjemalti's hair, once, fingers trembling as if with fever.

"Trident Bearer," he rasped and turned to look at his chief, standing sad-eyed behind him.

"Trident Bearer."

"It is so, old friend," she said gravely. "Come aside, and let him who bears the burden now move on to embrace glory."

He hesitated, as if he had imperfectly understood her words, and one stepped forward from the crowd to put a hand in his. "Come, brother."

He went where he was led then, looking back over his shoulder until at last he was tugged into a tent.

Anjemalti looked at the chief. "It meant something to him, this." He shook the Trident, lightly.

She smiled, sadness plain in her face. "As it might, since once he had borne it."

"But he's idiot," cried Corbinye, slipping her knife away.

The chief shook her head. "That came later," she said. "When it went from under his hand."

Corbinye froze, then turned to look at Gem, standing so fair and so strong with all his plans and his cleverness. "Anjemalti…"

"Not mad yet," he said lightly, turning his face aside from her gaze. "Or no madder than always." He bowed to the waiting chief. "Lead on, I pray you."

They met no other folk until they were past the tents and going along a stony ridge. Gem pointed at the ship lying quiescent near a tumble of boulders.

"What ship is that?"

Ven kelBatien Girisco glanced over. "Of the former Trident Bearer Jarge Menlin and his companions."

He frowned. "And Jarge Menlin is—where?"

"There," she said. And pointed.

The woman could only be Saxony Belaconto, striding along with purpose. Corbinye felt surreptitiously in the back of her belt, fingers closing on the palm-sized weapon she had concealed there. Carefully, she pulled it forth and dropped her arm straight down along her thigh.

Witness for the Telios stepped back, eyes on the fat man, who looked ill, truth told. Ill and frightened and more than a little mad. He ran, where the woman merely strode, and skittered on stones, breathing hard in the unkind air. Witness felt tensions building, webs of power weaving themselves as event took sudden note and began to converge—

Anjemalti the Seeker, Trident-bearer, Beloved of Shlorba, Whose other Name is Chaos—Anjemalti the Chief went forward, and met the fat man.

"That's mine!" The fat man's voice was thin with exertion or heat, or both.

"Hello, Jarge," said Anjemalti, stopping and standing easily, the Trident caught in the crook of his arm and the sun making gold of his hair.

"Mine!" shrieked the other—and he lunged, clumsy and desperate.

Death's Warrior brought her gun up—and held her hand as Anjemalti shifted, half-twisting to avoid the lunge.

The fat man's hand closed on the Trident's shaft and he gave a shout that began as hosanna and became a strangled cry; his eyes went wide and his muscles tensed—and gave up their duty, all at once.

Anjemalti went down with the fat man, getting a shoulder under the vast weight, trying with youthful valor to break the other's fall. Witness for the Telios could have told him there was no need for it—the fat man was beyond feeling the scrape of stones against his flesh.

"Dead." The bright-haired Seeker said the word as if he did not know what it meant. "Dead."

"More's the pity," said the woman Saxony Belaconto. "But I don't doubt you'll do as well, Master ser Edreth."

He recoiled, but there was no need for that, either. Death's Warrior still held her gun, and this time her aim was clear.

CHAPTER FIFTY-EIGHT

IT WAS DARK *inside the GenShip,* the verse ran through Milt Jinkins' mind, *dismal dark and quiet.*

Or, he thought irritably: Dismal dark and noisy. "Song-makers don't know anything about reality," he muttered and heard Ria laugh behind him.

"Songs aren't about what's real," she said. "No more real than heroes."

Milt sighed. She was right, he knew. Songs were about romance, and there was nothing romantic about the groaning, ancient system imperfectly cooling the air, or about smooth treacherous metal floors underfoot, or about rust patches, or about having to light your own way through some dark, decaying rabbit warren with a couple of repair lanterns hastily jury-rigged to accept batteries stolen from an emergency beacon.

"Here's a branching," said Ria and put her hand on his arm. Ria was leader in this endeavor—she having done salvage work before.

While she went a few steps down this way and a few steps up that way, lantern held high, scanning the walls for who knew what mysterious signs, Milt activated the portable comm clipped to his belt.

"Remote team three-three-six to Ship three-three-five. Read me, Dez?"

"Read you right steady." Dez's voice was startlingly loud in the noisy dark. "Any more sections coming loose?"

This was a joke, designed to make Milt cringe for his reactions when the breakaway section had fled the GenShip. However, he refused to feel guilt for his reflexes. Fifty times out of fifty-one, so he told Ria, his reactions would have been right on. Who built ships with breakaways the size of a moon?

"Not that big," Ria had said, and then: "GenShip crews are crazy, boy."

"Everything's stable," he told Dez now. "Dark, deserted. Cooling system's a bit rickety—ambient temp eighty-two, Fahrenheit. If it starts to climb, we'll back out. No use frying."

"Ria's the one thinks there's more to it than the metal rights," said Dez. "Happy with a share of that action, myself."

"Whyn't you say so?" demanded Milt. "Could've talked her out of it."

Dez laughed. "I'm too old a fool to try and talk Ria out of anything," he said. "I remember—"

"Hold it!" Milt's voice was sharper than he had intended. Dez cut off in mid-sentence and Milt tipped his head, trying to track the sound, a bare whisper of sound, half-heard under the din of the dying cooling system...

"Milt?" the comm inquired. "Ship three-three-five InRing to Remote three-three-six. Read me?"

Milt sighed and shook his head; thumbed the comm. "Read you fine. Thought I heard something new—damn ship's coming apart at the seams. Spooky, you know? Like the ghost ship stories the older kids used to tell the young ones in creche..."

"This way, boy!" Ria's voice echoed eerily off the metal.

"Partner's chosen the course," Milt told the comm. "Remote three-three-six out."

"Luck," said Dez. "Out."

She had found the engine room, or near enough. The walls were banked with machinery; here and there a status light glowed yellow. Milt stepped in and held his torch high.

"Wow."

"Easy to say." Ria was obviously pleased. "Might be more than salvage here, boy. Might get price as a working ship. Golights say she's able."

"It's an antique," he said absently—then her other words acquired meaning. He spun to stare at her in the light-lanced gloom. "If she's *able,*" he demanded, "why was she abandoned?"

Ria stared at him.

"We're leaving," Milt said, determination fed by abrupt terror. *And he heard a sound behind him, there in the ship where he knew there was none alive,* his memory provided, crisp and clear from childhood. *He heard a sound behind him and he was afraid to turn and see what was there—and he was afraid to stand one heartbeat longer, with his back to it, exposed—*

"We're leaving," he snarled again, but Ria still stood there, eyes wide on him. He snapped forward, grabbed her wrist and yanked her with him as he spun back toward the door—

And let out a sound halfway between a gurgle and a scream.

A—spider—was blocking the doorway, its eyes orange and hideous, its mouth able to cut the likes of Milt Jinkins in very half, its body round and as high off the worn decking as his waist, suspended between eight legs, each of which ended in—a claw.

He swallowed another scream and dropped Ria's arm; fumbled in his belt for the gun and brought it unsteadily up.

The spider's lantern eyes blinked. There was a sharp hiss and a sense of something flying in the dimness and Milt felt sticky cord wrap tightly around the wrist of his gun arm. He screamed and the spider yanked.

Desperate, he pulled back and another sticky rope snapped tight around his knee. Milt fell, tried to claw a fingerhold into the metal floor, felt the spider thread tighten around him and screamed again, for Ria to help him, to save him, to shoot it, kill it—

She may have tried. He heard more thread hiss by, heard a shriek that was none of his, followed by a strangling sob.

Milt had once known how to pray. He heard himself babbling the old words, as the spider pulled him in. In the end, it made no more difference than Ria's curses.

CHAPTER FIFTY-NINE

Using the Trident as a brace, Gem climbed slowly to his feet.

Witness stood off to one side, his face blank in that particular way that meant he was totally enclosed in his Witnessing.

Corbinye had put away her gun and stepped forward, sliding a steadying hand under his elbow. He looked at the ruin of Saxony Belaconto's face; at the blood that soaked her shirt, shuddered and closed his eyes.

"Was it necessary…" he began, and let his voice die out, because, of course, it had been.

"She was your enemy," Corbinye said. "What would you?"

"A moment of weakness, cousin. Forgive it." He opened his eyes and turned his head with the intent of smiling at her—and instead twisted free of her hand, crying out, "No!"

The turret of the grounded Vornet ship was moving, slowly and with deliberation, adjusting angle as it turned, until it was pointing down the ridge, to the sparse green base— Pointing at the tents of Tremillan Tribe.

"Devils!" Ven kelBatien Girisco screamed, snatching at her belt. She plucked loose one of the dangling trinkets and hurled it at the ship.

There was an explosion, minor, kicking up clods of earth and small stones, not quite halfway to the ship. The chief screamed again, this time something wordless and potent and ran forward, fingers working at another of her belt-fobs.

"No!" That was Corbinye, three steps gone on a course that would intercept the running woman, and the turret was moving again, homing in on this nearer meat, freeing the tents of danger and they would *both* die—

Gem leapt, slamming into Corbinye and knocking her to the hard earth. He held on grimly as she struggled, letting even the Trident go so that he could keep both her hands from around his throat, shielding her body with his own.

The second explosion was louder—the chief may have scored a hit.

The third explosion was louder still and the ground they lay on kicked and buckled, slamming them backward, to land with identical breathless cries amidst loosened dirt and rock-shards. The Trident slapped hard across Gem's legs and Corbinye twisted so fiercely he feared for her back and let her go, twisting himself to come up in one smooth motion, Trident held ready.

The earth outside the ship was splintered, torn, ravaged, glazed here and there to glass. Witness was on his feet a little distance beyond the worst of the devastation, a cut leaking bright red down his square cheek.

Of Ven kelBatien Girisco, Chief of Tremillan Tribe, there was no sign at all.

The turret was moving. Grindingly slow, as deliberate as fate, as inevitable as pain, the turret was again taking aim upon the tents below.

"None to warn them," Corbinye's voice was grief-laden. "*Hyacinth* downhill and more. No weapons here to stand against that. Valiant—oh, valiant, Grounder Captain! Your courage should have bought their lives…"

Gem stared, watching the black muzzle making its fatal, deliberate adjustments, feeling the weight of the Trident in his hand. He looked at it; saw the perfection of the new circuitry, the winking brightness of the jewels, the baleful eye of the Fearstone. He lifted it, weighing its balance in his hands.

He began to walk toward the ship.

"Anjemalti!" Corbinye's voice, carrying panic, fear and other things, which almost he could name.

"Bold, O Seeker!" The voice of the Witness rose even above the moan of the ship's engines, audible now as he walked closer.

They let him come quite near, those within the ship. Let him come nearly to the edge of their closest range, before the turret began to move again, away from the tents, sweeping down as it moved to cover him.

Milt awoke to light, and people, and the knowledge that he was bound, hand and foot. He lay on his side on a cold metal surface. His impression was that he had been roused by a kick.

"Come along," said a cool, hauntingly familiar voice. "Open your eyes, Grounder. I know you for wakeful."

Reluctantly, he did open his eyes, to the sight of scoured metal and a pair of boots—black leather and so thin he could see the outline of the feet within them. The hems of the blue trousers worn over the boots were frayed and the fabric had a slight shine.

"So," he said to the boots. "My eyes are open. Big deal."

"And ready to converse," the voice commented. "Eil."

He had a bare moment to wonder what an "Eil" was before another pair of boots crossed his line of vision and he found himself suddenly hoisted by the cords binding his arms behind him. His shoulder-joints popped painfully and he took a sharp breath.

"Get your feet under you!" a man's rough voice snarled in his ear. "Are you even too stupid to stand?"

He twisted and managed to make his feet obey him. For one moment he stood, swaying and off-centered by the tightness of the cord binding his legs together. Then Eil withdrew his hold on the arm-ties, Milt tottered—and crashed to his knees.

The cool-voiced woman sighed. "It will do. Look at me, Grounder."

He craned his neck to do it, hating the attitude of supplication. She let him look his fill and when he had memorized her from her short, pale hair, to her enormous black eyes to the hash-mark on her fraying sleeve, he said, "You're the one who was organizing the evacuation."

Surprise flickered in her bony face. "Mael Faztherot," she said, "Acting Captain and First Mate. You will have a name."

"Will I?" His voice carried an unwise suggestion of snarl, and she frowned.

"Churlish, are you not, Grounder?"

"You want my opinion?" He glared at her. "I think I've got cause to be a little rude. You scare me to death, you tie me up, you don't *un*tie me, you—where's my partner?"

She regarded him blandly. "Partner?"

That frightened him. He stared at her dumbly, tongue darting out to moisten lips gone suddenly dry.

"Your name," she prompted him.

"Milt Jinkins," he gave it around the terror in his heart. "There was a woman with me—my partner—when the, the—"

"When the Arachnid found you drawing weapons upon it," she finished for him, "and took steps to defend itself." She paused. "It seems to me that I do recall another Grounder. Perhaps I will let you see her. After you answer some of my questions."

"I want to see my partner!" Milt cried. "And I want to see her now!"

Shockingly, she laughed. "But you are scarcely in a position to insist upon anything, are you? Churlishness does not buy your partner peace. Recall it, and answer well. What is the frequency of the reporting line into the mother ship that hangs outsystem?"

He stared. "I don't know," he said finally, with no hope of being believed.

She shook her head. "Now that is a pity, because there are several other things along this same line that I need most desperately to know. Perhaps an aid to your memory?" She snapped her fingers and Milt heard the small clicking sound he had heard in the hallway just before Ria had called him to the control room. The—Arachnid?—hove into view and extended a claw.

Milt whimpered and bit his lip.

"Come," said Mael Faztherot. "Why make it painful? I will have the data eventually, you know, and it matters not at all to me if you are alive at the end of my questions. If it matters to you, then speak, and live to tell tales to your children."

"I—I don't know," Milt whispered, staring at the Arachnid in fascinated horror.

"Ah, stars take a stupid Grounder!" the woman said, sounding thoroughly out of patience. "Eil!"

The first blow went across the side of his head, just above the right ear, hard enough to snap his teeth together through the end of his tongue. The second disintegrated his vision into a flare of piercing colors.

"Come, man," said the woman. "You're a pilot, and I'm loath to see such ruined. Tell me the frequency and have done."

He turned his head aside and spat blood. Looked at Eil—a towering brute with the same startlingly pale hair and out-of-proportion eyes—and then at the woman.

"Frequency ten eighty-eight," he said, not caring that his voice shook, "on a duplicating sub-light and hyper-band."

A look of infinite sadness crossed Mael Faztherot's face. She sighed and shook her head. "Eil," she said.

CHAPTER SIXTY

"BUT," VELN SAID, and not for the first time since breakaway, "how can we *know* what's to do, Uncle? All very well to say we're aiding the Captain against enemies of the Ship—"

Finchet threw him an amused glance. "That's insufficient for you, is it?"

Veln stamped his foot on the slate floor and glared right regal, for all he was every bit of ten Standard Years old. Finchet was hard put to hold his laughter inside.

"All the universe," Veln said, in the tone of one reciting Regs for those of less encompassing intellect, "is the Ship's enemy. The Crew must ever be, be—"

"Vigilant," said Finchet, running an eye over the various gauges set into the back wall.

"Vigilant," repeated Veln, unmollified, "and ready to give battle. To die, if Ship or Captain demands it."

"Well?" asked the Gardener mildly. "What's amiss, then?"

"The Captain sets most of the Crew to battling The Combine, while he and, and—the Grounders—while they go to *aid* other Grounders, who are also our enemies!" cried Veln. "Surely you see that's *wrong*! My father—"

"Your da was a fierce man and a hard one, and I mean no dishonor when I say so. There's no dishonor in the truth, nor ever there was, no matter what they might be teaching you tin-side." Finchet frowned and rubbed his chin, considering the hot young face before him. "It's no sense saying what Indemion would have done in such a wise," he said, in a milder tone, "for truth is that he'd have never got himself tangled in Grounder affairs. He was a Ship's man, your da, and he thought always of the Ship's best." He shook his head. "Not to say that he always thought right or well. But he did his best. No dishonor there, either."

Veln's jaw was set. "But the new Captain—"

"Well, and there's a case like I was telling you, about your da not always thinking right. He's the one set the boy among Grounders, see it? Small wonder now he says folks is folks and undertakes to solve for Crew and Grounder. He's got ties, does your cousin Anjemalti. Think on it and see how it makes sense. Would you have him honorless, and turning his thoughts from his friends, because the Crew that threw him out suddenly crooks its finger and calls him home?"

The boy was looking a bit less sure. "But he takes— Grounders—instead of Crew—"

"Veln, Veln! And what's Corbinye but Crew to the core of her?" Finchet held up his hand. "Or are you thinking like some, that she slighted us? Tale I heard was she died for the Captain's sake—her duty, will you say? And for doing her duty she gains a reward—a new body, comely and strong, so that the Captain not lose her service. What's ill with either of them in that?"

Veln blinked. "What I heard—"

"Wisdom," Finchet interrupted tartly. "Listens to all, and thinks on itself." His eye snagged on a certain reading, there along the wall, and he stood. "Here's time for business now, boy. Attend me."

Together they went to the board, and sat down in the piloting chairs. Finchet touched a series of colored wooden buttons, and shutters peeled back from eight small screens situated at eye-level.

"You see these sharp, boy?"

Veln squirmed in his seat, craned, and sighed. "It would be better if I had a higher seat, I think, Uncle."

Finchet nodded. "There's the pillow off the bed," he said, checking readings and comparing them against the images held in the screens. "Or, if you like, there's the Book."

The boy stared. "Use the Book to sit on?"

"It's been used for ruder things," the old man returned, and threw the child a grin. "Hurry, whichever. I'm set to need your eyes right quick."

Veln ran quiet across the stone floor, nimbly avoiding the furniture, ducking under the strings of herbs and onions hanging from the rafters to dry. He returned somewhat slower, the Book clutched to his chest with both arms, placed it careful on the chair-seat and reverently lowered his rump.

"Better?" Finchet asked.

"Yes, Uncle."

"Well enough." Finchet made an adjustment to the resolution and then glanced over to the boy.

"We're set for a step-orbit. Best we can do—and that on an emergency system I doubt me was ever meant to work. Wouldn't have tried it, truth told, except the Captain got that Arachnid to come in and put things in top shape. Anywise—we're going down to the planet, step by step. Take us a little more than two Ship's days. Reason we're doing it this way, aside from it's never smart to just set down on a strange world without some situation study, is the Captain is desirous of maps. You scan it?"

Veln frowned. "The automatics can map while we're on the way down, Uncle. There's no need for us to watch—"

"Ah, but there is. This world is prisoner of The Combine. The Captain needs understanding eyes on these screens—eyes that know the shape of a fortress, or an anti-ship gun, or a transponder site. Hear what I tell you, young Veln?"

The boy's eyes were very bright. "Is—we're going to invade? Make the planet ours?" He drew a deep shaking breath and leaned across to grip Finchet's hand. "Is this the, the Promised Land, Uncle? Is this what GriffithPod sent the First Captain and Crew to find?"

The Gardener shook his head. "Starwind, child, what do I know about GriffithPod's intent or the First Captain's commission? If you've been allowed the Logs, then you know more than ever I do." He chuckled and withdrew his hand. "What I know is present orders, present course and present possibles. Are you able to scan five through eight?"

Veln was sitting very tall, shoulders square, eyes shining. "Aye."

"Do it, then. If there's aught out of common—even if you don't have its name—press yon blue button to note it. If you've got something you know will be bad for us, let me know about it, too. I'll be spending part of our last orbit calculating landing coords. Won't do to set us atop a barracks of Combine Marines!"

Veln laughed at that and turned his face attentive to the screen, right hand poised over the blue stud. After a minute of watching him, Finchet bent to the weary task of monitoring his own screens.

CHAPTER SIXTY-ONE

THE GUN SWEPT down and Corbinye moaned, certain that the next instant would see it fire. Certain, certain, that he was dead, and not a thing she might do except run forward and die in his wake, and still Anjemalti walked onward, oblivious alike to the gun, his death, her anguish.

The gun swung closer and compressed a little, firing tube sliding into locator as those who had its keeping fine-tuned the setting. It shuddered once, all along the barrel, then froze as Anjemalti strode into range—

—And out again, swinging under the lowering muzzle as Finchet might stoop beneath a branch slung too low across a Garden path.

"Hah!" The cry broke from her lips as her heart lurched back into life, beating with a joy as excruciating as it was short-lived.

True enough, the gun had stopped and Anjemalti now walked well inside the ship's safety ring.

But as she watched this and that of the ship's minor hatches and go-ways began to cycle; armored doors began to slide away, ramps to descend.

From the first such stepped a figure prudently clothed in a light, non-vacuum suit. And as this figure stepped from the end of the ramp, it raised a high-powered rifle to the ready.

Corbinye found herself racing forward, palm gun snug in her hand, running after Anjemalti without thought, nearly as heedless to danger as he, rejoicing that here at last was a service she could render—a danger she might, with skill and with luck, shield him from.

The pathway was as a long shining ribbon, stretched out before his feet. He need only follow it from where he had been to the place where it was necessary that he be. Follow the ribbon and strike truly at the vessel of the enemy. Do these things and his enemies would be delivered unto him— this he knew.

The voice had told him so.

Questioned, Gem could not have said when first he had apprehended the shining trail, nor when he had first heard the voice. It might have been that they manifested simultaneously, at the moment when he had given over his dread of the gun and, subsequently, of his own death, and allowed the blazing need to *stop them* override every sense.

They will not kill the Bindalche, he promised himself, stooping under the gun's barrel without breaking stride.

NOR SHALL THEY, MY BOLD, the voice assured him, caressingly.

They will have no hesernym, he continued, half-chanting as he followed the glimmering trail. *They will cease to hound me. They will be powerless!*

YES, the voice soothed. EXACTLY SO, BELOVED. YOU MAY STRIKE THEM POWERLESS. YOU ARE SO STRONG, SO CLEAN OF THOUGHT. DRINK THEM FOR ME, MY BRIGHT, MY ONLY, MY WARRIOR! DRINK THEM DRY AND SLAKE ME. I HAVE THIRSTED SO LONG!

The pathway was widening and before him he saw the ship of the Vornet; saw it as a spider's web of energy, crossing, recrossing, pulsing with life. There was a dark cloud hovering over it, seeming, indeed to cross the trail, diminishing its brightness. Gem hesitated, but the voice only laughed.

EVENT FORMS TOO LATE, it cried. FORWARD, BELOVED! WHAT IS IN A CLOUD TO STOP YOU?

Yet still he tarried, and it seemed that the path grew less bright, the ship of his enemy less vibrant with power. He heard, where he had heard nothing but the voice for some while, the unmistakable sound of gunfire, and he half-turned from the path—

THEY WILL BEST YOU! taunted the voice.

They will not! he snarled, remembering Shilban's body slumping in the arms of his tormentor; seeing again Corbinye's eyes widen with shock on beholding the face that never was hers…

He heard another sound—a human voice, crying out in anguish and in love—"Anjemalti!"—and he tarried a heart-beat longer.

There was a coarse cough near at hand and Gem screamed, going to his knees upon the pathway as his shoulder took fire from pain. The Trident fell from nerveless fingers—and he caught it in his other hand, flinging to his feet in the next instant and running along the blurry, disintegrating pathway.

He hurtled into the cloud and screamed again at a cold that was agony. But he did not halt his pace. Somewhere—somewhen—a voice was murmuring, caressingly, passionately, calling him all sorts of beloved, urging him on to the ship, promising him worship, an eternity of sensuous delight—none of it mattered; indeed, he barely heard it.

He broke from the cloud and charged on, the ship looming in his sight, energy lines pulsing. He all but flew the last feet to the hull he did not see, Trident raised for the strike.

And as he brought it down, into the very center of a power-knot, the thought that lifted above all others, even above the gloating of the voice, was: *Corbinye!*

They'd not done much that was good by the boy, and quite a bit that was ill. Ria knelt by him in the GenShip's gloomy Common Room, her finger tracking the rickety wrist-pulse and her mind busy.

She was hardly bruised, having only endured a bit of routine slapping about by the captain's bullboy, in order to verify what Milt had told them. The accuracy of that information was what had frightened her, not the blows, for she knew Milt's head to be stuffed with ballad-hero nonsense. He would have never spat that data free.

And so they had beaten it out of him, as he must have known they would.

"Boy," Ria murmured in the dark, "you're almost too stupid to live." She sighed and ran knowing fingers over him, wincing at the damage. "Almost too stupid to live," she said again, sitting back on her heels.

The GenShip crew had taken their lights and their comm-links—only sensible. She considered and discarded the idea of using the GenShip's comm: She could count on Dez to get antsy after a bit and send someone over to fetch them. The most urgent task at the moment was making sure Milt was alive when that happened.

Ria frowned in the direction of a ceiling dim—couldn't very well call it a "light," after all—and mentally retraced their progress through the ship. They had—she was almost certain they had—passed a sick bay of some sort.

She came to her feet, ignoring the protest of her bruises, peeled off her jacket and tucked it around the boy, who moaned a little, and twitched, and then was quiet.

If she went careful, there was enough light to navigate by. Sick bay would likely have a stretcher and a blanket. And she might luck into bandages, pain killers...

"I'll be back soon, boy," she told her unconscious partner, and left him, walking slow and cautious in the warm, noisy dark.

"There!" Veln hit the blue button and snatched at Finchet's sleeve. "See it, Uncle? Screen eight and sliding..."

Finchet made adjustments, captured image and data from Veln's side of the board and fed them through the cruncher.

"What is it?" the boy demanded excitedly. "An ocean?"

"Not likely that," the man returned, sorting the data deftly and with a growing sense of dismay. "Oceans aren't ringed in by walls, young Veln. They come and go as they will…" He leaned back in the chair as his mind grappled with the enormity of what he had just seen, what the cruncher assured him was true.

"Then what *is* it?" Veln said impatiently, and Finchet sighed.

"It looks to be a dam, boy. A big dam."

CHAPTER SIXTY-TWO

HER FIRST SHOT struck the rifle-wielder high in the arm, de-flecting his aim. He spun, rifle rising again, and squeezed off a shot that tore into the earth just aside of Corbinye and she returned another shot, cursing the poor palm gun, with its modest firepower. A marksman could score on such distant targets, but the chance of a mortal wound was negligible.

The man with the rifle staggered, slipped, or so it seemed, and tumbled off the ramp. Corbinye gave attention to two other potential assassins, encouraging them to keep their heads prudently down.

Anjemalti was directly ahead of her, still walking in that leisurely, almost dreamy way that allowed of neither danger nor death. Corbinye broke her stride for an instant and scored a shallow wound across a gunwoman's skull, a bright red rib-bon showing sudden against black hair. Satisfied with her work, fearing that the palm gun's charge was nearing a state of deple-tion, she stretched herself into a flat run, meaning to catch up with Anjemalti, to use her own body as a shield...

She saw him hesitate in his steady walking. Saw him stop and half-turn, as if he had just become aware of the mayhem around him, of the gunfire and the shouts and the straining hum of the ship's systems—

She did not see the gunman lying in the shadow of the ship take careful aim with his rifle, though she saw others, who were just as deadly a danger to him.

"Anjemalti!" she screamed, meaning to warn him, and saw him start; saw the flash of the hidden killer's gun and heard Anjemalti cry out at the same instant—saw him go to his knees, Trident falling from shocked-open fingers.

She slammed to a halt and stood tall there amid the storm of projectiles. Stood tall and took careful aim, pulling on every ounce of her skill. Stood, untouched, for a wonder, and pulled the trigger, hating the man who had wounded him—

She missed; heard her bullet whine off the hull of the ship.

Anjemalti was on his feet, not so blackly wounded as she had feared, though the blood flowed freely down his arm, dripping off slack fingers. He turned toward the ship and with a speed she did not think he had in him leapt forward. The gunman in the shadows shifted to take better aim and Corbinye screamed, charging forward, gun up—fired, and fired again and again—four times, before the little gun coughed empty in her hand and by that time the rifleman lay still and Anjemalti had lifted the Trident and slammed it, prongs first, into the skin of the ship.

She expected an explosion, or a flash of light; a choir of angels—*some*thing that would begin to balance the death of the Bindalche chief, Anjemalti's wound, her own terrors—

There was instead—silence.

Absolute, utter silence as every light on the ship went out and the gun drooped in its turret and the engines simply—stopped.

Before her, Anjemalti's fingers gave up their hold and he slumped, sliding bonelessly down the hull. In the silence, she began to walk toward him, and heard one last sound: The cough of a long-range rifle.

The pain that followed the sound seared and she cried out. Then her knees buckled and she fell, unconscious before she hit rock.

There was indeed a stretcher in sick bay, and a blanket. And much, much more.

Ria settled the boy into a very modern doctoring unit, punched appropriate buttons and got a gratifying reading. She okayed the outlined course of treatment, the machine buzzed to life and she stretched out on the abandoned gurney to stare at the relatively bright ceiling and think.

The line of the GenShip captain's questioning said plain that she meant a strike at the Big Ship. Ria didn't think she could take the Big Ship, even with the codes and line approaches. Getting docked was one thing, after all. Taking control of the tower was something quite else.

Still, Ria conceded fair-mindedly, a Combine Star Class mothership specially outfitted for frontier duty was a prize a GenShip captain might work to win. You couldn't blame her for trying. Though she'd probably earn death for trying—her and as many of her crew as were caught. The Combine was not forgiving of piracy and the GenCaptain surely knew that.

Ria frowned at the ceiling. The more she thought about it, the odder it seemed that the GenCaptain would abandon a working, if elderly, ship in a gamble for an admittedly sparkling ship of The Combine. Even if her act of piracy succeeded, she would have made The Combine her active enemy, which was foolhardy in the extreme. The Combine would think nothing of dispatching hunter ships to track down and destroy the pirated Star cruiser.

And if she lost her gamble, which seemed the most likely outcome, she would have annoyed The Combine and given up her ship—all for nothing.

Ria sighed and blinked at the fading ceiling. "GenShip crews," she muttered thickly. "They're all crazy."

With that comforting thought in mind, she fell asleep.

CHAPTER SIXTY-THREE

STAR CLASS TWO, Number Six-Three-One-One-Niner; the *Combine Felucci*, known to both her crew and the outriders reporting to it as the "Big Ship," rode placid among the starfields surrounding Spangiln System.

Third shift had been dealing with the various alarms and excursions emanating from the InRing and the mood on the bridge was one of high good humor only slightly leavened by puzzlement. A treat like a GenCrew abandoning ship within Combine space didn't happen every tour, after all, and the joke was made more precious by the startlement of the InRing pilot who had been setting his salvage beacons when the garden pod jettisoned. The shift historian liked that bit best and played the tape several times, chuckling and shaking her head.

The garden's destination bothered the security guy, and made him less than patient with the historian's antics. He snarled at her and the shift chief called them both to order and the historian shrugged her shoulders and went back to trying to trace the GenShip's numbers. Security muttered and bit his lip; cleared his screen and tried again to plot a trajectory for the garden pod while he worried about whether or not it was manned. The historian would probably know the answer to that, but he was reluctant to ask her—yet.

The mood on the bridge steadied as people settled back into their routines. InRing communications dropped back from the novel to the comfortably boring; OutRing reported no sightings of GenShip escape pods or of anything else out of the ordinary. The shift hit the half-way point and began to slide down toward quitting time. Security finished running his possibles and stretched where he sat. The shift chief got up and ambled over to the refreshment bank to draw his midshift jolt of caffeine. The historian cussed mildly and leaned back in her chair, running distracted fingers through her already untidy curls. She cleared her throat, preparatory to addressing the bridge at large, but the quartercon man beat her to it.

"Holy shit."

"Attack globe in place, Acting Captain," the second mate reported respectfully and Mael Faztherot nodded.

"Open comm lines," she directed, leaning back in her chair and laying her hands casually along the arm rests. "Release override program."

The mood on the bridge was one of vast disbelief as all stations stared at the overscreens, which showed a ring—nay, a globe—of ships, encircling the Big Ship at a uniform one-quarter light-second in all directions.

They were largish ships—each the size of a small yacht, or an InRing siege-rider—built along old, but very serviceable lines. There were guns, several to a ship; also old, but potent enough; serviceable. The historian cleared her throat.

"Generation Ship lifepods," she said, as if any of the shift doubted it.

Security moved a hand toward the toggle that would alert his section chief—and jerked it back as the ship-to line crackled to life.

"This is Mael Faztherot," a woman's cold voice washed over the bridge, "Acting Captain and First Mate of what had been the Ship *Gardenspot*."

Security bent to his board, isolating the line, starting a tracer, barely heeding the words that issued impossibly from the sealed bridge line.

"It has been brought forcibly to our attention that our Ship has fallen into disrepair, that, indeed, it presents a dangerous environment in which to engender and raise our children," the GenCaptain continued. "We have thus abandoned it and several of your battle-sworn are even now in the process of claiming it for themselves. This is good."

The tracer went bad, the entire board shuddering into a mess of crazy readings. Swearing, sweating, Security punched up the auxiliary board and initiated another trace.

"The ship we have abandoned is reparable," Mael Faztherot was saying, "but we are sadly destitute. Since The Combine is in part responsible for this state, since it denies us work, and hounds us from system to system, it seems only just to us that The Combine give over this Star Class ship in trade for which the Crew of *Gardenspot* does freely give its ship to The Combine."

The tracer ran a flutter of insane readings and went dead. The third aux board refused to come up at all. Security looked around wildly.

"They're into the scan lines!"

Quartercon swore and began slapping at keys. The shift chief jumped for his board, spoke four words into a dead mike, slapped up an aux board and threw the mike down. He stood looking helplessly up at the overscreen; at the unmoving globe of ships, each with guns pointed dead center, directly at the Big Ship.

"You have fifteen minutes," Mael Faztherot said, "to surrender the inner system keys to me and begin an orderly evacuation of your vessel. If evacuation has not begun within that time, we will take you by force."

The secure, intruder-proof bridge comm went dead. The shift chief didn't move.

Security levered himself out of the chair and looked over at the historian.

"I'm going to the captain," he said. She nodded.

He made his way across a bridge that was pandemonium as each crew member came to the conclusion that his station was dead, that even ambient readings might be untrustworthy.

He was astonished, and not really relieved, to find that the door to the main corridor opened at his approach.

Veln had long since fallen asleep, drooping like a thin, fair doll in his web of shock straps. Finchet had debated carrying the boy to bed and had decided to leave him where he was, cushioned by the straps, in case the going got rough.

He now had occasion to celebrate the wisdom of that decision, though not the leisure. For the going had gotten very rough, indeed.

Finchet gamely struggled with the controls, fighting to keep the Garden stable in a turbulence that threatened to overturn them. He had expected atmospheric agitation, though he had not expected so much—nor that he would encounter it so quickly. And he had expected that the Garden would fly only slightly better than a rock.

But there, he thought, fighting for equilibrium in a planetary overwind that might easily disorient a starship, the Garden had never been built to fly—or only to fly in the direst emergency. The most the builders had envisioned was the Atrium descending under its own power, carefully guided by a net of workpods. They could have never thought of *this* madness, with an ancient gardener and a sleepy boy trying to bring the thing down as if it were a proper ship...

The Garden shuddered, began to tip, and Finchet leaned to the board, pulling this lever, playing that dial, as if the physical work would correct the list.

For the Garden had to stay oriented in its certain manner as it descended—treetops must invariably be *up*, rocks, stream beds and moss must always be *down*. Not like a proper ship at all, where up and down were dismissible relativities, saving only that the pilot was correctly oriented to the board.

Incredibly, the agitation grew; the Garden rocked and somewhere Finchet heard a *snap*, as if a branch had broken from one of the trees in the glade. Swearing, he slapped up the last-ditch stabilizers: those to be used to aid landing.

Within his webbing, Veln stirred, moaned and then screamed to wakefulness as the Garden bucked and outside a tree gave up entirely under the strain, shattered and came crashing across the cottage roof.

CHAPTER SIXTY-FOUR

ANJEMALTI THE SEEKER dealt the ship its death-blow and Witness for the Telios was already running, secret heart and duty completely at one.

He saw Death's Warrior fall, the bright blood blooming like roses across the back of her white shirt and he raised up his voice in song, that this latest of her sacrifices not go unmourned.

A man stepped forward, blocking the way to the Smiter, gun raised and eyes glittering murder. Witness killed him with a knife-stroke, breaking neither stride nor song.

He heard, above and between the sound of his own voice, the speech of guns and the panicked words of the gun-wielders, who only now noted that their ship was dead. Between and below the pounding of his own feet upon the hard earth of home, he felt the pounding of others—many others—and his secret heart soared.

At the base of the dead ship, Anjemalti moved, dragging himself erect by fingertip holds upon the hull. He tottered where he stood and made a grab for the Smiter, which came willingly into his hand. Witness for the Telios stopped his running and his song, and dropped flat to the ground beneath the last of the foolish bullets, his eyes upon the Seeker's face.

Anjemalti leaned on the Trident like an old man upon his staff, one arm limp and red to the fingers, his hair wild as windchaff and his fey eyes gleaming cold.

"Surrender!" he shouted and his voice was neither old, nor worn, nor anything else so human. "Surrender or die!"

The gun-wielders stirred, and one among them laughed. Witness heard the shot, saw the flash as the Trident ate the projectile.

"Surrender!" Anjemalti cried again. "Your ship is dead and you are at the mercy of the Bindalche, who have no cause to love you."

They muttered at that, and Witness heard some say that there were a lot of them, uphill and down—look, look at the dust they raised...

"Fools!" snapped a voice from among the others. A figure strode forward, yanking at the ribands holding the war-helmet in place and throwing the helmet itself aside, revealing a woman's luxurious hair.

Bold, she stepped forward, rifle riding her hip—across rock and baked earth, to the place where Death's Warrior lay.

A grin, full of tooth and malice, she sent to Anjemalti, then she pulled the bolt on her rifle and lowered the muzzle until it lay against Corbinye's head.

"Surrender?" she taunted. "Think again."

One-handed, Anjemalti raised the Trident.

The gun-woman laughed. It seemed to the Witness that he saw her finger tighten on the trigger—

The first bolt kicked her backward, rifle snapping upward, releasing its charge into the sky.

She got her feet under her, swung the rifle down, and braced herself, Anjemalti square in her sights...

The second bolt consumed her, rifle, hair and war-suit; swallowed her in one fiery flare that left nothing at all behind, save a glassed-over ring of earth where she had been standing.

"Surrender!" Anjemalti shouted a third time and his voice carried such blood lust Witness' secret heart went cold. "Surrender, or I'll eat you all!"

"Trident Bearer!" A voice Witness knew all too well cried from the rear. "The Telios and the Bindalche are here in your service. Shall we rend now the enemies of our world? The Trident Bearer need only ask!"

The gun-wielders stirred and Witness for the Telios came to his feet, dared face half-away from Anjemalti and the Smiter—and saw the green of Telios robes, forming a barrier along the high ground, while below spread the hundred of Tremillan Tribe, their weapons bright and bristling.

One of the gunners moved, jamming the safety up on his weapon, unslinging it from his shoulder and throwing it far from him.

In a moment, all the rest had done the same and Anjemalti the Seeker nodded and lowered the Trident and leaned against it, looking nothing but ill and wounded and mortal weary. He turned his head toward the green robes grouped upon the high ground.

"These are my prisoners," he said, voice shuddering. "Secure them for me."

Then he let go the Trident and fell.

The board sparked and something blew with a sharp *snap!* Finchet swore at screens gone dead, tried to slap up an auxiliary board that wasn't there and coughed as he took a lung full of rancid smoke.

"Number Six screen gone," Veln was saying, voice steady as a veteran. "Data Bank Two blown. Forward stabilizers on the wobble." A pause. "The front half of the house is down, Uncle. We're trapped in here."

"Gods be thanked it's not the back half," said Finchet, daring a moment to glance behind him, to the wall of rubble, and the place where the bed had been; "else we'd lose our chance to bring her down."

Veln threw him a sick look. "Bring her down? We're blind, Uncle. Surely we can't go down—"

"Oh, we'll go down," Finchet said grimly. He glanced over at the boy and did him the grace of saying it straight. "No choice on that."

Veln's mouth tightened in a face already hullplate gray. Finchet nodded.

"How much wobble in that forward 'lizer?"

The boy glanced at the readings, frowned, and called for a recalibration. "Fluctuating," he said eventually; "twenty to forty percent."

"Strain." Finchet nodded again, took his hands from the board and closed his eyes, feeling the Garden around him; feeling how it bucked and tipped, but mostly—mostly, by the gods of space—kept orientation. Maybe...

He opened his eyes.

"Assign your board to main," he told Veln. "Tip that chair back and engage the crash-webs. You've been taught the Hemvils?"

"Yes, Uncle."

"Use 'em," Finchet directed. "I want you limp as a willow wand, hear me?"

"Yes, Uncle," said Veln, and did as he was told.

"Good boy," said Finchet and then forgot everything but the boards.

The timer on the healing unit chimed and Ria opened her eyes, rolled off the gurney and went to pop the hood.

Milt looked up at her with drug-hazed eyes, blinked and rasped out, "Ria?"

"Who else?" she wondered. "You're not dying on me, are you, boy?"

Memory stirred—his face scrunched and he shivered some, but the grin he gave her was real. "Naw. You don't get off as easy as that. Old woman."

"Yah."

His eyes sharpened still further. "Still on GenShip?"

She nodded. "Dez taking his time."

"Might be busy," he said and he was suddenly entirely back in his face. "They're going to take the Big Ship."

"Going to try," Ria agreed and put a hand on his shoulder, though he hadn't tried to get up. "Nothing we can do about that. Just sit tight. Plenty air. Probably a canteen. We'll look, pretty soon. Light's not so bad, after your eyes adjust."

"Yeah." The urgency had left his face, leaving it drained and grayish in the dim light. "Might take a nap."

"Good idea," she said. "I'll look around. I'm not here, you wake up, relax. Be back soon."

"Those big spiders…"

"GenCaptain probably took 'em with her," Ria said practically. "Look useful. You tuck in."

Milt closed his eyes, opened them. "Ria?"

"Now what?"

"You've got blood on your chin."

She cocked an eyebrow at him. "Thanks I get," she said and dragged a sleeve across her mouth. "Better?"

"Better," he returned. "Thanks."

"Go to sleep," she said, and stood by the side of the cot until he did.

It was not to be expected that the captain of The Combine ship would be so fainthearted as to surrender his secret system codes without a fight. Mael Faztherot perfectly understood his position in the matter.

It was with no tinge of anger, then, that she gave the order for the first pass.

Three of the Crew's lifeships, manned by three of the Crew's best pilots, broke formation and went sweeping toward The Combine ship.

Surprise played for them—by the time The Combine had understood that they were under active attack, it was too late to adjust range. Each of the three lifeships fired, as they had been instructed. Each scored a hit upon nonessential targets.

Each swept perilously close to the docking bays of the huge vessel, discharged their payload and, mission complete, went tumbling away.

Surprise did not play so well on the out-trip. One of the Combine gunners gained control of his board—or rode the luck high—and scored on one of the smaller ships, destroying it in a soundless flare.

Mael Faztherot gripped the arms of her chair and forced herself to watch as the two remaining scrambled for safety—and made it, as the voices of the Combine techs came clearly over the pirated lines, cursing computer readings that went from senseless to mad.

Mael Faztherot relaxed deliberately back into her chair and looked across at her second.

"Now?" he asked, eyes gleaming in anticipation.

She drew a careful breath and let it slowly out. "Now," she said, drawing a sleeve back so she could monitor the wristcomp, "we wait. And trust, if you will, in Grounder madness."

CHAPTER SIXTY-FIVE

SEVERAL OF TREMILLAN Tribe came forward, weapons leveled, and herded together those of the Vornet ship, who went docile within a ring of warriors up the hill to the Grotto of the Telios.

Green robes fluttered on the edge of Witness' vision, where he knelt in the broken earth by Anjemalti the Seeker.

"I greet you, Shlorba's Eyes." Thus, the voice he knew as his own. His heart shuddered, but he kept to duty.

The green robes rustled and she who had borne him moved out of vision's edge—then came entirely within his range as she knelt at the other side of the Seeker.

Carefully, she pulled back her sleeves; carefully, turned Anjemalti over; carefully, and with great reverence, laid bare the wound. She conjured a kit from the depths of her robe, brought out padding and twine. Carefully, she tied the rough dressing into place and raised her eyes.

"We will carry him to the Grotto and give him better there. Does your Witnessing tell you if the Trident still claims him?"

He drew a deep breath and met her eyes without a quiver.

"The Seeker's work is not done," he said.

She bowed her head; raised it.

"The Smiter is altered."

"It is," he returned, forcing her to ask the question.

She did so without apparent anger: "By what means?"

"Anjemalti the Seeker, seeing with eyes beyond those of men, was given to know both the Smiter's injuries, and that which would heal them."

"Praise to Anjemalti the Seeker," she murmured. "Praise to his eyes, which saw, and to his hands, which built." She glanced at him sharply.

"We have tended the woman with the braid. She is of some importance to the Seeker, ah? One would know her status."

"She is Corbinye Faztherot, Death's Warrior."

"Hah." Surprise there, and no little wonder. "We bear them both to the Grotto. Have you Heard the Smiter's will?"

He was silent for a time, eyes dreaming on the Trident. When he returned to himself, Anjemalti was gone, but his mother still knelt on the earth, patient and tireless.

"Let there come one who has neither fear nor desire," he said, noting how his voice cracked and how his head felt airy and overfull with light. "The Smiter will go with such a one, as far as Anjemalti's side."

"One shall come," his mother said. She stood, and shook out her robes, and left him.

He returned to the Witnessing, hovering in a place not unlike trance, though no dreams came to him there. Floating, he marked neither the failing of the sun, nor the five Bindalche warriors left to guard his honor. He was brought again to himself, indeed, by the merest spider-touch upon his shoulder and a slight, old voice murmuring, with bewitching irreverence, "Shlorba's Eyes, open, and see the world."

He looked up into the Gatekeeper's wrinkled face without comprehension and she smiled, eyes gleaming in their net of wrinkles.

"I am come to carry the Smiter to the Seeker," she told him gently. "Bear me company, do."

As if he had choice. Mechanically, he got his legs under him—and almost cried out at the pain of cramped muscles. His thoughts floated high above his head, distant and cool as the night clouds now forming.

The Gatekeeper bent and picked up the Trident. Held upright, it towered far over her head, and looked too heavy for her frail hand.

As if reading his thoughts, she chuckled, deep in her hood. "No dishonor, should an oldster use the Smiter as a staff. True, Eyes?"

"True enough," he heard his own voice tell her. "Anjemalti the Seeker uses it so, more than not."

"No harm, then," she concluded and turned uphill. She took two steps and looked over to him, extending a bird's claw hand. "Three steps to home, Eyes, as I know the way. We'll release these others to the care of their kin, and you will bear witness, as you must. Three steps, I promise you; then we tend your hurts and settle you down to Witness more seemly."

"All Witnessing is seemly," he heard himself say. "It is what must be done."

"Indeed, it must," she agreed, and captured his arm in her thin, strong fingers. "Walk with me now. One step, eh? Two steps…Three steps and—"

Home.

The ground shook, trees screamed, rocks split, streams left their courses.

Finchet battled the controls, beyond swearing—or praying. He rode the buffets, kept fall as slow as he dared, trusting more to his instincts than to instruments that flickered and flashed and gave forth giddy, useless readings.

He'd lost all but one screen; that one was enough to show him the ground rushing up at a rate that would have terrified him, had he not passed beyond terror some time ago.

The wind slapped them into a hard spin. He did nothing to fight it, all his fight going to keep the Garden *upright;* to save what he could while trees broke and died around him and the boy lay unconscious, stretched over a Book that was as useless to him now as prayer.

The ground came roaring upward; in the grainy screen he saw distant hills and an unending gleam of water. The wind gave them a last, playful tap and finally let them go.

Finchet sucked in his breath and sent all remaining power—pitiful though it was—to the stabilizers and sat, hands taloned above the useless controls, staring at the dark screens, waiting for impact.

Without the computers the Big Ship might as well just throw the docks open and invite the GenCrew on board. That the pirates had managed to subvert the System One codes and render all instrument readings suspicious was—disturbing. In light of this disturbance, the captain ordered the ship to System Two, and sent the techs scrambling for the access hatches.

CompTech Kandra Dinshaw swung the jitney off the main track and onto the Core A repair spiral. She kicked the speed up and whirled down and around—three full times around—before slamming on the brakes and rolling out.

The access hatches for the main computer cores were mechanical, designed for exactly the sort of unlikely emergency that faced them now. Kandra set a key the size of her palm in a keyhole bigger than her fist and turned, putting her back into it. The tumblers resisted for a second, then fell—click, click, click!—and the hatch sprang open.

She ran her fingers over the items hanging from her utility belt, nodded, and chinned herself on the overhead bar, scooting feet-first into the core.

Carefully, she worked her way down-core, shining her light overhead and keeping a sharp eye out for the axis numbers. At 38-6-I, she stopped and squirmed into position, reminding herself that there were good reasons why a opsystem changeover needed to be made mechanically. What if the ship were being invaded, as it was being invaded now? A computerized realignment could be read by the enemy, who could then conceivably capture the second computer's codes…

Sweating, but in position at last, Kandra felt in her belt for the hex wrench, fit it over the first of three holding bolts and applied torque.

The bolt spun and popped out into her hand, as did the second and the third. She eased the panel aside, squirmed some more and slid eventually into the changeover bank.

Her light picked out a dazzle of multicolored wires, gleam of metal and plastic surfaces, dull tubing and the glitter of amber spider-eyes, watching gravely from atop the first turn-joint.

Kandra froze, staring at the tiny insectoid. "What the—"

The spider blinked, one yellow eye after another, then turned on dainty gold-wire legs and minced away from her, down the joint—and disappeared into the less-than-hairline crack at the juncture into the second computer.

"A *spider*?" Kandra demanded, snatching at her belt-comm. A shower of static rewarded her effort to call the bridge and she cursed, and backed out into the core, swearing all the way.

She braced her shoulders against the core wall and thumbed the link again. There was a sprinkle of static, then Security's voice, snapping: "Yes?"

"Dinshaw," she told him, snapping herself, "CompTech Seven, dispatched to Core-A, computer realignment. There's a fucking *spider* in the backup!"

"Spider?" Security's tone was not encouraging.

"Spider," she reiterated. "Amber glow-eyes, eight legs, all out of gold wire, nice little transceiver body—a *mechanical*, you reading me? The backup computer's subverted!"

"By a spider." No belief there, maybe a touch of wondering if she'd cracked. Kandra gritted her teeth.

"By a *robot*," she snarled and glanced up at a sound— a very slight sound—in the core above her. Her light picked out the legs, the huge, shining body…"Oh, *hell*…" she breathed.

"What?" demanded Security, and Kandra shrank back against the core wall and knew there was nowhere to run.

"There's another one," she told the comm numbly, watching it come down-core. "Another spider. And it's *big*…."

CHAPTER SIXTY-SIX

HE WOKE SCREAMING, pursued by demons that whispered false delights, bloody talons outstretched to rend him.

Half-dazed, he fought the rich, scented furs, breath rasping, eyes wider than nature had ever intended—seeing nothing.

"Corbinye!" One sensible word in a tangle of fever-garble. Both of the room's watchers stirred at that. One rose and approached the bed, wrung out the cloth until it was damp and laid a thin hand against his shoulder, pushing him gently back.

"Down, child. Be still. *Still.* Good." She smoothed tangled yellow hair back from his brow and laid the cool cloth there. Blue eyes stared blankly into hers—and blinked, brows pulling together.

"Who are you?" he asked, with the wondering half-interest of a child.

His voice was rough, for all its innocence. She reached again and brought the bowl of inthil-juice to his lips.

He drank thirstily, and when he had drunk his fill, he turned his mouth away and asked again, "Who are you?"

"The Gatekeeper," she said, and put the bowl back on the stand. Facing him, she set the hood back, so he could see her clearly. "Gatekeeper for the Telios. The place is the Grotto of the Telios, where the Smiter rests—betweentimes. The healers have dressed your wounds and the singers have been praying for you this while. The Grotto is safety. No need for ill dreams here."

"Ill dreams…" He frowned and shifted a little where he lay, as if to see around her.

Guessing at his intention, she moved aside. "The Smiter is with you still. See—there it—"

A violent shudder shook him and he twisted as if he would fling himself off the sleeping ledge, save that the furs ensnared him.

"Take it away!"

The Gatekeeper stared. "The Trident Bearer speaks?"

"I said," he repeated, with awful clarity, enormous eyes bright as if with fever, or with that certain excitation which from time to time overcame those who bore the Trident, "take it away. I want none of it. It belongs to the Telios and I have returned it to the Telios. I'm done with it! Where is Corbinye?"

The Gatekeeper wet her lips, wondering if this were honest delirium or something sinister and beyond the ken of mortalkind. "I—" she began, meaning to say that she would go for one of the Five, but she did not get so far.

"Anjemalti." Two broad hands reached past her, possessed themselves of the Trident Bearer's shoulders and pressed him firmly down into the furs. "Be still. It is not thus that a man comports himself."

"You!" The Trident Bearer glared up. "You know its history—who better? Do you want me mad, with a legion of dead men bleeding on my hands? Is this friendship?" He twisted away from the hands that held him and sat up, his face near level with that of Shlorba's Eyes.

"I say to you *I do not want it!* Take it away and let another fool take it up!" He drooped back against the pillows. "I want Corbinye," he said in a milder tone. "Fetch her for me, if you love either of us."

"Death's Warrior may not come to you, Anjemalti," Shlorba's Eyes said sadly. "Her hurt was more potent than yours and the healers have labored hard, yet without full confidence in the outcome of their labors. And I cannot in anywise go away from here. For, though a man may love a man and a man may love a woman, I am Witness for the Telios and that is no duty I may lay down simply because it has failed of being joyful. It is not a duty I chose, who was happy in study and in song and never yearned for greatness." He closed his eyes and opened them, his mouth tight.

"My heart must always bow to duty," he said, "until such time as duty lays me down."

The Trident Bearer's eyes were less frenzied. The Gatekeeper allowed herself to hope that the madness had passed.

"And you wish me, an outsider and none of the Bindalche, to emulate you—to willingly sacrifice my self and my soul to—that."

"You are Chosen of the Smiter, Anjemalti, and you please the Goddess well. It is not Recalled that all who have borne the Trident have gone mad, though some have. It is Recalled that many who have lived to lay the Trident down walked away whole, with light in their faces and joy in their hearts and were the most blessed of men thereafter."

The Trident Bearer closed his eyes, leaned his head back and said nothing.

After a moment, Shlorba's Eyes sighed. "There is no one else who may bear it," he said softly, "while the Trident craves your touch. When the time is come to lay your burden aside, Anjemalti, your heart will know it. Until that time, any who seek to take the Smiter from you will die. Recall Jarge Menlin."

From the Trident Bearer, a sigh, long and shuddering. He opened his eyes and looked hard into the face of Shlorba's Eyes. Then he turned his head and stared at the place where the Trident lay, ringed 'round with holy stones, a pall of incense above it.

The Trident Bearer rubbed at his head, discovered the cloth still there and brought it away, holding it silently out. The Gatekeeper took it from his hand and dropped it back into the bowl.

"So." He began, methodically, rationally, to put aside the covers. "If Corbinye is as ill as that, I will go to her. She should not wake alone, without kin by her."

"Healers say you must rest," protested the Gatekeeper, and found herself caught in the brightness of his eyes.

"I will rest," he told her, "as soon as I am at my cousin's side. The healers may complain to me, if the arrangement offends them."

Shlorba's Eyes stepped back, and the Gatekeeper was shocked to see a smile on his mouth.

"Spoken like a man, Anjemalti. Gatekeeper, the Trident Bearer requires a robe."

She looked at him, whom she had known from the moment of his birth, and saw there was nothing she could do to sway him from his course. A glance at the other man's face revealed the same calm madness. Sighing, she went to the alcove and fetched the Trident Bearer his robe.

He was a boy again, running along Garden paths he had known his whole life—paths magically remade by the one he pursued. He had known Marjella Kristefyon nearly as long as the Garden, but never had he known her so beautiful, so gay, so desirable.

They were both fourteen, and in the Garden it was spring. Finchet stretched his strong young legs, knowing he would catch her at the next bend in the path—

The path pitched and buckled and Finchet fell—kept falling as trees broke above him and crashed down, everywhere at once. He rolled into a ball, shielding his head with his arms, face pushed tight into the dirt. Within the chaos, he thought he heard Marjella screaming. Or maybe it was himself.

He must have swooned, for the next sound he heard was the steady *thok-thok-thok* of an axe biting wood, and he carefully unwound his cramped body, and opened his eyes.

Above him, tilted at an insane angle, broken straps dangling down, was the pilot's chair. Finchet stared at it for several minutes, trying to make sense of its presence in light of his race with Marjella, and the continued sound of the axe.

Memory sorted itself, slowly, until he finally knew himself for sixty-four, with Marjella dead this weary round of years, and her son, grown to adult, and Captain in his own right, who had ordered the ploy that might well have killed the Garden.

"Well and it's the Captain's part," Finchet muttered, "to say what loss the Crew can take." He closed his eyes then, the better to attend the whirling of his head, and listened to the rhythm of the axe strokes.

These presently stirred him to a curiosity sufficient to overcome lethargy and he climbed painfully to his feet, moaning just a little.

The cottage lay wasted all about him, stone walls crushed beneath the corpses of hundred-year trees. The control wall alone was upright, speared by a broken branch, ready to crumble at a touch.

The axe wielder was Veln. Even as Finchet watched, the boy let the blade sink to the ground and rubbed at his forehead with a hand that shook.

Finchet shook out his legs and began to pick his way across the rubble. The boy turned, a grin turning his face young again, despite the grit that stained it.

"Uncle! Are you—how are you?"

"Well enough," he returned and stopped to cough. "Smoke," he said to the boy's suddenly anxious eyes and offered a grin of his own. "Told you we'd get down. True speaking, young Veln?"

The smile came back, but wearily. "True speaking, Uncle."

Finchet nodded and made a show of surveying the path that had been cut. "Been busy, I see. Belike you've a plan."

Veln pointed away across the tumble of ruin, beyond the edge of what had been the cottage and into the maze that had been a forest. "Access hatch."

"True enough." Finchet thought a moment, considering the boy's sweat-soaked shirt, grim face and trembling arms. "Happen we can get ourselves there without cutting us a boulevard," he said. "Let's have a sit-down and think it out."

They sat cross-legged among the wood chips, the boy straight-backed and tense, the old man leaning his shoulders against a log.

"If we go lightly," Finchet said, "happen we'll make it across to the hatch without trouble. You've uncovered a rope?"

Veln pointed shakily to a careful pile in the corner of two locked branches. Finchet frowned; nodded.

"Rope, small axe, knives, canteen, Book, belt comm— well done, young Veln! We're in a fair way to being out and about and seeing where we've come to rest." He looked closely at the boy. "You're wanting to start now, or rest a bit?"

"Now," said Veln with decision, and Finchet nodded again, creakily stood and bent over the careful little cache.

"We'll rope us together, for safety's sake," he murmured, more to himself than to the boy. "I'll take the large axe and one of the knives and a rope coil over the shoulder…"

"And I'll take the small axe, a knife, the canteen," said Veln.

"Right you are. Then I'm for the comm. The Book can go down the back of your shirt." He plucked the items out, one by one, and handed Veln his share. He had just made certain of the comm snapped to his belt when he felt a tough young body slam into him and thin arms go tight around his waist.

"Oh, Uncle, I'm so glad you're all right!" Veln cried out, words muffled by reason of his face being buried in Finchet's side. "I was so afraid—you were breathing, but when I tried to straighten you, you moaned and I thought you were broken and so I was going to cut a path and go—and go for help…"

"There now, there now…" Finchet put his arms around the heaving shoulders. "You did well, boy—as well as any could. It's only that us oldsters take our knocks a little more to heart. I'm right as right can be. We'll just rope ourselves together and stroll on out of here, eh?"

Snuffling, Veln nodded, and pulled back and stood patient while Finchet knotted the rope around his waist and measured out a length and tied the opposite end about himself.

"All right, now."

"A stroll," he heard the boy say behind him, and they swung out toward the hatch.

Of course, it was much worse than any stroll. It was a nightmare of tricksy footing and rolling logs; stones that turned under unwary boots, and branches crashing down random-like. Whole groves had gone down in impenetrable tangles, so that twice they had to make lengthy detours, and those weren't the worst of the bad moments.

Hours later, they reached the hatch, both of them grimy and sweating and trembling, and they took turns chopping at the vegetation piled before it. When it was clear, Finchet stepped forward, sending a prayer to the gods of stars and space that it wasn't jammed tight, leaned all his weight against the crash bar and *pushed*.

Against all his expectations, it popped open and he was catapulted quite neatly into the arms of the person directly before him.

Caught, Finchet blinked against the strong light—sunlight!—and got his captor's face into focus. It bore a marked resemblance to a face he had seen before.

He cleared his throat. "I'm a friend," he said into the Grounder's startled eyes, "of Witness for the Telios. It'd be thought a kindness if you'd take the boy and me to him."

CHAPTER SIXTY-SEVEN

THE ROOM WAS smaller than the one where he had awakened, and its walls were covered with fur. A fire burned in a pit near the center. Against the back wall was a bed, and on it a prince's ransom in furs.

A diminutive figure hurried forward as Gem crossed the threshold, waving small hands distractedly.

"Please, she is very ill. She must rest and not be in any way distressed. Please leave. We will send word."

Gem stopped and looked deep into the hood, seeing a face as young as the Gatekeeper's was old. "Do you know who I am?" he asked.

The boy pushed his hood back irritably, revealing black braids and a ring of white metal piercing one ear. "You are the Trident Bearer," he said. "But she's *ill*. She might die, the healers say. Please, you must not call her now—take someone else!"

"You, for chance?" asked Gem and saw the boy's face tighten. He reached out and touched the earring lightly with a fingertip. "What does this signify?"

"I train to be a healer," the boy said. "Let me fetch another to watch in my place, Trident Bearer, and I will come with you."

"Brave heart. But I am wounded myself, you know, and bound to rest. I've only come to sit with my cousin, that she not waken kinless." He glanced over at the fur-piled bed. "And if she should die, I would be with her then. Can you permit me these things, healer-in-training?"

The boy hesitated and from behind him, Gem heard the Gatekeeper's soft voice. "How will you stop him, little one?"

The boy's shoulders sagged. "True enough," he allowed, but then he looked sharply up into Gem's face, and snatched at his robe. "Swear to me," he said, "that you will not disturb her rest."

The Gatekeeper's gasp was audible. Gem smiled, seeing for a moment not this small apprentice, but a thin yellow-haired waif, with fierce eyes and demands of his own. For Edreth's sake, he extended his hand and laid it briefly on the child's dark head.

"I swear."

Satisfied, the boy stepped back and Gem walked on to the bed. He thought he heard the Gatekeeper's voice, but failed to note the words. Nor did he note that shortly thereafter she left him to the care of the small apprentice. All his attention was on the bed, and the one who lay there, so still.

Her face was pale against the richness of the furs, the honey skin gone to ivory. Lines there were upon her brow, aside her eyes, around her mouth, as if even in sleep she were pain-full. The long golden hair lay limp and lusterless, snagged here and there like spiderwebbing, and the hand atop the furs looked strengthless, fingers curved and impotent.

Gem sank onto the stool at the bedside, watching the labored rise and fall of her breast, his own breath strangled in his throat. Carefully, he slid his hand over her cold, lifeless one, and intertwined his fingers with hers.

"Corbinye," he murmured, softer than her breathing, "it's Gem."

He sat quiet then, holding her hand, watching her face and thinking of nothing, or so he would have said to any who asked. He may even have entered a doze, for he did not see that her eyes were open until she spoke his name.

"Anjemalti?"

"Yes," he leaned forward, so that she might see him more clearly, and tightened his grip on her hand. "I'm here, Corbinye, and well enough, though I seem to have a gift for getting shot in the shoulder…" He fancied he saw a smile quiver on that tight, tired mouth and smiled himself.

"I promised your physician, there, that I would not tire you," he said, nodding to where the boy kept vigil by the fire. "But I hope you won't mind it, if I stay by."

"I will sleep easier for it," she whispered. "Gods keep you, cousin." Her eyes hazed for a moment; cleared. "How fares the Vornet?"

"In the keeping of the Telios," he told her. "I expect we'll have to decide what to do with them eventually. But you must rest."

"In a moment," she said, but then lay still, breath coming in shallow gasps, cold fingers gripping his weakly.

"Corbinye…" Fear brought tears to his eyes, and the boy's frantic voice cried from memory: *She might die!* "We must get you to *Hyacinth*. The healing unit…"

"I doubt I would survive the journey," she whispered, as if it were of no moment. She seemed to wilt further beneath the furs; her fingers slackened in his and her eyes drooped shut. "I am happy you are with me, Anjemalti…"

Around the terror in his heart, Gem murmured, "Sleep, Corbinye." He touched her cheek, laid a finger against her lips. "I will be here when you wake."

"Sleep…" she murmured, and subsided, breath evening somewhat, her hand curled, resistless, in his.

He leaned back, seeing the signs of death in her, thinking of *Hyacinth*, so near, yet inaccessible to one in such desperate need. That Corbinye should *die* for the sake of a kilometer's travel…

There was a sound, as of something scrapping against stone, and Gem started, half-turning on the stool—

And bowed his head to the green-robed figure standing at the end of the bed, hood pulled up and hands tucked into wide sleeves.

The figure returned the courtesy, pulled its hands free and set back the hood, revealing the pleasant face of a man of middle years. "Trident Bearer," he said softly. "I am Third of the Five Telios. The Gatekeeper spoke to me of turmoil, and revolt against being chosen. It is for the Telios to teach and for all Bindalche to provide those things the Trident Bearer asks for." He slipped his hands back into his sleeves and stood, apparently willing to wait thus all day.

Gem stared at him. "I ask for the life of this woman."

Third of the Five moved his shoulders, face expressing infinite sadness. "The Trident Bearer is not a child."

"No," Gem agreed. "Nor is he quite a fool. I require the following items, and I require them *now*: Any and all information regarding the Trident's past deeds, its manufacture and its ultimate purpose."

Third blinked, bowed. "The Trident Bearer need only ask," he said formally. "Runners shall be dispatched this very hour to each of the holy troves. The writings shall be brought you with all haste, though I regret that you may not have any but the current writings *now*."

"It is sufficient," Gem said. "You will teach me—immediately—the manner in which I may communicate with the Trident."

Third tipped his head, puzzlement showing in his face. "Communicate?"

"Communicate," Gem said sharply. "Play no games with me, sir. I am ill and my cousin is failing before my eyes. Shlorba's Smiter has chosen me, so you say, for partnership in its present endeavor. That is well, I shall be its partner. But I have received the tuition of a master. I have skills and necessities of my own. I am no child to be molded to the Smiter's whim, nor an empty vessel to be filled and, mindless, used. If this is to be a partnership, the will of Gem ser Edreth shall be active within it."

"Ah." The man's eyes were shining, and he bowed most deeply. "The singers shall be told of this!" he cried, and held out his hands. "I had been taught that the Smiter speaks, but the lore you demand is not mine. I will go now, with the Trident Bearer's permission, and send the First of the Telios. She may teach you these mysteries."

"I don't care who teaches me," Gem snapped, his eyes on Corbinye's waning face. "But I will have it taught at once."

"At once," Third reiterated, bowing himself feverishly out of the room. "At once, Trident Bearer."

Gem took a deep breath, closed his eyes—and opened them, startled, at the unexpected pressure of fingers upon his.

Corbinye's eyes were open, watching him with some puzzlement. "It—*speaks,* Anjemalti?"

He sighed and reached out, cupping her cheek in his hand. "It speaks," he said, and the tears that had pricked at the back of his eyes spilled over. "Corbinye, do not leave me."

The Grounder's name was Borgin Vo Riss and he professed himself more than willing to lead the way to the Telios. He then offered the information that evening was fast approaching and hinted that perhaps the aged one and his boy would care to bide the night in Borgin's village and set out for the Telios on the morrow.

"Not a bad notion," Finchet allowed. "We're a bit done up, truth told."

Borgin was glad of the old one's wisdom, and said so. He also said that his chief would welcome the opportunity to speak to one who claimed friendship with Witness for the Telios. He waved his hand and two stepped forward from the half-dozen warriors he had brought with him to investigate that which had fallen from the skies. "These may carry your burdens, father."

"Gracious of you," Finchet said. "But we'll carry our own."

Borgin effaced himself, took rapid thought and waved his hand again. Water bottles appeared from among the troop. Borgin offered his to the old one, who drank thirstily. Rifta, his second, gave the child to drink, and for courtesy each of the six then took a mouthful before all moved out, the boy and the old man safely enclosed within a ring of warriors.

Finchet stumbled, and wished he hadn't been so stiff-necked about the offer of having the axe, at least, taken from him. Still, it wouldn't do to be without a weapon, with them far from Ship and not knowing the Captain's estate. Though this Borgin seemed reasonable enough, and as willing to aid them as if they were Shipmates.

The village, come upon abruptly at the base of a hill, was settled in among some scraggly trees—sticks merely, Finchet thought, with thin, ill-nourished leaves—maybe twenty tents and a handful of more permanent structures, all set up in a rectangle, facing in on an cleared space.

In the cleared space there was activity: A group of young ones, each seated before a flat stone. All the stones were the same shape, Finchet saw, as if deliberately worked that way, and on each was an array of smaller stones, twigs and bright bits of pottery.

Finchet stopped. Around him, the ring of warriors stopped and Borgin glanced aside. "Aged one?"

"Like to look over here a tick, if that's permitted." Finchet pointed at the group. Borgin bowed and stepped out of the way.

"Surely."

One person, a bit older, Finchet thought, than the ones at the rocks, sat on a stone in the center of things, from time to time calling out a phrase in what might be these Grounders' native tongue. When she did, each of the other children moved their hands in rapid pattern over their rock, slapping at this twig, or that shard…

"What do you make of this, young Veln?" Finchet asked.

The boy shrugged, barely glancing at the flurry of activity. "Grounder madness, Uncle. Nothing to do with us."

"No? Look again. Seems to me it looks familiar, but I'm further away from my lessons than you are."

The girl on the center stone called out another phrase and quick hands flashed across half-a-dozen rocks. Veln stiffened; stared.

"It's a board test," he said slowly. "She must be calling the drill-patterns…"

"Thought so," said Finchet, and nodded to the girl, who had turned to look at them curiously. "Borgin and his mates carry spears, and these younglings are learning their drill-patterns. Wonder why."

"There must be a ship, Uncle," said Veln.

"Must there? Doubtless you're right." He straightened, sighing a little at the complaint of his back muscles. "Well, let's not keep the chief waiting, young Veln. Happen he'll have something fine to feed us."

CHAPTER SIXTY-EIGHT

ANJEMALTI THE CHOSEN would travel to the Vornet ship, forsooth, there to demand of the Smiter. Power the Smiter must relinquish, in kind of what had been eaten, to spark the motor that would bring the healing unit to life.

That in turn would save the life of Death's Warrior.

Witness for the Telios could scarce contain his secret heart. This was the way the very oldest Memories went: That Smiter and Seeker were each half of a whole great enough even to shatter event and rework worlds. The very greatest of the Seekers were thus partners of the Smiter. The rest, Witness suspected within his secret heart, were merely toys of the Goddess.

First of the Five was less exultant than Witness' heart. For the twelfth time she said to Anjemalti, "There is no need to put yourself to the strain of travel, to the danger of crossing the Smiter's will. The Smiter itself can be used to animate. The old tales are very clear, Trident Bearer…"

"No," Anjemalti said, his dozenth repetition, also, though now not accompanied by the shudder that had wracked him upon first learning of the Trident's power in this wise. He looked hard at First Telios, blue eyes brilliant to the point of insanity. "Understand me. It is not *animation* I seek, it is Corbinye's *life*. Do I make myself sufficiently plain?"

First Telios sighed and slid her hands into the wide sleeves of her robe, a gesture of resignation Witness knew well. "Yes, Trident Bearer."

"Good," Anjemalti said and stood, stamping his feet into his boots. He plucked a cloak from the bench, swung it around his shoulders and twisted the brooch shut. "Then let us begin."

The night was far advanced, but their way was well lighted by the servants of the Telios. The drained Vornet ship was merely an easy stroll down the hillside in the coolness, even for one recently wounded. Gem used the Trident as a staff, as was his habit, and reviewed the instructions he had gained for its proper use.

As he understood it, the Fearstone was the key to communication with the Trident. He had a moment of disorientation and nearly stumbled on the stony path as Shilban's voice chided him out of the night: "*Sarialdan* isn't alive, it's just a dumb transmitter. All it does is transmit fear, boy. Just fear."

But First of the Telios had taught him that *Sarialdan* transmitted *more* than fear. Transmitted, in fact, the whole range of emotive energy. Gathered it, refined it and released it encoded along the various paths swirling around the Trident's length, opening and closing synapses, tripping switches in sequence, to produce a predictable outcome.

All that was needed was practice.

First of the Telios had also taught him that the Trident had become less and less effective over the years. The wise had understood that this indicated a lessening of the quality of those who Sought. But here came Gem ser Edreth, with a Trident made whole, capable again of miracles—she had thanked him for showing her this lesson. She had requested, diffidently, that he allow the singers and the scribes to hear the way of the Trident's mending, so that, if any damage should occur in the future...

Gem put that thought away; concentrating instead upon the technique she had given him to clear his mind and smooth his emotions. He must see himself standing at the center of a great peace, so the instructions went, with all of his inner resources spread before him, yet apart from him. He must see his emotions—his anger, his love, his fear—as tools to his hand. *Interfaces*, he had translated for himself, as the wristlet was the interface between his thought and the spiders' actions.

Still, the spiders had never, for all their faithful service, sent their own thoughts and necessities back along the line to the mind of their creator.

"It speaks," he had said to First of the Telios when she came to him.

She had bowed her head. "I had heard that it was sometimes so, Trident Bearer. But not always. You are indeed among those Chosen for greatness."

Of the mechanism by which it spoke, of the *probability* of its speaking, she had no wisdom. The old tales told of the Trident speaking, but only the Trident Bearers had ever heard it.

"Delightful," Gem had murmured then, and directed her to teach him what she did know, which, in its way, was considerable. Gem only hoped, for Corbinye's life, that he had learned enough to do what must be done.

Gem walked up the ramp, leaning heavily on the Trident now, nodded to the Bindalche standing guard at the gaping hatch, and hesitated, caught by the one who stood to the right, flowers and feathers braided into his hair, a wide belt hung with amulets 'round his waist.

"You are the chief now of Tremillan Tribe?" he asked.

The other laid his hand flat over his heart, "I am Ven Cabrise EnTallia, Trident Bearer," he said warily. "I thank you for your notice."

"No trouble," Gem said. "Ven kelBatien Girisco was a great chief. I honor her sacrifice for her people."

In the flickering torch light, the man's face altered, wariness melting. "I will tell the singers so, Trident Bearer." He hesitated, then added, "Joy to you."

"And to you," Gem returned and stepped into the ship.

Torches had been set here and there on the silent bridge, casting dancing shadows. Out of kindness for First Telios

and Witness, following him into what must seem to them un-
relieved blackness, he plucked one of the torches free and
bore it with him down the narrow companionway, past crew
quarters, galley, gym and finally into the doc's office. There
he pulled a fire extinguisher from its bracket and set the torch
in its place, so that the dancing light illuminated all corners of
the tiny space—more or less.

He found the emergency generator, bent to get a grip
on it—and suddenly gasped as his wound protested. Straightening, he set the Trident on a convenient cot and beckoned
to Witness.

"Help me with this."

First of the Telios bridled. "Shlorba's Eyes is bound to
watch, and to recall truly for the Telios."

"Yes," said Gem, mustering what patience he could, "and
as soon as he helps me hook up this generator, there will be
something for him to witness."

"It is not done—" First Telios began, and then clamped
her mouth as Witness strode past her and went to the Trident
Bearer's side.

"Where must it be, Anjemalti?"

"There." The Trident Bearer pointed. "Cable's not long
enough to reach from here."

Shlorba's Eyes bent, grabbed hold of the built-on handle
and heaved, a moment later placing the generator in the spot
the Trident Bearer had indicated.

"Thank you," said Gem calmly and yanked out a cable,
clamped it into place on the healing unit, pulled out another
cable and seated it, then bent and flipped several switches set
in the face of the generator. He walked over to the cot where
he had laid it and picked up the Trident, but he did not immediately go back to the generator.

Instead, he leaned across the cot, catching First Telios'
eyes with his. "Understand this: If that generator comes to life,

send for Corbinye immediately, place her within the larger unit and seal the door. Wait until a chime sounds and then help her out. Do this *first,* even if something should seem to have happened to me or to the Trident. Do you understand me?"

She gave him back, stare for stare. "I understand your words," she said coldly.

"Will you obey them?" Gem asked softly, wondering at the note of danger that made the softness hard.

Credit her for toughness and a long life lived imposing her will upon others as strong-willed as she. First of the Telios did not drop her eyes. But she did lick her lips. "I will obey them," she said and Gem nodded.

"I am happy to hear you say so," he said, still with that deadly softness; then he turned back to the generator.

He took the stance that had become most natural to him, since First Telios had not been able to teach him one better—Trident-end braced against the deck between his boots, both hands wrapped just below the Fearstone, fingers entwined. He leaned on it slightly, because he was so tired, and looked at the generator between the wickedly sharp tines.

He took a deep breath and strove to clear his mind, to set aside his irritation with First of the Telios, his worry for Corbinye, his terror that this might not work, that she would die after all, in spite of the best he could do. He, who had killed her once already.

Deliberately, he shut each of those concerns off, making his mind a clear white space, where he seemed to hang, weightless, the universe narrowed to the generator, seen between the barring of the tines.

Within the white space of his mind, he spoke: *I want that operating.*

It seemed to him that his words echoed, as if they went far beyond himself and his mind, into a region unthinkably vast.

Faintly, really much too faintly for it to be more than the

trickery of one's own tired ears, he heard a trill of laughter. Then nothing.

Frustration spiked, and fear of failing. He felt the Trident warm in his hands, saw *Sarialdan* glow to surly life—and deliberately closed his eyes, breathing deeply and evenly, clearing his mind of everything. He must consider his emotions tools, so First of the Telios had taught him. But what did he know of emotion? It had been Edreth's care to show his apprentice the path around such things, so limiting to a thief's success.

Never give your name to the roomgirl. Never, never ask hers. Keep all at arm's length, or further. Trust no one. Reserve your care for your craft and for your spiders. A thief is always outside—an intelligent observer—aloof, uninvolved...

"Corbinye," Gem whispered, unaware that he spoke aloud. "Linzer. Shilban. Edreth. Edreth, you lied..." For what but love explained sacrifices made on behalf of a child not of his body, the son of his soul, the heir of all his worldly goods? What but love had forced Edreth into that last mad scheme, when he might as easily have followed his own advice, stayed aloof and turned his wayward 'prentice loose... The scheme where he had taken his death, yes, and never a word of blame...

The Trident had warmed his fingers to the point of discomfort. He gripped it tighter, seeing only the past, where Edreth was busy weaving protections around the only thing he had ever loved, striving to make it invulnerable....

Gem gasped, shuddering as the tears came, bent his head—and felt the flare of heat, saw through closed eyes the flare of light—

And heard, in the sudden, fire-shot darkness, the hum of a generator, coming to life.

Ria had her walkabout and Milt had woken from his nap. They'd wandered down to the canteen and puzzled out the sequence for drawing rations, and they'd dawdled over the meal, talking some, and then not, with the din of the life support system all around.

Ria finally pushed back from the table and looked at the kid, seeing her worries plain in his eyes.

"Let's find comm," she said. "See what's taking Dez all year."

"All right," said Milt and came with her, down the rickety halls to the core, and up a couple levels to dead center.

Ria grunted satisfaction and hit the prime chair, fingers flashing over the antiquated board, calling up the lights. Milt wilted into the assistant's chair and leaned back, watching her and surreptitiously wiping the sweat off his lip.

"Out line?" Ria muttered to herself, and a second later: "got 'er. Now for beam-adjust. And now for Dez." She punched the buttons with assurance, taking a tick to send Milt a grin.

The line crackled live and Ria sang out their ID and their position, adding a: "So, Dez, what's keeping the party? You fall asleep?"

No answer.

Milt stiffened at that, and Ria frowned. "Must have wrong line," she muttered and went through the routine again, running the translations in her head.

"Yo, Dez! InRing crew three-three-six on GenShip attention required quicktime! Get us outta here, man. Vacation's over."

Only line-crackle came back to them. Milt ran a shaking hand over his face, fingertips coming away wet.

"Try General Alert," he said, but Ria's fingers were already on the board, slapping up the emergency numbers, chanting the Company's Mayday with the precision of a prayer.

The lines buzzed empty.

Ria sat back hard in her chair, staring at the old board, seeing the places where the metal was worn dull, and where toggles had been replaced with wood, rather than plastic; the places where the colors had worn right off, so you needed to know the drill by rote…

"They did it," the kid whispered next to her. "They've got the Big Ship."

"Shit," said Ria, and bit her lip, thinking about a long, mostly misspent life. Thinking about ending it here, on a ship so old it gave her the spooks… She put her hands on the arm rests and levered herself out of the chair.

"Where're you going now?" asked Milt.

"Engine room," Ria said grimly. "Going to see if we can get this buggy moving."

CHAPTER SIXTY-NINE

IT WAS A four-day walk to the Grotto of the Telios, though
Finchet thought Borgin Vo Riss and his group of hearties
could have quartered the time, left on their own.

Still, they set an old man's pace, and after the first day
Finchet was glad of it—and glad of the Grounder custom
that dictated he be waited on by those younger. There was no
wood-chopping and assorted camp tasks for him, though Veln
drew a man's share of those.

The boy brought him a horn cup, full to the brim with
water, and Finchet had seen enough of the land by now to
know how great a gift that brimming cupful was.

"Thank you," he said and took a sip of the tepid liquid
before asking, "You doing well, are you, young Veln?"

The boy grinned at him out of a grimy, exalted face.
"Well and more than well, Uncle. Have you ever *dreamed* of
such a place?"

"No," said Finchet, with perfect truth, and took another
sip, holding it in his parched mouth before swallowing. "You
still have the Book?"

Veln looked, Finchet thought, a little hurt. "Of course."

"That's fine," he said. "You keep that close, hear me? If
something untoward comes my way, you get the Book to the
Captain. That's my rede."

The boy straightened, face losing a little of its heedless
joy. "Yes, Uncle."

Finchet smiled and reached out to grip the thin young
arm. "You're a good lad. Go on with the rest of your
chores, now."

He was left then, with his water and his thoughts, but
not for as long as that. Another shadow found him where he
sat on a rock out of the way of the bustle of mid-day camp

and he looked up to see Borgin, hands clasped diffidently before him.

"'day to you, lad."

"Fine day to you, father," the warrior said in the gentle voice he reserved for Finchet and for his chief. He hesitated. "It is permitted that one sit and converse?"

"Sit away," Finchet returned, waving a hand at the various rocks nearby.

Those, however, would have put Borgin on a level with the old one. He made one of the complicated hand-signs he was prone to and sat himself down on the ground.

Looking up at Finchet he said, "We will be with the Telios this evening, father. But I feel you should know that it is likely that Shlorba's Eyes—Witness for the Telios, your friend—may not be with them. His duty is such that he may, indeed, be very far away."

"Your chief told me that," Finchet said unworriedly. "We'll take the chance of him not being to home. Mayhap his folk will know how to get a grip on him. Unless you're thinking the Telios won't let us in."

Another flash of those big fingers. "The Telios gladly house any seeker. It is my duty to say that, though we come to the Telios this evening, your seeking may not yet be done."

"Understood. The Crew's been seeking for centuries, so the logs say. Reckon the boy and me can seek a little while longer."

"The old one is wise." Borgin bent his head, looked up. "What shall become of the growing things?"

"Good question," Finchet said and then stared off into the never-never, rubbing his fingers absently down the satin finish of the cup.

He came to himself with a start and glanced down at the warrior, patiently waiting. "Land hereabouts is dry," he offered.

"Old one, it is so."

"Been that way since when, you know?"

"Since The Combine came and broke the backs of the Bindalche," Borgin said in a flat voice, as if it were something he had by rote, "hurling us down into barbarism and building the Dam to be Hated upon Traitor's Point, just beneath the polar ice cap." He blinked and added in a more normal tone. "The Telios will know more, father. I have only the tales."

"Hm. Saw that dam on the way in. Better for everybody, she was gone…"

Borgin looked up, pure joy in his eyes. "The old one will show us the way to kill it? To free the land and renew the Bindalche?" He came to his knees, yanked the big knife out of his belt and laid it flat across Finchet's knees. "I am yours!"

"No," said Finchet firmly, "you aren't. Bless you, child, I'm no Captain. You want to be swearing knife service, you wait 'til you talk to Captain Kristefyon—he's the one for knowing how to go on with things and how to get broke mended. Now take that up and put it away. I'm too old a fellow for such foolishness."

Borgin looked crestfallen, but he picked up his knife and stowed it and sat back on his heels.

"Father?"

"Eh?"

"How shall I find this—Captain Kristefyon? If he is so great a chief as you say, I will cede him the use of my blade."

Finchet sipped the last dregs of the water gratefully and put the cup aside. "We're hoping to find him with Witness for the Telios," he said slowly. "He's the one who needs to decide about the green things, too, see it? Hoping he'll be in shape to decide it soon. Though, truth said, he's a bit fond of chancy adventures. If we find him dead, then we're on our own, for the Garden will never lift again, that's certain."

The other man frowned. "Why does your Captain travel with Shlorba's Eyes, O aged one?"

"Because my Captain is promised to carry around something called a Smiter or a Trident and where he goes—"

"So goes the Eyes of Shlorba," Borgin breathed reverently. "Your Captain is Trident Bearer, old one?"

"Just said so, didn't I?"

"Indeed, indeed, you did!" Borgin leapt to his feet so suddenly Finchet flinched on his rock. But the warrior simply stood for a moment, back bowed, face tipped open to the sky, arms outstretched. The moment passed, and he was as suddenly bent forward, hands moving incomprehensibly.

"Father, your instruction is most excellent. Accept thanks from the center of this one's heart. You bring tidings of greatness for all Bindalche." He straightened, a grin that had nothing to do with humor illuminating his face. "That it should happen in my lifetime!" He collected himself with an effort. "The boy approaches with your meal. Eat well. A blanket shall be brought to you, so that you may rest for the final stage of the journey. O joyous—" He turned away and strode back toward his mates.

Finchet shook his head and took the slab of dried meat and the handful of small sweet fruits from Veln and then sat with the meal in his hand, staring very hard at nothing.

The book was old—as old as the oldest he had seen in Shilban's house—bound in heavy leather. A picture had once been painted on the front cover—the chips of color that remained were purple, and green, and gold. The edges of the pages were gilded and those pages were not, as Gem had expected, thinner, more supple leather, but a thick, fine-grained paper that had taken the ink well and held it without fading.

"The second of the Books of the Telios," said First from her station at his shoulder. "We have lost the secret of that ink, alas, and later books are not so easy to read as this."

Gem ran his fingers lightly over the pages, noting the ridges where the pen had scored the paper. "And the first Book of the Telios?" he asked.

"Is written on rock walls and on tablets of marble, malachite and gold. It may not be brought to you. You must go to it. If you think it will avail you. The Seeker must know that we have those among us who have devoted long lifetimes to the study of that single Book."

"Hm," said Gem, more than half-concerned with the study of the Book within his hands. "And is the Smiter spoken of from the very beginning?"

First of the Telios moved away, tucking her hands into her sleeves. Witness, watching the Trident in its resting place across the room, spared a moment of his attention to look at her face.

"The Bindalche," she said slowly, "were without the Smiter for many years. So the Books teach us."

Gem looked up sharply. "So the Books teach you," he repeated. "In what Book does the Smiter first appear?"

She avoided his gaze. "The old writing—you understand, it is very dense, very difficult to follow. The Books that come after this one are faded, some pages impossible to read…" She squared her shoulders and looked at him straightly. "The first clear mention of the Smiter is in the third Book," she said. "There was a battle…"

"Between the god and his children, the goddess and the younger god," said Gem and Witness for the Telios came to his feet, staring.

First of the Telios also stared; regained her composure. "You have that tale from the Smiter?"

"No," said Gem, "from a very old book, on a planet called Henron…" He glanced over and Witness saw humor in the depths of the large, fey eyes. "A fragment only—the kernel myth. Never any clue of what the myth might mean—or if the god had a name."

Witness for the Telios sank back to his seat upon the floor and disciplined his mind for duty.

Gem turned back to the Book before him, looked to First. "I will study this and consider what best is to be done from here," he said, in tones eloquent of dismissal. "Please, if you will, let me know when the other volumes arrive."

She stiffened, but retained enough sense of what was due the Trident Bearer to bow with courtesy and retire.

Gem ran his fingers once again over the fine paper with its ridges where the pen had passed over. He opened to the middle and studied a page there; opened to the end and did the same. He inspected the binding and frowned at the remains of the illumination upon the cover.

Then he laid the Book carefully back down upon the table and stood. Without a word to Witness, he passed from the room into the second chamber, where Corbinye slept off the effects of her wound and its healing.

The healing had not been as complete as he had hoped for—she was still weak, exhausted—but the learned of the Telios and the physician incarcerated with the Vornet crew both agreed that she was out of any danger. Rest and nourishment, they all had counseled, quietude and exposure to the kindness of those who loved her.

This last had been from the youngest of the Telios healers and Gem had thanked her most profoundly, while he wondered in his heart where there were any who cared for Corbinye, besides himself, inept at love, and Witness, who bowed to duty first.

He was forced to hope that his ineptness would not hinder her progress and he visited hourly, speaking with her if she were wakeful; just watching, if she were asleep.

Presently, she was restless, tossing and twisting under the fur covers, as if she could find no easeful position.

Gem leaned over and smoothed her hair, murmuring her name, bidding her, softly, to lie still. She did quiet somewhat, to his surprise, and he straightened the furs over her and turned to go.

A slim hand caught his and he looked up to see her eyes open and bright.

"I put you to a great deal of trouble, cousin."

"No trouble," he protested and then grinned wryly. "Less trouble than the damned Trident, at least, and not nearly so much as First of the Telios."

She chuckled, her fingers stroking the hand she held him by, so that he nearly snatched it away before forcing himself to be patient with the touch and ignore the flame it ignited.

"Are you hungry?" he asked her. "Thirsty? I can send for something…"

"Only wakeful," she said and pulled on his hand, urging him down to sit beside her on the bed. "Talk to me, Anjemalti. What have you been about while I've been sleeping the day away?"

"There's a book," he began, meaning to tell her the tale of the Books of the Bindalche, but he got no further than that before the mat was thrust back from the door and one of the servants of the Bindalche burst into the room.

"Trident Bearer, your pardon! There is come several of the warriors of the Bindalche, escorting an old man and a boy. They say they belong to you, Trident Bearer, and send the names Finchet and Veln."

CHAPTER SEVENTY

FINCHET FOLLOWED THE short green robe down the stone corridor. He kept one hand firm on Veln's shoulder and one ear on the comforting slight sounds made by Borgin and his mates, keeping pace behind.

They traversed several corridors, going deeper and deeper into the mountain. Finchet took care to memorize the turns: Right, right, right, left, right, left, left and—

"This is the place," the robe said, sweeping a leather curtain back and stepping hastily aside. "The Trident Bearer is within."

Finchet sent a sharp look into the depths of the hood, finding a pair of wide brown eyes in a face no older than Veln's.

"Huh," he said and pulled Veln close, so they both went over the threshold together.

The first thing he saw within the room was the Captain's trident, gems all a-gleaming in the firelight. And sitting before it, bland-faced as ever, was Witness for the Telios.

Finchet stopped and raised a hand. "Good to see you, lad."

Witness inclined his head. "Gardener. Veln Kristefyon. A man is joyful to see you both well."

"Very nearly didn't," Finchet said. "Captain about?"

Witness turned his head and Finchet followed his gaze to the right and middle of the room, to where a stone table stood, with a gaudy big book upon it, and a slender man in a dark gray robe standing behind both, his long yellow hair neatly tied in a tail down his neck and his eyes Crew-sized and blue.

"Well, now, there's a sight for worried eyes," said Finchet, letting Veln go at last and coming straight across the room. "Feared we'd find you in several odd pieces. Happy to know an old man can be as wrong as a young one."

Gem smiled and held out both his hands. "Hello, Uncle."

The old man gripped the young one's hands and cocked a grizzled eyebrow. "Uncle, is it? Well, and it's true enough, gene-wise—cousins, aunts and uncles, all. Doubtless that's the long and short of why we're dying out."

"Doubtless," Gem agreed. "But tell me, do—in what way was I wrong?"

"Hah." Finchet stepped back, glanced over to tally Veln and Borgin's crew. He looked back to meet those bright eyes. "Garden crashed."

The eyes moved, flashing to Veln, then back. "You both look hale enough. Have we lost the whole wood?"

"Might well make a recover," Finchet allowed. "Given workers and an agreeable system. How-to's in the Book. Thing is, somebody's been adjusting this system already, Captain. Big dam up under the pole—saw it on the way down. Winds not how they ought to be, according to what the Book tells me, stream-flow—what there is—altered." He shook his head. "Don't look that good for the Garden, present conditions prevailing."

"So the operators of the dam must be persuaded to reason," said Gem. "Who might that be?"

"The Combine, that one says," Finchet jerked a thumb at Borgin.

"He says truth," Witness put in from the floor. Gem nodded, eyes gleaming.

"Why, in that case, I think we really have no problem at all, Uncle. We've already doubtless annoyed The Combine by taking their ship—" He looked up. "*Have* we taken their ship?"

Finchet fished the comm out of his belt and laid it on the table next to the book. "Not a peep out of this since we hit, but it took a fair bit of knocking about."

Gem nodded again and rested his fingers lightly against the comm-case. Out of his sleeve came a spider, waltzed down the back of his hand and onto the comm. It walked to the place where the power pack was seated and vanished inside the unit.

"Let us assume for the moment," Gem said, "that we have been successful. Already then the Crew of the *Gardenspot* is struck from The Combine's guest lists. How much angrier can they become over a little thing like a dam on a world that doesn't even belong to them?"

Finchet grinned. "Reasoning worthy of a Kristefyon, that. Your mother'd be proud to hear you. I recall me—"

But what he recalled was not to be shared at this moment. A big voice cried out, "They will kill the dam!" And a big body surged forward, falling to its knees between Finchet and the table, offering a knife high on outstretched palms.

"Captain Kristefyon, have me! I am Borgin Vo Riss of Wyalin Tribe and these are mine hunt-mates. I pledge us all to you, only send us with Finchet Gardener to destroy the Dam to be Hated!"

Elegant eyebrows lifted above astonished blue eyes. Gem reached across the table and took the offered weapon up in two hands.

"Rise, Borgin Vo Riss."

The warrior stood, face lit with a hatred akin to holiness. Gem weighed the knife in his hands, looked into the other's eyes.

"You know that I bear Shlorba's Smiter."

"I do."

"And you know, I presume, the old tales, which should be sufficient warning of all the ill that might befall you as a servant of the Trident Bearer."

"Let me kill the dam," Borgin breathed. "Trident Bearer, let me only come near it and know it is to die. I shall gladly die myself, and sing your praises to the goddess ever after."

"I may well hold you to that," Gem said, and extended the knife. "I accept your service, Borgin Vo Riss. But I ask that you allow each of your hunt-mates to speak for themselves."

One by one they came forward, then, fell to their knees, and offered up their names and their knives.

One by one, the Trident Bearer accepted their service and when he had gathered all of their souls into his hand, he stepped back and beckoned the child waiting at the door.

"Take these and let them bathe and eat and rest. Tomorrow, I shall send for them."

"Yes, Trident Bearer," said the child and swept the leather back from the door, stepping aside to let them pass into the hallway.

When they were gone, Gem looked again at Finchet and the boy. "You'll be wanting the same things, I expect. But before you go, perhaps you would like, Uncle, to step into the next room and visit—"

"I am here, Anjemalti," a resonant, beautiful voice said from behind him. He turned to see Corbinye, clad in the loose blue robe they had given her, one hand braced against the wall.

It was Veln who moved first, who cried out, "Aunt Corbinye!" and who flung himself against her, arms going tight around her waist.

She swayed, and leaned into the wall, put both arms around the boy and hugged him tight to her. The face she raised was beatific and she smiled at Finchet like a goddess. "Uncle."

"Corbinye. You all right, girl?"

"Mending," she said, and gave Veln a fierce, final hug before pushing him gently away. "Go and get fed. Rest. Visit us tomorrow."

"Likely so," said Finchet, cocking an eyebrow at his Captain. "You'll be telling us how to go about blowing up this dam then, I expect?"

"Possibly," said Gem serenely. "I'll have to ask the Telios what they know."

"Hah," said Finchet and went over to give Corbinye a hug and proper kin-kiss. When he looked again, there was the short green robe back again, or another just like it, holding the curtain aside and waiting for them to leave. He gave Corbinye another squeeze, flung his arm around Veln's shoulders and headed hallward, giving a nod each to Captain and to Witness.

He coaxed Corbinye back to her room and called a servant, as she asked. By the time he returned to the table, Number Four was standing atop the comm-link, purple eyes glowing.

He offered a palm and the spider clambered into it, then up his wrist and arm, leaving the skin at last to cling to the inside of the sleeve. Gem sat down and thumbed on "receive."

There was a small bloom of static, followed immediately by a voice: "GenerationShip Five, Class One, on cycle three of fifteen. Scattered Crew orient to second world perihelion and activate ID beacons. You will be tagged and recovered. Any who have taken damage, load assessments onto BroadCode, establish emergency measures and wait. You will be tagged and recovered."

Slowly, Gem put out a hand and hit "send."

"GenerationShip Five, Class One," he said. "Captain's override and scramble. Mael Faztherot to the comm. If she is not available, I will speak to—"

"Mael Faztherot here, Captain," her cool voice held an undercurrent of pure glee. "Your plan was perfect in every particular—success is ours! The mother ship is taken and the outriders scattered. We have only to pick up our blade-ships and complete refinement of the key codes." There was a pause, as if she heard her own exuberance and stopped to school herself. "What are the Captain's orders?"

Orders? Well, and there it was. He had hardly thought past the taking of The Combine ship and returning the Trident to the Bindalche. One plan had succeeded, but the second had failed, and he was caught here, surely as if the Vornet still held him in their intrigues, not to mention Finchet and his crew of Grounders, mad to kill the dam…He glanced over at the Trident; laid his hand upon the Second Book of the Telios.

"How fares The Combine?" he asked Mael Faztherot.

"Those we captured were put into a cargo pod and towed to *Gardenspot*, where they are even now unloading. The outriders are but momentarily confused by our attack. They will be back, Captain."

"Doubtless." He stared hard at the wall opposite him, weighing needs and desires and fears. Eventually, he touched the "send" button once more.

"Collect your ships, then do me the favor of making a pass over the pole. I need a map of the dam I am told is there. Download the information to *Hyacinth's* bank."

"Yes, Captain. And yourself?"

"Myself?" He shrugged, wryly. "I am detained rather longer than I had anticipated. The Garden took damage in descent and must be attended to—and it is not so easy to return the Trident to those who should hold it." He frowned. "There is something…"

"The Captain need only command," Mael Faztherot told him, and he very nearly laughed.

"On a planet called Henron, within the Renfrew System, there is—was—a library. If it still exists, it is in OldTown and the one who had owned it was named Shilban." He bit his lip, nodded once, though there was none but Witness and Trident to see.

"I want that library."

"Orders received and acknowledged," Mael Faztherot said. "Are more specific coordinates available?"

He closed his eyes, called up the grid-map of Henron in

his head and read off the location of Shilban's Library. "If it is still there," he repeated. "Understand that we are speaking of bound books—in some cases, of scrolls and hieroglyphics. Many of them are fragile."

"I understand. The utmost care shall be taken in the loading and the books shall be brought back to you here." A small pause. "The Captain has further orders?"

"How goes the recoding?"

"The engine codes have been removed and replaced with clean codes. We are presently operating with the backup computer while PrimeComp's signature is rewritten. We have work boats out repainting the visuals."

"Good," Gem said. "When you are ready, call and I will give you coords for a courier boat landing. I have here several prisoners who should be returned—alive and hale—to Henron."

"It will be done," Mael Faztherot assured him.

"Good," Gem said again. "I have no further orders. Proceed with your necessities."

"Captain," she said, respectfully. "Acting Captain out."

For some little time he sat, staring at the comm-light, then finally moved a hand and turned the comm off.

So, then, he thought, the Ship will map the dam, and I will need to hear from the Telios what they know of the thing and if there is a Combine garrison there, then to get the Garden sorted, and The Combine will be back, no mistake on that. Defenses will have to be made. Perhaps the Ship can leave us outriders, and I will need to study the Trident, refine the operating system, study the Books…A hand gripped his shoulder gently and he gasped, starting so badly he knocked the comm to the floor.

"Anjemalti," her voice was soft, the scent of her as she leaned over him like the finest intoxicant. "Anjemalti," she said. "You cannot solve it all tonight. Come to bed."

"Bed." He looked up at her, the lovely face, the space-black eyes, the hair that had been newly washed and hung unbraided across her shoulder and over one breast. "Bed," he repeated, "is where you should be. To rest and regain your strength."

"While you worry yourself into a despair," she said with a touch of her old asperity. "Very good." Her fingers tightened on his shoulder. "Come to bed, Anjemalti. I swear to let you sleep."

Desire washed through him, and a yearning near pain, yet still he hesitated.

"Go with her, Anjemalti," Witness said from his corner. "A man may."

Corbinye laughed and he felt her hand leave his shoulder, felt warm fingers sweep down the side of his cheek. "We have been given approval, cousin. What more would you?"

He laughed himself then, and pushed back from the table, and let her take his hand and draw him across the stone floor and through the curtain to her chamber.

After a time, Witness got up from his place before the Smiter, walked over to the table and bent to pick up the fallen comm-link. He placed it carefully beside the Book, then stepped into the center-space and did certain exercises to ease his body and clear his mind. When those were done, he returned to his seat before Shlorba's Smiter and began to order the beginning of this, the greatest of the Telios' most recent Memories.

His name was Anjemalti Kristefyon and he had been born a Chief of star rovers. While he was yet a child, event did move upon him, and the star rovers cast him out, to be caught by a master wise in the ways and intrigues of event. The boy grew and learned, at the master's behest, a new role and a new name, so event for a time was confounded. Thus, in respect of the master, whose wise trickery preserved the outcast for the Smiter, the tale begins:

His name was Gem and he was a thief…

WEB
OF THE
TRIDENT

SHARON LEE &
STEVE MILLER